D1607332

Spare Time

God Bless you all!!

Michael Murphy

This book is a work of fiction. Any resemblance to actual events or persons, living or dead, is entirely coincidental.

"Spare Time," by Michael Murphy. ISBN 978-0-9856747-1-7 (Softcover) 978-0-9856747-2-4 (Hardcover) 978-0-9856747-0-0 (eBook)

Published 2012 by M&J Enterprise, LLC 35810 West Greenfield Road, Sylvia, KS 67581.

A special thanks to my dad who taught me I could do anything I put my mind to … to my children and grandchildren who give me both joy and pain … to all my friends who were an encouragement throughout this process ... to Juli and Pamela for their special contribution ... to my wife who has stood by me through thick and thin, I love you … and to God, to whom I owe everything. Thank you!

Chapter 1

HE IS SITTING ON the deck of their new house. He loves this place, everything about it. At the moment, the weather is perfect. It is early evening; the sun is still high in the central plains at this time of year. It can still be hot, very hot … it was over 100 just a few days ago. But today it did not reach 80, and it will be in the mid-40s tonight. The first frost is just a few weeks away. He has a satellite radio on a news channel, but he can also hear the aerator on the pond — it sounds like a waterfall. An occasional hummingbird visits one of the feeders, their wings buzzing as they dart back and forth. There is an intermittent quack from of one of the ducks feeding on the pond and the muted sounds of some wild turkeys feeding nearby, and several deer feeding in a field northwest of the house. *It doesn't get any better than this*, he thinks to himself. Well, it would be better if she was here. He has his computer resting on his lap, checking emails and working on some marketing materials for their business. The radio is mostly background noise as he concentrates on his work. At times something catches his attention and he pauses to listen, then returns to his work. The news … he can hardly stand to listen to it, but then he has to keep himself informed … ignorance is not bliss for him.

He has given the country's situation much thought over the years, but never has he been so concerned. It is the way of politics, different people with differing ideas take power, the country wanders some but is it hard to make dramatic changes … it normally takes a major crisis to make monumental changes … a world war, a depression, 9-11. He never believed it possible that a major transformation could take place without something like that … until now. The President and Congress now are either unbelievably inept, or incredibly devious, or maybe a little of both. People with no business experience making laws and regulations affecting business, no medical or medical administration experience making laws and regulations affecting healthcare, people with no farming experience making … well, the picture is clear … to him anyway. In a country founded on freedom, as the "land of opportunity," he hears a comment on the radio made by a member of Congress: "And guess what this liberal will be all about? This liberal will be all about socializing, uh, uh … would be about basically … about taking over, the government running all your companies." Okay, he believes in the First Amendment and does not believe people should be silenced. In fact, the more people hear things like this the better. This is a member of Congress talking in public? Do they not realize the blood that was shed to allow them to stand up and make a fool of themselves? The problem is that there is a portion of the country, probably only about 20 to 25 percent who believes in this, but they are a noisy lot, and they have the major media outlets on their side. They are the "entitlement class" — they believe people are entitled to all sorts of things. They believe the government rather than God gives rights. It is dividing and bankrupting the nation. These things drive him a little crazy and he wishes someone would do something about it.

Chapter 2

Mike or Michael

COMPLICATED … IF YOU ASKED him for a one word description of himself it would be complicated, or complex. His wife might say he is both complicated and complex. He would tell you we are all a product of our lives and experiences; some learn and grow from these things while others make excuses. He does not like excuse makers, as personal responsibility is of the upmost importance. He would tell you he lives in the greatest country ever founded, and in large part, what makes this the greatest country are the founding principles. These principles are closely tied to the principles handed to us from our creator — personal responsibility, respect for our neighbors, and following the rules of law. We are a nation of laws, not of men … this is why we had the revolution. God said He is not a respecter of persons; and the same principle applies under our system — the reason, "justice is blind." He would also tell you that we are quickly losing our nation as we depart from the founding principles.

He is an only child; his father was a tough disciplinarian, his mother coddled him. His father was demanding and had high expectations, his mother wanted him to have things she did not … material things, college and such. As a young man, he of course preferred the coddling to the hard line. As he matured, he learned the discipline served him better and prepared him for the real world. His father had served in the South Pacific during WWII and later reentered the military to serve in the Air Force. As a result, he did not go to the same school for an entire school year until 7th grade; he learned to adapt, and as an only child, easily occupied himself.

One of the best things his father taught him was that he could do anything — anything that was important enough in his mind. He quickly learned to do almost anything he tried; he would jokingly say he wasn't smart enough to know he couldn't do something, so he just did it. He quickly mastered several different firearms and was an excellent marksman. When he learned to fly he completed his private certificate in just over five weeks. He built a dream house for his wife and himself, a large log house, by himself.

He has a good sense of humor, enjoys pranks and practical jokes going both ways. He is not afraid to cry, as he does not believe it has any bearing on his manhood. The things that sadden him most are children who are molested, women who are abused and reflecting on the sacrifice of our founders and soldiers who gave us the freedoms we all enjoy. He has a quick temper, but learned early on to control it … his mind quickly thinks of things to say in response to situations, but, this too, is best left to time lest he say something best left unsaid.

He always wanted to fly, but financially it was not feasible. He started going to college to please his mother, but his heart was not in it. He went two years and quit. He then thought of going into the military and letting them teach him how to fly. He went back to college and talked with recruiters who tested him for his aptitude for aviation. He scored so high they about flipped out trying to get him signed up. As it turned out, the Viet Nam War was winding down and there was a glut of pilots, so rather than take a chance on "flying a desk," he backed away and left college again.

Some thought he'd had more than his share of hard times, but he believed everyone has burdens to bear. It is part of life and makes you what you are — it is what defines you. A girl he'd dated while in college was killed by a drunk driver on her way back to college from a weekend home. He married his best friend's sister and after less than six months of marriage she was killed in a car accident. A nagging irrational thought sometimes haunted him that if a girl liked him it could be a death sentence … yes irrational and not something he ever entertained as actually possible … yet these losses made it hard for him to fall in love again for while.

He would tell you he'd had more than his share of successes. He had an entrepreneurial spirit and often was involved in a business venture of some sort. Many people believe a salary is an assurance of income. To him, it was a restriction on income. A salary was all you could make, but if you put your time and money at risk, you have the opportunity to make many times more. This takes discipline and perseverance; many people do not have these attributes anymore. He also laments the fact that the government — from local levels up through the federal levels — places such restrictions on entrepreneurs that it is nearly impossible to start a business from scratch. It also takes a hunger for success, another thing lacking in today's entitlement society. This being said, he never chased wealth. Instead, he chased freedom, challenges and opportunity — financial security was a secondary benefit of his efforts.

His biggest success is his wife. He knows he is not an easy man to live with; she is one of the few who ever seemed to understand him. His biggest fault with her is not listening. He tries to do better, but there is still room for improvement … you might need to ask her. She is a positive thinker; she looks at his better qualities and endures his faults. He knows he has let her down and at times has hurt her. This in turn hurts him … he gets no joy from this.

His opportunity to learn to fly came in an unusual way. One time, a cousin of his father was taking lessons and invited him to ride along. The instructor, a character named Pinky, turned to him in flight and asked, "You seem pretty interested in this, why don't you take lessons?" He replied, "I can't afford it."

Pinky, thinking like many people that it was a matter of stopping something else like drinking or some other vice would open up some funds said, “If you really wanted to, you could come up with the money.” He actually had come back to the plains for a few months prior to a commitment as caretaker of a church camp in Northern California. He was just doing odd jobs for some spare cash and gas money in the meantime. He said, “I really only have enough to keep up with bills, I don’t drink or smoke or spend it on anything foolish, I just don’t have it.” A few minutes passed and Pinky turned and said, “I think everyone who really wants to learn to fly should have a chance. You can start taking lessons and pay me when you can. You can even work some of it off.” He took his first lesson that afternoon, he soloed within five hours. The FAA requires a minimum of 40 hours to take the check ride for a private pilot certificate. He had 39.5 hours when Pinky signed him off, and he got the rest of his total and cross-country time on the flight to the check ride.

At this time in aviation, the only way to get hired by an airline was to either come out of the military or to know someone. He loves flying. He takes every opportunity to fly something new, and he made some contacts that would serve him well in the future. His vast experience in a wide variety of aircraft made him useful to government agencies as they confiscated aircraft used in drug smuggling and other illegal activities.

Due to the deregulation of the airline industry by the government in the late 70s, the airlines began to grow at an unprecedented rate. Suddenly the airlines needed more pilots than the military could supply. He applied and was offered a job by two of the largest airlines in the world at that time. While nearly every pilot hired has a four-year degree, he did not. However, he had three times the total pilot time of the average new hire and had flown over 60 different aircraft. This, in addition to his businesses, made him a desirable employee. He was obviously ambitious. He was quickly asked to come in and work in the training center and taught the B-747 for a few years. He loved the challenge of training in different aircraft. In a relatively short time, he was type-rated in nearly every aircraft the company used. As he says, "We are a product of our lives and experiences. This and the people we meet as we go from opportunity to opportunity are what make us what we are, and what puts us on the paths we choose." He also had a tendency to get bored — one reason a typical nine-to-five job would never suit him. He felt the need to be continually challenged.

9/11 changed him … 9/11 changed a lot of people … and the nation. There are the families directly impacted by the loss of loved ones, and he was affected by this and more. He lost friends and colleagues in this ruthless attack, and the airline industry was forever changed … his country was forever changed. He remembers as if it were yesterday, commuting to work in Los Angeles and changing planes in Denver the first day planes were allowed to fly again. President Bush gave a speech that evening on TV; the terminal was uncharacteristically quiet anyway with so few passengers … you could have heard a pin drop as he spoke about the attack and what the country would and should do in response. Yes, there is evil in the world and we all experienced it that day … we all learned that things would never ever really be the same.

There are many quotes he liked, most by some of our Founding Fathers. But there is one, which once heard, ate at him; it gnawed at him, demanding action. "Silence in the face of evil is itself evil: God will not hold us guiltless. Not to speak is to speak. Not to act is to act." — *Dietrich Bonhoeffer*. Bonhoeffer was a preacher in Germany prior the Third Reich. It is obvious what he was referring to, many people just turned their heads while terrible things happened. The people loved Bonhoeffer or Hitler would have had him killed straight off. They spent years trying to get him in a way so as not to inflame the population. He was hung just 23 days before the Nazis' surrender.

How did we get here? How did our country change so much? Is it like the old story of the frog put in a pan of cool water that is cooked before he realizes things have changed so much? What would our founders think if they could be put in today's United States of America to observe? What would someone from post Civil War say? There is no doubt there are differing opinions as to how our country should be run, what our constitution means and how it should play into today's America. He is a traditionalist. He believes our country is special, that it is a result of our founders and their "Great American Experiment." The question our founders asked, "Can man rule himself?"

Throughout history, people have been ruled by monarchs and dictators. There were efforts in Rome and Greece to do some sort of democracy, but a true democracy is a dismal failure … it is quite simply mob rule. It disturbs him to hear reporters talk of democracy … likely most reporters have no idea what sort of government we have … a constitutional republic. The story goes that after the constitution was ratified a lady asked Ben Franklin what sort of government they had given the country. He reportedly responded, "A Republic … if you can keep it." Indeed. Our first attempt was futile — the Articles of Confederation — was too close to anarchy.

"Democracy is two wolves and a sheep voting on what to have for dinner. Liberty is two wolves attempting to have a sheep for dinner and finding a well-informed, well-armed sheep." — *James Bovard* "A democracy cannot exist as a permanent form of government. It can only exist until a majority of voters discover that they can vote themselves largess out of the public treasury." — *Alexander Tytler*

Politically, most people nowadays look at themselves as either "right" or "left." This view comes from Europe, but in reality that is not really true in America. If you look at a line and put anarchy on the right end and communism/fascism on the left end, you get a better picture of reality. The Articles of Confederation were very close to anarchy, there were not enough rules to protect the rights of the individual. The further to the left you go on this line, the government has more control and the individual has less freedom. This was another revolutionary thought — that individuals had God-given rights.

Few people know that the original words in the Declaration were rights to Life, Liberty and Property. Property? Yes, remember monarchs and dictators do not like the common man to have property, this was special. However, at this time, slaves were property. Our founders realized this could be used as a guarantee to slave ownership — which for the most part they were in favor of dissolving — so it was changed to happiness. The 3/5's clause regarding slaves is thought by many to be a belief that the blacks were less than a person. In reality, it was to even the field for voting; the South wanted to count the slaves as people in relation to representation but did not want them to vote.

It is amazing to him that we have access to the writings of the founders, enabling awareness of their thought processes, but many people do not care. Our second attempt with our current Constitution added more protection for the people … protection FROM the government. Many today want the government to do things FOR the people … this underscores that entitlement mentality.

At the turn of the last century there was a huge push by progressives to change our country and undermine our Constitution. In Europe they were called Fabien Socialists. George Bernard Shaw is a well-recognized writer from this time and many like his plays and writings. How many know he was a Fabien Socialist and promoted the extermination of people who he viewed as non-productive for society? He promoted the gassing of these people who were not able to justify their existence and he also defended Hitler's mass murders … nice guy. We had our despicable people as well … Margret Sanger for one. This founder of Planned Parenthood and her followers warned of the *menace posed by the black and yellow peril,* spoke of purifying America's *human breeding stock* and purging America's *bad strains*. These *strains* included the *shiftless, ignorant, and worthless* class of antisocial whites of the South. These promoters of eugenics believed they could determine who deserved to be born, live, procreate, or die.

Now, should these people be silenced? Absolutely not! We have a free country and as long as it is just talk, let them talk. He believes the vast majority of people will see these sorts for what they are and they will be minimized by their own words. However, we have a free press that has decided to take sides, who reports on what they want and ignores what they do not want exposed. A true free press reports and the people can decide what to believe or side to take. And this brings us to what he has decided to do. He is not a reporter; he does not have a newspaper, radio or TV station. What he does have is a love of his country and a belief that if the people know they will choose what is right for the country. This is a government "of the people, for the people and by the people."

The progressives claim their agenda is social justice; using the government to "even the playing field," or "make up for past injustices." Is it a fact that some have been treated unfairly? Is it a fact that some have had an unfair advantage? Certainly. But once an injustice has been done, the best thing to do is learn from the mistake and keep it from happening again. Any time the government tries to do something for, or to a group of people or businesses, there are always unintended consequences. It is best to move on and keep it from happening again.

These are his opinions, and everyone has theirs. Often our opinions are based on the facts we have combined with our personal experiences and beliefs. For instance, most children believe in Santa Clause … but once they learn the facts, they change their mind. This is what has led him to a decision. He thought; what can one person or a small group of like minded people do when there are over 300 million people in the country? Educate them, and let the chips fall where they may. With a press who has chosen sides, it will have to come about in another way. There are people with a voice who need data and information, there is the Internet and word of mouth.

There are people who operate in the dark … they are Marxists, communists, and socialists. They push the buttons they can, they parse the information they put out. They have willing accomplices in government and media as well as a small number of the people. He believes if their full story is brought to light, enough people will wake up and take action. Now is the time. The various Tea Parties and other similar groups show there is a hunger for becoming involved and making educated choices. He has to devise a way to get the information and then make it public … he has his work cut out for him. If given clear options, he trusts most people will make the correct choice and save the country.

He has a core belief — people view the world and other people through their own views and beliefs. Now this seems very simple, but he does not believe most people recognize or understand it. For example, you may not believe you have racist feelings, but if you believe many other people do it is likely you do as well … honest people believe most others are honest, and so on. Most traditional thinkers believe in God and that people have a duty to help their fellow man who is in need.

Progressives believe people are selfish and will not help others so the government has to step in and redistribute wealth. Traditional people typically give more to charity than progressives. What is better for the country, people who care for each other or a country who takes from the haves and gives to the have nots? People sometimes point to the story of Robin Hood who robbed the rich and gave to the poor … however, this is not accurate. Robin Hood robbed the government and gave back to the people … remember the Sheriff of Nottingham was the government. These things are constantly on his mind.

Chapter 3

Janis

CAN SHE BE DESCRIBED in one or two words? Not a chance. Kind, compassionate, trusting, trusted, intelligent … she is all these things and more. She is his wife. He knows he is a better man because of her … a lot of people are better because of her. They have been married nearly 30 years, and on the way to forever.

She has three sisters and was raised mostly by her mother. Her mother named her Janis, with the unusual spelling so it's "spelled as it sounds." She later thought it should have been Janus. Her father — she loved him dearly — but he loved other women as well and was not around as he should have been. As a result, she has many half brothers and sisters. Money was tight … she tells of accidentally dropping a carton of milk once when she was small, her mother cried as there was no money to buy more. She was devastated. The family only had a pickup, and when they went places as a family, the girls would have to ride in the back in a big wooden box. They would sit in the dark and wonder where they were and how much longer it might be. Later on, they had a topper shell … hey could see … however, bathroom stops were accomplished via a three-pound coffee can with sand in it.

She married young, soon after high school. She remembers the day she fixed her husband breakfast early, packed his lunch; he flashed a smile, kissed her and went to work. A little after seven that evening the phone rang, there had been an accident. He died in a fall, leaving her a young widow with a son 2 ½ and a daughter only 3 ½ months old.

Michael had taught the high-school-age class at church. Before she was married, she was one of four girls in the class. She'd make comments later that he'd dated all the other girls before her, and he'd reply, "Yes, but I didn't marry them, I saved the best for last, I married you." They understood each other having both lost a spouse, something that is hard to understand if you have not experienced it. He thinks losing a child might be tougher, but he never wants to learn that first hand. Her grandfather took her aside when they got serious. His wife had not been supportive of him or his desires. He told her, "He is a pilot; his job will require him to be away on birthdays, anniversaries and holidays. Make up your mind if this is okay or don't marry him." Good advice. They would eventually become foster parents; they had a son and adopted a daughter.

She is supportive of his entrepreneurial endeavors; she has a good business sense herself. She was a stay-at-home mom, as both believed that children should have a parent raise them in lieu of a daycare center. As the children got older and more involved, she followed a long-time desire to give back, and went to train as an EMT. She began as a volunteer in a local first-responder unit, ultimately becoming an EMT-I. She was asked to work for the county EMS after the kids were all out of school, and eventually took a full-time job with them. Her co-workers were amazed at her compassion and ability to relate to the sick, injured and their families … and they to her.

One day, as they waited in line in a store to buy a few items for their shift, a young girl with Down syndrome just came over and hugged her. Her partner said, "Let me guess, you have no idea who that was." She replied, "No, I don't." This is normal for her, people sense that she can relate and understand.

She is also strong. While he is a very strong personality and likes to be in charge while he is around, she is content to let him have that role while there, yet not afraid to take charge when he is away. The small town where they live wanted someone sharp to run for city council, she answered the call and served several years in that capacity. She sees the good in the world over the bad. She understands there is evil in the world, but she has a positive attitude and seeks the positive. She has always been politically aware, but not vocal about politics. She loves children and is dismayed at the prospect they might not have the same freedoms she has enjoyed. She has educated herself in the beliefs of candidates, and has become very vocal in defending freedom and voting, often entering discussions with the unaware to teach them history and what the result of our nation's direction might be.

She dreamed one day of owning and running a bed-and-breakfast, as she loves meeting new people and learning about them and their experiences. They discussed over the years the desire to have a log cabin in the mountains; they even had property for that dream. Sometimes responsibility gets in the way of dreams … aging parents and the need to help care for them makes the cabin dream inappropriate … but the B&B might be a different story. It took him 2 ½ years, but he built a large log house on their rural property where they also raise alpacas. This will be a source of income in retirement, a place to care for parents and a nice place to spend the rest of their lives in the quietness of the Central Plains.

She supports his new ventures; she never questions whether it is the right thing to do, but she does ask good questions to make sure all aspects have been thought out. She will be a key component of the team; most likely never directly involved, but an intricate part of the puzzle nonetheless.

They love their new house and their lives. Some couples just get comfortable and go through their lives; they're content and if that works for them, well that's just fine. Many couples at this point in their marriage have settled in or gone their separate ways … looking for something vague, for something perceived to be lost or missed. They are not like that, they continually challenge each other and they continue to grow together. Part of their thought process in building the new house, and keeping the old farm house and house they raised their family in, was to use them as income sources in retirement. Another part of their thinking was to have sufficient space for all of the family if needed in an emergency … such as a national crisis in which there was serious shortages of food and utilities.

They can live off the land and exist here much better than in a city environment. Better to be prepared and never need it, than to be caught off guard wondering how you will care for your family. He remembers an old western where an unlikely group of misfits and an outlaw end up together; none of them would likely make it alone, but together they make a formidable force. They make it to a cabin an old lady in the group knew her son had built. She thought her son a God-fearing man as he had cut out crosses in the heavy window shutters. The outlaw recognized the crosses as a place one could point a rifle at oncoming threats; up and down, back and forth … it all depends on your point of view.

Chapter 4

THEY ARE SITTING IN the screen porch drinking their morning coffee watching a few ducks swim around on the pond behind the house. They've been discussing some things about the B&B and after sitting in silence a few moments he begins, "I've been thinking about something, something I want to become involved in."

She is not surprised, his mind is always working… working isn't the right word … flying, that's better. "What's this going to cost?" She asks.

"Not what, but how much, huh?"

This does not surprise him. While she trusts him, she is always concerned about finances … it's just part of her … and he likes that about her. She waits.

"It probably will not cost anything, money-wise, but it will take some time."

She cuts him off, "Like either one of us has much of that to spare."

This is true, they are involved in so many things that the inside joke is to say "I'll get that done in my spare time."

"I know," he continues, "but I'm not sure we have much of a choice. You know that saying by Dietrich Bonhoeffer I told you about?"

She asks, "The one where he says something about seeing evil and doing nothing is evil?"

"Yes, in a nutshell that's it, and there's the part where he says God will hold us accountable."

They pondered that thought in silence for a few moments and then she asks, “So, what is this evil you have seen that needs to be confronted?”

He takes a sip of his coffee and replies, “We live in a big country, I mean square-miles big. The population is large, but in the shadow of India and China, not so much. There are a lot of patriotic people out there as we have seen at Tea Party rallies, people who want to see us come back to our basic principles.”

She wonders aloud, “So the evil has something to do with …?”

“The move our country is making away from God, and The Constitution. I believe a return to the basic principles that the country was founded on, will save the nation.”

“I agree,” she says, “but how do you plan to change the whole nation by yourself?”

“I don’t … by myself that is.”

He spends the next several minutes explaining his ideas and when he was finished she says, “I think this could actually work … I wonder why no one has ever thought of it before?”

“I don’t know, I suppose someone might have tried it and failed, but we have nothing to lose and everything to gain, so let’s give it a shot.”

They sit in silence and finish their coffee while watching the ducks swim and bob their heads under for something to eat.

A few weeks in the future:

He turns on the computer and prepares for the video conference. It is amazing to him how technology has changed in such a short time. It seems just yesterday that letters and occasional phone calls were all you had. Now, you can connect with people from anywhere in the world, see and hear each other.

They all begin to pop up on the screen and within a minute everyone is on.

"I'm sure glad you all took the time to make the call," he says.

Brenda replies, "You really have me thinking with the bit of information you gave me the other day and I just couldn't wait to see just what you have in mind."

"Well, I did sort of try to pique your interest a bit, but partly I did not have everything lined out as I wanted … and partly this conference is to get input from all of you. This is not just my deal … I hope to get started … but it will take the minds and work of many to be successful. First off, let's all introduce ourselves … and let's just use first names for now … first names and what you do for a living; I'll explain my concerns later."

"Well, since I already spoke up … my name is Brenda, I'm a nurse."

"Bernie, engineer … hydraulics, not trains."

A few chuckles.

"My name is John, airline pilot."

"Keith, I drive a delivery truck."

"I'm another John, college professor."

"Knut, heavy construction."

"Great, sounds as if we have a nice cross-section of America as far as occupations go. I know it is late and I will keep this as short as I can, but will be here as long as it takes to answer your questions and get your input. Everyone on this call has some things in common; you all love your country, you all have a sphere of influence, and most importantly, I trust each of you. I do not know what we actually might be up against as we try to implement this, maybe nothing, maybe a lot of pressure in various ways. I want to make one thing clear … you all are here as volunteers, I do not want or expect any of you to suffer in any way for your efforts here. If anyone wants out at any time, please just let me know and there will be no hard feelings. All I ask is that you keep all this within the group."

They all nod or voice approval to move on.

"My thought is to implement these ideas within your circle of trusted friends, so each of you will work with this group and your personal group. The success of this effort is going to lie entirely on the personal responsibility of key people throughout the country."

Knut asks, "So what exactly are we going to do on this scale that will have a national effect?"

"We are going to make the federal government irrelevant." He pauses and watches the expressions on their faces … he sees confusion, doubt, shock … pretty much what he expected.

Chapter 5

HE KNOWS THE COUNTRY is deeply divided. While this is in itself disturbing, he realizes when two people are in a room there are likely two differing opinions. Opinions are like heads … we all have one … and we all believe ours is better; this is just the way human beings are. If we are talking about who makes the best car or truck there can be much debate, often our beliefs are carried from our family's choices and personal experience … "My grandfather drove a Ford, my dad drove a ford … so I drive a Ford." This opinion is not really thought out or based on any fact, it is an assumption drawn from the thought "my grandfather and dad drove them because they were best."

He is reminded of the story where a young bride wanted to fix a ham for a special occasion. She thought her mom made the best ham she ever tasted so she called her mom to ask how it should be prepared.

Her mom said, "First you cut the ham in half, then …"

The daughter cut her off, "Why do you cut it in half?"

Mom thought a moment and admitted, "Well, I'm not sure … my mom always did it that way … I'd have to ask."

So the young girl thanked her mom, hung up and called her grandmother. "Granny, I was talking to mom about preparing a ham. She said to start by cutting it in half and I was wondering what that did, help get the juices all through the meat, or what?"

Granny chuckled and replied, “Honey, I never had a pan big enough to hold a whole ham!”

Sometimes our beliefs are built on a false premise. Many of us are ignorant … and many do not even realize the true meaning of ignorance, they equate it to stupidity. There is a big difference between the inability to learn and an unwillingness to learn. The dictionary defines ignorance: lacking in knowledge or training; unlearned: an ignorant man. 2. lacking knowledge or information as to a particular subject or fact. Ignorance has nothing to do with intelligence; it is related to a desire to know, to learn.

He remembers an example of this; a man recently made this public statement: “The issue with the Constitution is that people don’t read the text and think they’re following it. The issue with the Constitution is that the text is confusing because it was written more than a hundred years ago.”

There is no need for any explanation as to how moronic this statement is.

He spends much time alone, as an only child this is normal for him. It is not that he prefers to be alone; it is just how it often works out in relation to his job commute, his ranch, and his wife’s job. His mind is always running, racing, thinking. His memory is very good and he can work out a problem, design something, hatch a business plan; all in his head without notes.

When he is not working on something in his mind he reflects; on his life, family, and history … he loves history. In school he relished studying history; he is analytical and likes to figure out what happened and why … this is simplistic in a way, sometimes things are not so clearly cut and easy to figure out. However, often there are trends, events and ideas that keep raising their heads … the common thread that allows an observant person to follow and even predict an outcome …thus the saying, “those who do not study history are doomed to repeat it.” Being raised in the Northeast he was fortunate to live in areas where Revolutionary War battles were fought … being at the places where things happen help them to come alive.

Freedom. Our ancestors and millions since came to this country for freedom. There is the old test … put a fence around a country and see what people do … try to get in … or get out. Tens of millions have come to this country … they would have climbed a fence to get in. Compare to Eastern Europe … a fence was put up there and no one tried to get in … they wanted out. Freedom. But are we free? Certainly compared with many other countries we are. What if we compare our freedom now to the freedom of 50 years ago … 100 years ago … 200 years ago? Our country is very young when you really think about it … many countries have been in existence for hundreds and over a thousand years. So are we free? He thinks not … not really free. Simple things come to mind; the kids who set up a lemonade stand to raise money for a charity … only to have the police shut them down because they did not have a $500 permit.

He reflects on how words and their meanings change over the years. The progressives had a big following in the early 20th century … until the people learned what their policies were doing to their lives, their freedom. Progressive became a name people hated, so they started calling themselves liberals. This was a co-opting of a term that was already in use, what we today call libertarian. Interesting that again the term used for them has become one tied to something undesirable, so they have returned to the term progressive … history repeats itself, again.

What happened in the early 20th century? Well, he remembers something our founders warned about. Ben Franklin said, "People willing to trade their freedom for temporary security deserve neither and will lose both." These men were truly brilliant … they did not all agree, but they worked together and gave us a document that has served our nation and ultimately the world for over 200 years. So what did Ben mean?

He considers the Eighteenth Amendment to the Constitution, the prohibition of alcoholic beverages. A nation cannot legislate good behavior or common sense. There are always unintended consequences to any legislation … and the result of prohibition is certainly well documented. Many things that were a result of progressive legislation were initiated in the early 20th century ...farm programs have destroyed the family farm, rules to end child labor have prevented young people from working and learning a good work ethic, and regulations for auto safety have increased the weight and cost of cars and lowered their fuel efficiency. There are cars that get close to 100 mpg, but they do not meet "safety standards," yet motorcycles are okay. For some perceived security and safety we have given up real freedom. We have decided that a mouse or a fish is more important than people and property. We have decided the government can come take our property if someone else can generate more tax revenue than us.

The Constitution was made so it could be amended and has been over the years as the people deem it necessary. The beauty of the process is that an amendment will always be there so we can know of the mistakes ... such as the 18th. It takes another amendment to repeal, so the mistake is always there for us to know.

Another progressive amendment, the 17th, really changed the entire design of our government. The original intent was for the people to be represented by the House, the states were represented by the Senate. This amendment took the states representative and gave it to the people, so the states lost their ability to control the federal government. Was this consequence unintended as some are? He thinks not.

Freedom ... He sees the government as something that is reactive rather than proactive. In order to save the nation, the Constitution, and freedom ... it will require proactive rather than reactive solutions. Historically when efforts have been made to effect change, it has been reactionary. If it worked at all, it did not last. Look at history; do not do what did not work before. There are multiple problems in the country, largely as a result of generations of people who do not know *true* freedom and responsibility. One of his favorite commentators, the late Paul Harvey, used to say, "The increase of freedom requires the increase of responsibility." We are back to the founder's question, "Can man rule himself?"

The simple answer is, "Yes"… but there are conditions … responsibilities that are required of each person to enjoy the freedoms we so desire and love.

So the problem is not laws or the lack of them … it is a matter of controlling behavior and desire from within. Some people might be dissuaded from robbing a bank by the threat of imprisonment after capture … but most will not entertain the idea because it is not right to take things which do not belong to you; and there will always be some who will do it regardless. When the country first began, the Articles of Confederation ruled the nation. Created during the throes of the Revolutionary War, the Articles reflect the wariness by the states of a strong central government. Afraid that their individual needs would be ignored by a national government with too much power — and the abuses that often result from such power — the Articles purposely established a "constitution" that vested the largest share of power to the individual states.

Under the Articles each of the states retained their "sovereignty, freedom and independence." Instead of setting up executive and judicial branches of government, there was a committee of delegates composed of representatives from each state. These individuals comprised the Congress, a national legislature called for by the Articles.

The Congress was responsible for conducting foreign affairs, declaring war or peace, maintaining an army and navy and a variety of other lesser functions. But the Articles denied Congress the power to collect taxes, regulate interstate commerce and enforce laws.

Eventually, these shortcomings would lead to the adoption of the U.S. Constitution. But during those years in which the states were struggling to achieve their independent status, the Articles of Confederation stood them in good stead. As he reflects on the problems and possible solutions he makes a connection. It is something he has known all along, but it is something he just did not fully realize.

Chapter 6

THE PROGRESSIVES IN THE early 20th century, to be successful, had to destroy two things; God and our founders. This is the time frame when authors of textbooks started calling our founders “rich white slave owners” in an effort to demean them. “In God we trust” was added to our currency in the middle of the century in an effort to fight back at the attempts to remove God from our history, as was “Under God” added to the Pledge. He understands well that our founders were not unified in their beliefs, but they all understood the value of morals and virtue. To rule himself, man must have good morals and virtue.

He considers how the Progressives accomplished their goals; propaganda. When many think of propaganda they think of Germany and the Third Reich, of Joseph Goebbels. Not many think of Woodrow Wilson and Edward Louis Bernays. Diaries of Goebbels show much of what he knew of propaganda he learned from Bernays. Much of Bernays early work was done in advertising … which of course is propaganda. The Wilson administration used his work to gain the public’s support for his programs and plans. Ever hear of the slogan, “Make the world safe for democracy?” This is Bernays work to gain acceptance of entering WWI after running on the platform to stay out of the war.

Another way to turn the feelings of the people is to start with the children. Vladimir Lenin once said, "Give me four years to teach the children and the seed I have sown will never be uprooted." He vaguely remembers copybooks ... books young children use in school. There is a sentence at the top of the page and the child then practices writing the sentence on the lines below. Imagine if someone could put certain thoughts where the children wrote them over and over what that might do to their thought process? Well, he knows this is not a theory, it happened. A well-known author wrote a poem; the idea is that the copybook heading is a timeless gem to be learned and retained.

The Gods of the Copybook Headings
1919
Rudyard Kipling

As I pass through my incarnations in every age and race,
I make my proper prostrations to the Gods of the Market-Place.
Peering through reverent fingers I watch them flourish and fall,
And the Gods of the Copybook Headings, I notice, outlast them all.

We were living in trees when they met us. They showed us each in turn. That Water would certainly wet us, as Fire would certainly burn: but we found them lacking in Uplift, Vision and Breadth of Mind, so we left them to teach the Gorillas while we followed the March of Mankind.

We moved as the Spirit listed. They never altered their pace, Being neither cloud nor wind-borne like the Gods of the Market-Place. But they always caught up with our progress, and presently word would come. That a tribe had been wiped off its icefield, or the lights had gone out in Rome.

With the Hopes that our World is built on they were utterly out of touch. They denied that the Moon was Stilton; they denied she was even Dutch. They denied that Wishes were Horses; they denied that a Pig had Wings. So we worshipped the Gods of the Market Who promised these beautiful things.

When the Cambrian measures were forming, They promised perpetual peace.

They swore, if we gave them our weapons, that the wars of the tribes would cease.

But when we disarmed they sold us and delivered us bound to our foe,

And the Gods of the Copybook Heading said: "Stick to the Devil you know."

On the first Feminian Sandstones we were promised the Fuller Life

(Which started by loving our neighbour and ended by loving his wife)

Till our women had no more children and the men lost reason and faith,

And the Gods of the Copybook Headings said: "The Wages of Sin is Death."

In the Carboniferous Epoch we were promised abundance for all,
By robbing selected Peter to pay for collective Paul;
But, though we had plenty of money, there was nothing our money could buy,

And the Gods of the Copybook Headings said: "If you don't work you die."

Then the Gods of the Market tumbled, and their smooth-tongued wizards withdrew,

And the hearts of the meanest were humbled and began to believe it was true.

That All is not Gold that Glitters, and Two and Two make Four—
And the Gods of the Copybook Headings limped up to explain it once more.

As it will be in the future, it was at the birth of Man—
There are only four things certain since Social Progress began —
That the Dog returns to his Vomit and the Sow returns to her Mire,

And the burnt Fool's bandaged finger goes wabbling back to the Fire—

And that after this is accomplished, and the brave new world begins

When all men are paid for existing and no man must pay for his sins

As surely as Water will wet us, as surely as Fire will burn
The Gods of the Copybook Headings with terror and slaughter return!

Kipling wrote this poem in 1919 after he lost his son in WWI. As is clear from the language of the poem, mentioning "Social Progress," the "brave new world," "robbing selected Peter to pay for collective Paul," the dangers of disarmament and immorality, and with the overall structure following the evolutionary narrative, the subject is the progressive movement that attempts to reduce human life to scientific, animalistic principles. The poem reminds us constantly that old wisdom is still wise and true even if we have lost faith in it, and the last line echoes the toll of the first two years of the Russian Revolution. It echoes the 100-million death toll from communism, the ultimate progressive movement for the scientific reformation of society and humanity. And it echoes in the toll of 40 million abortions in the United States since Roe vs. Wade.

As God and the founders and their principles are essentially taken out, belittled and diminished, the country has been in decline. The more selfish the individual becomes, the more likely they are to lose the ability to rule themselves. The Constitution does not guarantee we will not be offended, but that is how much of this is accomplished; demands of God being removed so someone is not offended. Thomas Jefferson actually spoke to this over 200 years ago; "The legitimate powers of government extend to such acts only as are injurious to others. But it does me no injury for my neighbor to say there are twenty gods, or no God. It neither picks my pocket nor breaks my leg."

He realizes this conclusion will not be shared by all; this will be like any other opinion. However in recent years he believes there have been enough changes, people have taken a greater interest in their country. Ten years ago if you asked him, "You think they will have free sessions teaching The Constitution in our area?" he would have told you, "You've got to be kidding!" Guess what? They are being held all over the country. Why? People are beginning to realize that they were shortchanged in their education, and that our elected officials are not following The Constitution. Most elected officials seem to excel in the ability to become elected and little else. While there are some excellent ones, most count their ability to bring tax dollars to their state or district as most important.

So ultimately the problem is control, who is in control? Most politicians believe they are in control, and they essentially are. Career politicians, not what our founders intended nor what is in the best interest of the country, but that is not the pressing issue. The Preamble to the Constitution; We the People of the United States, in Order to form a more perfect Union, establish Justice, insure domestic Tranquility, provide for the common defense, promote the general Welfare, and secure the Blessings of Liberty to ourselves and our Posterity, do ordain and establish this Constitution for the United States of America. We … the … people.

There has become an elitist mentality in recent years that we the people are not smart enough to know what is best for us. He believes the elitists are morons, or evil … possibly both. There certainly are evil people involved, people who have their own best interest at heart. There are people who are ideological, who have good intent, but their ideas will not work … never have … never will.

Some will point to Europe, that style of socialism; it is now on the verge of total collapse from the weight of debt trying to do things from a central government … and the U.S. is stepping in to help prevent that collapse, lest they pull us down as well. He believes it will sink us all.

He remembers being taught in school about the "First Thanksgiving." He learned how the local Indians saved the pilgrims by teaching them how to plant corn and other crops. In reality, they spent several years in preparation for their endeavor. Before sailing to the new world they signed a pact, and had a socialist community. Everything was commonly owned, everyone shared the harvest. They forgot they were working with humans. There were some who worked hard, and some who just coasted … why not, they got the same ration as those who worked hard. In short order they all about froze to death and starved … many did. Most of the new colonies started this way and in all cases half or more of the settlers died. The solution was a free market. Colonists were given land they could use to farm, trade, or do whatever they chose. Immediately they began to thrive.

At one time, when their children were young, he gave serious consideration to home schooling. His job taking him away for days at a time did not fit well with that idea and his wife did not feel up to the challenge at that point in her life. There was one statement by the first major progressive president, Woodrow Wilson; "I have often said that the use of a university is to make young gentlemen as unlike their fathers as possible."

The people, the groups … the forces behind what is changing America are unified … but they are not the same. He realizes they both have the same goal … to replace our current system. What they replace it with is where they disagree. These people and groups range in beliefs from an oligarchy to an open society (ruled by something like the UN) to pure communism/Marxism. They operate on the theory of "the enemy of my enemy is my friend." He realizes his country has done this many times, aligning with Osama Bin Laden and Sadam Heusen being recent notable examples. So what happens when their mutual goals have been achieved? There will then be another power struggle to gain complete control. He does not have a feeling which might overcome the other … what he knows is we will no longer have a sovereign United States of America, and we will lose what freedoms we still enjoy. Whatever it is and whoever it is, things will not be the same and it will be easier to stop than to undo it … and stopping it will be nearly impossible.

Control … who *is* in control and who *will be* in control? He believes there are enough true patriots, those who love the Constitution and want to see a return to something closer to what the founders left us to stop this dangerous slide. This is not a Republican vs. Democrat problem; there are progressive Republicans and there are conservative Democrats. The forces on the other side are unified and organized. Even though they form a minority of the population, they seem larger due to their organization. They do have one huge disadvantage … they are trying to be reactionaries and revolutionaries … his ideas will set a clear choice between something radical and something positive …he believes the people … enough people … will make the right choice.

Chapter 7

HIS WIFE REMINDED HIM of the story from childhood about the Little Red Hen.

> Once upon a time, a little red hen lived in a small cottage. She worked hard to keep her family fed. One day, when the little red hen was out walking with her friends, the goose, the cat, and the pig, she found a few grains of wheat.
>
> "Who will help me plant this wheat?" asked the little red hen.
>
> "Not I," said the goose, "I'd rather swim in the pond."
>
> "Not I," said the cat, "I'd rather sleep on the hay."
>
> "Not I," said the pig, "I'd rather lie in the mud."
>
> "Then I'll do it myself," said the little red hen. And she did.
>
> Time went by and the wheat grew, but so did the weeds.

"Who will help me pull the weeds?" asked the little red hen.

"Not I," said the goose, "I'd rather swim in the pond."

"Not I," said the cat, "I'd rather sleep on the hay."

"Not I," said the pig, "I'd rather lie in the mud."

"Then I'll do it myself," said the little red hen. And she did.

All summer the wheat grew taller and taller. It turned from brown to golden amber. And, at last, it was time to harvest the wheat.

"Who will help me harvest the wheat?" asked the little red hen.

"Not I," said the goose, "I'd rather swim in the pond."

"Not I," said the cat, "I'd rather sleep on the hay."

"Not I," said the pig, "I'd rather lie in the mud."

"Then I'll do it myself," said the little red hen. And she did.

At last, the wheat was harvested and put into a large sack, ready to be taken to the mill to be ground into flour.

"Who will help me take the wheat to the mill?" asked the little red hen.

"Not I," said the goose, "I'd rather swim in the pond."

"Not I," said the cat, "I'd rather sleep on the hay."

"Not I," said the pig, "I'd rather lie in the mud."

"Then I'll do it myself," said the little red hen. And she did.

The next day came and the little red hen was hungry.

"Who will help me bake this flour into bread?" asked the little red hen.

"Not I," said the goose, "I'd rather swim in the pond."

"Not I," said the cat, "I'd rather sleep on the hay."

"Not I," said the pig, "I'd rather lie in the mud."

"Then I'll do it myself," said the little red hen. And she did.

At last, the bread was baked and the little red hen called to her friends once more.

"Who will help me eat this bread?" asked the little red hen.

> "I will," said the goose.
>
> "I will," said the cat.
>
> "I will," said the pig.
>
> "Oh, no you won't!" said the little red hen. "I found the wheat, I planted it, I weeded it, and when it was time to harvest it, I did that too. I took it to the mill to be ground into flour and at last, I baked it into bread.
>
> "Now," said the little red hen, "I'm going to eat it with my family."
>
> And she did.

Now, this is a harsh lesson in personal responsibility, reaping the rewards of your labor, tough love. He realizes there is a huge difference between helping those truly in need and helping those who will not do what they can … however the forces behind the change exploit this and try to make everyone feel bad for those without … no matter the reason. He believes this is why the power has to come out of Washington; it is impossible for a department in the nation's capital to understand the difference in those in need and those who are lazy … but on a local level that difference can be known.

Americans are looking for a hero. We always have wanted the hero, the triumph of good over evil. He grew up in the era of Superman and other super heroes, western films where the good guys wore white hats and the bad guys black. This has nothing to do with skin color, people become absurd with their PC garbage; it is simply the difference between right and wrong. He does not want to be a hero and has no intention of becoming one. Several years ago he remembers *Time* magazine made their "Man of the Year" the American soldier. This is his thought … make the average American citizen "Man of the Year."

He realizes the people who are trying to fundamentally transform the nation will not sit idly by and just watch this happen. Most of them have spent most of their lives trying to accomplish their goals, and they are close … very close to realizing those goals. He has seen them go after people who oppose them; talk show hosts, journalists, politicians and average people (Joe the Plummer comes to mind). They are ruthless and will stop at nothing to tear them apart, go through their background, and look for anything that can be used to destroy. Most will wilt at this, and many are put off from even trying for fear of their wrath. For this reason he plans to work completely in the dark, and use a few very close friends to control the information. He will be completely open with them and they will have the option to back away at any time with no hard feelings. He will feel personally responsible if anyone is hurt in any way as a result of helping him, no matter the reason or how noble the cause.

He does wonder if these people will become physical in their attacks. He has seen some of the "underlings" do things at rallies, people with tempers and no self-control … these things happen. But desperate people do desperate things … might some group or person do something drastic if they see their goal slipping away? He will have to keep that thought close; he is not worried about himself, but about his wife and friends. Could he ever forgive himself if his efforts led to someone's harm or death? He does not want to learn the answer to that question.

The idea is quite simple … and seemingly impossible… make the federal government, the aspect which gives the entitlements, irrelevant. We do need the federal government, and he remembers how the Articles of Confederation failed … and led to our current constitution. The entitlements are bankrupting the country, and morally bankrupting those who are "along for the ride" which is the more costly of the two. He knows the country is two or three generations into this and many know no other way. They expect healthcare, food, housing and more … some just one or two things, others everything. Some need it due to no fault of their own, others are just lazy. How can an agency in Washington D.C. know the difference? They cannot. How can he? Well, he cannot either, but this is his idea and the solution will come to him in time, and with the help of his friends.

His idea is to keep it simple, and keep it with a grassroots appearance. He remembers the story of the man with two sons; the man was dying and wanted to see which one had learned enough to take over his business. He told them, “I will pay you $10,000 a day for 30 days, or I will pay you a penny the first day, and then double it every day for 30 days.” The first son jumped on the 10K, while the second, after some thought, told his father he’d take the penny. The first son laughed at his brother and went off to work. At the end of the month, the first son had $300,000 and was quite happy … until he spoke to his brother. “How much did you end up with after starting with a penny?” he asked. His brother replied, “10.7 million dollars.” What???? He knew the value of compounding interest.

So, quite simply, his plan is to grow the group as in the story of the two sons. He does not know if the idea of six degrees of separation is true or not … does not really matter … it’s close enough. His idea is to involve each of his friends who will in turn start a group. Each of those will in turn start a group with their friends and so on. Each one will be autonomous and give the rest the ability to operate if one should be shut down for some reason. He knows some will lose interest or fall out for one reason or another. He believes the entire country can be covered while he only has to deal with a few of his closest and most trusted friends. Two things make this workable; once it is started it will have a life of its own, and if the forces behind the transformation decide to go after the operation they will not have a place or a person to attack … at least not one that will have any national affect.

Chapter 8

Capt. John

Easy going and loyal … that's how he'd sum up John. They'd been friends for more than 25 years; he'd helped John get his first "real" job flying. He remembered it as if it were yesterday. A small company in the area had lost their pilot due to a medical situation and they'd asked him to fly some and help them find another pilot. He'd made a trip to a smaller airport near a Midwest city and as he'd done several other times, asked around if anyone there was interested in a job. This day a young man said yes, he knew someone. John was up giving a flight lesson, he was the head instructor in a small flight school. The young man who he spoke to wanted the head instructor job so he was going to get rid of John to get that job. Now he could have just taken the job offer, a much better deal, but his eye was not on the better opportunity. John took the job right off, loaded up his old Chevy pickup and drove to the Texas Panhandle. He was impressed that John would just go at the word of a stranger, but then most people seemed to trust him. John was eager to learn everything; he'd help do anything from cutting firewood to putting new shingles on a roof. He and his wife called him their son, with a smile, and John liked it. They introduced him to peanut butter and jelly sandwiches; they were amazed he'd never had one before.

Very traditional, freedom loving and patriotic, John loves his country…and is frustrated by the changes toward socialism. The moral decline of the country is a big concern as well. He soon moved to a larger company flying a King Air, and then on to flying corporate jets for a large oil and gas company. He then landed a job at a large airline … a job that now has him in a position to move around the country with ease. This is perfect for operations, often things can be accomplished while on company business. Any prying eyes will not find anyone making a specific trip on any passenger list.

The phone rings twice, "Hey Mike, where are you?"

They sometimes have layovers in the same city and when possible they get together.

"I'm at home … I've got something on my mind, you got a minute?"

"Sure, what's up?"

He takes a few minutes to briefly explain his idea.

John asks, "You're serious about this aren't you?"

"As a heart attack."

"And you think this will work?"

"Who knows, but someone has to do something … doing nothing does not work, we know that for sure; you on board with this?"

"If you're involved you can count me in, at the very least we might get to see each other a little more than normal."

"That's a great side benefit … I'll be in touch soon. Thanks John, I knew I could count on you."

Bernie

Quiet and unassuming … yes, that would sum him up. They'd been friends since junior high with similar interests, primarily skiing in the Northeast where they were raised. He had lived in several countries growing up; spoke fluent German, French and Spanish. His father was an engineer; officially anyway … there was always a question as to whether that is all he was. They drifted apart in the early college years, different schools and all … it would be nearly 20 years before they reconnected. Bernie's father had passed away, and he was taking care of the necessary affairs. He took a chance that Mike's father still lived in the same house. They reconnected and have been close ever since.

It is amazing how similar they still are; aviation, love of country, traditional values, the Second Amendment … all important to them. Bernie had a low draft number during the Viet Nam War and rather than be drafted as a "ground pounder," his dad made some calls.

His father had been a member of the resistance in WWII. As a Jew he was taking a bigger chance than many; his fluency in several languages allowed him to become unassuming in his work against the Third Reich. No questions were asked, no need to know what his father was in later years. After his father made some calls; he went into the Army as a pilot flying the C-130. Once basic and flight training were completed he "disappeared" into the background and spent his time during the war doing things we never officially did. He came out of that experience in a body cast after being shot down in a country we were never in … officially.

Two events stuck out in their minds from their youth. Bernie built a canoe out of wood and doped fabric. On its maiden voyage they took it out on Lake Champlain and paddled out to Valcour Island. Interestingly, this is the same channel Benedict Arnold anchored his fleet waiting for the British Navy. The water was just a few inches from coming over the edge, they paddled around for a while, went ashore a bit, and then paddled back. They did not talk much about it then, but after they had families of their own they agreed, "No way would we let our kids do anything that stupid!"

The other event was mostly memorable; a ski trip to Tuckerman Ravine in New Hampshire on Mt. Washington. There is no lift, skiing down happens only after a walk up the slope. The easiest part is 40 degrees with the toughest areas going to 55 degrees. Skiers have to camp out in the snow if they want to stay up high … it was a memorable experience for a couple of teenage boys.

Bernie followed his father's footsteps in engineering, working at the state level of government in two different states. He has connections that are important to our "endeavors," and skills that will make him an invaluable member of the team.

He answers his cell on the second ring, "Mike … what's up?"

"Same ole same ole Bernie, I have an idea I want to run by you, got a minute?"

"Sure."

They talk for a few minutes. Well, he talks, Bernie listens …

After giving a high-level overview he asks, "You want in on this?"

"You know Mike, there are some things you and I do not agree on, but I love this country and do not like what the federal government is doing to us. I think this could work and I am willing to work with you and give it a try … count me in."

"Thanks Bernie, I'll be in touch soon and we'll start some planning."

Brenda

Compassionate and dedicated … yes, this pretty well sums her up. In his mind he likes to break things down to the simplest terms. He'd gone to high school with her, but they ran in different circles. It was years later when they "found" each other online through a mutual friend. He now felt he knew her better … understood what made her tick. She has an amazing sense of humor — an ability to light up any conversation with her quick wit. She herself had been through a lot both physically and emotionally … and she readily would say her belief in God and sense of humor is what kept her going.

She got the call one day several years ago, as her mother had a serious fall and was in critical condition, in a coma, and not expected to live. As a nurse she took charge and refused to believe this was the end, and after six long months, the impossible happened … her mother came out of the coma. This would be enough to try anyone's constitution, but not Brenda … she had more to give … and would.

Some curious signs and symptoms began to appear … ALS, Lou Gehrig's disease. As the disease progressed, and her mom lost the ability to speak, they would share notes. One day after several quick notes she told her mom, "Are you ever going to shut up?!" Her mom would toss her head back, her mouth agape in a silent laugh. Her mother loved to sing and dance, had a voice like Doris Day. Brenda would have a friend come over, they would put on some music, hold her mom between them and dance … moving to the music. Yes, compassionate and dedicated. Not long after her mom passed, she lost her father as well. When you meet someone on the street, you often never guess the obstacles they have overcome.

She had her own personal struggles as well. An accident and subsequent surgery threatened to leave her wheelchair-bound for the rest of her life. Was this acceptable? Not hardly, not for this woman. Shear will and determination brought her mobility back. She loves life, loves to travel … don't get her started on Italy unless you have some time.

He listens to the ringing on his cell, "Hello?"

"Brenda," he says, "I have an idea I'd like to share with you … I could use some help."

"Sure, what's up?"

He spends a few minutes introducing the plan and asks, "You interested?"

"You've piqued my interest … I do want to learn more."

"Great, I'll be in touch soon, catch you later!"

Yorka or Knut

He might struggle to come up with one or two words for his friend, or “brother” as they often called each other. Another complex individual with many talents, a keen sense of personal responsibility and honor; and these are the things that have kept them close for more than 30 years. They both shared a love of aviation and it was flying that initially brought them together.

They first met when they were working for the same company flying on a government contract doing aerial photography for the USDA. It was tedious and boring, but it was a great time builder. Logged total flight hours are the basis of experience for any pilot, most new commercial pilots begin as flight instructors, or CFIs and build their time that way. An aspiring pilot would do well to fly 500-600 hours a year doing this, but the flying they did doubled that.

He came from a family with money … but it had not always been like that. Immigrants from Norway, they worked part-time jobs to pay the bills while building a business and pouring all the receipts back into the business. Progressives would look at them as the lucky ones who had been blessed with wealth, yet in truth it was hard work, work most people would not put into anything for anyone which brought them to their current place in society. They helped people behind the scenes, gave jobs to people who were in need when they did not need an employee; they were the kind of employer to which the workers were fiercely loyal.

The two of them flew to Alaska together shortly after Mount St. Helens blew its top. It was amazing to fly over what appeared to be a lunar landscape. The power of this natural phenomenon was unbelievable. They were also awed by the beauty of the land, flying in a small Cessna 180 at low altitude seeing things missed by most of humanity. They made a pact of sorts early on in their friendship. Since both had daughters, they were keenly aware of the predators that prey on young girls and women. They decided if someone was to rape one of their wives or a daughter, taking the law into their own hands was not out of the question. If they knew who had done this terrible act, well, they both owned their own plane and taking a bound and gagged rapist on a one-way flight to go night skydiving over the desert sans parachute was a likely outcome. This causes some conflict, we are a nation of laws and vigilante justice is not the norm … who knows what you might do in a situation like this … until you find yourself in it.

The experiences they shared over the years would fill a book. Needless to say, they were close, and if one needed the other for anything, only a phone call was needed to bring help … and now was one of those times. At the time of the trip to Alaska, Dan Aykroyd and Steve Martin were doing their skit of the "two wild and crazy guys." They came up with the names of Borka and Yorka for each other …

The phone rang three times and then, "Borka! What's up?"

"Not much, Yorka, you have a minute?"

"Sure, I was about to fly out to a job site and give a bid, but I have a few minutes."

He goes over his idea briefly and asks, "You want to help us with this?"

"Who's us?"

"Well," he said, "Janis for one and then several friends around the country … one I think you know, is John."

"I was just curious, actually. Of course you can count me in; I'll do it in my spare time."

This joke is not just between him and his wife …

"Great, I know you have to run, I'll be in touch."

"See ya, Borka."

"Later, Yorka."

Kenny

Rough looking with a kind heart … that describes him well. In his youth his life equaled his appearance … heavy drinking led him to a lot of tough times and heartache. Over the years he learned his lesson … he still slips up on occasion, but most of the time he is responsible. He and his wife have a child with cerebral palsy. They care for him at home and do many things for him on very limited funds. He would do almost anything for Michael or Janis, but this is a special feeling for them and not shared with just anyone. He had broken his leg badly and had been off work for quite some time. It was healed and he needed to look for work, but he did not have any clothes to work in or to wear while looking. Janis heard about it and bought him some jeans and shirts to wear. This big tough man cried that someone cared enough to do that … and he did not want charity … promised to pay them back.

She told him, "Someday you'll meet someone who needs help and you will be in a position to help them. The best way to pay us back is to help someone else."

He thanked her and the relationship between both families had been solid ever since. There was much friendly joking between them, and they also relied on Janis for medical advice. Their mentally challenged son admired Janis for all the times she'd helped him, and he was in awe of Mike since he was a pilot and could fly airplanes.

When the idea first came to him he knew he had to find people around the country that could help. While Kenny lived in the same area, he felt there would need to be some help locally since the airline job and these efforts would keep him away at key times.

The phone rang twice, Kenny answered, "Hello, Janis, is that you?"

"No, it's Mike."

"Darn, I saw the caller ID and hoped it was Janis … why would I want to talk to you, she's prettier than you!"

"That she is, Kenny, but you know her husband is the jealous type … you'd better be careful!"

"Ha, I know that! What can I do for you my friend?"

"I'm working on a project and I might need your help."

"Okay, where do I need to be and when?"

"You might want to know what I need, might be defusing a bomb or something," he said with a chuckle.

"If you want my help, you have it. I know whatever it is, it's legal and someone probably will benefit from it."

"Kenny, you must not know me very well … but you're close."

He gives him a summary of what he has in mind.

"You think I'm going to be any help to you in this?"

"I know you can, and will."

"Okay, whatever you want, let me know."

"Great, Kenny, I'll be in touch soon."

Keith

They are cousins … well … second cousins … their fathers are first cousins. They did not grow up very close geographically, but Keith lived near his grandmother so they saw each other quite often from very early years. Keith's father's middle initial is E and many people had the habit of calling him J. E. or John E. to differentiate him from another John. Mike took to calling all the kids the same way, so Keith became Keithey.

Keith has an older and a younger brother and sister, but the two of them always seemed closer. Over the years they double dated, took trips together, and they both learned to fly about the same time. They took a memorable trip together one summer … he had a Land Cruiser so Keith and another friend headed for the mountains of Colorado and Wyoming. They stayed away from the typical tourist destinations, staying on jeep trails and back roads working their way from south central Colorado all the way to northwest Wyoming … hiking, camping out, fishing … young men enjoying what young men enjoy.

When he went to flight school for his commercial, instrument and multi-engine ratings he tried to get Keith to join him, but Keith's parents wanted him to go to college … which he did and got his four-year degree. After college they roomed together, Keith worked as an aircraft mechanic and Mike flew for a small oil company in the Texas Panhandle. After they both married they continued to live near each other and spent time together as couples playing cards and visiting often.

Keith and his family moved to the Northeast where his wife was from and for several years they did not see each other much, but they did stay close and in touch. A job opportunity allowed Keith to move back to the Midwest, eventually making visits and time together more frequent. Keith is a God-fearing man who loves his country, is willing to do the right thing even if it might not be the popular thing, and he is completely trustworthy; vital for putting the ideas to work.

The initial call was unanswered, but he knows his work sometimes keeps him from answering right away so he left a message to call back. His phone rings, he sees the caller ID and answers, "Hey Keithey!"

"Hi Mikey," he replies, "You called?"

"Sure did, I've got something I want to run by you, have a minute?"

"Yes, I'm on break now so have about 10 minutes, what's up?"

He spent the next few minutes giving a brief synopsis of his ideas, and when he is finished Keith says, "Wow, that's an interesting idea, you really ready to try this?"

He nods to himself and says, "I've given this a lot of thought, Janis and I have decided it is better to try it and fail than to not try and fail."

"Makes sense, what do you need me to do?"

"So you're on board with this?"

"Sure thing, Mikey, I don't want to be left out!"

"Great, it will be great to have you working with us on this. I have to get some things worked out and I'll be in touch soon … thanks and have a great day!"

"You bet … you too, catch you later …"

Deborah and Professor John

As he gets out of his rental car his mind begins to race … how long has it been? Years, many years … 33 to be exact. Is contacting her now the right thing to do? Yes, she could help make contact with an important person and it could save him valuable time. He must be cautious and not let on why he was here, at least not until he knows he can trust her. He has not taken the time to thoroughly vet her, maybe a mistake, but he does not believe it is. How could he, his life might depend on it and he is not normally one to be so cavalier about something with the potential to be this deadly.

He'd known her since she was 15 and he was 20. She had come to her grandparent's farm in the central plains, his grandmother and uncle lived there and he'd been living there and working for his uncle. He was raised in upstate New York, but had left to find what the world had to offer. He saw her that first time and was immediately smitten, her radiant smile, sparkling blue eyes, flowing blonde hair. They spent some time together, had a good time riding around the country on his motorcycle. They didn't date, just spent time together; talking, laughing, enjoying life. City folk would have frowned at the age difference, but in this rural community it was not unusual, and they both were well known and trusted. The night before she left to go back to California they'd walked down a lane at her grandparents, held hands and kissed briefly. It was an awkward moment, they even lost their balance a bit and got a laugh out of that.

They kept in touch through occasional letters. In those days long distance calls were cost prohibitive and of course the Internet and cell phones were ideas from futuristic comic books. The following year he married his best friend's sister, but lost her in a car accident just six months later. For a while he lost his bearings. He had a cousin in Northern California who told him to come out and get away, get his life back on track. He did. And not long afterwards his mind returned to that young girl from the southern part of the state. He called her, could he come for a visit? She seemed excited and said yes.

Over the next few years they'd dated some, but distance made a true relationship very difficult … well, impossible … and was he ready to expose his heart again after losing his wife? Not quite.

The last time he saw her it was a shock. He lived in the Texas panhandle flying for a small company and had gone to his grandmothers for Thanksgiving. She had come to her grandfathers from college in Abilene, Texas for the same reason. It was Sunday night … why hadn't they crossed paths before this last minute? She seemed happy to see him, they talked for a while, he had thought she was going to college at a well-known school in Southern California where her father worked, he had no idea she was so close, especially by the plane he now owned. He suggested they might get together and she said that would be nice — maybe a little more polite than eager.

After she walked away, a friend told him, "You know she's engaged, getting married next summer."

That explained it, she was intelligent, good looking and ambitious … lots of guys looking for a girl like that, and with no encouragement from me she moved on with her life. He'd felt they'd had a connection, but connections need nurturing.

"Hello, Deb."

She turned, did she know this man? He smiled, she looked in his eyes. You've got to be kidding, where did he come from? After all these years he walks up to her now, why?

"I know you hate Debbie, you prefer Deb or Deborah?"

"Deb is fine … you prefer Mike or Michael?"

"Either is fine, whatever you like is fine with me."

An uncomfortable silence followed, he said, "You drink coffee?"

She said, "Sure."

"I'd like to talk to you if you have some time, you busy?"

Why on earth would he want to talk to me now, out of the blue like this? Last time she'd seen him he seemed interested in getting together, but he never called or wrote. She kept up with him some through family and friends after that last time. She figured she'd read him wrong and moved on with her life.

"I have some yard work to do; I have a roommate moving in next month and lots to do to prepare for that."

"I'll help if I can have some time … it's …. important."

"There's a place close we can get coffee, I'll decide later if I want your help."

Still independent, he smiled.

She said, "I'll take my car so I can leave when I want."

"Deb, I will not hold you hostage, I'll bring you home the minute you want, I respect you and the life you have now."

A steely look, then it softened and she smiled, "Okay."

They made the short drive with few words, both obviously deciding how to proceed. They sat at a table with their coffee, "So, you have a roommate moving in, I thought you were married."

"*Were* is the operative word, been divorced nearly four years."

"Sorry to hear that."

"Things just … got …out of hand. I learned there are more ways than adultery a man can let his family down."

"I don't know what to say … "

"Don't have to say anything; it's just the way it is." She continued, "I left while we could still be friends, we have four boys together and things relating to them, we need to be civil."

"You still love him?"

She thought briefly, "I suppose so … like a hamster … which is sad."

Sad indeed.

"So you have four sons?"

"The good lord knew I couldn't handle girls after having all brothers."

He smiled.

She said, "What about you, married, kids?"

"Yes, married nearly thirty years, four kids, two of each. She'd been widowed and had two; we had one and adopted one. I say we have hers, ours and theirs."

She smiled, finally. She still had the twinkle in her blue eyes as well. He'd dreamed of her after that last time they'd seen each other and he began to wonder if this was a mistake. No, he was strong and he knew she was as well … and this was business anyway. He'd be on his way after he had what he needed. He felt a twinge of guilt at the thought of using her, but he was not hurting her or anyone close to her, so he wasn't technically using her … was he?

"I noticed you limping a little, you doing okay?"

"Tore my knees up skiing over the years; already had one knee replaced and the other one needs it."

"That's rough, at your age to already have both knees replaced!"

"Hey, I had fun and this is part of the price, it is what it is."

He already had sized up the fact she was not one to cast blame, for all she'd endured over the years and she just took things in stride.

"So, your ex, is he the guy you were engaged to when we last saw each other?"

"What are you talking about? I met him a few years later when I went back to California."

He said, "You were engaged when we saw each other that Thanksgiving, that didn't work out?"

"I wasn't engaged, where did you hear that?"

His mind was spinning … "Sandy was standing there when we were talking, when you left she told me you were engaged and getting married next summer."

"I don't know where she got that idea; I wasn't really even dating anyone at the time."

Now both their minds were spinning, this seemed like it happened yesterday. He'd wanted her, wanted her badly; and not in a sexual sense, it was about hearts. But she was engaged, so he watched her walk away … and now he knew the truth.

He snapped out of his thoughts as she said, "So that's why you never called me, you thought I was engaged?"

He felt foolish, "Yes."

Now he felt guilty for a different reason, he could have made her life better … but for a misplaced comment that was not even true … Murphy's Law.

"Well, that's life. I'm very comfortable with my life now, I don't look back and worry about things, and it doesn't change anything so why lose any sleep over it?"

Great attitude, great woman. Someone was very stupid to have let her down to the point she had to leave. His guilt was torn between what might have been, a different road he might have taken, and the fact that he had a great wife and family … guilt was not the right word, but he would not take time now to figure that out. Like she said, it is what it is …

"You know," she said," when we met that summer, do you remember kissing me?"

He said, "Of course."

She continued, "That was my first real kiss, I wrote a story about it a couple of years ago for a class I was taking. Actually it was about the lane at my grandparents … it was my favorite place in the whole world as I was growing up. It was special not only because it was my first real kiss, but that it happened where it did."

This is not how he expected this meeting to go, but he is learning so much that filled in so many blank spaces in his life … spaces he never expected to fill.

"And you remember when you drove your motorcycle down to see me in Malibu?"

"Absolutely."

She continued, "I'd just gotten over a relationship and I was a little confused about how I felt. I knew I liked you, but I wasn't sure at that point if it was just a physical attraction … I know now it wasn't."

"Yes, I was still hurting from losing my wife, it had only been four months, and I was not sure what I felt either." He continued, "Knowing what I know now and how I felt about you then, last time I saw you I should have told you I loved you. I had just come out of a relationship and was not ready to expose myself like that … certainly not to someone who was engaged; my heart wasn't up to the rejection."

She said, "I understand, just know if you'd said that I would have told you I loved you too, but I wasn't ready to expose myself either."

They were both young and it was a vulnerable time for both of them … they were so close, and yet so far.

"Deb, I need a favor."

"Just ask," she says…

After all these years he walks up out of nowhere, they give each other the Reader's Digest version of their lives and without knowing his motives or what he wants … she says, "Just ask." She must trust him completely, so he has no choice but to trust her as well.

"You're taking a night class taught by a professor who is a former president of a major corporation …"

He gets a cold stare … not surprising.

"What is this about?" she asks. "How do you know … you've been following me?"

She is outraged; he should have seen this coming.

"This conversation is over, take me home, now."

"Okay, I told you I would not keep you hostage."

He stands up and follows her out the door; she gets in the car and slams the door.

He gets in and without looking at her he says, "Deb, this is important, people's lives may be at stake, our country is at stake, I just thought …"

"Well you didn't think this through very well did you? You showing up like this is weird enough, but to sound as if you've been sneaking around following me … I just don't need this or want anything to do with it."

"Deb, I'm sorry … this was a mistake."

He starts the car and backs out. He knows her well enough to know that any further conversation would only make things worse. Driving back to her house in silence, he pulls up in front and put the car in park, but left it running.

She opens the door, but does not move to get out. She sits there a moment, and then closes the door. She looks straight ahead and says, "Michael, I don't know what this is about. I thought I knew you, I did all those years ago, not sure now." She continues, "I like this man very much and I will do nothing that will have any chance of hurting him or his wife."

"I understand … let me explain what this is all about." He hesitates, but continues, "This is not easy to talk about …"

She sits quietly and waits.

"Maybe I should start at the beginning."

"That might be a good idea."

"Well," he says, "this might take a while."

"I've got time."

"I thought you had lots to do; lawn, moving, etc."

She looks down for a moment, then right in his eyes and says, "You said it was important, that lives might be at stake. I trust you, not really sure why, but I do. I'll take the time to hear what you have to say and help you, if I think I should."

"Okay," he says, "I'm putting a lot of trust in you, whether you help or not, I have to have your word that this goes no further than between us."

"I have no problem with that, unless this is illegal."

"No, it is not illegal, but some of the people we are, uh, working against will not be very happy if we are discovered … and some of them are not very nice people."

"Go on," she says.

"I assume you live in Texas largely because you love the way Texans view their freedom and hate the way the federal government is infringing on the states."

"That's a big part of it," she admitted.

"There are … forces, for the lack of a better word, at work trying to undermine our Constitution and government. There are wealthy individuals, there are groups, unions … and they have joined with hard-line socialists, communists, and Marxists, to achieve their goals."

She asks, "Some of those don't necessarily get along, do they?"

"Well," he says, "the old, 'enemy of my enemy is my friend' comes into play. The problem is that once they achieve their common goal, the violent ones will take the others out and have full control … always works that way if you look at historical revolutions."

"You're saying a revolution is possible?"

"Not possible … it will happen, unless someone stops it."

"I don't know …the military can control things if the police can't …"

"Think about it, Deb. It is not going to be a typical uprising where things are so clearly defined. Imagine you have another huge crisis … let's say something that makes gas go to seven or even ten dollars a gallon. What does that do to our economy? What does that do to the average family?" He continues, "People cannot afford to drive to work, certainly not vacations…what happens to the price of airfare, groceries? How long do you think the store shelves will stay full? People will beg for the government to help … and there are those who want this crisis to put the next phase in place. What will happen in the cities when people are hungry, cannot afford electricity, or gas, and food is not available? … You think people will sit quietly and wait?"

"Hardly," she says, "but the military will …"

He cuts her off, "The military can help hand out food, but if there is unrest and riots … you know about *Posse Comitatus* don't you?"

She thinks about the law written after reconstruction that prohibits law enforcement action by the military on anything but federal land. "Yes, but I'd forgotten about it."

He continues, "We are in uncharted waters here. We went through a revolution, which in some ways was like another civil war… and of course the Civil War. Both were fought for the same reason, freedom … one was for the freedom of all, one was for the freedom of a group that did not enjoy that marvelous part of our nation. In a way this will be over freedom, but the ones pushing this are trying to restrict the freedom of most under the guise of 'social justice' trying to even the playing field." He lets that sink in, "You add in all the unrest in the Middle East, which has some of the same players by the way, and the reach for a global government … sovereign nations will becomes a thing of the past. Imagine a world without the United States of America."

Neither of them wanted to think of that.

"I know you are not ignorant, you see the news and have a feel for what is going on …"

Yes, she does and says, "But the people always do the right thing eventually, they sometimes get it wrong, but it works out."

"Yes, it has … but we have never had these … forces behind it before … pushing the buttons so to speak. I think it is time that some people on the constitutional side started pushing a few as well."

She is thoughtful for a moment, "I understand what you are thinking, but this is a big country and surely this will require a large number of people and money … who's backing this, and how do you know you are not being used?"

Good question.

"Well, it might not take quite as much as you might think and I'm sure I can trust the guy, it's me."

She is surprised, "I had no idea you might be involved in this sort of thing, I guess I thought you were more likely just involved doing your own thing. I always knew you were ambitious, just figured you would try to make a good living, nothing like this. You still fly?"

"Yes, I'm a captain for a major airline. Our group is made up of people I've met over the years I know I can trust, and we all have a love of country. We have different political views in some cases, but we all love our country and the Constitution ... that's what keeps us together. We all volunteer our time; some are involved in government, others in various industries, and one other pilot. Our job as pilots allows us move around the country without raising any suspicion." He adds, "I'm on a layover now."

"What will you do exactly?" she asks.

"If you can trust me, I'd rather not go into all that now … in time."

Her gaze shifts down towards her lap, "Alright, I'm sorry I got upset with you earlier … that just hit me wrong, and John is a nice man and I still want to make sure nothing creates any issues for him."

"I understand and I can assure you he will be fine, we are always very careful, and I just need some help from him. There is something he tried to do in the past that will fit in nicely with what we are doing; I'm hoping he will want to try it again. I might have been able to approach him directly, but felt it would work better if he were to be introduced to me by someone he trusted."

"I do know him well," she says, "I've been to their house and know his wife, they are wonderful people."

"I was told I could trust him completely, that he is a true patriot, and I just need him to know he can trust me."

"I can introduce you to him tomorrow, when do you have to leave town?"

"Not until 3:15, so anytime in the morning would be great."

"Plan on coming by my office at 9 … you found me here, I'm sure you can find my office."

"I'll do that. Now, let's get some of that lawn work done."

She protests, "You don't have to do that."

She does not sound convincing.

"A deal is a deal, and you're not walking very well, let me help."

"Okay, for a while, but I have plans tonight so I'll have to get cleaned up and ready before too long."

"Have a date?"

"I don't know if that's any of your business…but yes."

"Good," he says, "Hope you have a nice time."

They get out of the car and go around to the back of the house. They catch up a little more on the past 30-plus years and have a pleasant conversation.

When she has to get ready he tells her bye and leaves, "See you in the morning, hope you have a nice time tonight."

"Thanks," and a nice smile as she turns to go inside.

"Good morning," he says as he knocks lightly on the door which is standing mostly open.

"Good morning, you're early."

"I'm a pilot, if you're on time, you're late."

She smiles.

He asks, "How was the date?"

"You would ask," she says.

"Oh, I'm sorry … never mind."

"No," she smiles, "it was actually sort of comical; at least if I laugh it feels better!"

He waits.

"This was an online deal, so we'd never met in person. I'm very careful and always meet in a public place; they may have my cell number, but never my address."

"That's smart for sure."

She continues, "We met at a mall, good public place. I thought if the initial meet went well we'd go get something to eat at a nearby restaurant. The guy is Indian, from the country, and has lived here for over thirty years. When I suggested we eat he led me to the food court in the mall. This wasn't what I had in mind, but thought it was not a big deal. He told me to order what I wanted; I picked a Cajun place … love things really spicy so I had it loaded up. I got a bottle of water and he paid. I then asked what he wanted … I was a little taken aback when he said he'd just eat off my plate."

"Wow, this guy must be a little out of the dating deal, or something!"

"Yes, a little! Anyway, he took a few small bites, and he began to sweat. Now it was really hot, but I did not think it was that bad. He had a few more bites, sweating even more. After a while he took my bottle of water and took a drink … I didn't touch it again. Sweat was pouring off him by the time I was finished and his shirt was soaked. We walked out to the car, he tried to kiss me, I gave him the cheek and told him bye and drove off. I got several messages from him that he had a great time and wanted to get together again! I told him there was no connection there and that was that."

"Ouch," he says, "does not sound like I remember dating very well, or that was pretty bad."

"Pretty bad, to put it mildly! Let's go introduce you to John." She stands and limps out of the office and down the hall, he follows right behind.

The door to the office is open, she knocks lightly and the man behind the desk looks up.

"Come on in, Deborah … who's your friend?"

"John, this is Michael … Michael, John."

John stands and they shake hands, "Nice to meet you Mr. …"

"No mister, John is fine … if you are a friend of Deborah's you're a friend of mine."

"Thanks, I appreciate that."

"Did Deborah tell you she's my favorite student?"

"No, but that's not really her style so I'm not surprised."

"No, you're right … that's not her. Back at the beginning of the semester I gave a pop quiz, asked the students to tell me who all the elected officials are who represent them in city, county, state and federal government. I was quite disappointed that most did not do well; Deborah here did better than most, but still missed several questions. I gave the test again a few weeks later; Deborah got them all right … the only one. I gave it to them a third time, she aced it again, but I was most disappointed she was the only one again. So many want to complain, but have not educated themselves enough to participate."

He notices Deb is a little uneasy with the attention.

"Deb, I appreciate you introducing me and helping me out. I know you have work to do, I'll either catch you before I leave or call you later, thanks again for everything."

He flashes her a smile which is returned, "Bye, talk to you later … John, see you tonight at class."

"Sure thing, Deborah; so, Michael, what can I do for you?"

He pauses for a second before answering, "First I want to thank you for giving me a few minutes on such short notice and without any idea what this might be about."

"Not a problem, Deborah told me you were an old friend and that I could trust you … that's good enough for me."

He replies, "I've heard some good things about you and I think you can be great help on a project we're working on. I understand you love your country and what it was meant to be and that you worry about where it appears to be going."

"Yes, that's all true."

"My wife and I have been talking about doing something for some time; recently I approached some close, long- time friends and briefed them on our ideas."

"You've piqued my interest, go on."

"Without going into much detail," he continues, "we are distressed about a central government gaining so much power, taking it from the states as was designed by our founders."

John nods in agreement.

"They are doing it based on an idea of social justice, which is almost a code term for Marxism. They are putting us on a course which I believe will cost us our nation as we know it."

"I agree," John says.

They talked for a few minutes about his ideas and he asks, "Are you interested in working with us on this?"

"Absolutely, you can count me in," he replies.

"Thanks, I really appreciate this. If I can have your cell number I'll be on my way." They exchange cards and he says, "Sure nice to meet you John. I look forward to working with you."

"Likewise," John says.

Chapter 9

HE IS SITTING ON the deck and quietly picking the guitar in his lap and singing an old Gordon Lightfoot song.

She says, "If I could read your mind I'm not sure if I could take it."

He smiles up at her as she leans over and kisses him on the forehead. "I'm sure you couldn't, and I want to keep you around so I'll spare you," he replies.

She continues, "Where are you on your idea? Are you about to get started?"

He sets the guitar down and says, "Yes, we are going to have a video conference tonight actually. With most everyone working regular jobs and John flying, we have to meet late to get everyone on … and you know John, he likes to go to bed early, so hope he stays awake."

She smiles, "Yes, he might turn into a pumpkin."

He smiles as he goes into the small office. One would think a house this large should have a bigger office. Actually, the office is his walk-in closet off the bedroom. When he was building the house he kept telling her, "I don't know why I'm putting such a large closet in for me, I don't have that many clothes!"

He thought about just making that area extra space in the bedroom, but she told him, "My closet is big enough for both of us, why don't you make that an office? It will be in our private area and if we have guests we don't have to worry about anything lying around in sight."

She's practical like that, and he likes it. He turns on the computer and gets ready for the video conference.

(*Return to the video conference in progress …*)

Knut asks, "So what exactly are we going to do on this scale that will have a national effect?"

"We are going to make the federal government irrelevant." He pauses and watches the expressions on their faces … he sees confusion, doubt, shock….pretty much what he expected. He continues, "Not entirely irrelevant, but the part that is dragging our nation into debt and ruin. We have several generations of Americans who are used to watching the federal government do what they do, sometimes grumbling, sometimes happy, but having little control. I decided after looking at history to stop making the same mistake."

Professor John says, "Einstein said the definition of insanity is doing the same thing over and over and expecting a different result."

"Exactly my thought, thanks John. What led us to this was a vicious circle. We as Americans, neighbors, God-fearing people got busy and started leaving things to the government; our personal retirement, our healthcare, the poor and underprivileged … of course not everyone, but enough. Then taxes went higher to cover the extra expenses, we have to work longer hours to pay the taxes and don't have time to care for our neighbors in trouble, besides, we pay taxes for that, right?"

Keith says, "I never really looked at it that way, but you're right, but how do we get out of that cycle?"

He says, "It is simple in theory, but will not be easy. First, you have the people who are used to the status quo and comfortable with the way things are. Then there will be the people in power who gain their power by controlling things. The government is set up to operate this way and going against the system will be difficult as well."

Knut adds, "I've watched as taxes get higher and the Fed keeps printing money and causing inflation, people have less and less disposable income. Where in the past a man could make a decent living and the wife could raise the kids … now she has to work to make ends meet. Now the kids are in daycare, the family keeps getting poorer and further apart … there has to be an end to this."

He nods and says, "That's why we're here, and we all understand that to continue on this road will ultimately lead to the destruction of our nation … that destruction is well under way. Who on this call thinks the children of today have as good a shot at success as we did?"

No one speaks.

"Exactly, that's why we are doing this and why we must succeed."

All of them on the conference vocalize some sort of agreement.

"But I have to tell you I have some big concerns."

"Like what?" asks Keith.

He continues, "I can't put my finger on it, but I have a gut instinct that someone or some group will not only not like this, but will try to stop it; that's why I asked you to just use first names and your job … a couple of you know each other, but otherwise you do not know a last name or even what city the others are in. Our best bet is to keep it that way to keep it more difficult to tie us together. Please as you start your own groups do the same thing, better to prepare of the worst and expect the best."

They all readily agree.

Brenda asks, "So what exactly are we going to do?"

"Quite simply," he replies, "be good people, good citizens, good Americans … and encourage … teach others to do the same thing."

Keith says, "I know you don't think we are not that already, there must be a little more to it than just that."

"No, you're right," he says, "but we are going to have to be a little more involved than in the past."

Captain John says, "I think I understand … you want us to become more active and involve others to do things … say a church group or something like that."

Professor John adds, "So the idea is to help those who are in trouble so the government does not have to."

"Essentially … yes," he says. "I believe if we can ultimately get every community in America to take care of those in need; housing, food, medical assistance … wouldn't it be better for all involved to have local help over federal?"

Brenda asks, “What about people who are already using the system, those who are getting help because it is just easier than working?”

He nods and says, “Well, we can’t do anything about the ones already getting a free ride with the government, but the beauty of this is that locally we can easily know who really needs help and who doesn’t. I also believe that once people see how much more efficient the local efforts are compared to the federal government they will want to stay. We will also be in a position to help them move forward in their lives, with a job or whatever they need.”

“The old deal of give a guy a fish or teach him to fish,” Keith says. “This might also draw some of those on government assistance away to something better as well.”

“Exactly. This will take some time to formulate, to enact, and fine tune. I’m sure there will be some good ideas to help it work that will come along; we all need to be open minded. Ultimately the key to this working will be that it moves into other aspects of the communities; putting different people in elective office, changing the way people think about their neighbors, and so on. I think that is it for now; I want to give you all a chance to think about this and come up with your own ideas, anyone have anything they want to ask or add?”

“I think you have our attention,” Professor John says. “I like the general premise and want to sleep on this some.”

“I appreciate that John, and I look forward to your input.” He says, “I’ve been toying with this for quite some time and I’m still working on just how to implement it, I certainly need all the help I can get, anyone else?”

No one speaks. He thanks them for their time and they are all appreciative for being included in this project and then all sign off the conference.

As he comes out of the office she asks, “How was the conference?”

“It went well, I think I have a good group to work with, people who are dedicated to the country and their families. I also feel they will have some good input in time as they get their minds focused on the task at hand.”

She takes that in and asks, "Do you have any misgivings about this?"

He is not surprised by this as she has a keen sense and while not a pessimist, looks for problems that might arise. He appreciates the fact she sometimes picks up on things he has overlooked.

"I suppose three things come to mind. First, I'm hoping, but not convinced, that the people will take the lead and make this work … I know they can … I just don't know if they will."

"And …"

"I have watched over the past few years, people who cross the powers that be. You have the kooks who can and do cause problems, but there have been legitimate threats from the political powers, those who push the buttons so to speak. Some of these people have to have security teams that rival the Secret Service."

She looks at him with a blank look on her face, but her eyes show serious concern. "I don't think I am going to like you being involved in something that might be that dangerous, I've grown accustomed to you and don't think I'd like to train your replacement."

At least a bit of humor.

"I appreciate that, I am going to take some precautions to be on the safe side. To begin with, we are only using first names so I am the only one who knows my group, and then each subsequent group will be the same. Only one will know each in the group. Then we will operate under the radar; the ones who have had issues I am aware of are on TV or the radio and have a big target on their back. Trust me, I like our life here and certainly will not do anything to hurt you or us … if I can help it anyway."

"I know," she says, "it's just that we've worked so hard and waited so long for what we have. Sometimes it would be nice to just sit back and enjoy it … but I know we could not do that if there might be something we could do to help … neither of us is like that. I know you will be careful, and you know I am behind you all the way. And you said three," she reminds him.

He smiles, “The thing that scares me the most … even if it works, we might be too late. Things have progressed to a point where immediate change will not be possible, the country might have to “reset,” and that will not be pretty.”

“What do you mean by reset?”

He sighs, “Depending on just what different factions do and how people react, and given the current state of our economy, the economy could collapse. That would lead to massive shortages of everything, chaos in the cities … it won’t be pretty.”

“Let’s hope and pray it does not come to that.”

“Yes, especially pray.” They hug and then walked toward the deck to relax a bit in the quiet of the night and watch the night sky; the brilliance of the stars in the country is something most in the city never see.

Chapter 10

IT JUST SO HAPPENS that on his next trip he has a layover in the same city where Bernie lives.

"Bob," he tells his first officer, "I have an old friend who lives here; he's meeting me in front of the terminal. I'm going to stay with him and he'll bring me back tomorrow. I'll let the crew desk know where I am, and you have my cell just in case, right?"

"Sure thing," Bob says. "Enjoy your visit and I'll see you in the morning."

"Have a nice evening, see you then."

"Hey, Mike."

He hears the voice and then spots his friend, "Hi Bernie, good to see you."

"Great to see you too, you hungry?"

"I sure am, is there a good steakhouse around?"

"Well, we think it's good, but you being from cattle country might not agree."

"I bet it will pass, most of the time you get a pretty good steak about anywhere in the country, some better than others, but good nonetheless. You can't say that in Paris. Lousy beef smothered in some sauce they think makes it passable."

Bernie nods agreement, "That's for sure, let's get out of here."

They get in the car and he asks, "Bernie, what are your thoughts on our project since you've had a couple of days to think?"

"I've thought of little else since our conference," he replies. "I've got some thoughts to run past you while you're here."

"Good, I was hoping you'd have some ideas. Let's talk about it over the steak, how's Ellen?"

They talk about family and catch up on various things since they last saw each other on the drive to the steakhouse.

He orders an iced tea and rib eye medium rare, Bernie orders a beer and prime rib medium.

After the waitress leaves Bernie says, "Mike, you know I do not agree with you politically on everything, but I've got to tell you I really like what you are doing. As I see it you are just trying to get us back to the people we were … the people our founders hoped we'd be. I know they were not perfect men, but they knew we had to have a life of honor and respect for others. Our society has become so self-centered; this feeling of entitlement has to change."

"Exactly," he nods. "You have some ideas on how to go forward with this?"

"I do. Unemployment is high and many are looking for work and assistance. I'm thinking I can get a number of people to go to the unemployment office once a week or so, take a sack of groceries in, hand it to someone, say God Bless you and walk away. If asked what or why we'll just say it's one American helping another. If someone wants to try and pay us back, we'll just say 'when things improve for you, pay it forward.' I know there are other things we can do, but this is a good start."

He is smiling and says, "I knew when I involved all of you, each of you would have some good ideas. There are situations that are different around the country and you each know what will work best in your area. Part of why I chose each of you is the strategic parts of the country where you are all located."

The waitress brings a basket of hot rolls and honey-cinnamon butter, they both take one and pause long enough in the conversation to butter a roll and take a couple of bites.

"Well Bernie, so far this is a pretty good place!"

Bernie smiles and says, "I thought you'd like it, this is a favorite place of mine."

He goes back to the plans, "I think this is a great idea for several reasons. First off you help people in need directly, and then you set them up with a desire to continue the work on their own. As word gets around this will be noticed and word will get around. I'd expect someone will be interviewed by the media eventually, if it is you or your group of course it needs to look as if it is local and spontaneous … if it is someone subsequent to you they will of course believe it is local and spontaneous."

Bernie replies, "Of course, that is no problem. I figure we can start something else and this will domino and take on a life of its own."

"I agree, and not to mention the fact we are such a mobile and spread-out society, people will tell their friends and family, and it might pick up speed completely outside our efforts. My initial thought is for this to take a couple of years, but it could happen in half that time if things go right."

Bernie nods in agreement as the waitress brings the plates with sizzling meat and says, "It's not polite to talk with your mouth full!"

They both laugh and dig into their meals. Small talk is punctuated by the sounds of silverware on plates and satisfied sighs.

He says, "Bernie, you did good … that was great!"

"Yes it was. You ready to go to the house?"

As he rolls his bag into the house he says, "I'm anxious to see all the work you did, the pictures were impressive."

"Well, thanks … but not near what your project was."

"No, but remodel work is always tough, there are always unexpected problems and it always takes more time and money than you plan."

"Ain't it the truth, ain't it the truth," Bernie sighs.

A trim attractive woman meets them at the door; "Ellen, this is my friend Mike I've talked about. Mike, Ellen."

"Hi Ellen, nice to meet you; Bernie has told me a lot about you."

She raises an eyebrow and looks sternly at Bernie …

"It was all good, really!"

They laugh as they all go inside. The evening is spent reminiscing over events of their youth, and wondering how they ever survived.

The next morning on the way to the airport he asks, "You carry all the time?"

Bernie says, "I can't at work, government buildings and all, but the rest of the time yes, always."

"Good, I'm not thinking this project will make us any more at risk than we already are just walking down the street, but you know me … prepare for the worst…"

"And hope for the best," Bernie finishes.

"Yep."

Bernie asks, "Is it worth the time and effort for you to be an FFDO?"

Federal Flight Deck Officer (FFDO), a program whereby pilots are trained by the U.S. Marshal service to carry firearms for defensive use in flight.

"In the big scheme of things, yes. A potential hijacker knows about the program, and even though it is voluntary for each pilot, no one knows if there are no guns, or one or two in the cockpit. The HK 40 cal is a pretty good deterrent."

"I'm sure it is."

"You still have the Uzi?"

Bernie replies, "Yes, haven't shot it in a while and keeping the Federal Firearms Permit for it is a pain."

He smiles, "Yes, anything with the word 'federal' in it is a pain." He gets out of the car in front of the terminal, grabs his bags.

After the goodbyes, hand shake and a back slap he says, "Sure enjoyed it Bernie, thanks for everything."

"Me too, I'll be in touch."

And with that he disappears among the passengers as he works his way toward the operations office.

Chapter 11

HE ARRIVES HOME AFTER his trip, unpacks his bag and goes to the stack of mail that has accumulated in his absence. There is nothing out of the ordinary; a few bills, magazines and the obligatory junk mail ... nothing that requires his immediate attention. His wife is visiting a friend, and said she would be home soon after he arrived. He plays a minute with the dogs, they are happy to see him as usual. He goes to the gun safe and retrieves his Glock 36; a compact 45 caliber that is his preferred carry weapon and places the H&K 40 cal in the safe. While he is required to maintain a level of proficiency as an FFDO, he takes it much more seriously.

When his state first allowed concealed carry he was quick to accomplish the necessary training and background checks.

His wife asked, "Are you anxious to shoot someone?" largely in jest, but somewhat serious.

He replied, "I hope I never have a need to use it. Ever. But better to be prepared and never need it than to need it and not have it."

He has taken several defensive handgun courses over the years learning not only to shoot well, but to also read people and understand a situation before it develops into something deadly. Living in the country as he does it is easy to keep a target range set up and shoot whenever he likes. It calms and relaxes him, he enjoys it very much. His wife joins him on occasion, but she lacks the passion he has. She has no problem with guns, her father was a serious sportsman, and she shot her first deer at the age of nine.

She arrives home and sees his truck in the driveway; she is pleased he is home. As she opens the door she hears the sharp report of the 45 and smiles. She goes inside and to the bedroom, there is a sliding door out to the wraparound porch; she slides it open and watches as he moves quickly from one target to the next, leaving two neat holes near the center of each.

As he reloads she speaks, “Welcome home!”

He turns and smiles, “Hi honey, I’m home!”

She asks, “You going to be much longer?”

“No, actually, I was just going to come in after one more clip.”

She watches as he expertly places the seven rounds in the targets, then turns and walks up the hill to her, gives her a hug and a kiss.

“How was your trip,” she asks?

“Great, good crew, weather was nice … and I got to see Bernie.”

“That’s nice, how is he?”

“Doing well, looking forward to retirement. I got to meet Ellen, she’s really a nice gal … they’re good together.”

“Good to hear that, he certainly deserves better than what Jill did to him.”

He nods, “That’s for sure.”

“You hungry?” she asks.

“Not too bad, maybe a light snack and we can cook out on the grill for supper.”

“Sounds good, I’ll get some steaks out of the freezer.”

“I had a big steak with Bernie last night, how about some BBQ chicken?”

“Oh, okay, that’s sounds good to me too.”

While the chicken is on the grill the phone rings. He looks at the caller ID, smiles and hits the button to answer, “Hi Brenda!”

“Hey Mike, are you at home?”

“Yes.”

"I never know with you, but I had a great idea and wanted to bounce it off you, see what you think."

"Sure, go ahead."

"I've been trying to think of what I could do for the project that would not only help, but that I would love to do."

He says, "That's important, it needs to be something you are personally passionate about."

"That's what I thought too. Tell me, what rules the world?"

He thinks for a moment and then it hits him, "The hand that rocks the cradle."

"Right, that comes from a poem about motherhood. I thought who better to help bring things back than mothers?"

He smiles and says, "And everyone knows not to get between a mother and her kids! So what do you have in mind, how do you plan to move the idea forward?"

"I'm thinking I can get a group of mothers together, and we can get a Web site up that will help mothers all over the country. We can offer information on how to do things for the family that will save them money and make them more self-sufficient, help to teach their kids more about our country, and becoming more involved in communities."

"Brenda that's perfect; what a great idea!"

"I hoped you'd like it, I can really see this working and I am so excited about it I can hardly stand it! I have some friends in mind that can help me get this going; I think we can get started within a week."

"I knew I could count on you, I think this is just what the nation needs now. So many people have withdrawn from society, just trying to make ends meet, letting things go, families are falling apart … kids being raised by daycare centers and schools. Putting parents back in charge is what we need … this is fantastic!"

"I'm sure you're busy, I'll let you go and I need to make some calls."

"Thanks, I have some chicken on the grill; we're going to eat soon."

"Now why did you have to say that? You're reminding me I have to feed John!"

"Sure, like you forgot you have a husband … forget your girls too?"

She laughs and he hears a click and she is gone.

"Who was that on the phone," his wife asks.

"Brenda, she wanted to run her idea by me. It's about involving mothers across the country; it's an amazing idea."

He pulls the meat off the grill as she puts salad and veggies on the table. As they eat he tells her more about Brenda's idea.

"Wow, she's really got a handle on this doesn't she?"

"She sure does, glad I thought to include her in the group! I was sure the best way to move this idea forward was to get several people thinking and let them do what was passionate to them personally. The idea seems to be coming together, now let's hope the implementation goes as well."

They have a nice supper and a quiet evening at home. The next morning he is up early, he leaves the bed without disturbing her and goes to the kitchen to start coffee. He scans his email while that is brewing and then steps out onto the deck to enjoy the morning with his first cup. It is cool, clear and calm; the reflection of the far bank of the pond is mirrored on the glassy surface. His mind wanders and settles on an old friend.

Max passed away about three years ago, he was in his mid-80s and had lived a full life. Max had three daughters, but treated him like a son. After going to an antique tractor show with Max and the youngest daughter she told her sister, "Dad treats Mike just like one of us!" She did not mean that as a compliment as he had a tendency to order rather than ask; however, Max's orders were not burdensome or out of line. Max loved to tell stories and he had an amazing memory, he knew if he'd told you a story before or not. Before he'd proceed, he'd wrinkle his eyes and get a big grin in anticipation of the "punch line" before he began. He loved his grandchildren and as each one grew, began to walk, speak, and read … there was always something amusing or to be proud of. Each one was special, but he sure was proud of Andrea when she was accepted at the U.S. Air Force Academy.

Max held a Private Pilot Certificate and loved to talk planes and flying with him. They would talk world events and politics some. Max said once, "I'm glad I'm old, I won't have to see the loss of our nation like you will." He wondered if Max would appreciate the ideas they were working on; he believed so. Max was one to insist on personal responsibility and self reliance. He believed you did your job, you helped those who could not do for themselves, and you did not enable people to be lazy. You did not do things to draw attention to yourself; he learned that lesson early on. Max's dad was called *Fat*. Now Fat was thin, so maybe one can get the picture.

A boy at a neighboring farm could ride a horse standing on its back and he complained to his dad, "I can stand on Bo's back but he won't go."

"Well get up there and I'll make him go."

Now Fat was cleaning chunks of ice out of a water tank with a pitchfork. Max climbed up on Bo's back and held the reigns. Fat jabbed the horse in the rump with the pitchfork. The horse took off as if shot out of a cannon and Max went head over heels to the ground.

His dad looked at him and said, "Boy, no one likes a showoff."

Max was raised old school for sure.

Janis was at work and he was doing some things at home when he heard the call on the EMS radio to Max's address. He dropped what he was doing and went to see if there was anything he could do. Max had collapsed and was unconscious on the floor, having diabetes and other health issues complicated things as well. He helped max's wife get ready to go with the ambulance, and as the stretcher went by with an unconscious and somewhat blue Max, he said his goodbyes knowing this was not likely to have a good end.

The next day he stopped by their house, and the middle daughter saw him and came out and hugged him thanking him for being there and helping … and "Would you do the service?"

He was shocked, honored and scared. Max believed in God, but had no love for preachers. He believed himself capable, but how to get through this for a close friend? He could not turn them down, "Yes, I'll do it for Max."

It was one of the hardest things he ever did.

Chapter 12

"HI JOHN."

John looks up from his desk and sees him standing in the doorway.

"Hi Mike, have a seat."

He is on another layover and had called John the day before, and was told to stop by while in town.

"Thanks for taking the time to come by in person. Calls are okay, but I like to see a man's eyes when I talk to him."

He picks a chair across the desk and after a quick handshake sits down.

"I agree. The eyes are the window to the soul, glad to stop and visit."

John continues, "Yes they are. I have some ideas I wanted to run by you for our project. Since my background is with big business I wondered if there might be a way to help put this in motion from that angle. I'm actually getting to work on something I wanted to do years ago. While I was a CEO I had some ideas like this, but I could never get enough others to feel passionate enough about it to get it going … That, or there were economical issues we had to deal with and just could not expend the resources. I think as an outsider with the connections I have I will actually be in a better position to give it a shot. Anyway, I think major corporations can do two things. One is to start some programs in communities where they operate to help those in need both in physical aspects and in training. These will not only be helpful, but as a charitable act will help on the bottom line in tax breaks. Second, we can offer incentives for employees to become involved on a personal level, together I believe we can make a serious contribution to the project."

"John, this is why I picked you for this, I just knew your love of country tied with your background would make you a valuable asset to the group. Actually I was aware of your previous effort and hoped you'd have the passion to move it forward. I have no doubt this is a winning strategy."

John looks at him with a questioning eye, "I don't guess it matters how you knew about that, but I am curious."

"I have a friend, who did not work for you, but your two companies had some mutual interests and he told me once."

"Well, I'm glad you like it."

"You know, I am thrilled with the ideas each of you have. Even if one person could ever come up with what you all are putting together, there is no way they could ever implement everything. I knew bringing you all together was the only way to do it. Not only do you each have the ability and connections to make it happen, you have the passion to do what is important to you."

"I agree, and I am really glad you included me. By the way, how does Deborah fit into all this?"

"I had lost contact with her over the years. When I found where you were now I happened onto her in the process. I just used Deb to introduce us, I did not know if I just dropped in on you without any knowledge of who I was you might be skeptical."

"That's probably a pretty good guess, I stay busy and you would not believe some of the things that pop up. I likely would have not even taken the time to see you, which would have been a huge mistake."

He smiles and says, "Well, I guess sometimes Murphy's Law works in reverse."

They both chuckle at the inside joke and John says, "Yes, sometimes it does happen. Say, are you going to include Deborah in this?"

"I think she could be a great help, however my group is pretty well set. Each of you however will have your group to work with. While I know most of yours will be others with big business backgrounds, Deb has some great skills and would be an asset for you. I'd suggest you take advantage of having her right here to help you on your efforts."

"Thanks, I agree she'll be a great help to me. I'll get with her soon to help me get this going."

"I think you'll have a fine team, keep me posted with your progress. We'll try to have a conference call or online conference from time to time, but since each of you are on your own with your ideas I am certainly not micromanaging this, I just want to keep up with what each of you are doing and how you perceive it is going. If any of us hit a snag, someone might have an idea to get things going."

"Sounds like a plan, thanks again for taking time to stop by, I've got to get going here and I guess you need to head for the airport soon."

"Sure great to see you again John, good luck and we'll be in touch."

He stands, they shake hands and he leaves the office.

Once out of the office he starts for the parking lot, then stops and turns around heading the opposite way down the hall. He comes to an office door and knocks lightly.

"Come in," the feminine voice says.

He opens the door and smiles, "I was down the hall talking to John and thought I'd better stop in to say hi."

"Darn right you'd better say hi, if I found out you'd been here and didn't stop in it would have cost you."

The voice is stern, but the eyes tell a different story.

"You had your knee replaced since I was here last didn't you? How's it going?"

"It's going great, the doctor is really pleased with the progress; doing physical therapy, really tough, but getting better all the time."

"That's great news, I know you were not happy with all the physical limitations you had before."

"Hardly … hey, I'm really glad you stopped in, and I would tear you a new one if you did not come by, but I've got a conference coming up I have to get busy on …"

"Okay, I understand and I need to head for the airport soon. I told you before I'd fill you in more later on what I am up to … I think John is going to talk to you soon and you'll learn more then."

She has a bit of a puzzled look on her face, and then says, "I'm not sure I'm up to all the cloak and dagger stuff, but I'll play along for now."

He smiles, "You'll be a great asset to what we are doing, and I think you'll like it."

"You seem to think you know me pretty well."

"We probably know each other better than either of us would admit."

She smiles, "Probably so … probably so … bye Michael, talk to you later."

"Bye Deb," he says and turns to leave.

As he heads for the car his cell rings. He looks at the caller ID then pushes the green answer button and says, "Yorka, what's up?"

"Hello Borka. You at home today?"

"No, actually I'm on a layover. You remember John, the professor from our video conference?"

"Sure."

"Well, I just left his office. He has some great ideas, looks like the project is off to a great start with some excellent ideas."

"That's what I was calling you about. I have to go check out a new crane in a few days, if you're going to be home I'd like to stop by and see you, we can talk about it then."

"I'll be home tomorrow afternoon, when did you have in mind?"

"How about I come by tomorrow evening and spend the night? Been a while since we had much time to visit, we can talk about this and got all caught up. That'll break my trip up and we can have some time to relax and visit."

"That'll be great, I'll let Janis know … look forward to seeing you."

"Great, see you tomorrow."

They both click off, he gets in the car and his mind is spinning again before he reaches the lot exit.

Chapter 13

HIS TRIP IS UNEVENTFUL; he has a good time with a good crew. The joke for airline pilots is the job is hours and hours of boredom punctuated by moments of sheer terror. That's not really true; he supposes that if someone does not have a passion for their job as he does it could be true, although most of the terror is simulated in a simulator on his annual visits to the training center … thankfully. In his mind, the drive to the airport and home is the most dangerous part of his job.

He pulls into the drive to the delight of the dogs. He gets out of the truck and loves on each one as there is vigorous tail wagging and the occasional jealous growl as they each jostle for position.

He steps inside and hollers, "Hi honey, I'm home!"

Their personal statement they both make on arrival.

She answers from upstairs, "I'll be down in a minute."

He pours himself a glass of sweet tea in a large-mouth quart Mason jar and takes the first sip as she comes down the stairs.

They hug and kiss briefly and she asks, "How was the trip?"

"Excellent, great weather, good crew, good layovers … sure glad I love my job!"

"You're a lucky guy, in more ways than one." She says with an impish grin and slaps him on the butt.

"That I am … that I am," he smiles in return.

"I was just up putting fresh sheets on the bed for your brother, when is he getting in?"

"He didn't say for sure, I imagine depends on how his day goes, but I bet he's here for supper."

"Yes, he does seem to like my cooking."

"Everyone likes your cooking," he says with a smile.

"Well, you are certainly complimentary today, what's on your mind?"

"Oh, the usual," he grins.

"That's going to have to wait; I've got more to do before he gets here."

"Oh, he'd understand. I can just explain why you're behind and I'm sure he'll … ouch, that hurt!"

"Poor baby, look for sympathy someplace else, you keep your mouth shut about our personal affairs."

"Yes dear," as he heads to the bedroom to change and unpack. He's a foot taller than her but sort of enjoys playing like she's got the upper hand physically.

He's checking emails when he hears the helicopter. He steps out the back door onto the deck and sees the dark blue, almost black R44 helicopter approaching to land on a hill by the pond. After lightly touching down there is a period of time as things cool off before shutting the engine down. As the rotors slow he comes in closer and the door pops open.

"Hello, Borka! You sure have a perfect place here!"

"We sure like it, good to see you!"

They shake hands and work together to secure the helicopter for the night.

"You miss having a turbine helicopter?"

"In a way, the Bell and the Hughes I had were both good aircraft, but this Robinson is great, and the purchase and operating expense is so much better."

"I bet that's right, let's go inside, I'm sure Janis is anxious to see you."

"Hello sister!"

"Hello yourself," she says as they share a hug. "It's been too long since you've been here; you need to visit us more often."

"I know, maybe after I retire in a couple of years."

They all laugh; when they met 35 years ago he was going to retire in five years; over the past few years that has gone to the two-year plan.

"You two get washed up, supper is about ready to go on the table."

"Okay, I'll get him to his room and we'll be back in a few minutes."

"I get to stay in *my* room don't I?"

Everyone who visits loves the big room on the east end of the upstairs, they all claims it as theirs.

"Of course, you're the only one who has ever slept there," he says with a smile.

They both clean up and meet back in the kitchen.

"What did you fix me for supper, sister?"

"Lasagna, that's a good Norwegian dish isn't it?" she says with a smile.

"Sure, we shared it with the Italians and they claimed it for themselves."

They sit down and dig into the delicious pasta dish with salad and garlic bread. They're all hungry and conversation is minimal for several minutes.

"So, I've been thinking about your idea, I want to try something that might be a little different."

This piques their interest and they lean in a bit closer.

"You know as owner of a small business I understand the effects of government policy and regulation on our ability to make a living."

They both nod in agreement.

"I believe much of what you are trying to help resolve is caused by these regulations and policies. We have people out of work, losing their homes; we have families with both parents working long hours to support the family and there is no one to care for the children."

Janis says, "I see that all the time in my job, it's just heartbreaking."

"Yes, and maybe I'm more cognizant of the effects of these things coming from a socialistic country like Norway. Those policies lead to a cradle to grave entitlement mentality. My father had a serious problem with his arm years back, it was actually never really resolved and he lived with considerable pain. He had friends and family from Norway who thought this was a great thing. He could have the arm amputated and then the government would take care of him, unbelievable!"

"You know you're preaching to the choir here," he says. "We're living in a country that started much of this back in the thirties, how do we reverse it?"

"My idea is two-pronged; to get rid of the entrenched politicians who keep giving out goodies to be reelected, and replace them with people who have small business experience and understand what it takes to keep this country at work and growing."

He likes the way this is developing. On one hand there will be groups working to help people and their attitude towards their personal responsibility and helping their neighbors; and on the other hand changing the way government works to perpetuate the problem.

"I like it … I like it a lot. It makes perfect sense to help solve the problem we have and to stop the future creation of problems. We all know we do not live in a perfect world and never will, but we certainly need to remove as much of the evil as we can … and I do believe it is evil. I think it is evil to ignore those in need, to expect the government to help them, to create issues that put people in need, and to prop people up who have no sense of their own personal responsibility."

They spend the next several minutes discussing the possibilities and how it ties in with the other ideas the group will be working on, and they all agree it will be an excellent addition to the process. It is a nice evening and they each take a dish of ice cream out on the deck and enjoy the fresh air and the evening sounds; a pack of coyotes howling, frogs and crickets chirping. They have a long history and a lot of shared experiences. They spend the evening reminiscing about their trip to Alaska, numerous trips to the mountains, family vacations, diving trips, planes they've owned and flown … the conversation goes well into the night.

His Norwegian brother does not drink coffee. The next morning he gets a pot going then takes a cup out onto the deck to watch the sun come up over the trees in the distance, listen to the sounds of the morning, and enjoy the view of the R44 sitting by the pond.

"Wish that was yours sitting there?"

He turns to see his brother coming out of the house.

"That would be nice; I suppose I'd have to learn to fly it if I owned it!"

"You'd learn pretty fast from what I've seen when I let you fly mine in the past."

"Probably so, but I can't afford two planes like you."

They both get a big smile; they've been tweaking each other like that ever since they met. When they first met his brother had a Citabria, a tandem seat tail dragger. He'd never flown a taildragger, so called because instead of a nose wheel-like tricycle geared plane, it has a small wheel at the tail. The first planes had a skid instead of a wheel, thus the term tail dragger. After a few flights and learning the differences he fell in love with them. He owned several different ones over the years, culminating in the ultimate, a Cessna 185. He loves the 185; it historically has been used as a bush plane in rough terrain all over the world. With a STOL (Short Take Off and Landing) kit it has amazing performance hauling whatever you can stuff in it and using a bare minimum of ground roll for takeoff or landing.

"Well, your 185 is nearly a helicopter, you better not ever sell that."

"Not a chance, Yorka, not a chance."

After breakfast they walk out to the chopper and say their goodbyes. He then goes back to the deck to watch the rotors slowly start spinning as the engine starts. He watches as his brother goes through preflight checklists, allows the engine to warm up, turns to wave bye, then gently lifts off and flies away.

Chapter 14

PERHAPS HE HAS WAITED too long. Perhaps someone else should have started something long ago. Perhaps neither of these matters, it is impossible to know. While he is so busy with so many things, he still takes time to stay in touch with what is going on in the world. While he is concerned about America, Europe seems to be almost a basket case. Oh, the average person probably has no idea, and in fact many in the media and our government seem oblivious to the problems; but as a student of history he sees the telltale signs of collapse on the horizon.

America, in spite of the obvious problems Europe has experienced, seems intent on following the same path. Europe is much further "down the road to serfdom," but America does everything more efficiently; including screwing up. Greece is the first one that will fall; ironic in a way, so much of our history goes back to the Greeks. Their society has become accustomed to numerous giveaways, guarantees … including retirement under 50 years of age. How they think the remaining workers could ever pay for this in perpetuity is beyond him. Now the country is on the verge of bankruptcy, banks all over the world are worried they will lose their investments, and markets all over the world are reacting negatively.

The Greek government has no option but to cut, and cut deeply. Everything the government does … pensions, healthcare, college tuition, unemployment compensation, even trash collection is affected. Now, of course the population understands their country's predicament and gladly goes along with the necessary cuts ... no, this is not human nature. There are riots, serious riots; people are killed, buildings and property burned. A bad situation is made much worse. He is certain there is a significant segment of their society which recognizes the dire situation and understands the need to make serious changes — but it is mostly the young whipped up by anarchists and communists. His mind cannot fathom how people can be so misguided, so ignorant. What do they think will replace what they have? Where do they think their riots will lead? He thinks it is likely they have given this little thought. Young people often do not truly understand the way economies work, they just know everyone before them always got these things and suddenly they are the first ones to have them taken way.

Spain will be next. Spain bought the idea of man-made Global Warming and that they could do something about it. They invested a huge amount in green technology — incredibly expensive and the known technology could not possibly supply the demand. A few years into that failed experiment has led them to something like 22 percent unemployment. The remaining 78 percent will be unable to keep everything going for long. Once these two fail, the burden on the remaining countries of the EU will be unsustainable. With the "European Socialism" and the drain all the entitlements already have on the respective countries, banks stretched to the limit ... it will all fold quickly; Portugal, Italy and France likely next, then Great Britain. Germany is relatively strong now, but there is no way they can avoid the vortex of the EU as it spins down the drain. Some of the smaller countries might themselves survive, but all the banks will be laid waste and they will have no ability to do much.

What happens next? Who knows; possibly Russia, India or China more or less takes over financially. Perhaps even radical Muslims who have immigrated in huge numbers to Europe will try to take over. Whatever happens, it will not be pretty ... it will be disastrous economically and perhaps terribly bloody.

When it happens there, if the U.S. has not already put herself on a better track, she will surely follow. With a true worldwide depression, even countries like China and India, along with the oil producing countries, will have little market for their products and they will collapse as well. Only those countries, and to a greater extent individuals, who are prepared will survive. Imagine the chaos in the cities as unemployment goes to 20 percent, 30 percent ... even 40 percent. There is no food in the stores, and if there was, many have no money to buy; inflation goes through the roof. Government could not possibly care for that number of people in any sort of efficient way. And with so many hurting, there will not be enough good Samaritans with the ability to help. He really cannot get his mind around this, he prays it never gets this far … but it is possible. And it is very likely to get very bad even if it is not to the point of desperation in the worst case.

It is also complicated by other world events; if the world was just dealing with one major issue, but it is not. The world is tied together in sort of financial "mutually assured destruction." There is the worldwide issue of terrorism, there are the never ending problems in the Middle East, and of course the occasional dictator who decides to throw another monkey wrench in the works.

Who in their right mind would want to be president? He thinks if someone wants to run for president, this pretty much disqualifies them. They are either too stupid to understand no one can control all this, or so arrogant and think they can. He thinks of the story of George Washington; men came to him and asked for his help, they wanted him to serve in the new government. It is reported that he said, "Have I not given enough for my country?" He later went to them, his conscience getting the better of him … a reluctant leader. "That's what we need now, a reluctant leader," he thinks aloud. Someone the people recognize as a great person who has proven himself (or herself) in their life to be honest, virtuous … and maybe a little crazy.

The Russians were scared to death of Reagan, they thought him a little nuts, that he might just "push the button" for fun. They certainly knew he was not to be messed with. The idea of mutually assured destruction kept them at bay, something well known regarding nuclear war … but what about mutually assured economic destruction? He does not have any knowledge this is something that exists on purpose, but he believes it is a reality nonetheless.

Just as nations use the idea that if you fire a missile at me, I'll fire two back, then you fire more, I fire more … and before you know it both sides and everything in between is a nuclear wasteland. He believes the more industrialized nations agreed to a mutual assurance regarding economics, no one has an upper hand. However, this ties everyone together, so if one fails it raises the chances they will pull someone down with them. He is not a world economist, this may be nuts or over simplifying things and even completely wrong. All he knows is there have been numerous countries that have failed over the years and one just has to observe their mistakes to predict the outcome of countries that follow the same paths … this is not rocket science, it is common sense … something that is not so common anymore.

The ignorant see no problem here; they seem the think countries can just print money, like there is an endless supply. He spoke with a young lady once who was very progressive, thought the government should just give everyone free health care.

He simply said it would not work, and when she asked why not, he replied, "If you could get free gas, would that change your driving habits?"

"Well, I guess, why?"

Would you care how much gas you burned? Would you go places you can't now due to the cost? What would others do?"

She thought about it and replied, "Sure, who wouldn't?"

"So think about it with health care. If you never had to pay for a doctor or medicine, would you go more often, take more pills?"

"Sure, because it's free."

"Nothing is free, someone has to pay. If just five percent of the citizens suddenly started going to doctors and hospitals more because it was free, it would shut the system down … supply and demand. Next comes rationing, then what?"

"Huh, never thought of it like that."

Yeah, sure …

The forces behind the scenes in the U.S. back in the 60s and 70s … those involved in the Weather Underground. The Weathermen for example were a terrifying bunch. Americans seem to dismiss the idea we would have people like this. Oh, we recognize the singular nut here and there, a Timothy McVey or someone like that. But a group bent on the overthrow of our government by any force necessary? Well, unfortunately, yes. It was many years later that some of the intensity and what they were willing and prepared to do really came out and most Americans have no idea. Their methodology comes largely from a book entitled *Rules for Radicals* by Saul Alinsky. Many of our current progressive politicians studied Alinsky and his ideas for organizing communities to achieve objectives. If anyone has any doubt as to the intent of his principles, they need go no further than the opening page dedication: "Lest we forget at least an over-the-shoulder acknowledgment to the very first radical: from all our legends, mythology, and history ... the first radical known to man who rebelled against the establishment and did it so effectively that he at least won his own kingdom — **Lucifer.**"

It was revealed in recent years that the FBI had an informant within one of these groups. They bombed police stations, local government buildings, even the Pentagon. At a meeting once this informant asked about people who did not agree with them, what happens with them?

The response, "We know that historically ten to twenty percent of the population will not go along with us. We will have re-education camps to teach them what is best for them."

And what of those who are not willing to accept after re-education? "They will be eliminated; we cannot take a chance any will be able to fight back at a later date."

They were willing to exterminate 25 to 50 million people to see their plan through. Sounds much like Stalin, Mao … those two made Hitler look like a piker.

Are there people like this involved now trying to overthrow or fundamentally transform America? He believes so. The President wrote a book in which he clearly stated, "To avoid being mistaken for a sellout, I chose my friends carefully: the more politically active black students, the foreign students, the Chicanos, the Marxist Professors and structural feminists and punk-rock performance poets." He remembers his grandmother saying, "You are what your closest friends are." The President was not hanging out with Washington, Madison and Jefferson.

Two very progressive professors were involved in these movements in the 60s and 70s. They soon realized that an armed resistance would not be successful and another strategy was developed; to overload the system. They believed if the government was obligated to care for enough people the system would collapse and another would be put in its place … one with equal pay, "stuff," benefits … guaranteed income and thus an end to poverty. Yes, that does sound like communism.

Many bristle at the terms Marxist, Socialist, Communist; some gladly accept those labels. Redistribution of wealth is a Marxist principle … "From each according to his ability, to each according to his need (or needs)" is a slogan popularized by Karl Marx in his *1875 Critique of the Gotha Program.* The phrase summarizes the principles that in a communist society, every person should contribute to society to the best of his or her ability and consume from society in proportion to his or her needs. In the Marxist view, such an arrangement will be made possible by the abundance of goods and services that a developed communist society will produce; the idea is that there will be enough to satisfy everyone's needs. You might be able to do this with machines, but not people.

There have always been people it seems who want a Utopian society … he thinks America is as close as anyone has ever come; but as our founders noted, it takes virtuous people to make it work. Is America perfect? He knows it is not and never has been, but no other country has ever given opportunity to so many to succeed and prosper. No other country has given so much … financially, or has shed as much blood to help others. A Marxist society would not, could not, do as much for others. He believes America must survive, not only for Americans, but for the world.

Chapter 15

HE HOPS IN HIS truck and heads into the small rural town that is about four miles away. He wants to talk to Kenny and thinks it best to talk in person rather than on the phone. He pulls up in front of the house and shuts down the truck. Cort, their mentally challenged son, is sitting out front on a swing with his parents. He knows Cort loves planes and thinks he is something special because he can fly them; he has brought some old flying magazines for Cort to look at.

"Hi Cort!"

"Hi Mike!"

"I brought something for you," he holds up the magazines and is rewarded with a big smile.

He hands them to the young man and his mother says, "What do you tell Mike for bringing those for you?"

Cort lowers his eyes, embarrassed and mutters, "Thank you."

"You're welcome Cort, hope you enjoy them."

Kenny asks, "What brings you to the big city?"

Most people here use that term with tongue in cheek, the population is 300 at best and likely lower than that.

"I wanted to visit with you a bit … and bring those magazines; I heard someone accidentally threw his last ones away."

"Yes, things have been pretty sad around here since then …thanks for bringing those. Momma, why don't you take Cort in so we can visit here a bit?"

"Alright, Cort, come inside with momma."

Cort gets up and follows while looking at one of the magazines, he almost trips going up the steps.

"Thanks again for bringing those; he'll be so much easier to get along with for a few days! Now, what can I do for you?"

"Well, I filled you in with the project we're working on … I know your resources are limited and between your job and Cort I know things are tight."

"We're doing just fine."

"Oh, I'm sure you are … I was talking more about time. I know the demands on you, and I know you will never complain about it. There is something I could use your help on."

"Just say it, you know that."

"Yes, I know. I don't have any reason to believe anything might happen, but I'd appreciate it if while I am away on trips if you'd sort of check in on Janis, keep your ears open for anything odd or anyone strange?"

"You trust me with Janis?" he asks with a wicked smile.

"No, I don't trust you … I trust her!"

They both laugh and Kenny says, "You know I will, don't you worry about a thing."

"Thanks, Kenny, I really appreciate it … this makes it easier for me and is more help than you know."

"Not a problem, wish I could do more."

They sit and visit a bit more, taking about unimportant things, a good diversion for both of them and after several minutes he gets up and says, "Thanks again, I better get busy on some chores at home."

"Glad to help anyway I can, you just let me know when you will be away."

He slides into his truck, cranks the diesel to life, waves and drives off.

The one bright spot (so to speak) on the national scene, is a man who is on TV and radio. Some consider him a kook, but the number of national listeners is quite large. He listens to the shows when he can, the man is a libertarian for the most part; he is himself in many ways … personal responsibility is the mainstay of libertarian philosophy. Most talk show hosts like to hear themselves talk, say all the right things to tickle listeners' ears and keep the ratings up. This man is different; telling listeners to research on their own, learn history, educate themselves. He likes this knowing the listeners, even if it is a small percentage, will gain valuable information to help them in the future.

It is much like his father, when he was young and would ask how to spell a word or what a word's meaning was … "Look it up. If I tell you you'll never remember it."

How true. Just think about those adults who have no reason to read history and research current events will gain knowledge that will prove invaluable in the weeks, months and years to come. There are classes set up all over the country to teach the constitution free to the public. Two things make this amazing; people in America should know this already, and these people at least realize they are ignorant and willing to learn.

He has to leave early the next morning so he busies himself with chores and packs for his trip. This is one time things did not work quite right. His wife is working today and he has to leave early, so they will not see each other for a few days. They talk every night, but phone calls are not like sitting on the deck next to each other.

His trip is going well, in fact he gets a big surprise on this trip … make that two.

On day two of the three-day trip he is doing his cockpit prep while the first officer is doing the walk around inspection. The passengers are not boarding yet, and they have plenty of time.

There is a light knock on the cockpit door, "Captain, my name is Renee, and I'm ready for a briefing whenever you are."

He looks over his shoulder and says, "I'll be out in a minute." He finishes his set up and climbs out of his seat and steps back to the forward galley.

"Hi, I'm Mike … Renee, right? Have we flown together before, you look familiar?"

"I don't think so, I normally fly international, and I'm German-qualified and normally fly those routes."

"I used to fly international as well, maybe we crossed paths there some time or another."

"Perhaps," she looks at her paperwork and he hears a gasp and she snaps her head up and looks at him, "I just saw your last name on the paper work … we may not have flown together, but we've skied together, went to school together …"

"Renee … that's why you look familiar … my goodness, it's been …"

"1974, I flew out to meet you and some friends, we went to Steamboat Springs … I'd always wanted to ski the Rockies after being raised in the Northeast."

"Wow, this is unbelievable!"

"Yes it is. I almost wish we'd not figured it out until we got finished for the day … my mind is going to be really working overtime over this!"

"Mine too … but we'd better get the briefing over and get back to work before we have passengers in here."

They go over the cockpit entry procedures made much more complex since 9/11, the weather, and other information, and then he returns to the cockpit.

They had dated some, but mostly they'd been good friends. She was a year behind him in school, they'd skied together with friends and after he graduated they'd not seen each other until a chance meeting. He'd been on a ski trip in Vermont and had a bad fall. His thumb was all swollen and he was trying to work the cash register at his job in the grocery store. The head cashier had made him go to the doctor, who sent him for X-rays. He was waiting for the tech when she walked around the corner and said, "I wondered if it really was you." She had been to school and become an X-ray technician. His thumb was broken, and they dated a few times after that; however he left for the Central Plains that spring and any contact between them became occasional letters and calls, until that ski trip.

He'd not asked her to come as a date and she did not come for that. She was dating someone and while he might have wanted more, she had things in her life the way she wanted them and did not need to complicate things. The trip was fun, and as young people do, eight crammed into a condo meant for six, and the skiing was fantastic.

That evening they had dinner together and caught up on each other's lives over the past, what, 37 years? He does not feel old, but when he considers it has been 40 years since he graduated from high school, it does make him think. She is happy, married to the same guy all these years, five children, involved in volunteer work …

"Why did you leave the medical field, I would think it would be a little more conducive to family life?"

"I still have family in Germany and that job did not pay me to go see them, and this one does."

They talk for quite a while getting caught up, as the next day they are going separate ways so who knows when or if they will see each other again.

"It's getting late and I need to call Janis, I'm sure enjoying this, but better head for my room."

"Yes, I'm still sort of stunned over all this, but it has been great. Maybe we'll cross paths again."

"I hope so, but you and your husband must come and stay at the B&B … as a guest, not a customer," he smiles.

"We'd love to, let's stay in touch."

"Yes."

They share a quick hug and go to their rooms.

Once in his room, he slips into some shorts and flops onto a chair flipping the TV on to catch some news before he calls his wife and goes to bed. As the TV comes on he hears a familiar voice, "Brenda?" he says aloud. Sure enough, there she is on national news. They are talking about her "Mom" project, how a friend built a Web site and they are getting inquires from all over the country, and some from foreign countries.

"I can't believe how this is being received," she says, "I'm amazed."

The reporter is asking her more questions when his phone rings.

He looks at the caller ID and smiles, "Yes, Brenda, I see you on TV!"

"Can you believe this … I'm on national TV! I never thought in a million years I'd ever see this!"

"I've been flying a couple of days and have not seen anything, when did this all happen?"

"Just today! We launched the Web site, it was mentioned on some social media sites, and I guess it went viral. It shut down the server and we had to get a bigger … whatever it is … we had to get a bigger one!"

"Brenda, this is fantastic! What about money, is this going to require anything, you need help?"

"No, that's part of what is so exciting, we have people offering to help with their services, contributors are offering money to help … I guess there was a desire for something like this but no one had taken the initiative to do it."

"You did it Bren, you did it!"

"No, you did it, I never would have tried this but for you."

"It's okay, take some credit … no one is going to accuse you of being selfish … enjoy the time in the limelight, you deserve it!"

"Okay, I'll try … I might have to quit my job … been thinking about retirement anyway, looks like this might require full time from more than just me."

"Whatever works for you, I'm so proud of you, and happy for you … I think you have hit your true calling … I know you are a good nurse, but I can hear something in your voice … this is special."

"It sure is, Mike … thanks again, I need to go, talk to you soon!"

"Bye," as he hears the click on the line.

Well, this has been quite a day! He takes a drink out of a bottle of water and then calls home. It's getting late and he hopes she has not already gone to bed for work tomorrow.

"Hi honey," she says.

"I was afraid I might be late calling since you have work tomorrow."

"You know me, always want to get to bed early for work and never run out of things to do."

"I know … hey, you see the news tonight?"

"No, been busy running around the house and did not turn it on … what is it?"

"Brenda was on national news about her project, seems it went viral and her Web site and idea are taking off like no one could imagine."

"Sounds as if people were just waiting for her idea … maybe the timing for this is right … people are just so fed up."

He nods as he replies, "I think so, and the entrenched politicians and pundits are scared … they are on the attack. I heard a candidate say the other day that Social Security is a Ponzi scheme and he's catching more flack from his own party and advisors than the media and other party!"

She says, "Yes, I heard that, he even said it was unconstitutional."

"Yes and the mainstream commentators are all saying how this is suicide, it will drive away the moderates and he cannot be elected talking like that, but …. I also heard a pollster had a group of solid party members and some more moderate and he asked them about that comment and something like seventy-two percent liked hearing a candidate be honest and frank … find it refreshing."

"Me too!"

"No argument there … this is just so awesome … oh, something else interesting happen today."

He tells her briefly of meeting Renee and the subsequent visit.

"That's so cool; I hope they'll come see us sometime."

"Yes, me too … hey, it's late and we both need to get some rest. I'll call you before I start home tomorrow. I love you … good night."

"Good night, love you too," and they both click off.

He's not sure he can get to sleep after this day, wow. He sets the alarm and turns off the light. When he was young sometimes he would have his mind flying and unable to slow it down to go to sleep. He figured out once how to get through those times and he puts it to work tonight. He closes his eyes, relaxes and takes a slow deep breath. He clears his mind and thinks only of his toes … makes them relax and then he moves to his feet, willing any tension to leave his body and relax completely. He has never made it to his head, usually if he has to do this, sometime around the middle of his body he is so relaxed and his mind is not thinking of anything outside his body … he drifts off to sleep. Tonight is no exception.

The alarm almost startles him … this is unusual because he often wakes up about the time it is set to go off. He busies himself getting ready, shower, shave, pack and off to another day. Today is normal, no surprises. He drops his flight bag off at operations and then heads for his commuter flight and calls home.

"Hi, honey, I'm on my way to my flight."

"How does it look?"

"I think I'll have a seat, but the jump seat is always a backup."

"Okay, see you in a few hours. I have a few more errands and will be home soon."

"Okay, love you."

"You too, anxious to see you."

As it turns out an earlier flight had cancelled and the plane is full, so he has to take the jump seat. This is not a "regular" jet, it is a jet, but what they call an RJ … regional jet … used on routes that don't demand a full sized jet. They only have 50 or so seats and the cockpit is small, the jump seat cramped. At least he is headed home and it is a short flight.

The crew is busy and other than keeping his eyes open to help look for other aircraft, his mind begins to wander. One thing that has been an unexpected pleasure of this whole deal has been finding and catching up with people from the past. Life is like a huge jigsaw puzzle ... sometimes some pieces are lost so you keep finding and using the ones you have, putting each in its place. Historically those pieces remained forever missing, which was fine because the picture is so large we can't see that part of the picture as clearly from where we are now.

Finding some of these friends from the past is like finding those pieces and putting them in their place. While it is true if they had been made a part of the picture back then it would have changed the whole thing, now it is just part of history. It is just nice to know they were not forever lost.

Once on the ground he calls her and tells her he is on the way to his truck and will be home within an hour. He leaves the parking lot and flips on the satellite radio to listen to the news; maybe he'll hear more about Brenda's project. It is a time in the hour when they discuss business and he is pleasantly surprised at the guest … it is John.

It seems John has contacted several CEO's and has them all on board, some of these corporations are smaller, and some are huge. The reporter is asking him the basics of his plan and how he came about doing it now.

John replies, "This is something I wanted to do for many years but something always got in the way. I felt that since I am no longer tied to one company it made sense to work with several to get the ball rolling. This is not something we will compete on; we will cooperate as much as possible to keep from duplicating efforts. The timing just seemed appropriate with the problems the nation is facing, unemployment being so high, and so many corporations trying to make a profit with tremendous uncertainty in our economy. No one knows what the government is going to do so actually most companies have more cash now than normal as they take a "wait and see" course of action.

"We all got together and decided part of the reason for the uncertainty is people are waiting for the government and expecting it to take care of them. We thought if we can take charge of this it would take some of the uncertainty out of the mix."

The reporter responds, "Why would you want to expend capital on something like this when there are government programs already in place designed for this very thing?"

He can tell by the tone of John's response that patience is thin for ignorant reporters … "Well, if these programs are such a great deal why aren't they working? We believe that private agencies are much closer to the problem and can see exactly what is needed and where … the government has a one- size-fits-all program and is good for a few and insufficient for most. Since we announced our plans we've had a number of other companies contact us to see if they can be included and of course we will let them participate.

"I can see in just a few months we will cover every metropolitan area in the country, and since many of these corporations also operate in smaller cities as well we should be able to offer solutions to people in all but the most rural areas."

The reporter thanks John for his time and moves on to other news. He almost wonders if this is all a dream, two of the members' ideas have made national news in two days … success beyond his wildest expectations.

He arrives home to the excited yips of the dogs, much wagging of tails and dancing on hind legs, each jostling for the first bit of attention. She comes out of the house to meet him, it has been too many days and they stand by the truck holding each other for a few minutes, the dogs competing still for attention. They pull apart and kiss briefly, then he stoops down to love on each of the dogs; there is jealous growling and pushing until each has had what they feel is the appropriate amount of loving.

As he stands she asks, "You interested in having some guineas?"

"Sure, who has them?"

"Ricky called and says he has some that are getting close to being ready to be out and Martha wants him to thin his flock."

He smiles, Ricky and Martha are good friends from church. Ricky is a retired judge and Martha works at a college nearby. Ricky was raised in Texas on a farm and he loves his place in the country, raising all sorts of foul, sheep, goats, pigs, cattle … they even milk a cow and make their own cheese. Martha is onboard with all this, but she thinks Ricky has a little too much and is always trying to get him to cut back.

"Sounds good, I'll give him a call and see what we need to do to get things ready. Now, I have some news for you."

"Is this good or bad?"

"Oh, it's fantastic actually … I heard Professor John being interviewed on the radio while I was on my way home."

He tells her what he heard as he grabs his bag and they go inside.

When he is finished she says, “This is great, did you think things would take off like this?”

“You know, I don’t think I could have imagined it going this fast … now if the others don’t go this well it might be a big disappointment!”

They go back to the bedroom and visit while he unpacks and changes out of his uniform. He is tired and ready to unwind a bit so she says, “I have tea made, why don’t you go out on the deck and relax for a while, and I’ll bring you a glass of tea and then start supper?”

“That sounds great, but I can get my own tea.”

She slaps him on the butt and says, “Let me take care of you once in a while why don’t you?”

“Alright, I’ll get a phone and call Ricky.”

She brings him a glass of tea while he is on the phone. He sets up a time tomorrow to get the guineas and hangs up.

“He says he has about ten he’ll give us. He heard you mention once you’d like to have guineas to help get rid of ticks.”

“Yes, and they make good watch dogs too!”

“Don’t we already have those?” he asks.

“Well yes, but they are often in the house. The guineas will always be outside and will let us know any time someone comes in the drive.”

He is still being cautious and sees a definite advantage to another warning system, one that does not use electricity and cannot be bypassed. “My grandmother used to have guineas, I always liked them … maybe we’ll get some eggs from them as well.”

“Maybe, their eggs are really hard shelled; I hear they are great for hard boiled eggs. I still want chickens too you know.”

“I know, maybe this fall and winter I can build a coop so we can get some in the spring.”

“I’d like that, now I’d better start supper,” she says, then leaves him with the dogs on the deck.

He puts his feet up and sits back in the chair. This is nice, sometimes he wishes he could spend more time here like this, but he is a work-a-holic and knows that in a fairly short time he’d get bored … but spending relaxing time here on occasion is not only nice, it is needed. He watches the ducks on the pond … these came from Ricky as well. They also ordered some hatchling ducks online, those will arrive in a couple of days, and Ricky will raise them until they are ready to live on the pond. Ricky is all set up for this sort of thing and it just makes sense. The ducks are relaxing to watch, as they are not loud as some ducks can be. They feed on plants and algae in the water, and occasionally he can hear a muted quack. They enjoy the alpacas, but they decided they need to expand into animals that are more food-oriented. Alpaca is eaten in the rest of the world and some in America eat it. He knows before alpacas are to be a true livestock option in America the meat aspect will have to be developed, and one of these days he will convince her to try it … in time.

She will also have to learn that as the chickens, ducks, and guineas reproduce… they will have to be a food source as well. A friend told him, "Don't let her name them so she won't have such an aversion to eating them."

He replied, "Oh, we'll name them … Pokey, Slow One, Lunch, Supper, Dinner ..."

Part of that thought process is of course to prepare for the worst regarding the nation and the economy. It will not be fun to do without the niceties America has become accustomed to, but they will be in a very good position to "weather the storm" if need be. There are fish in the pond; deer, turkey and pheasant are plentiful. There is a small river just across the road to the south. They have a windmill that can pump water, though the house is large and is heated with a geo-thermal heat pump, it can be heated with wood. There is an old wood-burning kitchen stove in the farm house on the property, so they could even cook with wood if needed. He hopes and prays none of this is necessary, but …

He tips his head back and closes his eyes; it feels good to relax for a bit.

"Did you hear me?"

"What … uh, no. I guess I dozed off."

She says, "I thought maybe you had, supper is ready."

He gets up, grabs his tea glass and heads into the screened-in portion of the deck where she has a table set.

Chapter 16

THE NEXT DAY HIS phone rings, it is Keith. "Hi Keithy, how are things going?"

"Good Mikey, I just have a minute and wanted to fill you in on my participation in the project."

"Great, go ahead."

"Well, I was struggling with just what I wanted to do. I had sort of thought I'd try to do something within my company when John made his announcement and my company is planning to participate."

"Wow, that's great, Keith. They're one of the biggest employers in the country!"

"Yes, and that's where I come in. The company needs volunteers to help regionally, and I have volunteered to lead the efforts here. I just think I can be more effective doing this than trying to start something else, and I can get some close friends of mine who work around the country to become involved."

"I'm letting this sink in a bit, but Keith, you and your group could personally affect tens of thousands of people!"

"Yes, I just keep getting more and more excited about the prospects of this and where it will lead. Thanks for including me on the project. You know, I'm not so sure if this had come up and I was not looking for some way to help … I'm not sure I would have done this. It is so easy to get caught up in life and personal things; you sort of forget there is a world out there and that we have an obligation to help our neighbors."

"That's a good point, Keith. So many of us just get tunnel vision; remember Paul Harvey always said, "Increased freedom requires increased responsibility." We tend to forget there is a world out there and we have responsibilities outside our own family."

Keith says, "I need to go, I had a short break but I have lots of deliveries to make before I can go home. Thanks again, hope I can get up your way and see you soon."

"We'd love to have you … and thank you for what you are doing … this is a great help! Bye, have a great day!"

"You too, Mikey … bye."

He is an optimist, but also a realist. The news of the various projects getting off the ground is wonderful and fills him with optimism. He also knows dealing with people, that things can happen to let things fall apart … people are not committed, unforeseen obstacles and of course the forces trying to transform the country will not like any of this. Will the country as a whole take to this or will a majority prefer the government? He has the tendency, as do most people, to view the world through his own eyes and world view; who wouldn't prefer a personal approach to the government? Of course there will be the lazy ones who want a check with no strings or requirements, but they certainly would be a minority … or would they? Time will tell; he just hopes there is enough time.

The next several months pass, things are pretty much normal … the news is typically bad, sprinkled with word the various groups around the country are having an effect and it is growing more and more all the time. Of course the old saying of "If it bleeds, it leads" has the news consumed with all the gloom and doom and problems. Good news and happy people are just not newsworthy to the mainstream media. While the alpaca business is slow, nothing related to their upkeep has slowed; they still need to eat and be cleaned up after, breedings, births, and shearing all occur on schedule. He's gone on his trips, she has gone to work every third day, and things have progressed as expected. They have a couple of part time people to help with B&B needs if there are guests when neither of them can be there. They have not advertised much, preferring to retire first so they can enjoy the guests. The occasional guests are mostly from word of mouth by friends and family.

It is about time for the news so he pours himself a glass of tea and turns the TV on to a cable news channel. He gave up listening to any of the major network news years ago. It was so obvious they were biased and it just frustrated him what they reported, how they reported and interviewed their guests. He is horrified at some of the reports. The leader of a major union is shouting to his membership at a large gathering, "Let's take these sons of bitches out!" He is referring to the Tea Party … not really a party, a movement … normal citizens who are fed up with the direction the country is going, big government, and excess taxes and spending, moving toward Marxist principles, and are voicing their opinion and backing politicians who want to go back to the constitution. Now he has never heard any of them say anything this rash … and he's sure he won't. These patriots are peaceful and law abiding; some unions, not so much. He is a union member and this association does not make him feel anything like warm and fuzzy.

Next are reports of neo Nazi's in different parts of the world committing acts of violence against Jews. Then there is a video of a Black Panther leader teaching violence, including how to behead someone, to a group including children. "Good Lord … maybe we should just shut the world out, sit here at the ranch and let them all kill themselves," he says aloud. No … no, that is not an option worth considering. He knows there will always be evils and horrors, but it has to be the exception, not the rule.

Since he is a commuter to his job he sometimes puts trips together … back to back. While he does not really like to be away the extra days at once, he is rewarded by having more days off at home in a row and one less commute that month … in the big scheme of things, worth it. He has done what they call a trip trade, dropped one trip for another so when he leaves tomorrow it will be for five days.

When he flew internationally he occasionally was gone for over a week, and as Murphy's Law dictates, if something were to go wrong at home it would be when he was halfway around the world. Once the water heater went out, another time the air conditioner, another time car problems; these things bother him. He hates that she is left with problems like this to handle. Not that she is unable, but his makeup is to be a hunter/gatherer/protector. It is his job to provide, to protect, and to solve problems so she will not have to be burdened with things like that. It disturbs him to be unable to do his job as he sees fit. With all that is going on with this project and the normal day-to-day operations of the house and ranch, the odds are higher something will go wrong and she will be forced handle whatever happens.

He does not dwell on these things as he is not really a pessimist … he is a realist and understands things happen, and when they do, action must be taken to resolve the issue and then move on. Prepare for the worst and hope for the best.

His trip goes smoothly and nothing unusual happens either on the trip or at home. Time passes, the world keeps turning and in spite of the issues plaguing the world, there is as yet no major failure of a nation. Governments are still micromanaging, primarily using regulations to force companies to do business in desired ways, control behavior, etc.

Things at the ranch are going well, her job has its normal calls, and things with the project are really being accepted by the public. He hears some comments on a radio talk show and later on a news show that underscores that Bernie's idea is going well. People are doing random acts of kindness to complete strangers, and it is infectious; as people hear of it they just take it make up their own version and do things. He smiles as he thinks of how this has progressed. In reality, it did not take much time on anyone's part, very little financially, and it really has gone better than he ever imagined.

Churches used to be very involved in communities and over the years had taken a back seat to government programs. Now there seems to be resurgence in church groups taking the initiative in communities, helping those in need. Assisting with childcare for working parents, benevolent work for those hurting in many ways, and often the spiritual lift is more important that the physical assistance. This was his pilot buddy John's plan. They talk quite often, but oddly, seldom about this.

They had a layover in Los Angeles once at the same time. There is a Mongolian BBQ near the hotel they both enjoy and an evening there with good food and company is always welcome. It was one of those evenings John shared a few of the details he was implementing. It just made so much sense, good people doing good things. It is so unfortunate many in America believe “Separation of Church and State” exists in the Constitution. This leads to a fear anything accomplished in public and allowed or endorsed by the government is a violation of the Constitution. In reality, that phrase exists only in the minds of progressives and the uneducated. He thinks if progressives read the Second Amendment the way they read the First, gun ownership would be mandatory.

Chapter 17

HE SUPPOSES IF HE has any weaknesses for things it is guns and cars. That being said, he would never buy an expensive new car. He likes classic cars, fast cars. In his younger years he owned a number of different sports cars; MGB, two different Datsun 2000's, a TR-6 … and his favorite … the Porsche 356c. He sold the Porsche for twice what he paid for it and used the money to buy a family car. At the time it was something that needed to be done, but he sure wishes he still had that one. He does have a basket case Porsche 914 in his hanger he plans to rebuild one of these days … in his spare time.

He'd always liked Jaguars, loved the classic lines. He also knew they were a mechanic's nightmare … you could not own only a Jag; you have to have something reliable to drive while the Jag is in the shop. When he made captain he decided to treat himself to something special. He loved the V-12 XJS; it looks fast, and is. The 12-cylinder engine runs very smooth, but once again, is not normally reliable. His plan, to buy one that is not running or has high miles and put in a 350 V8, as there are a number of different kits available for this conversion. You get the looks and some reliability. He found a good one with over 120,000 miles on it thinking it would not last long … that was 10 years ago. He decided the low-mileage cars were ones that were plagued with problems and did not ever run right, whereas the high-mileage ones were the good ones.

He does not drive it very much, he takes his wife on dates in it and on occasion, when he goes somewhere alone, he takes it out. He has several friends who are sheriff deputies and he jokes with them about a high-speed chase, but that is not something he is serious about. While this car was made to really go and with the right tires very safe, this should only be done by a professional driver on a closed road (as the commercial says). He has opened it up a few times on straight roads with no traffic, the speedometer goes to 160, and it came very close to that. Slowing to 65 after that he felt he could almost get out and walk beside the car. When talking to one of his deputy friends he made mention of doing this once and was soundly reprimanded about inexperienced drivers and how dangerous that was. He'd replied that he agreed, the biggest problem being someone else that might happen on the scene, and reminded the deputy that while he knew what he did was not legal, he "drove" a 747 on the runway weighing over 750,000 pounds going over 200 mph, with only his feet on the rudder pedals for steering on takeoff roll.

He has a few errands to run today; typically he'd take the big diesel truck because there was normally something for the B&B or the ranch that required the bed. However today there were no such needs and the weather is nice. He'd had the car gone through years ago, any rust cut out, and a nice paint job put on. It had not been driven in the rain or snow since. He makes the necessary stops at a home center, bank, courthouse and grocery store. He is typically vigilant, mostly as a defensive driver, but in this city most in the country would consider small (population about 50 thousand) unusual things are noticeable. And seeing the same dark blue sedan with the same driver in the rear-view mirror after the third stop, the guy might as well have a neon sign on the car. Wondering what was up, he decided to make some turns, go places to verify he either is or is not being followed. The car was not always real close, sometimes several cars or some distance back, but it was still there. Surely by now the man in the car knows he's been spotted, so now what? He decides to head out of town, but not in the direction of home. Once out on the highway he verifies the car is back there about half a mile. "Well, let's see how bad he wants to follow me," he thinks as he presses on the accelerator.

As the speedometer goes past 100 he sees the car is trying to keep up, but is some distance further back. As he goes past

125 the car is rapidly disappearing in the mirror. He settles in at 140 and holds the speed for a few minutes, worried he will encounter one of his friends in law enforcement and have to explain what he is doing … to no avail he's sure. He comes to a crossroad with a tree row along it hiding the road from view until you pass. He hits the brakes hard and makes the corner and punches it again. He does not see the car at all, whether the man gave up or he just lost him does not matter. He goes a few miles, makes another turn and heads for home at normal speed.

What is this about? It has to be related to what he is doing, related to his idea, but why? What might be the reason for following him? If someone knows who he is, they also likely know where he lives. So the thought is they are looking for who he might meet with or a place he might go. By running they will think he has something to hide, which is fine because none of his efforts are focused locally. There are people locally involved, but they are part of other groups and do not even know him. Perhaps his caution in the beginning was well founded and a good plan … prepare for the worst, hope for the best. On the drive home his mind is a blur of thought about what this might mean to the project, and to him.

He arrives at home, puts the car in the shed, greets the dogs and goes inside.

Chapter 18

"YOU DRIVE PRETTY FAST," the voice says.

He is walking to his truck in the parking lot of a home improvement center; he'd left a large cart of supplies by the commercial pickup door and was going to drive up closer to load.

"Who are you?" He asks while trying to place the face, voice, something.

"That's not information you need," the man replies.

This gentleman, using that term quite loosely, has done several things that really put him on edge. He's glad to be wearing sunglasses so the man cannot see exactly where his eyes are focused.

"So I guess you're the jerk who was following me the other day?"

The man obviously did not like the "jerk" comment; good, keep him off balance and emotionally involved in this … whatever "this" is.

"Yes, that was me, and I did not appreciate your little game … and my employer was not amused either."

"So you won't tell me who you are, I suppose your employer is a big secret as well?"

"Let's just say," he goes on, "that it is a group of individuals with a rather large investment they've made over a long period of time and the things you are meddling with are putting that investment at risk."

"I really don't know what you are talking about."

The man chuckles and says, "Oh, I think you do."

He does, or at least assumes this is about his idea, the project and groups working around the country. It has more or less taken on a life of its own, just as he had hoped, and the general change in the way communities are operating has been in the news more often. As some politicians and liberal media try to make negative comments and say things to belittle participants, the people just put their heads down and work harder. He knew as people in power lost that power they would want to strike out, but how did anyone single him out? Out of all the people involved in this all over the country, how did they learn he was instrumental in its beginning?

"Okay, let me get this straight. Someone who will not give me his name, or tell me who sent him, or tell me exactly what he wants … expects me to guess what that is and just do it? Do I have that right?"

"You're a real smartass aren't you?"

"Me? Are you listening to this conversation? Who's the smartass here?"

The man is getting pretty upset, but is holding his temper fairly well.

"Okay," the stranger says, "I'll be a bit more specific so your thick skull can take it in."

This guy does not want to be the only one upset and is trying to get him riled up; it does not work. He trains in his job, in his defensive classes and on his own to always be in control. You cannot handle an emergency in an airplane full of people if you lose your cool.

"You started something that has grown to be a problem for my employers. You have started groups who are doing things that undermine years of work, and billions of dollars spent, and they want it stopped … now."

Well, he finally spelled it out, sort of. If someone were to listen in on this conversation they would have no idea what this was about, but he's played dumb long enough. Need to bring this to a close and send this guy home empty-handed.

"First off," he says, "I think you are giving me way too much credit. How can one person in a rural community have such an effect on so many people across the country? Are you telling me that simply being a good citizen and helping my neighbor is not allowed in your employer's world? That is a world I do not want to live in. I have no contact, none, with any organization or group around the country, no way to stop this as you say. Oh, and if I could, I wouldn't. Go home and tell your people I was not cooperative, that I am powerless to do anything. Tell them this is a great country, just enjoy it."

The man is not happy with the way this is going, he thought some pressure on this country boy would intimidate him and he'd fold like a cheap suit.

"That is not one of the options." The man says. "My orders were to try and reason with you and get you to see what you are doing is not in your best interest … or your wife, or the friends you have involved."

Well, this certainly took a serious turn … his senses have been on high alert and this only confirms his first impressions.

The man continues, "Your options are to make every effort to stop what you started or face the consequences."

"You going to poke holes in my tires? You've got a lot of nerve to come here like this and expect me to take any of this seriously. I'm busy and have a lot to do today, I'm done talking to you … take a hike."

The man does not move, at least he does not walk away. He does move, as he speaks he slowly pulls his jacket open showing a weapon, looks to b a 9 millimeter, "I was hoping you would be reasonable, but figured you'd be stubborn."

The man has been very overconfident, very careless. There was apparently no thought he might be armed. The years of training have culminated at this point … they were leading to this moment. He is not even thinking, as the man's hand closes on his weapon, he pulls his Glock and swings it up. The man realizes it is too late and tries to hurry his gun out of the holster. The sound is deafening. He is used to shooting with hearing protection and the sound in the parking lot reverberates off the cars and the building. Just as he's trained he fires twice, they are only five or six feet apart, missing is not an option.

The Glock 36 is loaded with 7 jacketed hollow-points, .45 +P, 230 grains each. The first round strikes center mass in the thoracic cavity, the hollow-point shredding the left lung and half the heart; the second hits a little higher and tears open the aorta and most everything else … the damage is amazing, and death is nearly instant. The man does not fly backwards like in the movies. The initial look of shock on his face is replaced with one of disbelief, and then nothing. The man's gun falls to the pavement, and he crumples in a heap with blood pouring out of the gaping wounds.

He has killed many times … but only animals. While he's trained for this and was as prepared as possible for this moment … there is just no way to really prepare for afterwards. After the adrenaline rush, comes the crash. He holsters the Glock and looks around. Only a couple of people in the parking lot are visible, but some are coming out of the store now and everyone is looking his way. He pulls out his cell and dials 911. The operator answers on the second ring, "I'd like to report a shooting." He gives the location, the operator asks some questions … anyone hurt, how many, etc. He is asked to stay on the line; he leans against his truck, takes a deep breath, and waits.

He can see the hospital from the parking lot, so he sees the ambulance and hears the siren right away. In a moment he also hears several other sirens, police and sheriff deputies likely. Suddenly he has a thought … a troubling thought. His wife is working today, and she is working the station at the hospital. He hopes she is not on the call, but then there is Murphy's Law.

The ambulance arrives first as he figured … he can see the worried look on her face. They park some distance away, protocol for situations such as this to not endanger the EMS personnel, until law enforcement arrives. First on the scene is a city cop who screeches to a stop a short distance away with the passenger side between him and the body.

The officer exits and keeps cover behind his patrol car and shouts, "Are you the one who called this in?"

He still has his cell to his ear talking to the 911 operator. She tells him to hang up and speak with the officer. Another city police car arrives and a sheriff's patrol pickup.

He hits end on his cell and lays it on the pickup hood and responds with a nod and "Yes" to the first officer.

Next question, "Are you armed?"

"Yes, it is holstered under my shirt," he responds.

He is instructed to remove it from the holster, lay it on the hood of the truck and move away, slowly. He understands these men are just doing their job and do not know but what the good guy is laying in a pool of blood and the bad guy is talking to them. He recognizes the sheriff deputy, Brian, an officer who was raised near his rural community. They know each other well; they have worked together on a few cases of burglary and theft, in addition to a community crime watch program.

He is asked to put his hands on the hood of the police car, as the city officer is looking for any other weapons Brian asks, "What happened here Mike?"

The city cop says, "You know this guy?"

"Yes, known him for years." His hands are cuffed behind his back and EMS is told they can come in. He can clearly see his wife has no interest in the man on the ground, but she has a job to do.

Her partner takes the radio from his belt and speaks into it, "We have one Code Black."

Brian speaks, "What happened here, who is that?" He realizes he does not have to say anything and just let the facts speak for themselves, but he sees no reason for this … but it does not mean he can be careless … anything he says can and will be used in a court of law …

"It all happened pretty fast, Brian. I have no idea who this is."

"Was he trying to rob you?"

The gun is in plain sight on the pavement next to the body.

"No, he was making some strange demands, said he'd been sent to stop me from doing something that was hurting his employer. When I told him I did not know what he was talking about and tried to leave he reached for a gun. I just reacted and got mine out first. I did ask who he was and who sent him, he refused to tell me. That's about all I know."

Brian says, "Uncuff him, I know him well, he is not going to be a problem. Besides, his wife is the lady over there with EMS and I think she wants to come over and make sure he's okay."

The city cop is clearly not entirely sure this is the right thing to do, but after looking at her and back at Brian who nods, he unlocks the cuffs. She has tears streaming down her face and she throws her arms around him and holds him tight. He is about a foot taller than her so her face is buried in his chest. He has a bit of a flashback.

It was her father's 60th birthday; he had flown a Piper Pacer to his father-in-law's ranch with two of their children and a nephew. When he was ready to leave the pasture where he'd landed, a piece of barbed wire caught on the landing gear. It flipped up and damaged the right aileron making the plane uncontrollable at a slow speed and low altitude. He made a split- second decision to crash the plane before it rolled over upside down which certainly would have been fatal to all on board. She watched that happen, and her reaction then was just like this.

Her partner speaks, "You okay Mike?"

"Yes Trace, thanks. This is not the best day of my life, but I'll be okay."

"You let me know if there is anything I can do, not just now, but in the days to come, you be sure to let me know."

"I will Trace, thanks."

She pulls back slightly and looks up at his face. "What happened here, I mean besides the obvious?"

"Let's talk about that later, I think they will need me to visit with them some more. I'll be alright, really."

She says, "I don't think you should be alone tonight, I'll take off the rest of the shift."

"Okay, but hang on a bit, I might be tied up for a while here. I'll call and let you know."

She hugs him again, kisses him and says, "I love you."

"I love you too, go with Trace and I'll call. Trace, take care of my girl, okay?"

"Sure thing Mike, don't worry about a thing."

"Thanks."

He asks, "Brian, what do we do now?"

"Well, we need to go down to the office and do some paperwork, answer some questions."

"Should I get an attorney?"

"Well, that's certainly your right, but between you and me I don't think it will be necessary. It looks pretty clear you were simply defending yourself; you are local, known and respected. I view most of this as a formality."

"Okay, can I go back in and have them secure my supplies? I had just bought several things and they are in a cart up by the commercial exit."

"Sure, I'll wait for you here." He goes and speaks to an employee who says he'll set it in the back, "Just let us know and you can get it anytime. Gee, that was something, what happened?"

"I'd better not talk about it now, they're waiting for me. I'll tell you when I come back."

He returns to the parking lot.

Brian says, "Get in and ride with me, I'll bring you back to your truck when we're finished."

They talk about other things on the drive to the sheriff's department, Brian's coming retirement, the new house and so on. They arrive and go inside, the place is all abuzz … a shooting in this county is not very commonplace. They go back to an office and sit down, a detective joins them. "Mr. Murphy, I'm detective Hedges."

He smiles … Mister … "Hi Jeremy, you forget you went to school with my oldest son?"

"Oh, I know, I figured you probably did not remember me."

"Yes, I remember you. Remember, you handled the case when my gun was stolen … the gun I used today actually."

"Hmmmm, that's an odd coincidence."

"Yes, it is."

They ask for his concealed carry permit, driver's license and begin to fill out forms and reports.

Another detective asks detective Hedges to step out, he's gone a few minutes and then returns. "The name Robert Hudson mean anything to you?"

"No, I know a Bill Hudson, but not a Robert, why?"

"That's the name of the guy in the parking lot. His DL is from Virginia, and you have no idea why he was here?"

He's thought about this, knew this question would come up. How would he explain that he and several other people decided to be good citizens and help others and that in turn encouraged others to do the same, the idea took off and then someone got upset about it? Honestly, this guy and his visit made absolutely no sense and the full truth would raise more questions than it would answer. He decided to keep it brief and not offer quite everything, at least not now. It would be easy to say later that someone trying to kill you for being a good person would not come to your mind, so play it a little dumb, leave out the chase the other day.

"No, I don't."

"What did he say to you?"

"It all happened pretty fast, and it did not make any sense to me, then or now. He blocked my path and told me the people he worked for wanted me to stop. I asked who he was, he refused to say … who he worked for and was told it was a group of investors. I told him I did not know what he was talking about, he insisted I did. He told me I had two options, to stop whatever it was they thought I was doing or suffer the consequences; he threatened my wife and my friends. I told him to shove off and tried to leave, that's when he pulled his gun. He certainly did not know I carried, he was deliberate and I think trying to intimidate me, that's why I was able to get my weapon out before him; he took it for granted he had the upper hand."

Brian asks, "You think this could be a case of mistaken identity?"

"I suppose," he says, "but that would make you wonder who the person is he was after."

"Yes, the questions just keep coming."

I think we have all we need for now," Hedges says. "You have any plans to be out of town?"

"You know what I do for a living, yes, I'll be away on a trip for three days, and I leave Thursday."

"Okay, keep in touch with us and I'll call you if I need anything."

"Okay, how about my gun?"

A hesitation, then, "Okay, we'll get it for you. Typically we'd keep it until everything is cleared up, but it appears you broke no laws … and to be honest, since we do not know really what this is about it is conceivable you could be in some danger. I'd feel better if you were able to protect yourself."

"Thanks, me too. I have other weapons I can use, but love that little 45. I have another 45, but it is not a compact and does not carry well."

They retrieve his Glock and he leaves with Brian to get his truck.

"I've got to tell you Mike that was the strangest shooting I've ever seen in our county."

"I don't doubt that, Brian. There aren't that many here anyway, thank goodness, one reason we like it here so well. Janis used to wonder why I carried, I think she thought it was a macho thing, but maybe she's better with it now."

"I'd think so, better that guy than you for sure; how are you doing?"

"Well, it will take some time to get over, but I will get over it. Had I shot someone accidentally I doubt I could handle that very well, and taking any human life is a tough thing no matter why. I'm glad Janis is taking the night off and coming home … probably would not be good to be alone tonight."

"Good for her, I agree."

He asks Brian, "You ever have to do this? I remember when that guy took a shot at you with a rifle; if you hadn't reacted as you did you wouldn't be here now."

"No, I haven't ever shot anyone. And that event is forever etched in my mind, that was not easy to get over … my wife sure was ready for me to find another line of work after that!"

"I bet she was!"

As they pull up next to his pickup in the parking lot Brian says, "Well, here you are. I'm sure we'll be talking to you quite often here over the next several days."

The scene has been cleaned up, the body removed and probably the fire department washed the area clean.

"I'm sure that is a fact. Anything I need to do?"

"Just take care of yourself, take it easy for a few days. Might not hurt to talk to someone, you know, psychologist or someone like that."

"Sure, I know someone, thanks."

"That 45 really did a job; I'd always liked my 9 millimeter and the fact it carries more rounds, but if you are on the mark nothing compares to the 45."

"That's why I use it, and actually I can shoot it better than a 9 millimeter. Thanks for everything Brian … we'll talk soon."

"Take care."

He gets out of the patrol truck and into his. He calls his wife and tells her he is finished with the reports and is going to get his supplies he'd purchased earlier and head home.

"Thanks," she says, "I will leave here soon and see you at home … Love you!"

"I love you too, see you soon."

He pulls up to the loading area and goes inside. The associate he spoke with earlier sees him and tells him to wait there and heads back to retrieve the cart.

As the employee brings the cart out he asks, "Can you talk about it now?"

As they load the truck he begins, "I supposed the basics will be alright. Did not know the guy, it was not a robbery, there is speculation he mistook me for someone else. All I know is he threatened me and my family verbally, I told him I did not know what he was talking about and to take a hike; he did not like that and reached for a gun … I got mine out first and you know the rest."

"Wow, more like a big city or even a movie … never thought anything like that would happen in this town … and certainly not in this parking lot!"

He's tired and ready to be at home; all this is really catching up to him.

"I know, still doesn't seem real to me. Thanks for the help, hope my next visit is not nearly so memorable."

"Sure thing, be careful!"

He eases out of the parking lot, glad to be on the way home.

Chapter 19

HIS MIND IS SO full of things on the drive home he's not so sure it is safe for him to be driving. At least he is out of town soon and driving down the highway towards his house. Traffic is light as is normal. How did anyone figure out he was involved in this at all, let alone the person who thought it up?

The idea that any of his friends would have talked is not realistic, they all knew to be careful, and once it moved to the next level of groups he was not connected at all. That answer may never be known, but more of a concern now … someone tried to kill him today, and made verbal threats against his wife and friends. He has to notify his friends, but his common sense tells him to not use any normal form of communication. And his wife … that really concerns him, and he will not tell her this detail. He will, however, make sure she is always armed. When she is at work she should be okay, but anytime she is alone she needs to carry.

He decides to use an overnight delivery service to notify his group as to what happened and to take all precautions … he'll work on that tonight.

He pulls into his drive and is greeted by the excited barks of their dogs, two Miniature Dachshunds and a long haired Chihuahua. Leaving the truck he stoops and pets them all, much to their delight, and then he begins to unload the truck. Just as he finishes, his wife pulls into the drive. She jumps out and quickly comes to him and holds him tightly.

She says, "That was the longest drive today, I didn't think I'd ever get here!"

"Yes, I agree. My mind was so full of stuff, I'm glad there was no traffic. I'm glad you came home, I would not want to be here alone tonight ... not out of fear of being alone, but just need someone to be with and talk to ... and I can't think of anyone I'd rather be with."

"Well, after thirty years together, you better not be able to think of anyone else you'd want to be with," she says with a smile and slaps him on the butt.

He says, "I think I'd like to relax in the hot tub for a while, might clear my mind some and relieve the tension. After the adrenalin rush earlier I feel exhausted."

"That sounds good, I'll join you."

They change and climb in the hot tub. The hot swirling and bubbling water is soothing, the muscles relax and his mind begins to slow and feel a bit more normal. Their conversation avoids the day's event on purpose, so they discuss other things and spend some time in silence.

He cooks some steaks on the grill while she prepares salad and baked potatoes. The evening has become more normal, but it has almost come to the point of avoiding the obvious, so he starts.

"I suppose I should tell you the details of today."

"Whenever, no rush until you are ready to talk about it."

"I'm much better now."

He gives her an accurate recount of the event, sans the threat on her and his friends, and the time spent at the sheriff's department.

She listens carefully then says, "I am so glad you had a gun and that you took the time to train. This is pretty bad, I can't imagine what it might have been like had I arrived on that call to find you on the ground."

"That's for sure, I had not really noticed until it was over, there were really no witnesses, only a couple of people in the lot and they were quite a distance away. If he'd been able to shoot me it is likely he'd slipped into his car and driven off without being seen well enough to be identified, and with him coming from out of the area he could have disappeared and no one would have know what happened."

"And I would have been a widow … again … not something I wish to experience, at least until you die of old age."

"I don't want either of us to experience it again. You know, since there is so little known about whom this was and why it happened, I want you to carry … anytime you leave the house, I want you armed. You shoot the Sig 380 well, it's not a 45, but it will work."

"Okay, I wish I had some of the training you've had."

"Me too, I'll spend some more time with you on that sort of thing here over the next several days. Since I don't know how they, whoever they are, figured this out I'm going to write the group and give them the news so they can all take precautions; I'll send them via overnight delivery … avoid the Postal Service, Internet and phone."

She does not like this sudden extreme caution, but says nothing. It is not that she does not like him taking the precautions, it is the fact it is necessary.

He writes the letters, avoids printing the labels from the Internet and hand-writes them all and puts them into the envelopes. He has included an alternate contact method. This will be a pain to set things up but until he can figure out how they were isolated, it is necessary. And each of them could be in danger as well. This thought concerns him greatly, he wanted so much for this to work as it has, but if one person is hurt … can he forgive himself if that happens? He knows the problem now is that even if everyone were to try and comply with these demands to stop, how can they? This has taken on a life of its own, it is unstoppable.

They go to bed late, he is exhausted. His normal joke; insomnia is him tossing and turning for 30 to 45 seconds before falling asleep, not tonight. He relives the event of the day over and over, the look on the man's face before and after being shot, his body on the parking lot; blood flowing freely out of the two large holes he placed precisely where he intended. In reality, it is not remorse over the shooting and death … he is worrying about his friends … and mostly his wife. What has he brought into their lives? While he had no choice today, he did have a choice getting into this … or did he?

Did Washington and the other Founding Fathers have a choice, did Lincoln, and did any of the many service men over the years who gave limb and life? He does not put himself in that class, but for the decisions to be made regarding love of country there is little difference … no, he did not have a choice. To watch the nation he loves be transformed into something akin to Europe or attempt to help restore it to its former glory … that is not a choice.

He will do everything possible to prepare his wife and friends. The project is on auto-pilot and does not require any input. There are literally millions involved, people who love their country as much as he does have awakened to what they nearly lost, and they will not be denied. With some resolution in his mind he drifts off to sleep.

He awakens to the smell of coffee; he normally makes the coffee, she says he does a better job … he thinks she just likes him to do it, which is fine. He feels fresh and much better, the sun is still low, but shining brightly. He slips on some shorts and pads his way from the bedroom to the kitchen. He sees her out on the deck with a steaming cup; he fills his and goes out to join her.

She hears the door open and looks at him, "Good morning," she smiles.

"Good morning, been up long?"

"No, just long enough to make coffee and come out, I just got out here."

It was probably her closing the door that woke him up. Funny, when she has to get up early to go to work, he rarely hears her alarm or her getting ready, sometimes barely wakes for her goodbye kiss; these sounds are all normal. When something unusual happens however he hears it, is awake and alert. He bends to kiss her and hears the phone.

"Who'd be calling this early?" he wonders aloud. He steps back in the house grabs a cordless phone and looks at the caller ID; Private. Often he does not answer calls like that, just because many are sales people or some organization looking for donations, lower your interest rate, etc. However the time and remembering Brian calling from his official phone in the past shows this … he hits the button and says, "Hello."

"Mike … Brian … sorry for the early call."

"That's okay; I'm up and just got a cup of coffee."

"Good, I have some information, you sitting down?"

"No, but go ahead."

He looks outside and sees her looking his way, he mouths "It's Brian," she nods and turns to look out across the pond.

"Robert Hudson … he's an FBI Special Agent."

What??? That's impossible!

"Mike, you still there?"

"Yes, trying to take that in, you sure? I mean, I don't get it. He never …"

Brian cuts him off, "He seems to have been acting on his own outside the Bureau. We found out late yesterday, but have been talking with them trying to figure some things out … it is still an open issue. They, the FBI, did not know he was out of Virginia, he certainly was not on official business."

Just when he thought the most bizarre thing that could happen had happened …

"Thanks, Brian, keep me informed will you?"

"Of course … you doing okay this morning?"

"I think so, no thanks to you with your call … just kidding. I'm much better this morning, had a little trouble unwinding and going to sleep, but slept well."

"Good, I'll be in touch," he says and clicks off.

"That obviously was something you were not expecting, what did he say?"

He is still trying to get this to make sense … that will not happen soon, "The guy I shot is, well, was an FBI agent."

The look of shock is expected and he is not disappointed.

"FBI, FBI ... what does that mean? Are you in big trouble?"

"Brian says the guy was with the FBI, but that the Bureau did not know he was here and he was not on official business."

She thinks about that for a moment then says, "That is really odd. What do you think it means?"

He's been trying to size up this new bit of information and it seems to be taking form.

"I'm not positive of course, but here's what seems most likely. I wondered how this guy found me … even how he knew who I was and that I had any connection with our project. I still cannot imagine how they figured any of it out, but it makes sense that it would take someone with access to some pretty sophisticated surveillance equipment."

She nods slowly and says, "And who but the government would have that capability?"

"My conclusion exactly."

She thinks about this for a moment and says, "If the government is trying to do something why didn't this guy do it as official business?"

"It's not the government; this guy is working for someone on the outside."

"Like a dirty cop?"

"Exactly … and it is not likely he is the only one. This sort of operation would take several. I don't know who is behind this, but I'm beginning to have an idea. I did not tell Brian or Jeremy anything about the project, but I very likely will. I hope they are not upset with me and they will still trust me after this."

"So this isn't the end, it's more like the beginning, isn't it?"

"I'm afraid so … I'm afraid so."

They refill their coffee cups and sit in silence a while to contemplate this new development and what it might mean to them, their lives. Suddenly the country's problems seem small.

The two days before his trip are fairly quiet. They spend the time together doing things around the house and the ranch. He considered calling in sick for his next trip, certainly no one would blame him, but he is feeling pretty good and to him the sooner things are back to normal the better.

Chapter 20

A FEW DAYS LATER while on a layover his phone rings, it is Brian. "Hey Brian, got some news for me?"

"Well, yes, but not about the case."

"Okay ..."

"I heard you were looking for some hay, I came across a good deal on some large round bales."

"You know, these animals do not have teeth on the top and if the hay is full of heavy stems they can't eat it very well."

Brian responds, "Henry told me that, this is pretty soft brome with a little alfalfa."

"That would be perfect, thanks!"

"Henry needs ten bales for his horses, a semi can haul thirty-four; how much do you want?"

"I'll take the rest, which should put me through the rest of the year."

Over the next several days at least there is some good news. As they go about their daily chores around the house and ranch there is usually a TV on a news channel or a radio on a news/talk station. He likes to have something on while she is content to have it quiet. He often is not really listening to every word, but it does catch his attention if something new is mentioned, and that is how he hears about more of the plan making the news.

It seems a large church near where his pilot friend John lives has become active not only in their neighborhood, but is setting the framework for a nationwide plan to help not only their own congregations, but the area communities. There is a wide range of activities; childcare for struggling families, counseling services, aid for utility bills, groceries.

An interview with a minister who says, "Over the years we have left the duty God gave us to care for the less fortunate to the government. We have decided no more. We believe it is our responsibility to care for those in need and to leave it for the government is not what God intended us to do. We fear that the dereliction of our duty has helped lead to the taking of God out of our communities and schools, which in turn has lead to the moral and financial decline in our communities and our nation."

The reporter then shows clips of different churches around the country which have joined in the effort, smiling faces of women and children who are being helped, and the smiles on those helping … everyone feels better.

He knew if things could just get rolling it would be infectious, at least he hoped it would. We did not get where we are overnight and getting back to our roots will not happen overnight either. We used to be a country that cared for our neighbors, and somehow we became a nation who did not even know our neighbor, and did not want our neighbor to know us.

Benjamin Franklin was once asked if America had a religion. "You desire to know something of my Religion … Here is my Creed: I believe in one God, Creator of the Universe. That He governs it by his Providence. That He ought to be worshipped. That the most acceptable Service we render to Him is doing good to His other Children; that the soul of Man is immortal, and will be treated with Justice in another Life respecting its Conduct in this. These I take to be the fundamental Principles of all sound Religion and I regard them as you do in whatever Sect I meet them." Franklin also once said, "Only a virtuous people are capable of freedom. As nations become corrupt and vicious, they have more need of masters."

As he contemplates this he thinks, "Better virtuous than burdened with more masters."

His brother's efforts also became national news during this time ... RTN … Replace Them Now. It seems a group of small business owners, fed up with high taxes, oppressive regulations and healthcare mandates have taken on the politicians … head on. While there are a few who will remain true to their values, Washington has a way of corrupting almost anyone … it must be the thing that "power corrupts." With few exceptions they suddenly become consumed with becoming re-elected … and they often believe they have to do favors in return for financial and other support.

Part of this stems from many looking at an office in Congress as a long term job, a career. Our founders looked at it as service, something you did for your country for a time and then went home to run your business, farm, whatever. Davy Crockett, while famous for his frontier adventures and his stand at the Alamo was also a congressman from Tennessee. He was famous there for standing his ground, sticking to his principles … and holding strictly to the constitution. He believed the constitution prohibited the federal government from giving charity, which was to be left for the people and private groups, churches. One example was a bill which was to give aid to the widow of a navy veteran … Crockett believed that was not a proper use of taxpayers' money and violated the constitution … he suggested Congress take money from their salary to give her … of course they refused.

Crockett narrowly lost his first re-election bid, and two years later was elected again. He believed his job in Congress was to defend the Constitution and to represent his district. In 1834 he published his autobiography. He went east to promote his book and was narrowly defeated. After this loss he said, "I told the people of my district that I would serve them as faithfully as I had done; but if not … you may all go to hell, and I will go to Texas." And he did.

Replace Them Now. This sounds much easier than it will be. The idea is they ALL need to go, while you might lose a few good ones, the overall end will be a positive. It will take something like this to break "the way Washington works"… or doesn't work. Small business runs this country. While there are huge corporations which have over 100,000 employees, more than half of the nation is employed by small business … businesses with fewer than 500 employees. Most of the owners of these companies have been demonized by progressives;

believe they are the lucky ones, the winners of life's lottery. The continual class warfare pitting the rich against the poorer, the progressive taxes (is that name a coincidence?), the regulations, the uncertainty … business owners have hit the proverbial straw … they have had it, and they are not going to take it anymore.

They have launched a program which will not just vote out the incumbents, but replace them with solid, constitutionally sound candidates with business experience. People who have never hired anyone, never made a payroll, never put capital at risk, never grown a business, never put self last for the good of the company and employees … how can they understand what makes the country work? How can they know what their policies do to a business and its owner? The answer is simple, they cannot. They spend their time being lobbied and listening to the one who donates the most to their re-election coffers. They are slaves to an ideology rather than the constitution.

The news reporters are shocked; they cannot believe the idea is a wholesale cleansing of Congress. This is of course a long-term goal. While the entire House of Representatives is up for election every two years, a Senator's term is six years. This will take time and perseverance, and of course they will not be successful in every race … but imagine half or two- thirds of the House being occupied by people whose only focus is to follow the constitution and does not care if they are re-elected. The climate in Washington would change overnight … and that is the goal.

The hay arrives and is unloaded. Of course Murphy's Law has to strike once in a while just to keep him on his toes. Years ago a spindle broke on his tractor while hauling a heavy load with the loader. The wheel was cracked, and he knew he should take it off and weld the crack … but it just never happened. So after the hay was off the truck and it had driven away he was moving the bales and putting them under the overhang of the barn. With three left to go, that wheel had given its all and the front of the tractor dropped abruptly … rats. Luckily she was still in town after getting off work that morning and picked up a used one for him at a tractor salvage yard. Another day on the ranch …

Chapter 21

SHE WORKS A 24-hour shift every third day. Since they live 35 miles from town she runs errands, shops, etc., after she gets off work so that first-day off time at home varies depending on how much she has to do. Her second day off is usually dedicated to tasks around the house, that is what today is. She enjoys painting, crafts, sewing, gardening; she loves the new house because there is a loft in the master bedroom just for her. She can leave her sewing or painting out and not have to clean up for guests. Today she is sewing for her granddaughters, making them something special; she is happiest when doing things for others and this is one of the things about her he admires.

She is busy in the loft and he is out tending to some things in the barn and the paddocks for the alpacas. It is a pleasant day, a good time to get a few things done he's been letting go. They got the guineas to run around on the farm and eat bugs; they are good at it and ticks are a favorite. Guineas are also excellent "watch dogs." They start raising a racket, which is normal anytime a car pulls in the drive. She is not expecting anyone, so she walks to the other end of the house where she can see the drive from an upstairs bedroom. She sees a strange car parked in an odd way, halfway between the old farm house on the property and the new house. A stranger steps out, dressed in a dressy casual way, slacks and dress shoes with a light jacket. The man glances at both houses, but works his way north toward the barn … where he is working. Normally this would not be a concern at all, but after the shooting they both are being more cautious. Something about this just does not look right, and as he always tells her, "Better to be prepared and not need it than to not be prepared and wish you had." She goes down to their bedroom and retrieves the Rugar Mini-14 Ranch Rifle. He keeps it handy for varmints and the ammo loaded in it is just for that.

He is busy securing some fence panels and does not hear the man approach. While he did hear the guineas, he had the radio on in the barn and was distracted by a discussion on the news/talk station, and it was close to time for the mailman.

He is startled when the man speaks, "Where's your big gun, hot shot?"

He snaps his head up to see a large man standing about thirty feet away holding a semi-auto handgun. He does not respond, he straightens up and carefully takes in the situation. His mind is racing, the man is right, he does not have his weapon; he stupidly felt safe here at home. Thirty feet is a long distance with a handgun, he remembers seeing video of gunfights where people 20 to 30 feet apart emptied clips at each other and no one was hit. Might he be that lucky?

"Cat got your tongue? Nothing to say before I remove you from this life?"

"Well," he says as he tries to figure out how to stall if possible. "How about a question?"

"Okay, maybe I can answer and maybe not; go ahead."

"Who's behind this, who's so upset they think they have to kill me? I mean, at this point, there is no way to stop things, killing me does nothing."

"Killing you gives satisfaction, sort of like society gets when they put a convict to death. Putting the convict to death does nothing for anyone but give satisfaction to society. And after I'm finished with you I'll go find your wife and kill her too," he says with a sneer.

"If you think I'm going to stand here while you shoot me, you've got another thing coming. I promise you, you will regret coming here."

While this was going on she made her way out onto the deck where she could see the two of them and her heart sank as she saw the stranger holding a gun on him. She practices with handguns but is more comfortable with the rifle; she killed her first deer at nine years of age. She raises the rifle and looks through the scope, a 3-9x50. The distance is about 150 yards; with this scope the man is huge. The clip holds a super flat-shooting 40 grain .223 bullet that will travel 3800 feet per second. This is an ideal bullet for this flat country, at that speed a bullet simply explodes when it hits anything; it's safer as a miss will not ricochet.

The man had been holding his gun pointing at her husband in a casual way at waist level, but shortly he raises it. She had always told him she did not think she could kill a person. His response was that you never know what you can do until you are in the situation; some who think they will, cannot and vice versa. She does not view this man as a person; it is like a rabid dog that is attacking your child. The crosshairs on the scope are square on the man's chest, she squeezes the trigger.

The comment of not just standing there does not set well with the stranger, who raises the gun and says, "No more questions and answers, time for you to go."

He is not going to be a sitting duck, as he sees the gun raised and the hand tightens on the gun he darts to the side and heads for the barn door as he hears a loud "whack" and a rifle shot. He knows the difference between a rifle and pistol shot, the difference is quite dramatic, and the shot was from some distance as well. As he slips into the barn he sees the man collapse where he was standing. He hides for a moment looking around the doorway; the stranger is quivering in death, but is no danger to him now. He comes back out into the open to see her coming in his direction; she has the Mini 14 in her hand.

He smiles, a varmint round for a varmint.

"Is he dead?"

"As a mackerel," he says as his dad used to say, never sure what that meant. He's positive, but bends down to check for a pulse, there is none.

"Here, take this."

She hands him the rifle and leans on him. She is shaking and the tears begin to flow. All the emotions, nearly seeing her husband shot, killing a man.

"I never thought I could do that." She sobs.

"It's okay; you did what you had to do."

The man is on his side, and he rolls him over on his back. Blood is seeping out of an ear and the nose, the chest is like a bowl of jelly. As he thinks back over the event of moments ago he realizes he heard the bullet hit the man, a bullet at that speed hitting a solid object makes a discernible whack as contact is made. It was information that was there but too much was happening for it to make sense until later. Even though the bullet was small, about the size of a 22 Rimfire, the speed made the damage massive.

He's not entirely all together himself. They hold each other a while; he tries to stay strong for her. While standing there he briefly considers just dumping the body, but it is a fleeting thought. Certainly no reason to hide this, the thought was just so whoever sent him might wonder where their hired gun went. One thing for certain, their lives are forever changed … will they have attempts on their lives until someone finally succeeds? Probably, and next time, if it were him, he'd use a sniper and just do it from a distance … there'd be no warning, a scary thought.

"I'd better call 911."

"Yes, let's get this over with; I want him out of here."

"Me too, let's go to the house."

They put their arms around each other as they go to the house.

He decides not to call 911; he has Brian's cell number and decides to call him. He listens to the phone ring several times and is about to hang up when Brian says, "Hi Mike, what's up with you today?"

He replies, "It's my turn, you sitting down?"

"I'm in my truck; I pulled over to answer the phone, that's why I did not pick up right away. What is this about?"

"Another shooting."

Silence … and then, "Did I hear you right, another shooting?"

"I'm afraid so."

"Where, when, who?"

"My wife and I are home, at the new house. I have no idea who this is, it just happened."

Before he hears Brian's voice he hears the siren, "I'm on my way, I'll get EMS and more help there as soon as possible."

"Okay, this one's not going anywhere either."

"I'll be there in 15 minutes."

He clicks the phone off and sits next to her to wait.

They hear the call on the EMS radio for the ambulance with the instructions to wait for SO; once again they have to hold back and wait to make sure the Sheriff's officers to secure the area for their safety. She is pretty shaken; this is not easy for her. He knows this will take her some time to recover; even seasoned officers often need serious counseling after a shooting. He hears a siren in the distance, sound travels well on the plains, so it still likely will be a couple of minutes.

He says, "I'll go to the door to meet them, you can wait here if you prefer. They'll of course want to talk to you, but I can take them to the barn first."

"Yes, I really don't want to go out there while *he's* still there."

"Don't blame you, be back in a bit."

She pulls the dogs close as he heads for the door.

He goes out the side door by the driveway. He can hear Brian's truck with the siren on, it is just a short distance away now. In a moment he sees the blue truck with Sheriff's Patrol on the door pull in. Brian stops in a cloud of dust, opens the door and steps out.

He walks down the drive and says, "Brian, thanks for getting out here so fast. Janis is pretty shaken up, she took the guy out."

A surprised look, "What's going on? We still don't have much on the last one, at least as to who was behind it and why."

"Well, I don't really know either, makes zero sense to me. I was over by the barn doing some repairs to a fence panel and was surprised by the guy. I'm here on my property and just did not think anyone would do anything here. I heard the guineas as she did. I'm more used to them squawking, thought it was the mail and did not really pay attention … need to change that notion. Anyway, she went to see what set them off. She saw the guy walking in my direction; since the other shooting we've both been extra sensitive to anything out of the ordinary. She grabbed a rifle we keep handy for varmints and came out where she could see us. When she saw him raise his gun to fire she put one in his chest."

"How's she doing?"

"She's pretty shaken up, I told her to stay inside and take it easy."

"Good, let's see where this happened." They walk together towards the barn; the man is laying there near the barn in plain sight. Brian asks, "Where were you?"

He shows Brian where he's been working and was standing when it took place.

"That's a pretty long shot; she handles a rifle pretty well doesn't she?"

"Yes, she killed her first deer when she was nine, so nothing new in shooting ability, but the target is quite different."

They hear more sirens coming now, "I can't really see an entry hole, what was she shooting?"

"I have a Mini-14 Ranch Rifle with a big scope; it is loaded with 40 grain high-speed varmint loads."

"That .223 is a good round. The military uses essentially that same round with a full metal jacket, zips right through with very little damage in some cases. The bullet must have literally exploded on impact."

"I can attest to that; not sure if the whack of the bullet impact or the shot was louder from here."

"I bet that's right," Brian agrees.

Brian calls on the radio that the scene is secure and there is one code black. EMS and two patrol cars arrive moments later and soon there are several people wandering around the scene. Brian discusses what he knows with the others, gives some instructions and then comes back.

"Let's go talk with Janis for a minute," he says.

They walk to the house and go in, the dogs bark at the new person in the room and then go lay down after assuring themselves Brian is supposed to be there. The three sit at a table near the kitchen.

"Hi Brian, sorry to put you through this," she says.

Brian replies, "Don't worry about me, this is my job; how are you doing?"

"Not so hot, I never thought I could do anything like this."

"I'm sure; why don't you tell me how all this came about?"

She recounts everything as Brian takes notes, asks a few questions which she answers.

"Am I going to have to go in with you?"

"I think I have enough for now, you might need to come in at some point. It seems obvious this is connected to the shooting before with Mike and we already have an active investigation going on that. We'll likely work them together, especially since we are a small department."

In the meantime the other officers are taking pictures and collecting any evidence they believe might be pertinent. The coroner arrives and makes the official call that anyone with eyes can make, the stranger is dead on scene. The body is picked up and carried away; a tow truck arrives to tow the man's car. About two hours after the shooting the last officer leaves and they are alone again.

"I don't know if I will ever be the same," she says.

"It will take some time, maybe you should talk to Dawn."

He is referring to a doctor friend who has been close to them for a number of years.

"I'll give her a call and see when we might get together."

"You know Dawn, she'll drop everything and be there for you."

"Yes, yes she will."

Chapter 22

OVER THE NEXT SEVERAL days she begins to feel more normal. The idea she had to take a life does not fit well in her world … she knows she had no choice, but she is one who believes in most cases reason can be used … "Why did this have to happen to us?" she asks herself. "All we did is to do nice things for people, help those in need. How can someone get to the point they have to kill someone that is doing good things? The world must be upside down." Yes indeed.

She takes a couple of shifts off to try and get her feelings and her mind clear enough she can concentrate on her work. He has a three-day trip and suggests he take vacation time and stay with her, but she insists he go on and try to keep things as normal as possible. He really did not want to go, but after Dawn says she will come out and stay with her while he is away, he decides to go.

These are not easy days for them, but each passing day sees new strength, and ultimately renewed desire to see things through. While there is occasional good news regarding some of the ideas going on around the country, there is still the ongoing work of the ones trying to change America.

One such moment was on the news one night while they were relaxing during her recovery.

"I hear all this, you know, 'well, this is class warfare, this is whatever.' No. There is nobody in this country who got rich on their own … nobody. You built a factory out there? Good for you. But I want to be clear. You moved your goods to market on the roads the rest of us paid for. You hired workers the rest of us paid to educate. You were safe in your factory because of police forces that the rest of us paid for. You didn't have to worry that marauding bands would come and seize everything at your factory … and hire someone to protect against this … because the rest of us did. Now look, you built a factory and turned it into something terrific, or a great idea. God bless … keep a big hunk of it. But part of the underlying social contract is you take a hunk of that and pay it forward for the next kid who comes along."

This is from a person who is running for U.S. Senate. The idea that someone can put their capital at risk, work hard to be successful … and then have it taken on some idea of social justice. They were not lying; they want to fundamentally transform America.

Brian's cell phone rings, he sees the name on the caller ID and answers, "Hi Mike."

"Hey Brian, you have a minute?"

"Sure, what can I do for you?"

"A couple of things, but I think it best we talk in person, any idea when we might get together?"

"Well as luck would have it, I'm just about ten miles from your place, are you at home?"

"I am, now is a good for me if you want to come by."

"See you shortly, I'll call in and let dispatch know I'll be out of service for a little while."

"Sounds good, see you in a bit."

Brian's sheriff's patrol pickup pulls in the drive.

They shake hands as Brian gets out, "Thanks for coming, like a glass of tea?"

"That sounds great."

"Sweet or regular?"

Brian smiles, "Sweet, but don't tell my wife."

"Your secret is safe with me."

He grabs two wide-mouth Mason jars with sweet tea and they go out on the deck. It is warm, but in the shade it is tolerable.

"So, what's this about, Mike?"

"I have two things on my mind. First of all, I haven't been entirely open with you on this issue with the shootings."

Brian raises an eyebrow, "Oh?"

"Well, it's not as bad as that makes it sound."

He spends then next several minutes outlining the project and it successes. Then he tells Brian about the chase that happened just days before the first shooting.

"You know, you should have told all this up front."

"I know, and I feel bad about it now. I know we were doing nothing wrong, but I was trying to keep our names out of the whole thing, publicly anyway. I guess I hoped it would just all go away … wishful thinking.

Brian sits there thinking for a moment, takes a swig of tea and says, "Well, while it does not look good that you withheld information, I don't see anything here that changes the big picture. Essentially you and some friends start being good people, and trying to teach and help others do the same; hardly justification for attempted murder on their part. I'll have to share this with the investigation, but I doubt it will have any bearing on things for you and Janis."

"Thanks, I felt that would be the case, but was worried you'd learn it before I told you and I could not let that happen."

"Thanks for that. You said two things."

He begins, "I have an idea to bring these people out, but I need help."

"What do you have in mind?"

"Now this is just my theory, but I see no other explanation; the first guy was FBI for sure, any word on the second one?"

"No, but we are suspicious the FBI is embarrassed and is not saying if he is as well."

"Anyway, he, or they, would have access to sophisticated surveillance methods. Our group does not meet very often, and for the most part we are all independent. We share ideas and each gives their thoughts, but then each of us is on our own, there is no central controlling entity. We meet on conference calls and video conferences. I would think it is not a big stretch to say the FBI would have the ability to listen in covertly."

"I agree they could, but why would the FBI be looking at you and your group?"

"That's just it, it's not the FBI, it is the FBI's equipment and ability, but it is rogue agents using it for … well, nefarious activities. If we are to believe the FBI, this guy was operating on his own. He's already breaking the law so what difference does it make what he does and what he uses?"

"Good point, so what do you have in mind?"

"I want to set them up. I've tried to think as if I were the brains behind this, which is tough because I am not like this at all. If I'd tried twice to kill someone by using a pro that was in close and failed, I think I'd use a sniper or even a team of snipers and do it from a distance so there is less chance of failure."

"That makes sense, so how do you go about making them do it when you want?"

"I've used an overnight service to get information to the group a few times, for instance when I told them about the initial shooting and for them to each be careful … I was afraid my phone might be tapped or something. I would initially send them the plan so we would all be on the same page. I then would call them and set up a conference. On that call, we schedule a meet time in person … a meeting here at the house. It would be plausible for us to get together for a face-to-face meeting to spend more time talking than a call or video conference allows. The dates and times will be agreed to by all, but of course they will not actually come. I can have some friends drive out to make it look right so there will be people and cars here. Of course I will need the sheriff's department cooperation and I'd like you to lead this on that end since you know this area so well."

"This sounds interesting, but I'm not so sure I can get the sheriff to sign off on an operation like this … might be too much risk to civilians."

"I thought about that, I'd have everyone come in at night. They will need to have daylight to identify their targets; they will be very hesitant after two failures to make another mistake. You and I can work on the outside, we hunt, we know how to hide and where they will likely be. This is our back yard; they will be on foreign territory; this will all be to our advantage."

Brian takes a sip of his tea, makes a satisfied sound and says, "You've thought this out pretty well. I'll run it by the sheriff, but between you and me if he does not want to go with it I'll likely do it on my own. I'm close to retirement; I can bow out and take the hit to save the department, and the sheriff."

He is impressed, not many would risk so much.

"Thanks, Brian … this means a lot to me, I will do everything I can to make sure you are getting a commendation rather than a kick in the butt before you retire."

They finish their tea and talk a few details, knowing there will be much more to discuss before the plan is enacted.

Brian says, "I better be going. I'll give this some thought and visit with you some more soon. I know we cannot discuss any of this on the phone, so I'll be in touch and let you know how this flies and we'll do some more planning."

"Perfect, I'd like to shoot for a date in about two weeks. That will give us plenty of time to prepare, and give them plenty of time to formulate some sort of plan to try … I just hope we're right."

"Me too … see you later."

Brian gets in the patrol truck and backs down the drive.

He goes inside and she says, "Brian like your idea?"

"He seems to, but is going to run it by the sheriff but indicated he'd likely work with me regardless. He'd really like to get these people, and I'd love for him to as well."

"Me too," she agrees, "but I'm not so sure I like it, are you sure it's not too risky?"

"Of course it's risky, but I have to take it to them, I believe it is much more risky to wait for them to just do something when we are not prepared. I'd rather be on the offense than defense any day."

"I hope you are right, I've sort of gotten used to you being around … if something happened to you I don't like the thought of breaking in someone else."

She smiles, and he smiles back … they have a good understanding of each other, confidence and trust. He knows he can count on her as well, and while he hasn't told her yet, he has plans for her in this as well. Her proven ability with a rifle will certainly be needed.

He sits down at his computer and begins to write the letter that will put this all in motion. He knew when he spoke with Brian that he would do this regardless of whether the sheriff's office would cooperate or not. After all, this is his life they are after, and he does not intend to be a sitting duck; and something needs to be done to try and uncover just who or what is behind this. His letter simply says that the group has been compromised; there has been a second attempt on his life. They can expect a call soon to set up a conference call. It is vital they all be on the call. The call will be to set up a face-to- face meeting at his ranch. They are to all agree to the date he sets … they are *not* to come. This is a set-up to try and flush out anyone who might show up, he will have police help (he hopes) to take custody of them if they do.

With the addressed overnight envelopes in his hand he finds his wife working in a flower garden. She loves her flowers and she has several very nice areas around the ranch.

"I have to run to town to get these out tonight, you want to go and grab a bite to eat?"

"That sounds nice, I have time to clean up a little?" she asks showing her dirty hands and pants.

"Of course, take all the time you need … up to about ten minutes, I don't want to miss these getting out tonight."

"I'll make it five."

She jumps up and disappears into the house. He walks around enjoying the sounds of the country and the view he has from the elevated wraparound porch.

She's back out in a few minutes, "You don't give a lady much time to pretty up."

He smiles and gives her a quick kiss, "You don't need much time for that."

She smiles and they hold hands on the way to his truck. On the drive to town they talk about the grandkids, some things at her job, the ranch and some politics. They arrive at the package store in time to catch their last pick up for overnight deliveries. They decide to catch some Chinese food at a place with a nice buffet. After supper he stops and fills his truck with diesel before heading back to the ranch. When they get back they are greeting by the dogs, yipping with joy and wagging their tails. The evening is pleasant, they both take their laptops out on the deck and get caught up on emails and enjoying the night air and sounds.

"Tomorrow is my last day off; I have a lot to get done so think I'm ready for bed."

She says, "I'm about ready too, go on and I'll join you in a minute."

"I'm going to take a shower, you?"

"Yes, I need one too."

"Okay, I'll get them going if you're coming soon."

"Be right there."

When he built the house he put a large shower in the master bath with two separate shower controls and heads. He constantly embarrasses her when people tour the house, he tells them, "We have two because sometimes we're in a hurry and we can both shower at the same time … and sometimes we're not in a hurry and it's nice for that too."

Tonight they are not in a hurry.

Chapter 23

THE NEXT DAY HE is up early, makes coffee and spends some quiet time on the deck, sipping his coffee, thinking … and looking. He plans to make a point on the call that the deck will be a great place to meet. He wants the possible sniper who might show to concentrate on this side of the house so he knows where to position himself. If he had to cover all sides it would be nearly impossible. The house is made of oak logs, not many bullets will penetrate them, if any. The only possibility might be a 50 BMG, but it would lose so much energy there would not be much left. There are some small windows on the second floor above the deck where he will position his wife. With lights off inside even during the day it is hard to see in. They can slightly crack one, just enough for a rifle barrel and she will have an excellent view to where a sniper would have to position themselves. Across the pond there is about 100 yards of shrubs and weeds. It is low and often has water standing or is muddy, especially if there has been a recent rain. Beyond that is a large area of trees. This would put a sniper at 250 to 300 yards, an easy shot for an expert, or his wife for that matter. Her job will be to watch and be a backup in case things go wrong.

He hears the door and turns as she says, “Good morning.”

“Good morning, sleep well?”

“Yes I did, you?”

“Sure did, I always sleep well after …”

She cuts him off, “Yes, I know, you always say that!”

“Well, that’s because I always do.” He smiles.

“What are you thinking?” she asks.

“I’m thinking out plans for our little surprise.”

"I figured; care to share it with me?"

"Of course."

He goes over his basic plans including what he wants her to do.

"I don't know that I want that kind of responsibility."

"You will be primarily our eyes from above. I, and hopefully Brian, will already be in place. Our ability to see very far will be very limited. From upstairs you will be able to see if someone is working this way and you can alert us as to how many and where they are in relation to us. You'll have a rifle, but it will only be for a backup in case something goes wrong. Let's face it, you've already proven to me and yourself that you are up to this. Neither of us expected this, or wanted this, but we have what we have, it is up to us to finish this."

"I know, but I don't like it."

"Neither do I, babe, neither do I."

They spend the day doing chores and things around the ranch and house. He knows each of the group will have their letter by midday so he plans to call them this evening. His trip is a three days and commutable on both ends, so he plans to have them be on a conference call in three nights. The planned meeting date will be in about two weeks, he has several days off in his schedule then so there will be plenty of time to execute the plan. He calls each of the group and tells them it is important they be on a conference call in three days and they all agree to make the call. He just hopes whoever is behind all this was listening in. They are.

Half way across the country the man smiles. There have not been many calls lately and the boss has been anxious for them to finish the job their partners bungled. The first one no one could believe, how could an ordinary guy get the best of a trained professional? The second one they still did not have much info on, they knew he'd been killed but did not know how or any details. Since the locals learned Robert was with the Bureau they were being a little more careful with the info they shared. Robert had been an important part of their operation for a long time. He'd put away a tidy little nest egg

… as they all had since they couldn't openly spend the cash they were paid … and had planned to retire soon.

Well, they all knew the risks, but had mistakenly believed this would be a simple operation. This time there would be no mistakes, nothing to chance up close, they'd do this from a distance. He'd never know what hit him.

He picks up the phone and punches in the numbers, a voice answers on the second ring, "Yes."

"They just set up a call in three days."

The voice on the other end is gravelly and thickly accented, "Good, hopefully you will get what you need to put this to bed for good this time."

"I hope so too. I'll keep you informed."

"Of course you will."

The line went dead. This time they have to get this right, no mistakes this time.

His trip is uneventful, and he has spent most of his down time in planning. He arrives home to happy dogs, steps in the house and shouts, "Hi honey, I'm home!"

She answers from the bedroom, "The doorbells let me know you were here, I'm back here folding laundry."

He takes his bag to the bedroom where she has laundry on the bed, folding undershirts, underwear, pairing socks. They hug and kiss, then she returns to her work and he unpacks his bag.

"I brought you some more to wash, know you are anxious for that."

"I didn't expect you to bring home clean clothes!"

He sits down to love on the dogs a bit, and then he gets up and changes out of his uniform into some comfortable clothes.

"How was the trip?"

It was good, you remember the co-pilot who was with me on the last trip you came along on?"

"That English fellow?"

"Yes, Trevor, that's him. We had a nice trip and a good time on the layovers. Fun to meet new people, but also nice to be with people you know … especially on this trip … had a lot on my mind."

"I'm sure. What do you want for supper?"

"Nothing sounds especially good or bad, whatever you want is fine."

"Thanks a lot." She hates it when he says that, she'd prefer him to say something, anything, than leave it up to her.

"You have the stuff for taco salad?"

"I think I have some taco meat in the freezer, if so, yes."

"That sounds good to me." She leaves to start supper and he sits there in their room and reflects on the plans for the conference call later. It is vital this appears normal, not contrived.

After supper he goes to his office for the call. He dials the number and the code for the conference line; he is the first one on and listens to music for a moment until the next caller comes on.

"Hi, it's Brenda."

"Hi Brenda, how're things going?"

"Great, I wish I could make a living doing this because I love it."

The tone sounds of more callers come in, and after quick hellos, they are all on the line. "I'm glad you all could make this call on short notice. There are some things that have come up and I know of no way to deal with it on conference calls or video."

"What's up?" John says, "I thought things were going extremely well."

"They are, but there are issues coming to light we need to address, I can't go into it more here. Bottom line, we need to meet in person."

Bernie says, "This is a slow time for me at work, I should have no trouble getting away, where did you have in mind?"

"Well, I am pretty centrally located; we have a nice big house that can hold us all."

"I think it is a great idea," Brenda says, "I'd love to see your place and also meet everyone else, when would you like to meet?"

"Time is important, but I know you all need to make arrangements to get away. I never really thought I'd have to ask you all to do this, but it is important. I'm thinking the twenty eighth for arrival. We can meet some that evening, but we should be able to take care of everything on the twenty ninth. If you need to come in or leave later on either one of those days, that is fine. Oh, and Janis told me to let you all know that if you want to stay longer you are more than welcome, sort of a mini vacation. We have a nice big deck overlooking the pond that will be a great place for us to talk. The weather should be nice and we can all sit around, relax and take care of business. Anyone have a problem with the dates?"

It takes a minute or two as people check their calendars and make comments. After some brief discussion they all agree to come.

"Thanks everyone, hard to believe this worked out as it did. I look forward to seeing you all here."

They all say bye and click off. He sits back in his chair and reflects on the call. He believes it went well, he just hopes it sold whoever might be listening. It did.

The man cannot believe his good fortune. He picks up the phone and punches in the number. The phone rings and then the familiar voice says, "Yes?"

"They just completed their call."

"And?"

"They are going to have a face-to-face meeting at his house."

Silence as that news soaks in, then, "About time luck went our way, when?"

"They arrive on the twenty eighth and meet on the twenty ninth; plenty of time for us to prepare a plan and put it in action."

"Just make sure there are no mistakes … and no witnesses."

"You can count on me, sir."

There is no response, just a click on the line. He had worried how this might all shake out for him. After two failed attempts and adding in the problem of the others in the group using cell phones in business names and other entities, they had been having a hard time pinpointing just who else was in this group. Having them all meet at one location was a stroke of luck. He picked up the phone to call an associate and put his plan in motion.

Chapter 24

IN THE NEXT TWELVE days before the "meeting" he has a lot to accomplish besides the couple of trips for his job. He walks the area north of the house looking for likely places a sniper might use. He does not know how many, but likely they will keep it small and manageable, two or three at the most. The group is fairly small and two good snipers could pick off all of them fairly quickly, the first few would be dead before the others had any idea what was going on and they could finish the job in the ensuing confusion … at least he knew this is what they'd be counting on. They would have to scout the area in the days before; they would not just come without any surveillance. His advantage was that he did not need to see the house from his hiding place, just their hiding places. He hoped he'd set things up so they would try on the morning of the 29th since he made it look as if they might not all be there in time to meet the 28th. Setting up for the morning of the 29th made the most sense.

The dogs bark as a vehicle turns up the drive; it is the dark blue patrol pickup Brian drives. He walks up as Brian gets out, they shake hands and he asks, "What brings you this way today?"

"I thought it best I didn't call, and I hoped you were home. I had to do a little arm twisting but I got the sheriff to go along with your plan."

"That's great, I'm glad you didn't have to leave on a bad note."

"Me too, it will be just you and me out here, but we will have back up close by."

"I think that will work, we can't have more than a couple of us out there, and if people aren't used to being still in a hunting situation they could sure mess it up."

"That's for sure. All I have is regular camo; you use a ghillie suit for bow hunting don't you?"

"Yes, I've had hunters walk right by me while I was sitting there on a log and they never knew I was there. Thought about saying something to scare them, but was afraid I'd get shot!"

"You have an extra one I can use?"

"Yes I do, bought it for my son when we used to hunt together before he went into the Army."

"How's Ryan doing?"

"Great, he's a Captain now. He talked about getting out but with the economy as it's been decided to stick with it. He had a tough time getting in a job he liked, but he seems pretty happy now."

"Wow, a Captain, seems only yesterday he was in grade school!"

"Tell me about it!"

"I'd better be on my way, just needed to let you know we are a go."

"I'll be in touch, I have a couple of trips before the 28th, and I'll need you out here to go over things in about a week, okay?"

"No problem, talk to you soon."

They shake hands again and Brian gets in his truck and drives away.

He goes on his first trip and then while at home after he returns Brian comes out and they go over plans and go out to the trees and give it a good look, careful not to leave obvious evidence they'd been there. Since it was a relatively small area that had a good view of the house it was not difficult to find the likely places for a shooter to hide and then to find appropriate spots for himself and Brian. His wife is watching from her vantage point upstairs.

He calls her, "Can you see both of us where we are?"
"Yes, but barely."

"Okay, you won't be able to see us when this is real, but make a mental note of just where we are now. Next week we'll count on you being our eyes if these people make their move."

"What if they come a different way or try something else?"

He does not want to think like that, but she is good at making him look at his plans and verifying he's on the right track.

"I've got to go with the odds. We'll be back to the house shortly."

He clicks off his phone and tells Brian, "I think we're good to go here, let's go to the house."

He makes a good mental note of just where their places are, as they will have to come back here in the dark. It is also possible, but not so likely, that anyone looking to use this as a shooting area will also come in the dark. This will be very unfamiliar territory; most likely they will come at first light.

Back at the house the three go over each ones duties, he is glad Brian is letting him run the show. Brian and he will be in position, she will be watching from the upstairs. Hopefully there will be enough light for her to see anyone working their way into position. Whoever comes will be careful, but will not expect anyone to be specifically watching for them.

They will all have a simple radio used by hunters and hikers, Brian and he will have earpieces, they will not be able to transmit but should not need to. He will carry the Mini 14, it is short and being a semi-automatic more versatile for this operation. Brian has access to one as well so that is what he will use as well. He has a Remington 700 in .243 she will use. She is used to this caliber; it is very accurate and will drop a deer at 300 to 400 yards, so a man should be no different. He hopes she is only a back-up and will not have to shoot, but if something unexpected happens or goes wrong he wants her to be in position and ready.

He tells her, "If you sit a couple of feet back from the window you will be very difficult to see, and don't put the whole barrel of the rifle out, just the muzzle."

"Okay, I still don't like this."

Brian says, “You know I could probably get a deputy to do this for her.”

“You know anyone who has her skills with a rifle, and has proven it to boot?”

“Point made and understood.”

They finish going over the details and Brian leaves them alone at home. They both have a few things to take care of in addition to their regular chores around the house and ranch, as he will be away for three days and she will be away every third day on her normal rotation at work. They both do their best to go about their activities in a normal way, but this looming event is never far from their thoughts. To him, the best outcome will not be killing any more people, but capturing anybody who shows up and getting to the bottom of who’s behind all this.

The 28th comes very quickly. He is up early and fixes coffee. She is off at 7 AM and comes right home so they can enjoy some relaxing time together with their coffee.

She asks, “You feel comfortable with the way things are set up?”

“Yes, it would have been nice to have been around all week to watch and see if anyone came for sure. I’m going out there in a little bit and see if I can see any sign someone has been there.”

“What if they’re there already?”

“No way, sitting out there for twenty-four hours? Only a Special Forces sniper doing a mission could do that … I’m willing to take the chance … and take a gun just in case.” He smiles.

They finish their coffee and have a bowl of cereal. While she goes about changing out of her uniform and some chores around the house, he slides the .45 onto his hip and grabs the Mini 14 and heads out the door. As he nears the trees he becomes very careful to not leave any obvious tracks and to look for any new ones since he and Brian were out last week. He approaches the first spot and is stricken by a combination of satisfaction and fear. It is very obvious someone has been here and built a "nest," a place to be comfortable while they wait and hide. He goes to the next spot and finds another. He carefully looks around and finds no other places. His feeling of satisfaction is of course being able to figure them out before knowing anyone might even come … the fear is over the fact they have actually come. This is real, not a game. It is one thing to deal with a sudden unexpected attack. It is quite another to know for certain it is coming. He has to believe he has the upper hand; they would not be here if they believed they had been compromised.

"Well?" she asks as he comes back inside, then she sees his face and knows. "They've been here haven't they?"

"Yes, yes they have, two of them."

This really bothers her. When were they here, they never close their shades, what did they see?

He reads her mind, "They most likely were concentrating on the deck area. Our bedroom is barely visible because of the cedar tree."

Small consolation, they've still been there … watching.

"I look at it this way, we know they are coming, they do not know we know that. We have the upper hand, the element of surprise. They will not see us in our camo suits, they will not expect anyone out there, and they will be concerned with being seen from the house."

She is somewhat comforted, but not completely.

The day is spent going over the plan, but mostly trying to be normal. He made arrangements for some friends to come for supper and stay overnight. They do not know about the plan and he feels a small twinge of guilt using them like this, but he wants everyone to act normal. The extra cars and people will be what they will expect. Brian will be one of them. He and Brian will go to bed at the regular time, but will get up at three. He wants to be in position well before light in case they come while it is still dark. He'd normally cook out on a night like this for guests, but to be on the safe side they stay off the deck this night. The house has just shy of 8,000 square feet, so space for this small group is not an issue. They had hosted the biannual family reunion with over 50, so this is easy … except for what waits for them in the morning. He takes the Mini 14 and the .243 down and cleans them both well, taking care to properly oil the important points … he cleans the .45 as well.

Brian comes in late in the afternoon. He wanted Brian there early so they could get him and his gun in before anyone else came. He gets his other ghillie suit out, Brian tries it on.

"Where'd you go?" he says and they both laugh at the old joke, it helps ease the obvious tension.

While Brian is taking the suit off as he says, "I slipped out there this morning and checked. They've been here; we were right on the places they would pick."

"Really? I was almost hoping we'd do this and nothing would happen."

"I guess it is the old 'good news, bad news' scenario; the good news is they've been here, the bad news is they've been here."

"Something like that. I have two other deputies I know well and trust who will be our back-up. They will be able to listen in on the radio frequency we're using, they will not transmit. When they hear Janis communicate to us that the shooters are coming they will go to the north side of the section, as that is where the snipers will have to leave a car. My men will hide and wait for instructions from me, or if something goes wrong, Janis can reach them as well. Their job will be to block any avenue of escape. They know these are not people to mess with, and they will shoot first and ask questions later. They know if these men come out something went wrong on our end."

"Sounds good, I love having things in place you hope to never need, more than wishing afterwards you'd thought of it."

Janis spends the afternoon preparing for her supper guests and making sure all the bedrooms are ready. She puts Brian in the room she'll use for her observation post. A thought comes to her that if she should have to shoot from inside the house what the guests might think. Oh well, can't worry about that. Their friends arrive and they all have a nice evening visiting, she makes excellent Mexican food and tonight is no exception.

Enchiladas, tacos, chips, salsa, and homemade sopapillas; good company and conversation keeps their minds off the morning plans, at least until bedtime.

After everyone is off to their room the two of them go back to the master bedroom and close the door, they look at each other and then just stand there holding each other. She suggests they have a prayer together and they do, asking for strength and guidance to see them safely through the night and the morning. With few words they go through their bedtime routine and slip under the covers. A kiss good night, he rolls over and is asleep in seconds. She does not know how he does it. She normally goes to sleep easily as well, but with something like this … it takes her a while to drift off.

He has a sense about time, even when he is asleep. He supposes he got it from his father who often knew within a minute or two the time even though he never wore a watch. He wakes up, wide awake and looks at the alarm; 2:58.

He sits up and touches her arm lightly, "It's time to get up."

"Is it three already? I didn't hear the alarm," and then she realizes he probably woke before it sounded. She likes to hit the snooze, it drives him a bit crazy, but in the big scheme of things not a major deal. He starts coffee for her so she can have that to help wake her up, he does not think he and Brian will have any such problem. He slips upstairs and finds Brian is awake as well. They go down stairs, using the night lights to see the way. They check their weapons, both carrying their Mini 14's and a holstered pistol. They slip on their camo suits, he gives her a quick kiss and they silently slip out the door.

In their earpieces they hear her ask if they can hear her. They both give her thumbs up. They do not speak; Brian follows him since this is his "backyard." They arrive first at the position Brian will occupy, and then he goes on to his spot. First light is a couple of hours away, his mind is in overdrive. He makes himself comfortable. He learned over the years bow hunting for deer, one of the hardest things to do was to be still. The key to that is being comfortable. One thing you cannot plan for is insects. If you are sitting there and a deer is approaching, you certainly will scare the deer if you swat or even shoo a bug. The stakes here are much higher than missing a shot at a trophy buck.

They wait. His mind is here, and then again it is not. He is listening intently for the sound of a foot, the scrape of a branch against fabric … sounds that do not belong. There are a lot of deer, turkey, coyotes and other wildlife here so it is not silent. He hears an occasional car on the highway two miles distant and a train on the tracks 7 miles south in addition to various animals that are mostly out only at night. The eastern sky is beginning to lighten a bit. It happens very gradually at first; suddenly you realize it is not completely dark. It is the new moon phase, so only stars were giving any hint of light. It is amazing how much can be seen using only the stars once your eyes adjust.

A cough. He knows Brian would never do that, besides it came from more to the north of his position. He hears the occasional crunch of a foot on dry weeds. Rookies, well, probably not, but they likely think the closest people are in the house and asleep. They will just be concerned with staying low and out of sight until in position. It is light enough now he can see fairly well, especially compared to the night sky. From his position he cannot see far, mostly just the spot that was prepared. He knows he is essentially invisible in his camo; he just needs to keep the gun covered by the camo until needed.

Brian in his spot hears them as well; both their senses are on high alert. A sudden crackle and voice in the earpiece almost surprises him.

"I see them, two of them coming your way from the north. They are on the west edge of the trees, wearing military- type camo, guess about 20 to 30 yards north of you."

Good girl, if it were him he'd be tempted to take them both out now. Sit still and watch them. He cannot see the house, but assumes she is following his instructions.

They are close now, very close. They are speaking in low tones.

One says, "You stay here, I'll take the other position. When it looks like they are all on the deck I'll give you a low whistle and we'll shoot together the first round, I'll start on the right, you on the left. Shoot until they are all down. We can then go in and make sure they are all dead before we head out."

It's chilling that he can speak so casually about killing several people. The camo-clad man comes into sight and settles into his spot. He is behind and to the side of the man, about 10 yards away. He'd told Brian to wait for him to begin, but that once he spoke to immediately let the other guy know he was covered as well so his man would not jump up and come over.

He closes his eyes for a moment and sees it all play out, he takes a deep silent breath and says in a low quiet voice, "Do not turn around, put your gun down, get on your knees with your hands behind your head … today is not a good day to die."

The man nearly soiled himself when he heard the voice. He had hardly stopped talking when he heard Brian voicing orders for the other man to comply as well. The man hesitates as if thinking about trying something.

"I am not alone, you can die or you can live. I'm not a cop so I'm not particular which you choose."

The man lets his rifle drop, gets to his knees and puts his hands on his head. Keeping the Mini 14 trained on the man's back he slowly eases up to where he can see the other man and Brian doing roughly the same thing he is doing. He takes some plastic cable ties out and cuffs the man as Brian does to his captive.

In his earpiece he hears, "Thank goodness, I'll keep a close bead on them until you are back to the house."

He waves a thanks, "That was from the house, you were in crosshairs the whole time, you never had a chance of pulling this off."

Brian brings his man over and says, "I need to call and let the others know we have them."

"Hold off a minute if you would, I want to talk to them first. Maybe you should take a short walk; pick up their rifles would you? I'll just need a few minutes."

He explains to the men, "You see, he is a cop and I don't want him to have to compromise his situation in regards to any interrogation he will make, I am under no such obligation."

Brian says, "Shout out if you need me." And he walks away.

So, who are you and who do you work for?"

"I'll take my chances with the cop," the first man says.

"Me too," says the other.

"We'd be killed if we talked," says the first man again.

"You don't seem to understand me, you'll be killed if you don't … and it won't be fast or clean."

"You don't have the guts or the stomach to," he says as his boot connects just below the jaw, slamming his mouth shut on his tongue and breaking teeth. The men are sitting with their hands bound behind them and they are completely helpless.

"Your bunch has tried to kill me, twice, threatened my family and now you were here to kill a whole group of people who have done nothing. I don't know how you got off on such a wild tangent … I suppose it was money …doesn't matter. It ends here. You can talk to me or you can talk to your maker and explain it to Him."

"You won't do that, you don't want to go to prison any more than us."

He chuckles and says, "You think a judge and jury in this part of the country would put me away for ridding the world of a couple of vermin like you? Shoot, the DA wouldn't even bring charges. Remember, this is my backyard."

He sees them as the reality of their situation sinks in. Would he kill them in cold blood? No, but he had to make them believe he would, and if they tried anything between Brian, his wife and him, they would not get far in any attempt.

"We work for an organization that is not happy with what you are doing, it is costing them a lot of money and money spent in the past has been essentially wasted."

"You haven't told me anything a seven-year-old could not have figured out; Robert told me that much before he died. I want names and phone numbers, now."

The man looks down in resignation, as he looks back up his face is a mess.

"You know, you're right, it was the money. At first, I felt like a traitor to my country; I'm a veteran. But they convinced me it would ultimately be better for the nation once these changes were in place; and it didn't hurt that I was compensated incredibly well and promised a top position under the new system. I have to admit when we discovered what one person had done, just getting things going and the people taking charge of their own lives, we had second thoughts. Then we sent someone to try and reason with you, to stop what you'd started and hoped it would end there."

"It was too late even then; this has taken on a life of its own. There is no central planning or organization, it is just people doing what they believe is best for their country, for their neighbors, for themselves."

"I know that now. I'll give you what I know."

"Brian!"

"Yes?"

"You have a pen and paper?"

"Always, be right there."

Brian is there in a few moments, "Okay, ready."

"I only communicate with three people; only know one name and only have phone numbers … I've never met two of them."

The man gives the name and numbers which Brian jots down in his notepad."

"I suspect their cell phones will tell if they are being truthful, we'll figure that out later."

"I am. I have nothing to gain by lying to you; in fact I'd guess I have more to lose."

"Go ahead and call your men, hopefully we have what we need to put an end to all this."

Brian speaks into his radio and calls his men to come down to the scene.

He asks the man he kicked in the face, "What's your name? First name only …"

"Bill, why?"

"Just curious, thank you for talking to me Bill. I know you are concerned as to what these people might try to do to you, but if we can shine some light on them they just might have to go away, one way or another."

"Maybe, I won't hold my breath," he replies. "While I don't know who we're dealing with, I do know what we are dealing with. They are used to having their way and they are ruthless in their efforts and methods. We are dead men walking; we failed on a mission's third attempt."

"I know this is not over, may never be until I am gone. One thing for sure, I'm not waiting around; I just have something else to do in my spare time."

After Brian's men arrive and take charge of the men, he finally begins to relax.

Brian says, "You okay?"

"Yes, I am now, thanks."

"I'll go with my men and help them. I'll get a ride out later and get my car and things."

"Okay, thanks a lot, couldn't have done it without you."

"No problem, glad to help, really."

They leave to the north as he turns to head back to the house.

As he comes around the side of the pond he hears a door close and she is now out on the deck. It's still early and their guests are all still in bed.

She has a big smile on her face and says, "I am so glad that worked out as it did, I wondered for a moment."

"Why is that?"

"I had the power on the scope turned all the way up to nine; I had a good look at that guys face. I thought he was going to turn and try to get you, the look on his face; I put my finger on the trigger. I knew you had said something to him because at first he looked like he'd seen a ghost, then he got a determined expression, but suddenly his face went slack and he dropped his gun. What did you say to him?"

"I told him it was not a good day to die."

"No day is a good day to die." she says, and he agrees.

He slips off his ghillie suit, puts it and the guns away in their room, and returns just as their first guest comes down the stairs.

"Been up long," they ask?

"Just long enough to make coffee, ready for a cup?"

They smile at each other as they walk toward the coffee pot.

Chapter 25

THE NEWS HAS BEEN reporting for some time about groups planning to protest on Wall Street. The first couple of weeks there are a few dozen, but not much happens. He thinks about people who have nothing better to do … how do they afford rooms and meals in New York City without jobs? Their signs are professionally done, unemployed people with professional signs … this is not grass roots; this is organized and financed by someone or some groups. He does a search online and finds a Web site for the group, the symbol at the top of the page is the raised fist of the communists … nice. There is a link to another group calling themselves the 99 percent. They bemoan being kicked out of their homes, having to choose between rent and groceries … suffering environmental pollution, working long hours for little pay … and on and on. They claim to be non partisan, yet most of the scheduled speakers are well-known and avowed socialists, Marxists and communists. Their Web site says it is built by anonymous. When asked who is behind it he says, "We are legion."

To someone who knows the Bible it seems another reference to evil; Jesus cast the evil spirits out of a deranged man into a herd of swine. When asked his name the evil spirits say, "We are Legion."

On a cable news station, a reporter known for going to the source to get the story is interviewing the young people who are chanting "Down with Capitalism!"

He asks several, "What do you want to replace capitalism with?"

He is rewarded in most instances with blank stares and silence. One attractive young lady does readily respond, but her answer is blocked by some other protesters and you cannot hear what she said. Giving his report he is asked what happened during that shot.

"It seems some of her friends did not want her response to be on air … she wanted to replace capitalism with communism."

A couple more clicks and simple searches reveal what he already knew; well-known progressive organizations and one wealthy individual … his name keeps popping up. This man was raised in Eastern Europe, but has made billions within capitalism … what can be his motivation? One would think living under such vastly different systems and being so successful under one, the choice would be simple. Maybe his motivation is not money … but then if this man is central in the major transformation of the nation, and even the world, then he will be well positioned; maybe money and ultimate power is the objective.

The old James Bond films always had a villain who wanted to control the world. Maybe this is no longer the goal of a made-up movie character … maybe this is really happening. If it is this or something similar, this will likely be the most dangerous man in the world. This is someone whose goals will not be denied. The wealth and connections will allow access to every corner of the earth. People who believe they can go along for the ride and assist however they can will believe they will have advantage in the new world order. The problem is, men with this wealth and power do not share, they use. When people are no longer needed they are eliminated. It is as the bank robbers who meet to divvy up the loot after a heist, and the one who planned it all kills his accomplices, not willing to share the bounty.

"If the person behind the attempts on our lives is this man …" he says aloud to no one. They say there are five emotions one goes through when they suffer a tragedy. He goes through each one in the next few moments; denial, anger, bargaining, depression and acceptance. It is said that one does not have to go through them in that order, and he doesn't.

He finishes with anger. If he were to have learned he was terminally ill with cancer, he likely would have ended with acceptance and gone on to live life to its fullest and fight the disease the best he could, but this is different. With this realization he does better with anger, and anger is probably too soft a word. He reflects on his home, his wife and family, all they've worked so hard for; but more importantly, the nation.

Until now he felt it likely there was a group who wanted to change America due to some sort of idealism, thinking socialism or communism was just better, or some version of those; the only reason it had not worked anywhere else was due to some minor errors. The thought one person is largely pulling the strings and many more either complicit or just ideology driven and helping … this has him furious. America is the greatest country ever on the face of the earth; he believes as did the founders that God had a hand in the forming of this great nation, that we all owe Him for our prosperity and might, that we have to be virtuous in our lives.

We are not perfect, America is not perfect, but she is closer than anything else. He will not let this man or anyone else take what he and his wife have built … but more importantly, he will not let this man take America without a fight. He believes his projects are going well enough, sort of on autopilot; that most Americans will fight for their country, their way of life, for their constitution. While there are plenty who will sit around and whine with their hands out, and those who are blinded and participate in this destruction out of ignorance; there are enough who will not sit still while their country is destroyed. There are also willing accomplices who are idealistic and have no clue as to the "horse they are hitching their wagon to." Most will not have to fight as he will, most will never know some of the struggles going on in the background.

He may not survive; in fact odds are he will not. He smiles as he thinks of a situation he once found himself in many years ago. He was outnumbered by a bunch of hoods that made it clear they planned to pound him into the ground.

He said, "Yes, you probably can … but you know something? Just before you get the job done you're going to wonder if it was worth it. I'm taking one or two of you with me, who's it going to be?"

Evidently, as Shakespeare said, "Discretion is the better part of valor."

They told him it was his lucky day and left him alone.

He does not expect to be left alone, and is not going to take this without a fight. At times he has felt great regret for not serving his nation militarily. Maybe this is his destiny, to serve in this way. Most heroes are never known, but the definition is the same: Ninety-nine percent of the time it's someone who's tired enough and hungry enough and scared enough not to give a damn. It is someone who has been put in a situation with few options.

The phone rings, it is Brian. "Hey, Brian … what's up?"

"I'm on my way out to see you and just though I'd better make sure you were home before I got too far along."

"I'm here, how far away are you?"

"Be there in twenty minutes."

"See you soon." and they both click off.

He didn't ask, but he is pretty sure this must be some news relating to the guys they caught on the sting. It's cool outside and they are getting a little of the much-needed rain the ground needs, he starts a pot of coffee rather than iced tea.

He's had a few sips of his cup when he hears the guineas start to squawk and the dogs bark. He gets to the door about the time Brian walks up.

"Hi Brian, come on in … coffee?"

"What cop would turn down a free cup of coffee?" he says with a big grin.

"Probably a sorry one!" he says as he pours a mug of the hot dark liquid. "I assume you have some news worthy of telling without risking the phone?"

"Yes, oh, that's good coffee!"

"Thanks, we get it from a roaster here in the state … we try to use products produced here in the B&B to help promote local merchants … glad you like it."

"Anyway, this has taken some time for us and our small department. We've tried to avoid using the feds since we are not real sure who we can trust."

He nods as Brian continues, "We followed the name and numbers up … the numbers were no help, pre-paid cell phones with no name tied to them."

"Figures."

"Yes, no surprise there. The name however was somewhat helpful. We were able to tie them to various other names, corporations, foundations, non-profits …"

"Really, anything that would hold up in court?"

"I doubt it would matter in the short term, my guess is it would take years and the use of undercover personnel … that's time, people and money we don't have."

"So who or what are we looking at here?"

"You ever hear of an outfit called The Surge Foundation?"

"Yes, yes I have."

"Really?" "I'm surprised … I'd never heard of it … guess I need to pay better attention."

"Probably so, what did you learn about it?"

"I guess I thought all these types of people died out back in the 60s … gave up, changed, faded away, something. I was amazed at the number of Marxists, radicals, and communists from the past involved with and employed by this foundation!"

"Yes, they have people who were active in the Weather Underground, SDS, and communist party … every group over the years that ever tried to undermine or overthrow the government. They work in concert with unions and every radical group, domestic and foreign. They were instrumental in writing that stimulus package back in '09 and the President's healthcare bill, and they are in the middle of this demonstration on Wall Street. Funny, I always thought until this that Congress wrote bills!"

Brian questions, "Me too, who ever thought the government let special interests write their own legislation?"

"Maybe Congress is not paid enough!"

"Right."

He pauses for a moment, "So, Brian, what else have you learned? Honestly, I sort of had this figured out … actually I was thinking about it when you called. Any chance a man named Volar came up?"

"Actually, yes … not directly, but he is tied to everything in some fashion; how did you figure it out?"

"Well, the pieces were there but I think I was too close to things to see it until now; I had to sort of step back. Honestly I would never have thought someone like me would have caught his attention, but he has had his eye on something for a long time … and I'm still not positive just what it might be.

"Bottom line, he's a very wealthy man who is accustomed to having his way. A lot of organizations who do not agree on very much have banded together to change our nation. I think each one believes they will come out on top and of course only one will. I am afraid it will get very bad at some point in the future … and that point is closer now than ever before."

"Mike, I'm sorry, but I just don't get it. You saying they are going to try and essentially destroy our country and then fight over who controls the rebuilding? … Who is essentially running the world?"

"That's it in a nutshell. I fear for our country Brian, for many who are unable to prepare … for what the future holds. The future of our nation has not been in such doubt since the Revolution and the Civil War. I think we are in for serious times win or lose."

They sit in silence for a few minutes sipping the steaming coffee in their mugs, finally Brian asks, "I guess I just thought our country was pretty safe, I mean sometimes politicians do things that upset us and things go in directions we might not like … but what you're saying is actually that our nation might not survive?"

"I'm afraid that's a distinct possibility, certainly if these people have their way. Other possibilities; they will take it down and do not end up in control which might even be worse and probably the best scenario is things fall apart, but the people of this great nation rebuild it themselves. Regardless, we are in for some terribly rough times in this country … around the world in fact."

"You don't think we'll just have a few bad bumps then recover, sort of like a bad recession or something like that?"

"Well, I suppose that could happen if we are lucky, but I think these people are so intent on their goals they will not give up. They will keep pushing as long as they see any hope of obtaining their goals. Remember, they want it to crash so they can build what they want, so just the collapse of the nation is not enough to drive them away. We, the people of this nation, have to stay the course and keep our constitution the focus. At best we will likely have a deep depression."

"Won't it be hard to keep everyone on the same course; how can that be kept organized?"

"That's a great question and I'm sure I do not have the answer. My focus has been to get people helping each other and that will be vital if we are to survive. That's not why I did it, but it is a nice benefit. I think we'll have to rely on some higher profile people who might be in a better position to lead."

He stands up and goes for the coffee pot to refill their mugs.

"Enough of that doom and gloom; you have any good news as to what we can do about the guys we caught and the information we gained?"

Brian sets his fresh mug down and shakes his head, "I'm afraid we don't have enough to do anything at all with the information we got, and the DA is not too sure we can even do anything to the guys we caught. While what they were planning was awful, they didn't carry it through and he doesn't think we have them on much more than trespassing."

"Well, between you and me, he's a moron … I've watched him boot more than one case and fail to bring charges more than once on something he should have. We've got two guys with high-power rifles sneaking up to secluded places, and you and I both heard them say they planned to kill everyone in the house. I'm not buying it that he can't make something stick, conspiracy, something."

"Hey, I'm just the messenger …"

"Yes, you want to take him a message from me? Good grief, these are people who are not only trying to kill me, but my wife and friends … let alone what they plan for the country. If he refuses maybe I should pay him a visit and ..."

"I'm thinking that might not be such a great idea, let me work on him some."

"All right; now, I have some ideas about what we might be able to do with some of the info we gleaned from those guys. I figure if there is nothing legal that can be done with it, we should not let it go to waste."

Over the next several minutes he explains his plan and when he's finished Brian says, "Are you serious? Are you nuts? You know what kind of trouble you can get into for this?"

He smiles and responds, "Let's see, we have a DA who won't bring charges on men who tried to kill me my wife and friends … I've had two attempts on my life and it appears there is no end to that until they succeed, the country is on the verge of collapse, and …"

"Okay, okay, I get the point. I'll talk to the DA and do everything I can to get him to take some action, and I'll do what I can to help you on the other, but I hope you understand my position."

"Of course, I would never have you compromise your job or pension. Don't worry; I'll keep you out of it."

As Brian leaves his thoughts begin to wander … he considers his options. There are few.

Chapter 26

THINGS ARE GOING MUCH faster than he ever dreamed; the changes in the country and the potential for serious problems. While there is much excitement with many people involved in the various aspects of his project across the country, there is determined opposition from the other side and a seemingly willing accomplice in the mainstream media. Most conservative talk shows continue to play the parties and ideologies against each other, one stands alone educating and pleading with people to wake up to the dangers. Mr. Volar is a constant subject on the radio program and he knows the danger to which this leads first hand. It was noted once that this radio host paid over a million dollars a year for security. It is a shame that in this great nation with the First Amendment one would have to high security to protect that … isn't that the government's job? Of course, who would expect the government you criticize daily to actually protect you … the million is money well spent.

There is a highly watched traditionalist on a cable news channel who is being a good watch dog as well, but he seems somewhat behind the "power curve," more reactive than proactive; seeming to wait for definite facts after events over predictions with history and facts. In normal times this is quite safe and sufficient … however, these are not normal times.

About six weeks ago he'd ordered three-dozen hatchling ducks; Cayuga, Welsh Harlequin, and Rouen. They wanted more ducks for the eggs and to help clean the pond, but they also thoroughly enjoyed watching the webbed fowl both on the water and off. Ricky had the facility to raise them so when delivered they went straight to Ricky's farm. Now they are getting their adult feathers and it is time for them to come to their real home. He'd put up a temporary shelter for the ducks and guineas they had, but now it is time to build something a little larger and more permanent.

"Pole" sheds are simple and strong. He had picked up the materials a few weeks ago and just had not taken the time to put things together. All he needs to do is dig four post holes for the four corner 4x4's, put on 2x4 nailers, rafters, attach the steel and it is nearly finished. This leaves a three-sided shelter which will give cover from wind and rain; he can add a front wall with window and door at a later date before the snow flies.

This takes only half a day, he finishes the enclosure using some portable dog-pen panels for fencing and a poultry net to protect from aerial predators. Owls have a nasty habit of killing chickens, and guineas by taking their heads off … they then leave without eating them. There are many things he does not understand … mostly with people … but this is one in nature which has him baffled.

He calls to verify Ricky is home, and then grabs two large dog kennels and starts down the dirt road for the 20-mile drive cross country to Ricky's farm. He has to smile about every time he thinks of Ricky. Ricky is a retired district judge and still practices law part time out of his home. His wife has her PHD and works at a local college. He is reminded of the old TV show *Green Acres* … Now there is nothing about Ricky or his wife that is similar to Eddie Alpert or Eva Gabor … it's just the idea of an attorney turned farmer. He enjoys the trip, seeing several deer, pheasant and a couple of coyotes. Before he knows it he is pulling into Ricky's drive.

Ricky and Martha bought a huge old farm house where a family had raised a large family and then moved on. Ricky has plenty of room for his collection of fowl and livestock; geese, ducks, guineas, chickens, turkeys, quail, peacock … and cattle, sheep, pigs, and goats. Ricky told him the other day they had not bought milk, cheese, eggs or meat for years; they will be ready if things collapse for sure. The guineas, turkeys and geese herald his arrival and Ricky appears shortly.

Average height, thin with an impish grin Ricky says, "How's Mike?"

"Good, Ricky … you?"

"Oh, you know, never had it any better! Ready to take some ducks home?"

"Yes, just finished the coop today so we should be all set. Janis is getting anxious to see them on the pond."

"Yes, well … they're still a bit young to turn loose. I'd give them another week or two before you let them run free."

They go to the little pump house where Ricky keeps his just-hatched fowl. It takes some effort and time to corral the three-dozen jumping, running and cheeping ducks. Once in the kennels and loaded in the back of the truck they take a breather.

"Everything working out okay for you in those two shootings," Ricky asks?

"Yes, at least as far as I know."

"You know, I realize you know people and they know you, but you should really have representation. Things can happen and you can find yourself in trouble even if you are not in the wrong; you know, Murphy's Law."

"Yes, I'll call you next time."

"Next time? What do you mean, next time? One in a million … ten million is ever involved in a shooting, you've been involved in two … and you say next time?"

They are good friends so he takes the time to outline just who he is dealing with, explains the project and how it all came about; he does not share his future plans, at least not now.

Ricky looks out across the prairie, and then down at the ground, then up at him and says, "I suppose there is nothing I can do or say that will change anything. Just know that I am here for you if I can help in any way. I know you will be careful, I just don't want to have to attend your funeral."

"I understand, better people than me have died for less. I just know I have to see this through and I really don't have a choice. I'm a marked man and my only hope is to cut this off at the head, if I do nothing I'll be on defense the rest of my life … I won't live like that."

They say their goodbyes and he starts the diesel engine and idles out the drive.

On the way home he thinks about their conversation and a realization comes to him that offers some hope. He knows it is very likely that to keep control of things and protect those involved, very few people know about him and the efforts to take him out. If he can possibly carry out his plan in an efficient way, there might not be anyone left who knows about him and his life might get back to some sort of normalcy. While the odds for this all happening might be slim, some chance is better than none.

He arrives at home and unloads the anxiously cheeping ducklings in their new home. He has a small tub of water in addition to their feed and drinking water … they attack the tub with much excitement and splash around before finding the food which they ravenously consume with just as much enthusiasm. He leaves them and heads for the house.

He's actually feeling pretty good; his new-found hope has given him a lift. He had not been moping around depressed, but he is beginning to feel that there will be an end to this one way or another. He pours a glass of tea and turns on the TV to his favorite cable news channel … the lift he'd felt just a few minutes ago is short-lived. The news is nothing that involves him directly; it is the progression of things that now has him down.

Once again he wonders aloud, "Maybe I should stop watching this?" No, not a realistic option … but the continual bad news is starting to wear on him, that and the personal issues combined have his endurance stretched pretty thin.

A young girl marching with the group against Wall Street is being interviewed as she walks. When asked if she thought this was a "patriotic march" she answered, "I don't — I mean, I don't think we know what we're doing enough for it to be technically patriotic (she laughs). I mean, come on, this is like crazy liberals, I don't even know what's going on."

The next segment has a story about a congressman who believes government regulations create jobs. "People have to be hired to help increase fuel mileage in cars when we raise the standard, when we cut emissions on factories people have to be hired to comply." Then the same man bemoans the fact companies are moving their factories overseas, that it is unfair to the workers, as if the employer owes them a job. He thinks to himself, "What the employer owes is a return on investment … morons, don't even understand capitalism." A company has to compete in the open market. If another company in another country can produce the same product for less, they can sell it for less. The U.S. company has to cut costs or go out of business.

The protesters are upset at CEO's making $50 million a year, but have no problem with an actor making $75 million for a movie, or an athlete making $120 million for a four-year contract. Evidence is produced by groups paying protesters … groups tied to Volar. They demand a living wage no matter their work status, free education, housing, food, transportation … "Let's see, they hate corporations, but they want jobs. Wonder who will hire them? Oh, right, the new government." He closes his eyes and takes a deep breath.

There is a story about U.S. Government agencies involved in the sale of guns to Mexican cartels which led to the death of an agent. The U.S. Attorney General tells Congress he knew nothing about it, and then some emails surfaced. Now the AG's options for a defense; either he lied or is incompetent. "I think it is both," he says to the TV.

Next there is a story about the aftermath of the U.S. using a predator drone to kill a terrorist in the Middle East. Seems the key terrorist had an associate with him who was also killed. The U.S. State Department had contacted the family of this associate to express its condolences. A family spokesman even went so far as to say he felt the department was not only apologetic for killing the man, a terrorist enemy of America, but upset for not giving its condolences sooner. By way of background, this particular terrorist was an American citizen who maintained an anti-American Web site while he lived in North Carolina. Two years ago he left for the Middle East to help produce an anti-American English blog. In an early essay he had described himself as a "proud traitor of America" and was also the author of *Make a Bomb in the Kitchen of your Mom*. He asks himself, *Good Lord, am I living in some sort of parallel universe*?

He stands and goes to refill his tea glass and walks out onto the deck. The afternoon sun, cool breeze and fresh air revive him. He thinks of a Bible story about the prophet Elijah. Queen Jezebel has vowed to kill Elijah by the next day so he flees to the desert. With the help of God he escapes, but Elijah is feeling sorry for himself. In a discussion with God he reminds God of all the great things he has done to no avail —

"I alone am left and they are trying to kill me." God diverts Elijah's attention from himself, and gives him some simple tasks, promises him a companion (Elisha), and also reminds him he is not alone; that there are 7,000 who have not bowed to the idol and are prepared to follow God.

As he thinks on these things he is reminded that he is not alone. There are his friends who are doing their part and possibly in danger as well. And there are some public figures, some in politics and some in the private sector who are doing their part. And there are countless constitutional patriots around the country who are willing to do their part. This helps ease his anxiety … no one wants to be alone. He knows he can count on his wife, children and friends … but he has to remember God is there as well. He also firmly believes God had a hand in the formation of this great nation and He will be there to help keep it. We often like the status quo, but he realizes there will likely be nothing and no one that will escape the rough times ahead.

He goes back in the house, the TV is still on and as he goes to turn it off something comes on and he stops. Good news for a change! An investigative reporter has been working on a story where random acts of kindness are springing up around the country. She is perplexed as there seems to be no person, company or organization behind it. She gives several examples around the country; people who are in line for some sort of assistance are given a bag of groceries by a stranger and told "God bless you," people who are homeless and hungry are invited into people's homes, fed and clothed, children who are from underprivileged families are assisted with meals on weekends when there is no school and they would otherwise be hungry. The story ends on the note that while she could not uncover the source of all this goodness, the country is better off.

He says aloud, "Yes, it is; we would not know the definition of good without God."

As the country has allowed God to be removed from school, courts, and the workplace, it has sunk to new lows; from greed to violence, to corruption. It will not end until we allow Him back into our country and our hearts.

Chapter 27

HE TAKES SOME LEFTOVERS out of the refrigerator and fixes himself a quick supper, and then showers and changes into something comfortable for the evening. He's had enough of the news and no shows interest him, so he turns on the satellite radio to a music channel he enjoys, and sits at his computer to catch up on some records for the alpaca ranch and upload some new pictures to the Web site. It's been a long day and he is tired, not just from the work but the emotional drain.

He calls his wife and they visit for a short time, but the call is cut short as she gets an EMS call and has to go. They say "Bye, love you," at the same time and he hangs up. He checks the S&W .357 Magnum that is hidden behind the bedside table, the Mini-14 is just around the corner as is a .410 pump shotgun.

"What a way to live," he says to himself as he turns off the light. The house is quiet; he lies back in the bed and sees stars through the skylight. He closes his eyes and is asleep in moments.

He wakes up, it is dark. This time of the year it is tough to tell time, it could be nearly 7 AM and still completely dark. A glance at the clock tells him 6:30, time to rise and shine. He starts coffee and fixes a quick bowl of oatmeal. As he sips his coffee he sends a text to his wife to see if she will be home soon. She has a few errands to run, but should be home by ten. He goes out and does the morning chores, his mind is on the next problem at hand … trying to figure out a path, tactics that will work … or at least have a higher probability of success.

Back in the house he decides to take a chance and turn on the TV while he pours himself another cup of steaming coffee.

His favorite talk radio host is being interviewed. The discussion is about current events and the solutions.

"Part of the problem we have is that our society is now the society of everyone gets a trophy! You know, everyone plays, no one keeps score, and everyone gets a trophy! No one knows how to excel, no one knows how to lose, and if 'I don't win' it isn't fair."

The interviewer comes back with typical progressive ideas and why it is important to include everyone and make them feel good about themselves, "What about the poor kid who is always last or is unable to play the sport as well as others?"

The frustration is evident on the face of the radio guy as he says, "You want the doctor who operates on you to be the one who was given a degree to make him feel better about himself, or the one who busted his butt to study and be the best in his class?" He doesn't wait for an answer to this rhetorical question and continues, "Nothing in life is fair, and we all have different abilities. If you aren't good at something find something you can do. Our constitution grants us equal opportunity, not equal outcome. Not everyone has the intelligence to be a doctor, not everyone can be a concert violinist, or ..."

"So you don't care if some are left behind, if some never realize their dreams?"

"I am absolutely inept at sports, I'm a complete klutz. If my dream were to be a professional basketball player, should I be allowed to and make big bucks doing so? Are you going to pay to come watch me play? What if my dream is to become an architect, but I just can't seem to get the idea of structural integrity down. When I design things the experts say will not withstand conventional limits of stress, should I build your house? I don't know whether you believe in God, but I believe God gives us all certain abilities, certain talents. It is up to us to discover what those talents are and cultivate them, be the best we can be within the limits of our abilities. You see the problem with inequality is people try to go against nature ... you can't bring the bottom up so you take the top down."

The interviewer is not convinced, never will be; you cannot reason with the unreasonable.

Turning on the radio to a talk radio station, the host and sidekicks are discussing the morning interview. They are incredulous as to how ignorant the interviewer was, ignorant in the classic sense of uneducated, operating from ideals rather than facts. They move on to the subject of the day, God and the nation. This host also believes the suffering our nation is experiencing is due to a drifting away from God. They believe as he does; it is a lack of morals and virtue, acting on the basis of greed, corrupt business practices and "crony capitalism." They believe the only way our nation will be saved is a return to godly principles and there is a plan to help people do just that; stop focusing on themselves and help others. There will be events online and in cities around the country planned in the months ahead to help give people guidance. Sounds familiar, but the big difference is the platform. This is not competition, it is help. No one is looking to take credit, but there is a mutual desire to return to basic principles.

Once again he is buoyed by this news, but he is hesitant to enjoy it … the emotional roller coaster is not an enjoyable ride. His wife arrives to the joy of the dogs and the racket of the guineas. He helps her unload her van and they go in the house.

"How was your shift?"

"We were pretty busy during the day, but luckily we were able to sleep all night."

"That's good, sure is rough when you are up all night, sort of like when I was flying international routes … no fun."

They spend the next hour talking about some of her calls and what he did; his talk with Ricky.

"Oh, you need to come out and see the ducks and how much they've grown."

They walk over to the coop and go inside the enclosed area.

"Oh my, they're bigger than I expected! They're getting their adult feathers, how pretty!"

"Yes, when I ordered them I thought I'd like the Cayuga best, but I really like the way the Welsh Harlequin look. It'll be great when we can get them all out on the pond."

"And eggs, I'm anxious for them to start laying."

He is as well, may come in handy in a crisis to have fresh eggs.

They spend the rest of the day taking care of normal day to day chores. Close to sunset all the fowl want to be fed and put back in the coop. After giving them feed and water he comes in, washes his hands, gets a glass of tea and sits at the bar while she prepares supper.

"Get everything done you hoped to?" he asks.

"Never do, everything always takes longer than you think … you?"

"I guess the same; there are enough regular chores for both of us it doesn't leave lots of time for extra things. Is that chicken noodle soup?"

"Sure is, getting cooler and feels more like soup these days." A friend of theirs from rural Mississippi had given her the idea of homemade chicken noodle soup; it is one of his favorites. Supper is good … two-bowls good; and a quiet evening at home together seems a rare treat.

"So, how do you feel things are going?"

"You mean the project or things in general?"

She pauses, "We haven't had a lot of time to discuss much of anything lately, so give me your take on all of it. I don't know if its women's intuition or what, but I just have a feeling things are going to get bad … really bad."

He looks at her intently and a slight smile appears on his lips. "You are very perceptive, or a psychic, or something."

"I've been living with you too long!"

He corrects her, "Not long enough … remember we promised each other … we're not finished yet."

She says, "You know what I mean."

"Yes, I do. Okay, first of all the project seems to be going well. I see things in the news from time to time I know is a result of it and occasional contact with the group seems everyone is happy with the progress. Also, our favorite radio talk-show host just announced a plan they will implement across the country that dovetails nicely with what we started."

"That's fantastic, but you don't seem excited about it. Why?"

"Oh, I'm very happy about it and it will be very important for the nation's survival. The problem is I am afraid this is too late to stop a crash. It won't stop it, but it is what will save us."

"I've been feeling we are in for very hard times … I mean like we might have to live off the land with no electricity and none of the regular niceties we normally enjoy."

"If that is all we experience we will be most fortunate. I think, while not likely, it is possible we could see a civil war."

She lets that sink in and responds, "That would be awful, but who would be fighting who?"

"I'm not entirely sure, and it could be quite variable and just depend on how things progress."

"I can see different scenarios. Most likely, the people behind much of this big push towards Marxist policies come from a background of violent groups. They conceded to work within the system to get their change, and they are oh so close."

"So you fear if they see it slipping away they might revert to their old ways to try and keep what they have and push it over the edge?" she asks.

"Exactly. And add to the mix the turmoil in the Middle East, the anti-Semitic sentiments not only there but in this country and others, and the economic turmoil as Europe implodes under their debt of social policies. There are just so many variables, if things hit just right we might skate through this with just a mild slow down …"

"And if everything falls just wrong it could be a worldwide calamity?" she adds.

"That's right, and if that happens all bets are off. Might some country try to take advantage of the situation and attack us? We have one distinct advantage; I mean the nation, our Second Amendment. Japan wanted to attack our mainland, but knew most Americans had weapons and would defend themselves. They knew they would be fighting more than our army."

She nods and asks, "Isn't it strange that the progressives are typically the anti-gun types, yet they are usually the ones to go violent?"

"Yes, they are full of contradictions like that. They also are the ones who are anti-death penalty and pro-abortion, soft on rapists and murders because they had a rough childhood, but let them hurt a dog and there is no penalty harsh enough."

She thinks about this for a moment and says, "Well, we just better be prepared for anything."

Chapter 28

HE'S UP EARLY THE next morning, fixes coffee and then as he enjoys his first cup, sits on the deck and reflects on … well … lots of things. His reflection seems to settle on a certain type of thing; things in his life that have not gone as hoped or planned and the way things were handled and worked out. While he has enjoyed many successes and he is not one to dwell on the rough times, these difficult situations often are what define and refine you. Loss of jobs, family, wife, accidents and countless other potentially life-altering events had hit him as it does most people in their lives. He likes to think he handled most of these in a better-than-average way, probably could have done better a time or two as well. The main thing is that he believes he learned valuable lessons each time, they made him stronger.

As he contemplates what is before him though, the stakes have never been higher. Sure, his life has been at risk before in situations, but there were circumstances beyond his control and he just had to handle things as they happened. This is different. He started this, although never believing his life would be in danger. He sees no way he could have accomplished what needed to be done without getting to this point; not with these people. He now finds himself making plans which, if they do not go well, could cost him everything. He has deep admiration for the nation's founders and their words never had greater meaning; "We pledge our lives, our fortunes and our sacred honor …" He thinks he might understand what these great men faced. He does not consider himself in their league, but he understands.

He leaves on a trip tomorrow so he has a lot to accomplish today. After breakfast he does the morning chores and then heads into town. He does not call because he is not sure it is safe, but he hopes Brian is on duty. He arrives at the sheriff's department and asks for Brian, he's working but not in the office.

"I have some information for him about a case, could you call him and see if he can meet with me this morning?"

The young lady does not seem eager to help, but asks his name and then calls dispatch to ask. In a couple of minutes she tells him, "Brian says he's close and will be here in about five minutes. You can wait over there."

She points to a row of chairs by the wall. He takes a seat and pulls out his phone to check emails while he waits.

In a few minutes he hears, "Hi Mike, what brings you to town?"

"I have something for you, is there a place we can talk?"

"Sure, follow me."

They go down a short hall to a small office, he takes a seat as Brian closes the door and sits behind the desk.

"You get anywhere with the DA on those guys?"

"Well, actually, I think so. I'm not exactly sure just what all they will be charged with, but he made an impression on the judge and so far bail has been denied … something to do with attempted murder of law enforcement will do that. Not sure how long he can keep that, but it should give us some time."

"And some leverage. Can I talk to them?"

"Oh, I'm not sure if I can make that happen."

"You know if I am going to make my plan to work I have to have a chance to talk with them, at least one. Bill, the one I talked to out in the field would be best … I think I can connect with him."

"Let me see what I can do, hang on."

Brian leaves and is gone for several minutes. When he returns he says, "I managed to get you five minutes, will that do?"

"Has to, when?"

"Well, now if you want. That might be best if you are ready, just in case something happens and they get released or something and you miss your chance."

"I agree, also if the charges were reduced they might get bail, but worse they might feel they have other options; I want them to think they have no options."

They go to the jail section of the courthouse. He is searched which seems a bit strange since they will be separated by glass and talking on a phone. He takes a seat in the spot as directed and waits. After about 10 minutes there is some movement in the room on the other side and then Bill comes into view, takes a seat and picks up the phone.

He lifts his receiver, "Hello Bill."

"Well, this is a surprise. I wondered who it might be, never thought about you … what do you want?"

Bills face looks better than the last time they talked, but it is still obvious his face was on the business end of a boot.

"I want to put an end to this thing and I'd like your help."

"Why would I help you?"

"Two reasons come to mind; one is I believe you to be a man who loves his country and does not want to see it become like the USSR used to be, and I think I can get you a break on your charges. Our state has a sentence called the "Hard 40," this charge qualifies and you'd get forty years with no chance for parole."

"You said you weren't a cop and I'm sure you aren't with the DA's office, so what makes you think you can help me … and why would you?"

"People here trust me, I can make no guarantees, but I will make every effort if you agree to help. I can offer you hope where there is none … and I need your help to do what needs to be done."

Bill looks down for a moment, runs his fingers through his hair, then looks back up. "You're right, I love my country and I got caught up and lost focus, got a little greedy. What do you want me to do?"

He spends the next couple of minutes explaining what he needs Bill to do, and when he's finished Bill says, "You really trust me?"

"Of course, but like Ronald Reagan said, "Trust, but verify. I have friends who are prison guards. If something happens to me because you double-crossed me they will make sure you become some big fat guy's girlfriend … that or have you beaten to death … maybe both. I hope you are the man of honor you once were and will use this as an opportunity to atone for your sins."

Bill looks at him with a hard look and says, "I believe you'd do it, and I do want to redeem myself, even if it just in my own mind. I'll do what you need."

"Thanks, Bill … good luck. Maybe someday when this is all behind us we can sit on that deck and reminisce about the old days."

"I won't hold my breath, but thanks."

He hangs up the receiver and heads for the door when he hears a tap on the glass. He turns to see Bill still there mouthing, "Thank you."

He smiles, waves and goes out the door.

He finds Brian after the visit. "Brian, this is important. Bill has agreed to help us. He will ask to make a call in a day or two and it is important he be allowed to make it."

"Mike, this is highly irregular, against anything considered normal in here. How do you know he's not lying to you? He could be taking this opportunity to set you up, get back in the good grace of his boss."

"That thought certainly occurred to me, but I really don't think so. I pay close attention to people's eyes. I remember the change that come over his eyes when we originally caught them and he decided to give us the name and numbers he did. He does not have a direct number, but he believes he can get a message to the big man himself. I looked deep in his eyes and I believe him; he is a veteran who now understands he crossed a line he vowed never to do. He needs redemption, and this is his chance."

Brian gives him a hard look, "I don't like this, but your instincts have been pretty good on this. While I don't really trust him, I trust you. I'll make sure he can make his call."

"Thanks, Brian."

They shake hands and as he walks off Brian adds, “You be careful, call me if you need anything.”

“Will do, thanks again.”

His commute to work is uneventful, thankfully. Weather can really mess things up, making him leave earlier than normal to make sure he makes it to his domicile in plenty of time to be properly rested for his trip; and almost worse, it can keep him from getting home after the trip is over. He’s looking forward to this trip because he has a layover in Los Angeles the same time John will be there. They have a tradition to get together there and go to a local Mongolian BBQ. It is outstanding and is a set price for all you can eat … however the older he gets maybe it ought to be all you should eat. He normally likes to bring his first officer along, but this time he will not. He is going to need John’s help for his plan and they need to be able to talk.

The restaurant is always busy and noisy, so people nearby will not be able to hear or understand much, and it is a nice walk so they will have that time as well. John arrives at his layover hotel first, so he comes over a couple of blocks to meet him.

“Hello Captain!” John calls.

He immediately recognizes the voice and turns to see the big grin on his friend’s face. “Hey buddy, good to see you!”

They share a hand shake and a hug, “Yes, I love it when this works out … I haven’t eaten all day in anticipation of filling up at the BBQ.”

“I’m pretty hungry myself. Come on up with me to the room and I’ll get changed.”

As they go up the elevator, “How are Cheryl and the boys doing?”

“She’s doing fine, involved with some things on the project. She really enjoys helping people and this deal is right up her alley. The boys are all working and off my payroll, thank goodness. Thought they’d never graduate and get jobs!”

He laughs and says, “Yes, now just wait until the first emergency and they want to move back in … with a wife and kids to boot!”

"That's all I need! How's Janis and your kids ... and grand kids?"

"Oh, Janis is busy keeping me out of trouble, and everyone else is doing great.

He changes clothes and they head off for the restaurant, it is about a mile and the weather is typical for a late afternoon in L.A.

"So, are you up for a little excitement?"

"Sure, what's up?"

He tells him about the sting and the capture of the two snipers.

"You've got to be kidding me, is this for real?"

"I'm afraid so, they seem to have me pegged. The first one was an FBI guy working on the side, we suspect the second was as well, but the Bureau was not entirely cooperative the second time, probably embarrassed. I'm not entirely sure about these two; I know the one I talked with is a vet."

"This is unbelievable, what are you going to do?"

He stops and faces his friend, "I'm going to take it to them. I've let them come at me three times, they set the time, the manner; I'm on defense. Not next time if I have anything to say about it. I may need some help. I promised myself when this all started I would not involve any of my friends if it got dangerous, but I may not have any choice."

"Mike, you know you can count on me. Just tell me what you need and when, I'll be there."

He puts his hand on his friend's shoulder and says, "Thanks, this means the world to me ... literally."

During the last several minutes of the walk he goes over his ideas for a plan. As they approach the restaurant he asks, "You still good with this?"

John stops for a moment and looks his friend square in the eye. "I told you, you can count on me and I meant it. Don't ask me this again, just tell me when and I'll be there."

He returns the eye contact for a moment, then turns to open the door. He knew he could count on John, but he wanted to make sure John was committed and knew what they were up against ... eyes wide open so to speak.

Their senses are met with the aroma of meats, vegetables, oils and sauces on the hot grill just inside the door. “Ah, that smells great … I’m hungrier than I thought!” he says.

“Me too.”

John holds up two fingers to the waitress. They take their time picking out the desired contents for their meals, waiting for the men who work the grill doing what is essentially a stir-fry, and then eating it along with rice. They each make two trips to fill their bowls, the conversation is about old times, planes they’ve flown, places they’ve been, moments they’ve shared over the years. It is an enjoyable time, as it always is when they are together … and as always it ends too soon.

They stop at a convenience store for a couple of items and then head for the hotels.

The pace walking back to their hotels is slower, enjoying the evening and the waning time together. His hotel is closer, they pause in front.

John says, “Don’t worry about me; I’m good with this, really.”

“I know you are willing, I just needed to know you knew what we might be up against. Hey, hope the rest of your trip is good. I’ll be in touch soon, this was great!”

They shake hands and share a quick embrace with back slaps.

“Had a great time as usual, you have a good trip as well. I look forward to the time we can add this experience to our memories.”

He smiles, gives John thumbs up and goes up the walk to his hotel.

In the room he readies his uniform for the next day and jumps in the shower. A good hot shower always helps clear his mind; the hot water on his skin, the steam in his nostrils.

With his eyes closed and the water streaming down his body he thinks, “Am I forgetting anything? If I were on the other side, how would I react?”

It is hard for him to think as an evil person might, but as the events have occurred over the past months another way of thinking has become imperative. If he could just walk away and it would all be over; well, that would be tempting. However he knows this is not an option, and he is also certain waiting for them would be akin to a duck sitting on a pond hoping the hunter in the blind doesn't see it. Not only are his options for action very limited, so is the likelihood of success … but there is a chance.

"The glass may not be half full, but at least it has something in it!"

He finishes the shower, towels off, slips on some shorts and flops on the bed to call his wife.

"Hi honey!" she says.

"Hi back … how was your day?"

"We had a few calls, enough to help the day pass, but not so many we were stressed. At least they were all pretty routine; falls, minor accidents and such … no code blues or major wrecks."

"That's good, I don't think I could do your job … well I could, don't think it is something I'd enjoy."

"No, you would not like it, and I would not like yours! You get to see John today?"

"Sure did, had a great visit … and we had Mongolian BBQ!"

"Am I going to have to order larger pants for you now?"

He laughs, "If I went there any more often you would!"

She becomes more serious, "You talk with John about your plan?"

"Yes, yes I did and as I expected he did not hesitate; he assured me he was more than willing. I worried he might not understand the consequences, but he does and is prepared to do whatever I ask."

"Is Cheryl okay with this?"

"I did not ask, but I know John and I know Cheryl. He won't tell her because she'd have a fit, and if anything bad happens she'll hate me forever … of course if things go wrong I won't have to hear it either."

"Don't talk like that," she says. "I know this is dangerous and I trust you, but I will not have you talking like failure is even a possibility. Positive thoughts only, I want to grow old with you."

"Yes, I'm sorry. On another subject, how's everything at the farm?"

"Everything is fine; they are getting all the open females bred. The ducks and guineas are running all over the place as if they own it."

"Well they do sort of own it. Having them forage around for bugs and insects is why we got them in the first place; anything else going on?"

"Not that comes to mind, how's your trip going?"

"Pretty good; the weather has cooperated, we've had good crews and no surprises."

"That's good, anxious to have you home! I have to get up early, so I'd better get off the phone and get ready for tomorrow."

"Okay, I need to hit the hay soon too. If all goes well I should be home tomorrow evening. I might stop and see Brian on the way home."

"Okay, let me know, see you then … love you, good night."

"Love you too, good night."

He clicks off the phone and turns on the TV. He needs to unwind and might as well see what is going on in the world. The "Occupy Wall Street" groups are still in the news. This event has become a joke, but actually there is nothing funny about it. Some in the media have compared it to the Tea Party events … one such event had about three-quarters of a million people on the Washington Mall. There was no trash, not one arrest; the people were considerate and respectful.

This group; not so much … murders, rapes, destruction of private property … all this and more going on in cities all over the country.

He sees a segment where a man from the former Soviet Union interviews OWS protesters. Now this is funny! The protesters hate capitalism and he responds with, "Oh really? What would you replace it with?"

Some actually say socialism, others beat around the bush but it is essentially socialist, Marxist or communist …to which he responds, "Oh really?"

He then reveals he is from the former USSR and is met with disbelief, or denial, or something like "Well, they didn't do it right, we will." Sure ...

There is something else going on in the world that scares him. Iran is trying very hard to build a nuclear weapon and the leadership hates Israel, speaking openly about its destruction and denying the holocaust. That's bad enough. Add in the fact that governments in Tunisia, Libya, Yeman, and Egypt have all fallen in the past year and the people behind these new governments are very much unknown. One thing for sure, the treaty which has existed between Israel and Egypt is no longer being honored. Israel is sitting in the middle of countries that hate them, and one may soon have nuclear weapons. If anyone thinks this would not affect the world's oil supply they are living in a fantasy land.

If Israel is attacked, will we become involved? They are an ally, the definition of that is, "An attack on one is an attack on both." He has no idea what this administration might do. There is every indication they have no love for Israel. He believes as did the founders that we as a nation should stay out of other nation's affairs and not become involved in nation building. If war is inevitable, you pound your opponent into the ground and leave. What does all this mean for the nation?

Problems without and within, even if things can be resolved within, the pressures from without could spell dark times. He turned the TV on to unwind, but now he is wound tighter than the main spring on a clock. He uses his relaxation technique to drift off and soon the alarm awakens him. It is a new day with new challenges ... hopefully they are simple and routine.

Chapter 29

THANKFULLY THIS DAY GOES smoothly, the weather cooperates for his trips and the commute home, the flights are on schedule … this is as good as it gets. He calls her cell and gets no answer; either on the phone or is a bad spot. Coverage in their rural home can be spotty.

He drops by the sheriff's department to see if Brian is in. As luck would have it he had just checked in for the night shift. They work rotating shifts, he'd been on days and then after his days off he began a run of night shifts.

"Hey Brian, how's it going?"

"Hey Mike, pretty good … you coming or going?" he asks after seeing the uniform.

"Just coming home, thought I'd check with you and not take any chances with phone calls. Any news on anything; has our boy made his call?"

"We don't have anything new on any of the other stuff, but he did make his call."

"Good, I have several days off now and I just may do a vacation drop on my next trip so I can have plenty of time."

"Okay, keep me informed and let me know if there is anything I can do."

"I will thanks. You stay safe out there tonight."

"I'll do my part, catch you later."

As he leaves the department his cell rings.

"Hi honey, I'm just leaving town, need me to pick anything up?"

"No, I just came home this morning and picked up a few things then … only thing I really need is you."

This puts a big smile on his face, "That goes both ways, see you in about thirty minutes."

"You hungry, did you get any supper?"

"Yes, I could use a bite to eat, but keep it light and don't go to any trouble."

She says, "I have some leftovers I can heat up after you get here."

"Perfect, see you shortly."

He clicks off his cell and goes to his truck.

The drive home is routine, not much traffic ever on this road with the exception of a holiday weekend. There is a reasonable amount of truck traffic, mostly hauling grain and cattle. The biggest concern is deer. He remembers back as a child, visiting his grandparents, deer were nonexistent then. When he was college age there were a few you might see from time to time. Now they are prolific and with all the farm crops for feed they grow quite large. Hunters come from all over the country to hunt the bucks with racks that will qualify to go in the big game records books.

Unfortunately, many are harvested with cars rather than guns or arrows. Janis has hit a few, luckily the last one was not too far from home and the responding officer gave him a tag, at least they got some meat in the freezer out of the deal. He figures if the worst comes to pass, there will be plenty of meat to eat.

He concentrates on the road and its shoulders illuminated by the headlights; looking for the telltale gleam of an eye or any movement that might be a deer … and his mind is elsewhere. He is still working on the details of this next phase in the operation. It is important he is the one in charge, the one calling the shots, keeping them on defense. Ideally, they need to feel they are taking the offense; in essence, a sting or a trap. After setting the last one they might be more cautious, but then they will not really know how this last effort failed. It is completely possible they might be a bit careless due to desperation. Three attempts, three failures.

To him this would make any further effort be incredibly concise, carefully planned and executed. However none of these attacks have had a high degree of planning or execution.

They are used to surprise and intimidation; will they change? He doubts it. His best guess is something involving several people on different fronts with overwhelming force. Deer have superior senses to man, it gives them an edge even though a man has superior weapons and abilities. Many a hunter has gone home empty handed after a deer smelled, or heard, or saw the hunter, and often the hunter never sees the deer. He will be like the deer, they will be the overconfident hunter, and he will send them home empty handed.

He pulls in the drive and shuts off the truck's engine. As he steps out he breathes the cool country air and takes a moment listening to the evening. The heat ticks of the hot engine as it begins to cool; a light breeze is stirring the remaining leaves in the cottonwoods, an occasional muted quack of a duck, and the humming sound of the alpacas. "Ah, it's good to be home," he says aloud.

He grabs his bag and goes inside, and is met by new sounds; the incessant barks of the dogs as they hear the door open and him bringing in his bag.

"Hey girls, it's just me!"

The barking ceases and is replaced by the sounds of their nails on the hardwood floor as they excitedly dance around his feet and rise up on their hind legs to get the first head rub. He bends down and gives them all some individual attention amid a few jealous growls.

"Girls, girls, girls ... settle down!"

As they settle down from the initial excitement he hears, "What about me? You have some of that special attention for me?"

He stands as she approaches and says, "Sure do."

They kiss briefly and hold each other for a few moments, enjoying each other's touch.

"Miss me?" she asks.

"Always, you know me; I'd rather be at home with you than anywhere in the world."

She does know him and knows that is the truth.

"Why don't you get into something more comfortable and I'll get you a bite to eat?"

"That sounds great, be right back," and he heads for the bedroom.

When he returns she has some leftover roast, potatoes and gravy heated up for him. He pours a glass of tea and sits down to eat. They talk about the past few days, what each of them did. She tells him all the news from the grandkids, friends and the rural community.

Their daughter had called about one of their grandsons he nicknamed Ralph. In math at school he was given a problem that required deductive reasoning to figure the answer. Now, we're talking third grade, so it is not terribly difficult, but part of the problem was to tell how he arrived at the correct answer.

"It was easy with the clues you gave," was his answer.

He tells her the latest from the rumor mills at the airlines and how the trip went.

After they are all caught up he stands and says, "Think I'll turn on the TV and watch some news."

"Okay, go ahead. I'll clean up here real quick and join you in a few."

She is in tune with world events, but does not really share his desire to know all the gory details. She would be happier to be watching one of the channels that centers on remodeling and decorating. This does not upset him at all, she has learned much and all the decorating in the new house is a result of her natural and learned ideas … she did a great job … but for him it is like watching paint dry, one area where they are not compatible.

He sits in the living room and clicks on the TV. It is good to be home, he leans back in the soft leather of the couch and looks up at the wood decking on the open ceiling extending 21 feet above, the two sky lights where he can see stars in the night sky. His eyes move down to the large open stairway from the upper floor. When he was building it, this was one area that gave him some pause, it required a lot of time to figure and then to construct it so it was symmetrical, functional and of course, looked good. He feels he found a good balance and is pretty pleased with the result. As the TV came on there was a commercial break, but now the news is back on.

There is a report on the groups marching against Wall Street. There are groups gathering in major cities all over the country. Their message is still very mixed, the individuals do not know who or what is behind them.

One comment in particular sticks out; "Our mission is to keep the pressure on so the authorities keep spending money." Was this a slip of the tongue? This idea to "overwhelm the system," make the government spend itself into oblivion, is right out of the playbook of the 1960s radicals. They are getting bolder. He remembers for instance when the mention of Marxists, communists and socialists by either side was not welcome. Now they proudly proclaim their status as a communist or socialist.

She joins him on the couch, "What were they talking about? I couldn't quite hear it all from the kitchen."

He fills her in briefly, "Good grief, these people are pulling out all the stops aren't they?"

"I think this is just the beginning. Some of these protests have gone violent; thankfully those are the exception rather than the rule. I don't believe the violent outbreaks are part of the current plan; it is some independent radicals or anarchists. When they feel they are running out of options, it will be widespread and well organized."

The next segment is dealing with the threats of Iran on Israel. He is not a foreign-policy expert and certainly there are intelligence sources he is not privy to, so having a policy in his mind that is workable is not really possible. Iran's leader says, every time a microphone is put in front of him, that he denies the Holocaust and plans to be the one who brings about the destruction of Israel, and then calls for a hastening of the return of the 12th Imam.

She asks, "What will happen if this nut does something?"

"Good question! Saudi Arabia is in a precarious position, they are no friend of the U.S., but then they rely on us for protection, and we protect them for the oil. I mean, the Saudi's have no military strength; there are several countries that could and would overrun them and take over their oil fields. The potential for a worldwide meltdown would be very high if anyone drops a nuke anywhere in the Middle East. Add to this mess the fact there have been many anti-Semitic messages out of the protesters on Wall Street, this whole thing may be tied together … either by design or coincidence … and I don't believe much in coincidence."

She lets out an audible sigh … all this really bothers her and while she says nothing, she is ready to change the channel to a decorating show.

Next the discussion is financial. If things weren't depressing enough already, Congress is punting their responsibility. The senate has not passed a budget in three years; they have to pass resolutions every few weeks to keep paying the bills. They cannot agree on how to reduce the deficit, the progressives want to tax the rich and do not want to cut spending while conservatives want to cut spending and keep taxes low. These are fundamental differences and the media is having a fit over the fact Congress can't get along … and of course the Republicans are demonized for not compromising … funny, the Democrats are never demonized for not compromising. He has no love of Republicans either; the progressives have a firm hold on many of them as well.

To him it is basically a law of physics. He knows how business works, they do not pay taxes; they pass them on to the customers built into the product's price as part of their business expense. And the people will make every effort to avoid paying any more taxes than they have to, most legally and some not.

She asks, "Why can't they work this out?"

He shakes his head, "The country is so polarized right now everyone is afraid to disappoint their base for one. But to me it is insanity."

She agrees, "It only makes sense to cut spending in this situation. The spending is so out of control compared to the tax revenues; it is like a family who insists they go on a European vacation, buy a new car and remodel the house. They have to borrow every cent and they are already stretched to the limit paying the bills; there is no way they can increase their income enough to matter."

"That's right, it does not matter how noble the cause. They could demand more from their employers, might get a second job, but they cannot possibly pay for their spending."

"Yes … the smart family would cut back on their spending before they sink the family."

He nods in agreement, "And a smart country would do the same."

The dialog on the news now is about debt. The national debt just passed 15 trillion dollars; it has increased by 5 trillion in just the past three years. If something is not done to reverse this trend our national debt will exceed 47 trillion is ten years. Current unfunded liabilities are 114 trillion, things like Medicare, Medicaid, social security and other programs; much of this is supposed to be funded by user taxes and fees … which the government has spent already on other things.

He says, "My biggest fear, that the plan to pay all this off is through inflation. That might get it paid off, at the expense and demise of most Americans."

"Can we watch something else? This is just too depressing."

He understands and feels somewhat the same way.

"I agree it is very depressing, but we have a nation at risk and ignoring it will not make it go away and might leave us more unprepared. We are doing all we can, but no one will be completely prepared."

"I know. It's just such insanity."

He agrees.

A recent partial audit of the Federal Reserve Bank reveals in the past three years the Fed helped bail out countries and banks to the tune of 14 trillion dollars.

"Where is the money coming from," she asks?

"I don't know, I'd guess they're just printing it."

"Won't that just cause inflation?"

"Looks like we've come full circle, doesn't it?"

One of the reports on the TV tells that the Fed owns more of our debt than China. China is often vilified for holding so much of our debt; it's just a business decision for them, they did not force it on us. The Fed carrying so much of the debt is another disturbing fact of news.

Most people do not know The Federal Reserve Bank is not a government entity, it is a private institution. Congress formed it in 1913 with the Federal Reserve Act to try and control fluctuations in the economy; it also handles the printing of our currency. There is a lot of secrecy surrounding the Fed, there have been calls for a full audit and accounting to allow the people of this nation see just what they have done and why; these efforts are blocked at every opportunity … a red flag in and of itself. When the Fed carries the debt, it is just another way to essentially print money.

"Go ahead and put it on whatever channel you like, I've seen enough for now."

She notices the change in his demeanor, "What's wrong? Something affected you, I can see it, what are you thinking?"

He closes his eyes and rubs his neck for a moment, "In normal times we dealt with one problem at a time in our nation ... that is, the people were concerned about what Washington was up to one issue at a time. They have learned to operate on many fronts and rather than an "all or nothing" outcome, with this method they will likely be successful on multiple fronts ... overwhelm the system ... overwhelm the opposition. We have all they are doing in addition to world events …"

"You aren't saying we don't have a chance are you? You don't think they will succeed with all this do you?"

He sometimes has feelings, feelings that have no basis in fact, a gut instinct. "I don't know what to think, you know I am normally a "glass is half full" kind of guy. I've never seen a time in history with so much happening at once … sort of like a perfect storm. Part of what makes it worse is the age in which we live; the information is available from all over the world in seconds."

She asks, "So in the past, events in other parts of the world or even across the country might not have had an effect, but now you are saying one event might cause or exacerbate another?"

"In a nutshell, yes."

Chapter 30

WHILE LAST EVENING STARTED off on a sour note with the news, the night was actually very nice. They relaxed and talked about simple, yet important things; their children, grandchildren, friends, and memories … fun times and experiences they've shared over the years. It was not spoken or even consciously thought, but likely something deep inside compelled them to share these things at this time; a sense of foreboding. They went to bed and lay next to each other, touching and enjoying each other's presence. Tired and content, they drifted to sleep quickly.

His eyes opened and he was awake as usual. She is normally slow to wake up, needs some time to get things going. He pulls the covers back, slipping quietly off the bed and pads into the bathroom. He peeks out the window, often there are deer eating in the yard just a few feet away and this is one of those mornings. He stands quietly and watches in the dim light of pre-dawn as several does and fawns munch on grass and leaves. As a bow hunter this is something he has seen many times while dressed in camouflage and sitting in a tree stand. While the deer seem content and safe, there is no doubt they are on constant alert. The slightest smell or sound will command their immediate and full attention.

He thinks to himself, "When your life depends on you paying attention, you pay attention. We as a society in America have become too lazy, too trusting, too dependent."

He slips into jeans and a shirt and then quietly leaves their end of the house for the kitchen and the coffeepot. He starts water running into the pitcher while he grinds the beans. The coffeepot is actually a commercial type that brews a pot quickly; in just a few minutes he's enjoying the first cup. It's too cold out to sit on the deck so he sits at a table just inside and looks out over the pond as the sky gets gradually lighter with the sunrise. Once it is fully light outside he slips on a jacket and goes outside. The bird coop is directly east of the house and as the ducks and guineas see him there is a cacophony of squawks and quacks in anticipation of their release. He opens the gate and throws them a little scratch grain as a treat. The guineas will forage around the farm and the ducks on and around the pond all day; in the evening he will feed them in the coop and close the gate to keep them safe from predators at night.

As he comes back inside she says, "Good morning!"

"Good Morning, sleep well?"

"Great, you?"

He nods and says, "Like a rock."

As she pours a cup of coffee she adds, "You snored last night, you normally only do that when you are really tired."

"I guess with all the regular stuff going on plus my mind has been running in overdrive. I suppose that helps to wear on me some too."

"Probably so, what are your plans today?"

"After doing the regular chores I have a few things around here to catch up on and I plan to get on the computer and drop my next trip so I can have plenty of time to complete this last phase of my plan."

"How confident are you this is going to work?"

He pauses a moment, "There are so many variables…if everything goes as planned it should go well, but then there'…"

"Murphy's law," she finishes his sentence for him.

"Yes, I'm hoping for it to work in reverse … in other words it hits "them" instead of us … things go wrong for them at the worst possible moment."

"That does sound better; you know I am praying about this."

"I'd be disappointed if you weren't, and I am praying as well."

While it is chilly outside, it is calm and the sun is shining, a beautiful day. He puts on a jacket and goes out to do his chores. Their oldest son works part time for them on the farm for extra money. They don't need a full time employee so it works well for both of them. It also assures him things will be cared for while he is away on trips and his wife is working. He stops and looks up into the clear blue sky, "A beautiful day for flying," as a friend used to say. He thinks every day is a beautiful day for flying, some are better than others, but flying is always fun. Okay, there are exceptions; hurricanes, tornados, ice storms to name a few.

Here in the middle of the country one seldom looks into a clear sky without seeing an airliner flying over and this is no exception. The plains are noted for their beautiful sunsets, but add in a few jet contrails and a few clouds it can be simply amazing; the reds and golden colors paint a brilliant picture. His father had been in the Army Air Corps and later the Air Force. When he was small he remembers his father would tell him and his mother when he would be flying close to the house at night. He and his mother would stand on the back porch and flash the porch light, his father would flash the landing lights in response; a silent connection for a moment, and a memory forever. Thirty-five years later this memory came to him as he was looking over the flight plan taking a B-747 from New York City to Los Angeles and realized he'd be flying right over his house. He called home and told his youngest daughter when to go out and look. A few hours later as he approached he turned on all the landing lights, hoping although he was 5 miles up she could see him. Later at the hotel he called and asked if she'd seen him. A friend of hers had been there too, they went outside and watched.

She saw the strobe lights flashing, but when the lights suddenly came on she exclaimed," There's my daddy!"

A silent, momentary connection…and a lifelong memory.

His chores do not take very long to complete and soon he is back inside filling his coffee cup. "Cold out there?" she asks.

"Actually not bad, there is no wind and the sun feels nice."

"Good," she says, "I have some things I want to get done before the snow flies."

"Don't waste this day, I'm sure days like this will be few and far between before long."

He takes his coffee back to the small office and turns on the computer. He looks over a few bills sitting on his desk and the screen comes to life. It asks for the password which he types and then waits for everything to load. He signs into the company system, goes to his schedule and drops the next trip. This put a pretty big dent in his pay for the month, but some things are more important than money. Besides, if things go well he might be able to make it up before the end of the month; and if things do not go well.....well, then it might not matter.

Over the years he has owned many airplanes. Early on they were used for pleasure and a way to help build time and experience. After he had a wife, children and a business they became part of the financial stability for the family; and family vacations could be quite unique. After his hiring by the airline it reverted back to mostly pleasure again; although he could often fly places himself in less time than it took to drive to the airport, go through security, fly to a major airport and then rent a car to drive to the final destination.

For his plan to work, he needs flexibility; flexibility to travel exactly when and where he needs. His plane will be perfect. While he likely will not need the full performance of the Cessna 185 for this trip, the ability to take off and land on an area the length of a football field is a definite asset; another thing to have just in case.

Most planes with as much power as the 185 has are faster; it gives up speed for its STOL performance. However it is plenty fast, he will be able to cover the distance for this trip in a little over six hours. It also gives him the ability to travel without the knowledge of anyone; and the ability to travel well-armed.

He turns on the pre-paid cell he bought in L.A. and thumbs in a number.

"Yes?"

"Just making sure, guess I'm a bit anxious."

"Everything fine on your end?"

"Fine as frog's hair."

That brings a smile; humor always helps ease the tension. "I'm glad to hear that. Everything's on schedule on my end, see you soon … bye."

"Later."

He punches in another number.

"Hello?"

"Just checking in, making sure everything is set on your end."

"I'm ready, you can count on me … don't worry about a thing."

"Thanks, you don't know how much I appreciate this."

"My pleasure, you just do what you have to do and don't worry about things here."

"I owe you big time."

"No you don't, and I won't hear that out of you again … bye now," and the line goes dead.

"Is everything set," she asks?

"Best I can tell, yes. I can only guess what is going to happen, play the odds."

"Are you sure this is the only way?"

"You mean short of doing our own version of a witness protection plan; changing our names and moving to Alaska? Yes."

"I know … it's just ..."

"Hard … I know. Remember, I promised you years ago…"

"I know, but some things are beyond your control."

"That's why I'm taking control now."

The rest of the evening and night is spent quietly; the TV is not on a news channel. They both enjoy professional bull riding and they decide to watch an event on the DVR they have not had the time to watch before. He packs a small bag for his trip, need to travel light. They go to bed early; neither of them wants to close their eyes, however, in the stillness of the country and the moonlight shining through the skylight, they both drift off.

His eyes snap open, the moon is down so it is dark. He looks at the clock radio by the bed … the alarm will go off in three minutes. He rolls out of bed, turns the alarm off and goes in the bathroom. He quietly dresses, picks up his bag and walks quietly over to her side of the bed. As he bends to kiss her bye she reaches for him and holds him tightly, then a long kiss. He knows she needs this so he makes no effort to leave until she releases her grip on his neck.

"I love you; I can't call until this is over."

"I know, love you too … careful!"

He takes his bag and quickly leaves for the small private airfield where the plane waits in his hanger.

Most people do not understand general aviation, the generic term for everything that is not airline. The rules and regulations cover everything from ultra-lights, to balloons, to gliders, to corporate jets. As long as he does not fly into a controlled airport with a tower or fly under instrument flight rules, no flight plan is required. Actually, a VFR (visual flight rules) flight plan is a request for search and rescue in the event you do not reach your destination. He will not file a flight plan for this flight.

He parks by the hanger, opens the doors and flips on the lights. He got a good deal on this plane many years ago, it was in rough shape. He had the STOL kit put on it and had it painted a burnt orange with black and white accent stripes. He drops his bag in the right seat, and then does a thorough pre-flight on the plane. He always fills the tanks when he puts the plane in the hanger after a flight, but a visual in each tank is still done. Once the visual inspection is complete, he rolls the plane outside, pulls his truck into the hanger and closes the doors.

Once in the left seat, he does the pre-start checklist, primes the 300 hp engine and turns the starter. The quiet of the small rural strip is broken as the engine roars to life. The down side, if there is one to this plane, it spent part of its early life on floats in Alaska. Being on floats allows a longer propeller for better performance, and this plane still has that longer prop. On takeoff, with the engine cranking out its full 300 horsepower, the prop tips are nearly at the speed of sound, and the scream of the prop can be heard for miles.

With the pre-flight checklist completed, and engine properly warmed, he taxis back to the end of the short strip. He lines up with the centerline of the runway and eases the power in until the throttle is at the stop. At this light weight, the plane is nearly airborne by the time the power is at its peak. The 185 rockets into the dark sky, and he is on his way.

She is still lying in the bed, the dogs tight against her warmth. She hears the scream of the propeller as he departs the airport nearly four miles away. She hopes this is not the last time she hears this, and she says a silent prayer.

He wears a noise cancelling headset, so the noise level in the cabin of the plane is very comfortable. He climbs up to 11,500 feet above sea level, levels off and sets the engine to cruise power. This time of year the winds aloft generally pick up in velocity, so his fuel burn with a significant tail wind should allow him to make this trip non-stop. The GPS gives him a nearly direct flight path deviating only slightly to miss a couple areas of restricted airspace. The air is smooth, he is doing what he loves, but his destination will be no vacation.

The man answers the ringing cell phone, “Hello?”

“Is everything in place, everyone properly prepared this time,” the gravelly voice asks?

“Yes sir.”

“Better be, heads will roll if anything goes wrong this time.”

The line goes dead.

Chapter 31

HIS THOUGHTS WANDER AS he flies eastward. Did he remember everything? Did he think everything out? Did Bill do the honorable thing, or did he try to redeem himself with his boss? "Thoughts like this do you no good," he says aloud. He turns his thoughts to when he and his "brother" flew to Alaska. That was an amazing trip with some unbelievable sights. He remembers camping out near Denali, the natives name for Mt. McKinley. They played volleyball in the daylight till almost midnight with a group of college kids who were working for a mining company picking up rock samples. One of the kids had a birthday, they could not find a knife to cut the cake, and so he fired up a chainsaw … frosting flying like woodchips everywhere.

The sun is up and in his eyes; the aviator sunglasses keep the glare to a suitable level. He grabs a candy bar and as he chews on the chocolate and nuts, his mind wanders again. This time, it is a flight in the 747 coming from Europe to the west coast. They flew as far north as 75 degrees, nearly 10 degrees north of the Arctic Circle. The northern lights were so brilliant; they were like a shimmering curtain of lights hanging to the north. They were so bright they lit up the cockpit with the reds, blues, greens and yellows. It lasted for hours as they followed the great circle route over Greenland and the northern reaches of Canada.

It is close to noon local time when he lightly touches down at the small airport outside of the metropolis of New York. He parks over a tie down spot in the transient area and secures the ropes to the tie down anchors and walks inside the general aviation terminal.

A college-aged girl is behind the counter and greets him with a smile, “Hi, what can we do for you today?”

“I’m going to be here a couple of days; would you top me off with 100LL?”

“Sure, would you like me to call a cab or something for you?”

“Thanks, but I have a ride …see you when I get back.”

“Have a nice day; see you in a couple of days.”

He walks out in to the parking area and sees a hand waving him over.

“How was the flight?”

“Perfect, John … good to see you!”

“Good to see you too, I still love seeing that 185 coming in to land … love that plane!”

“Me too …you have things all scoped out for us?”

“Yes, found a perfect place for your plan.”

“Good, let’s take a look.”

They pull out of the parking lot and turn toward the city.

Today is her day to work, and she cannot get him off her mind. Years ago when his job took him around the world there were many times she did not talk to him for a week or more; but for a number of years with the advent of cell phones she has become spoiled. A quick call or a text, it is almost like he is there all the time. To be unable to call him, to not know … it’s killing her, but she is better off at work. The day is going fairly well with enough calls to help her keep her mind off of him most of the time…most of the time.

“Is there ever a time of day the traffic is not bumper-to-bumper here?”

“Not any time I’ve been here,” John says. “The place is just ahead.”

John parks on the street just off the motel parking lot. It is what he would jokingly call a “No Tell Motel,” and it is perfect. He does not care if it is clean, or smells, or is noisy.

Neither of them will be staying here. He goes into the office, a scruffy old woman behind the counter coughs as she exhales cigarette smoke.

"Waddaya want, sonny?"

"Room for two nights."

"How many?"

"Ma'am?"

"How many in the room?"

"Oh, sorry … just me."

"Here, fill this out … need your ID too."

He pulls out his driver's license and fills out the form. She looks at the ID, then at him, and hands it back.

"That'll be $155 with tax … cash."

He pulls a fold of bills out of his pocket and pulls out the cash and slides it across the counter. "I'd like the last room at the end if I could."

"Whatever, don't make no difference to me."

She slides the key to him, "Thanks, ma'am."

He walks back to the car and gets in.

"All set?"

"Yep, got the end room too."

"Good, looks as if only the rooms close to the office are used most of the time."

"I doubt the vacancy sign ever goes out!"

"No kidding, glad we get better than this for our layovers."

"Ah, come on, I thought you guys stayed at places like this all the time!"

"Not quite, but maybe the reason my airline makes money while most others have gone bankrupt …"

"Okay, let's get something to eat … all I've had is a couple of candy bars since supper last night. You find a Mongolian BBQ for us here?"

"Didn't look for that, how's pizza sound?"

"Perfect, let's go."

"Hello, who's this?"

"I was told to call this number if a man checked in."

"Yes, where are you?"

She gives the man the address and room number.

"Is he there now?"

"No, he checked in but did not go to the room, I saw him walk back toward the street."

"He alone or with anyone?"

"Alone."

"Someone will bring you half the money, you get the rest after he comes to the room and you let us know."

"Alright …"

They arrive at a local pizza place and go inside. It is past the normal lunch hour, so the place is nearly empty. They take a table in a corner where they can see the door; a chubby bleach blonde waitress takes their order and leaves them alone. They talk about everything but the planned events of the next twenty four hours … there will be plenty of time for that.

The gravelly voice answers, "Yes"

"We pulled out all the stops, used all our resources, and it paid off. We got a call from a dump of a motel, he checked in."

"Is he there now?"

"Lady said he walked up, got the room and walked out without going to the room, went back out to the street. She has no windows on that side of her office, so she would not have been able to see where he went or if he was alone. She says she asked how many for the room and he said just one."

"What are your plans?"

"I told her I'd give her half the money now and the other half after she called to tell us he was there. My man will leave a little surprise for him when he returns."

"Let me know when it's over."

"Yes sir."

Half a world away, the pilots sit in a briefing room while a senior NCO and officer show a wide array of aerial and satellite photos of the target area. Two specifics are discussed at great length, the actual target and the defensive systems. There will be rendezvous points before and after for refueling.

This is an extremely dangerous mission, success is not assured, and all participants are volunteers. There are also many pictures taken at ground level, obviously from an agent close to the targets.

"John, you did a great job of picking this spot … you sure you haven't done this sort of thing in the past?"

"I think I would have remembered that!"

"Probably so, we better get to work."

Their eyes meet, nothing further needs to be said … when this is over they will be forever changed.

Night is falling at home and she is a nervous wreck. She feels so alone and she is terrified this is the way her life will be from now on …she does not know if she can handle it. She finally talks to one of her closest friends at work.

"Trace, can we talk?"

"Sure, Janis … I can tell something has been eating at you all day."

"This is just between us, okay?"

"You know you can trust me."

"Well, you know these attempts on Michael's life? Well, he's figured out who's behind it and he's gone to put an end to it."

"Why didn't he just call the police?"

"This guy has crooked cops, FBI, working for him. Michael believes we'll never have a moments rest."

"And you're worried he won't come back …bless your heart, I see why you are so upset. Why don't you just go home?"

"I don't want to be alone, especially not there."

"I understand … let me think about this, maybe we can do something to help."

John and he have taken their positions, now they wait. Between hunting and flying, they both have learned patience. When they were younger, waiting seemed interminable … now it is part of life.

In the secure bunkers on the other side of the world crews check, double-check, triple-check everything on the aircraft. The F-16C's, known as Wild Weasels for their ability to "ferret out" enemy defense radar are equipped with radar jamming and air to ground missiles, the F-15 Strike Eagles with BLU-118 Thermobaric warheads and BLU-113 "Bunker Buster" Super Penetrator warheads; they will effectively destroy everything above and below the ground in the target area. The tanker aircraft are located at another airfield and are in their final preparations as well.

The two men pull into the motel parking area and get out of the car. One stands by the car and looks around as the other goes inside the office.

"I talked to you earlier," he says and slides a thick envelope across the counter.

The old woman doesn't bother to take the cigarette out of her mouth, "He ain't been back since … been watchin'." She opens the envelope and thumbs the hundred dollar bills.

"Good, give me a key to his room."

She slides a key to the man and without a word he turns and goes outside. He flips the key to his partner.

"She says he is still away, I'll stay here and watch while you go take care of it."

"Sure."

The second man looks back and forth as he walks quickly to the room, opens the door, steps in and closes the door behind him. He is in the room only a minute. Suddenly the door opens, the man steps out, closes the door and walks back to the car.

"It's ready."

"Good." He steps back in the office and slides the key back to the woman, "I'll be waiting for your call," he says as he walks out.

They both have a good view of the entire event.

"I wish we knew what they said," John says.

"Yes, but probably doesn't matter … whatever they are up to, it's not good."

"No, but you talk about me, what about you? You seem to have their playbook."

"I figured if they found me in the middle of the plains, they could find me here. If I had not wanted them to find me I would have used a different name. They want to minimize anything in the open with witnesses. I figure a gun fight attracts too much attention, even in the big city where no one wants to get involved, someone might talk. I guessed they'd use a bomb. Question is, will it detonate when the door is opened, or is it on a timer related to the door, or remotely set off?"

"You plan to open the door to figure it out?"

"Nah, figured I'd let you do that."

"No thanks."

"I was where I could see in the office, he gave the old lady a fat envelope. My guess is after they think they have me, they'll kill her and get the money back."

"That's a shame."

"Yes, but she's greedy, and she has to know those guys are up to no good."

The two men drive up the street a few blocks to a local bar. They go inside, order a couple of drinks and take a table in the back. The one apparently in charge takes his phone out and punches in a number.

"Yes?"

"Everything is going according to plan here; you take care of things on your end and call me when you are finished."

"No problem."

Trace says, "Come on, I'm taking you home."

"But they'll be short-handed, we can't just leave."

"I talked to our supervisor. I did not tell him what was wrong, but everyone here knows about the attempts on Mike and they figure that is what is eating on you, that and you having to take one of the guys out. We made a couple of calls; two are coming to take our place so they won't be short. I'll take you home and stay there with you so you won't be alone."

"But …"

"Now, you are always worried about other people, let someone take care of you when you need it."

She sighs, "Okay."

Trace helps her load her things and they leave the station for her house.

There are several hours before the mission begins. The men all go back to their quarters for some sleep, if that is even possible. They will be brought in for a final last-minute briefing with the latest satellite information to verify nothing has changed before they launch just after dark.

They decided to keep their positions on the outside chance someone comes back to the motel to visually watch, but nothing is happening. Two couples come separately to rent rooms … probably by the hour.

"Do those girls look like the girl-next-door to you?"

"Not in any neighborhood I've ever lived in! How much longer you plan to wait?"

"Let's make them sweat a little; I'll be ready to move at about 2300."

"Okay."

"You think that old woman is stiffing us? You sure the guy is even there? I mean she might have made it up and just take whatever she can get. We might be sitting here wasting our time."

"She wouldn't be that stupid, she never would have gotten so old."

"You're probably right, I guess getting paid to sit in a bar and drink is not so bad anyway."

"Naw, there's worse things."

She pulls into the garage and Trace parks his truck in the driveway. They both get out and he helps her get her things out of the van and into the house.

"I'm already seeing this was probably a good idea, I'm sure I would not have been 100 percent if we had a serious call, code blue or a really bad 10-48."

"I know this will be best for you, I'll stay with you until we hear from Mike."

"Thanks, Trace."

"You ready?"

"Anytime, sure tired of sitting here, that's for sure."

"Me too. Get the car and wait for me."

"See you in a few."

Before leaving his hiding place, he double-checks his weapons. He walks out to the street in front of the motel and pauses; takes a deep breath and walks toward the motel. He walks steady, more casual than hurried. As he walks past the office he looks in the window and sees the old lady watching TV and smoking. He smiles and waves to her, she sort of flips her hand upward and goes back to watching TV. He does not break stride all the way to the room. As he nears the door he is nearly out of sight of the office, but he sees the old woman has the phone handset up to her ear. He walks past the end of the building and around the corner; the fence is about 6-feet tall. He's in good shape and hauling himself over only takes a moment. He sees John waiting, slips into the car and they are moving in no time at all.

It is after 11 when the man's cell finally rings. He sees the caller ID, and says, "Yes? Okay, thanks." He clicks off and says, "He's back…show time."

The other man smiles and says, "This is my favorite part." He pulls his cell out of his pocket, punches in a number and hits "Send".

The car is moving slowly down the road with its lights off. As he clears the trees lining the road he can see the large log house on a rise a couple of hundred yards from the road. There are several lights on in the house. "Good," he thinks to himself, "she's home." He knows she works 24 hour shifts, but does not know her schedule so he wanted to check at night when he would not be seen. There is no moon, but in the country the stars are bright enough for him so see the road as long as he drives very slowly. He parks further down the road out of sight from the house so he won't be seen leaving the car. He checks his weapon, and quietly slips out of the car and walks back down the road. He is used to the city, the night sounds of the country are unsettling to him.

The old woman hangs up the phone and goes back to her show on the TV. When the bomb goes off moments later, she soils herself.

"Well, you had that figured right."

"I'm afraid so, I just hope it wasn't so big it killed anyone…except me of course!"

"Where to, James?"

"Let's go to your room and get some sleep"

"Sounds good, I'm beat."

Before any police or fire responds to the blast the two men are parked on the street in front of the motel. The man in the passenger side goes in the office and returns moments later.

"She won't need this anymore," he says holding the envelope. "I think she had a heart attack, she is all blue and not breathing."

"Perfect."

They drive off into the night as flashing lights and sirens approach the motel. Two couples half-dressed and half covered with sheets and blankets are standing in the parking area in disbelief as police cars arrive.

The house is huge and there are doors everywhere it seems. There is a porch all the way around the house, there is no way to look in a window without being up on the wooden porch … he'll have to be very careful. He sees her walk past a window in the west end of the house, so he slips that way in the darkness.

The gravelly voice answers the phone, "Yes?

"It's finished, he went in, the device went off, and we left. No trail, no witnesses."

"Good, about time. What about the wife?"

"I have my best man on it; I expect a call any time now."

"Let me know, then take a few days off."

"Yes sir."

The man works his way to the back of the house careful to stay far enough out light from inside will not give him away. He sees a sliding patio door in the end of the house where she is, he works his way quietly up onto the porch beside the door. He'll be glad when this is over. He's been goosey ever since he got here, coyotes howling, who knows what making noises in the dark. "How can people live like this?" he thinks to himself. He takes a quick peek in the edge of the glass to make sure she is not in sight; better to completely surprise her. He puts his hand on the door handle, gives it a little pressure to test if it is locked; it is not. He pulls his gun out of the holster, and puts pressure on the handle to slide the door slowly open.

"Are you going to call Janis before we hit the rack?"

"She's working tonight, probably asleep by now. I think I'll wait until after I make my call in the morning from the airport, let her know I'm on my way home."

"I know she'll want to hear from you as soon as possible, but you are probably right to wait. We're not out of town yet either …"

The door slides quietly open, and then the world goes dark. She and Trace hear a dull thud and sound of the man as he slumps to the porch. She comes around from the master bath as Trace comes from the other end of the house and the dogs go crazy. Kenny is standing there with about a six foot two by four.

"Kenny, what are you doing here? Who is that?"

"Well, I don't know who that is," he says pointing to the unconscious man. "But Michael asked me to keep an eye on you while he was gone. He had a suspicion someone might try something …looks like he was right."

Trace bends down to check the man. "You really whacked him, might have cracked his skull, he's out cold."

"Well dang, I swung hard enough I thought to kill him; guess I need to work out a little more. I don't take too kindly to someone coming to mess with my girlfriend."

Trace raises an eyebrow and Janis smiles, "That's a deal between Kenny, Michael and I. I think we better call 911"

"Go make the call, you know the address. I'll stay here with Kenny and watch this guy. Oh, Kenny, I'm Trace."

"Nice to meet you, Trace."

"Wonder why we haven't heard from Joe?"

"I was wondering the same thing, suppose we should call him?"

"No, absolutely not … the phone could ring at the wrong time and mess things up something terrible. We'll hear from him. You know she sometimes works nights, so maybe we won't hear until tomorrow."

"Yeah, not our problem anyway, we got ours."

Chapter 32

THEY WAKE UP EARLY; both of them are early risers. They find a pancake house on the way to the airport and stop for breakfast. The waitress hands them menus, they order coffee and look over the selections.

"What are you having?"

"Not sure, but whatever it is, I want a lot of it."

"Me too … they have all you can eat pancakes."

"Sounds good, with a side of sausage."

The waitress takes their order, "So, how do you feel things went?"

"So far, so good; I'll feel better when the rest of it is over and I'm home."

"I bet."

The crews had some rest, but not much sleep. The mission weighs heavily on all of them. While the odds of success are not good, success is vital … thousands … millions might die … failure is not an option … and there will be no second chances. The final briefing is completed, there are no changes of any consequence, and the fighter crews are on the way to their aircraft about the same time as the tankers lift off into the night sky.

The police and EMS had come to the house last night. Brian was not on duty, but after hearing about the incident he came out to check on her. He was glad she had company and things seemed to be under control. He discussed privately with Janis what was going on, but had to admit he did not know any more than she did. The man's name was Joe Edwards; he'd had some serious arrests back east, but no convictions. He was in ICU at the hospital with a fractured skull, he was still unconscious … Kenny had really teed off on him.

The drive to the airport takes time with the morning traffic. They pull into the parking area and John turns off the car.

"I'll make my calls before I head in, when is your flight home?"

"There's a flight nearly every hour I can catch, so just whenever I get there and get on."

"It's late enough now Janis is off work, so I'll call her first."

He dials her cell, she answers on the second ring, "Oh, I am so glad to hear from you … everything okay?"

"Yes, I'm fine. I have one more thing to do, but I'm at the airport about to get in the 185 and head home."

"Well, I don't know what your night was like, but mine was certainly extraordinary."

"Have some tough calls?"

"Not exactly." She explains how Trace got her to go home early, the intruder and Kenny's intervention.

He is in disbelief and John is suddenly concerned by the change in his body language. "You have got to be kidding me, I had Kenny keep an eye out sort of out of an abundance of caution … never believed they would actually go after you, especially when they thought they had me up here."

"I know. I just want you home …please."

"I'm on my way. I'm sure I'll have to make a fuel stop, I'll call then … love you!"

"Love you!"

"What happened," John asks?

He gives John the limited details he has.

John is furious, "What is with these people? She certainly never did anything and was no threat to them!"

"Principle … it's the principle."

The F-16's and F-15's taxi out of their hardened bunkers to the end of the runway. Maneuvers and practice flights are common, so there is nothing about this to raise suspicions. Each pilot pulls his jet onto the runway and pushes the throttle to the stop, flames visible out the exhaust of each engine until airborne safely where they throttle back and wait for the team to form up. As the last jet joins the group they set their course for the rendezvous point with the tankers.

He is nearly shaking with anger as he takes the number out and starts to enter the numbers. He stops for a moment and takes a few deep breaths.

"Are you going to be okay?"

"You remember hearing about that Navy Seal who heard some punks outside his house one night? He got a gun and went to investigate, some pieces of crap had beat his dog and shot it?"

"Oh, yes … he could have killed them, but he chased them down and they were arrested."

"I feel like he did, I could drive back to town and finish this."

"And you'd be in prison … I know you … you would not do well in a prison."

"I know ..." He regains his composure, finishes entering the numbers, takes a deep breath, and hits send.

"Yes?"

"I'm calling you from the grave, I've seen your future and you're going to hell."

"Who is this?"

"I'm the one you've tried four times now to kill."

"Impossible, what is this, some sort of sick joke?"

His thick accent and gruff voice sound as if he is having a stroke … good.

"No, this is no joke, I'm deadly serious …deadly serious. Now, I'm going to talk and you're going to listen." All he hears is heavy breathing, he continues, "I do not know what motivates you, it can't be money, Lord knows you have enough. I wanted to kill you … guess I still do … but I think that would be too easy for you."

"I'm not going to listen to you any more, you …"

"I really don't care if you listen or not, it will not change the wheels that are already turning."

"Wheels turning?"

"Since you had some FBI people on your side we did not know who we could trust. I have a friend who has been in state government for thirty years and he has many close friends in law enforcement and the judiciary. It seems your practices over the years have made you many enemies. A few strategic phone calls to law enforcement and a couple of judges for warrants; all the calls to you, to the motel … all recorded. And I just learned about the attempt on my wife, that poor fellow is in ICU. You are history Mr. Volar; I won't take your life … but I will help take your freedom and your power. Oh, and if you get the wild idea to come after me again and succeed … I have a number of friends who know who you are and have promised if anything happens to me that they will hunt you down … you'll always wonder who is around the next corner, who's cooking your meal. Maybe you should hire someone to make sure nothing happens to me. This was strike three for you … you're out. Goodbye Mr. Volar."

He hits the end button and looks at John

"Think he believes you?"

"He'd better, I wasn't lying."

"You mean you …"

"Yes, you know Bernie in our group?"

"Yes…"

"Well, all that is happening. Volar is a very powerful man with unlimited resources and he will not just give up. I just wanted to have some leverage, take his mind off of me, and have him looking over his shoulder."

They agree that this is without a doubt going to be the highpoint of their experiences together. They go inside; he goes to the bathroom and then pays his bill.

The same young girl is there, she runs his card and hands him the receipt, "Did you enjoy your visit?"

"It was sort of like flying, hours and hours of boredom punctuated by a few moments of sheer terror."

"Well, if it was like flying you must have had a good time … have a nice flight!"

John follows him out on the ramp and helps by untying the ropes as he does the pre-flight inspection.

He turns to his friend, "Couldn't have done it without you."

"Glad to help, you know that. I hope this is all behind us now."

"Well, one problem down …700 to go!"

"Goodbye my friend."

"Goodbye."

John walks back to the terminal area as he goes through checklists and starts the engine. He taxis out, completes checklists, rolls onto the runway. Easing the power in, he is airborne in moments. As he passes a waving John he dips his wing in return and climbs into the clear blue sky. To avoid the higher headwinds he settles in at a cruise altitude of 6,500 feet. As he works his way westward, he wonders if their life can get back to some sort of normalcy.

The rendezvous with the tankers went precisely as planned, all aircraft are topped off and ready. The flight leader verifies everyone is in the green, the mission is a go. He banks to the north, when they are "feet dry" it is about 750 kilometers to the target, about 45 minutes at cruising speed. Once drop tanks and weapons are dropped, their return will be less than half that. As they approach the southern coast, alarms sound in radar facilities. This is normal, it is a frequent occurrence, the Israelis will fly north over the gulf and at the last minute turn and depart the way they came. Tonight they do not turn. At first the operators do not believe this is actually happening, surely they will turn. They do not, and then suddenly the screens go white.

"Why is this happening on my shift," the supervisor asks himself as he picks up the phone to call his superior. The line is dead. "How can this be?" He places the handset back on the phone and lifts it again, nothing. He takes his cell phone and places the call … he gets a fast busy signal … the call will not go through. While he wonders what is happening, he is more concerned as to what will happen to him for not sending a warning.

He lands at a small municipal airport for fuel. As the line boy fuels the 185, he makes a bathroom stop and calls his wife.

"Hi honey, I'm on the ground getting fuel, I'm about three and a half hours out."

"Great, I can't hardly stand it, fly safe and I'll talk to you when you get in … I'll meet you at the airport."

"Sounds wonderful see you soon."

He pays for his fuel, grabs a soft drink and a candy bar from the machines in the terminal, and walks to the plane. Once again, through all the normal prep, and soon he is airborne. He has never been more ready to be home than he is on this trip.

The Wild Weasels in the flight are worth their weight in gold. While the electronics on board are pretty much top of the line, newest generation equipment, the Iranians are using older, nearly obsolete radar equipment. The F-16's are jamming nearly every piece of electronic equipment, for now. It is believed the radar is more sophisticated closer to the target area.

As the jets work north the coastal radars begin to work again. The supervisor tries his phone; there is a dial tone, so he places a call. Apparently, however, where he is trying to call is now jammed as he gets either busy signals or no answer at any number. He finally does get an answer at a facility in the north. This facility sounds the alarm nation-wide; although there is little doubt what the target is … if indeed there are any aircraft. Fighters are scrambled to protect the target area from above. The fighters who are flying escort pick up the Iranian fighters as they lift off; they are carrying AMRAAM missiles. These are advanced air to air combat missiles which can be locked on a target, known as a "Fire and Forget" missile; they are deadly. Success of the missile is much better at closer range … so they wait. As the Iranian fighters climb and search for possible intruders, the Israeli fighters acquire, obtain missile lock and fire. In a coordinated attack, the fighters fire at the climbing Iranians. Within minutes, all threats are terminated.

As the attack group closes on the target area, they encounter more sophisticated defenses including mobile SAM missile launchers and radar. There are too many for the Wild Weasels to eliminate, but they effectively reduce the numbers dramatically. Several SAM's streak skyward and two find their mark, eliminating two of the F-15's. This is less than the planned possible loss, so more than enough bombs will find their mark.

Target acquisition is accomplished, weapons are released and the flight turns to their escape route. External fuel tanks are dropped, now with no bombs or external tanks they are no longer speed restricted so throttles are pushed to full afterburner.

Personnel in the targeted facilities do not have a chance. With alarms sounding every effort is made to escape to secure bunkers … but nothing is secure. The air burst thermobaric warheads decimate virtually everything above ground. The five thousand pound bunker busters do just that. Capable of penetrating 20 feet of reinforced concrete or 100 feet of earth before their 630 pounds of high explosives detonate, they devastate most of the underground facilities. What is not destroyed is made unusable or inaccessible. Iran's nuclear program has been set back years.

She is cleaning up some things around the house and has put some pork chops in the oven to slow cook for supper, along with some baked potatoes. She has the TV on one of the home improvement channels when programming is interrupted. This has her attention because these shows essentially never interrupt programming for anything. The news anchor is not really prepared, but this is news of such importance perfection is less important than timeliness.

"This just in from the Pentagon, Israeli Forces have struck Iranian nuclear facilities near Qom, Iran. There has not been a statement as yet from Iran, but in the past their leader has stated any such move by Israel or the United States will bring the world to a war that will bathe the Middle East in blood."

She stands there with her mouth open. “Dear Lord, where will this lead?” she asks herself.

He is so anxious to be home. He has no idea if all this worked and if Volar will leave them alone. He is descending to enter the flight pattern of the airport as he sees her van turn off the highway and then turn and drive up to his hanger. Winds are light as he brings the big tail dragger in, a couple of sharp “barks” of the tires and he is slowed to taxi speed with minimal brakes. As he turns in front of the hanger to park on the pad just in front of the hanger doors, the first thing he notices about her, she is not smiling … she has a serious look on her face. He cuts the engine and as the prop stops he pops the door open and she runs over.

“Is there a problem,” he asks?

“Israel just bombed Iran’s nuclear facilities.”

“What has Iran done?”

“It just happened, Iran has not responded, but in the past they have warned of serious consequences if anyone attacked their country. What do you think will happen?”

“I don’t know, honey, but I’m sure nothing good will come of this.”

She helps him open the hanger, back the truck out and push the 185 inside. Normally he’d fuel it up now so it would be ready for next time, but he is ready to be home and see what is going on in the world. He did not want to scare her any more than she already is, but he is afraid this is the first domino to fall. He had hoped the country would have years to try and heal its wounds; and that the world would hold together for a few years to give the nation the time it needs. If there is worldwide chaos due to financial issues *and* military conflict … well, all bets are off.

Chapter 33

ONCE IN THE TRUCK and on his way home, he takes the pre-paid phone and calls Brian.

"Hi Mike, are you home?"

"Just landed and put the plane away, driving to the house now … you heard the news?"

"About Israel and Iran? Yes. How did things go on the trip?"

"I am hopeful, we did not have any problems and it appears Bill did his part. I'd like to get with you soon to go over all that, but mostly wanted to let you know I'm home and about the Middle East situation … this could be the start. You need to get your family and close friends prepared. Won't happen overnight, but it will happen almost without warning and probably sooner than we think."

"After talking to you about this the first time I talked to them … some think I'm nuts."

"Welcome to the club … you do what you can and move on. I'm almost to the house; I'll be here for several days and have no plans to go anywhere. Make a trip out soon so we can talk."

"You've got it … see you soon, glad you are home!"

"See you …"

They pull into the driveway, he grabs his small bag and they both go inside. He pours a Mason jar full of ice tea, takes a long drink and says, "Mmmm, I've missed that!" He tops the glass off before going into the bedroom and flipping on the TV. He props several pillows so he is nearly sitting up and changes the channel to his favorite cable news channel. She joins him after a quick trip to the bathroom.

"Information is still sketchy as the attack was just carried out in the past few hours. Iranian officials say the attack was thwarted by defensive measures; that most of the attacking aircraft were shot down and the rest fled. Officials also claim retaliation will be swift and the elimination of the Zionist State will be complete. However, officials at the Pentagon say satellite images indicate significant damage to a remote facility near the city of Qom. Israel will neither confirm nor deny any knowledge of, or participation in, any military action."

"Well," he says, "it's still early … we'll learn much more in the coming hours and days. I suppose we can hope there will be pressure from all sides on Iran to not do anything, but I fear that "nut job" of a president in Iran will use this as an excuse to do what he wants to do anyway. He's a "Twelver," believes in the "12th Imam" who will come when the world is "Awash in Blood." They believe they can hasten the return of the Imam if they can create the world situation which would bring him."

"Sort of like if we believed there might be something we could do to hasten the return of Christ?"

"That's the way I understand it. Much of the Muslim religion believes the Twelvers are kooks; at least it is not the general belief. However, if enough within Iran believe it, doesn't really matter … they hate Israel and us and will take the opportunity if they think they can legitimately attack."

"What do you think this means for us?"

"Depends of lots of variables, whether Iran has other countries that join them; remember, leadership in the Middle East has had a huge shift and change in the past year. No one really knows just who is in charge and/or pulling the strings."

"On another developing story, billionaire Jorge Volar is under investigation for involvement in conspiracy to commit murder and attempted murder. There seems to be a connection between these charges and a mysterious explosion in a seedy motel near Uptown New York City where one person was killed, however some sources said that death was from natural causes. Sources with the New York State troopers office of investigation would not confirm exactly what or who the investigation was centered on … calls to Mr. Volar's office were not returned. Mr. Volar has been widely accused of financing many entities behind the Occupy Wall Street movement, as well as other groups supporting questionable union activities, those supporting a one world government, and others."

He does not react to this news, but she looks at him and asks, "You know anything about this?"

"Maybe."

She is not amused, "You'd better tell me everything, now. I don't want to learn it in the news."

He gives her all the details and leaves nothing out.

"How did you know he'd try a bomb?"

"I didn't, but guessed it most likely. I wanted him to believe I was coming after him. He would not want to take a chance I'd get through his defenses, so figured he'd try to get me first. I tried to make it easy for him to find me, I picked the motel for several reasons; it was old and not heavily used, it was easy for us to watch for them to make some sort of move, and we felt it was not likely anyone else would be hurt."

"The report said there was a death."

"If I were to guess, it is likely the old woman who ran the place. If they said natural causes she likely had a heart attack or something when the bomb went off. I actually think those men planned to kill her anyway, no witnesses."

"You were really taking a lot of chances."

"I know, but doing nothing was not an option … you know that."

"Yes … I know …"

The next morning as they are drinking coffee they hear the guineas squawking and the dogs get nervous and start barking. They look at each other; he rises out of his chair, pulls the 45 out of its holster as he goes to the door to look outside.

"Brian," he says and holsters the weapon. "Come on in," he says opening the door.

"How are you two doing today?"

"Pretty well, considering," she responds.

Brian looks at him with a questioning expression as he says, "We're both still pretty edgy and at this point there is no way to know if my trip was entirely successful, but we are hopeful. Coffee?"

"That'd be great, thanks."

He pours Brian a mug of the dark steaming liquid and they all sit at the table.

"I could come out here every morning for coffee!"

"That'd be fine, but we might have to put out a coffee kitty!"

"That would work … now, you know why I'm here … let's hear all the gory details."

"Alright." He spends the next several minutes detailing everything he and John did and what happened, and the phone call to Volar.

"That's like a spy movie or something, pretty cool!"

"There's nothing cool about it, Brian," she quips.

"I've had to use humor to get through this, but Janis does not appreciate that sometimes … and I understand why."

"Yes, sorry Janis."

"Not your fault, not anybody's fault … it just hits me wrong sometimes. I lost one husband and the thought of losing another to anything but old age …"

"Not to change the subject, but what about the Israel/Iran thing," Brian asks.

"Honestly, I have not even turned on the TV this morning … maybe we should see if there is anything new."

Chapter 34

DEEP IN A BUNKER near Tehran the Supreme Leader, the President, and several generals are in a heated meeting. The Supreme Leader, as usual, sits quietly and listens. Also as is usual, the President is in a tirade, worked up to the point spittle is at the corner of his mouth and bits on his shirt … as a rabid dog might look. The generals try to diffuse some the attacks, but to no avail. It is their fault the Zionists were successful? They think, "Is it our fault we have first generation equipment to defend ourselves against third generation weapons?" To say this aloud would be certain suicide, they walk a thin line between life and death. This little man is very dangerous, to cross him is to cross the Supreme Leader … unless the Leader will say or do something to give them hope. As it looks now, the expectation for them is to plan an attack on the Jewish nation. Whether to win or hasten the return of the 12th Imam is unclear, and likely it will not matter.

Behind the scenes, representatives from the various nations in the area are taking sides and weighing the options. In the past, Israel and the U.S. were solid allies and there would be no question as to where those lines would be drawn. However, now it is unclear if the U.S. will back Israel, Iran, or just sit back. Countries that would never cross the US out of fear, no longer have that to fear. Egypt and Tunisia come out in support of Iran straight away. Saudi Arabia is being very careful, they quietly allowed the Israeli attack over flight rights and also rely on the US for protection, but outwardly do not want to anger fellow Muslims and Arabs. Lebanon, Jordan, and Syria are more or less forced to ally with Iran due to the influence of Hezbollah and Hamas. This leaves Israel with the Mediterranean to the West, and countries bent on revenge and destruction on all other sides. Add the oil fields to the mix which are operated largely by Western oil companies, and suddenly the world economy is also in the mix.

He turns on the TV in the kitchen and the three of them sit in silence, sipping their coffee and watching the updates to the events in Iran. In the latest sweeps of the satellite, the photos show nearly complete devastation to the area widely believed to house the Iranian's nuclear facilities. Smoldering fires linger amidst the rubble, rescue personnel with heavy equipment lifting and moving remnants of buildings looking for any survivors. Speaking through interpreters a government spokesman bemoans the fact that all the Zionist bombs missed their intended target, what was leveled here was factories, schools, Mosques and houses. He evidentially is unaware that the viewers just watched before-shots clearly showing military vehicles carrying equipment, supplies and personnel.

Next is a round of pundits, each with their opinion on how Iran will respond, who will support Israel, what this means to the world in general. The ideas range from nothing to World War III.

"Well, that nails it down, doesn't it? I don't know anything about that part of the world and I could guess that close," Brian says.

"Yes, you have to sort of ignore what they say and look at each country, what they have to gain or lose, look at history … and then it is still a guess … too much volatility," he says.

She adds, "I'll wait until it is over, then tell you what happened."

"Thanks! I know what we will do … prepare for the worst …"

"And hope for the best," she finishes.

Brian says, "I had one more reason for coming out this morning."

"What's that," he asks?

"The charges against those two we caught out here were reduced and they made bail, they got out this morning."

"What? You're kidding aren't you," she asks?

"Well, you need to understand the whole story. Mike here talked to one of them and he helped with the operation back in New York. We talked to the DA and he agreed if things went well in New York and they helped, then charges would be reduced. Mike, Bill gave me this to give you."

Brian hands him an envelope.

He opens the envelope and reads aloud, "Mike, if you are reading this, it means things went well for you on your mission. I want to apologize again for what we did, I know we still will have to pay a price, but thanks to you that price will be more bearable. Thanks for all you are doing for our nation, I hope I can help in some way and try to make up for some of what we have done. I look forward to that visit on your deck. Sincerely, Bill." "Well, that was nice. I certainly hope he is sincere, it is obvious he helped me, I hope that bunch does not go after him now."

Brian says, "I guess time will tell; I need to leave. Thanks for the coffee and I'll be in touch, I'll probably need to get some tips from you as to just what I should be doing to prepare."

"I'd be glad to help, let's get together again soon."

They both get busy with morning chores. He is back inside first and pours himself another cup of coffee and sits down with his laptop.

"She comes in and asks, "Watcha doin'?"

"Well, checking email real quick then thought I ought to try and put together a meeting with the group. I think maybe we should expand our focus some. There are lots of people out there who would not have a clue as to how to make it if there is a major crash. This has me worried; we will survive just fine, but think of the chaos in the major cities ..."

"I can't imagine ... is it safe for you to contact them like this and have a meeting where *they* might eavesdrop?"

"Thanks, good point ... I guess I am feeling a little over-confident. Better to keep this under the radar just in case. I'll send an overnight letter and have everyone get a pre-paid cell to use, and then maybe we can just set up a regular time to get together."

"That makes me feel better."

He writes the letters and puts them in the envelopes. It is not urgent they go out today; he needs some materials for a project. Hopefully he can figure up a list and do both jobs with one trip. This is something he has put off for quite a while, there just is never enough spare time.

"I'm going out to the shop for a while."

"Okay, I'll be up in the loft sewing."

Once in the shop he pulls out the plans he'd printed out what, six or eight months ago? They had discussed putting up a greenhouse for years, there was just always someplace else in greater need of the funds or the time required. He has never been one to buy something he could build. This greenhouse will be somewhat unique; a geodesic dome. The neat thing about this design, it is strong, simple, and can be made any size. His plan is to build a forty foot diameter yielding about 1,260 square-feet of floor space. Using simple shelves can yield nearly 2,000 square-feet of growing space. He compares the total amount of 2x4's he will need to what he has on hand.

Back in the house she asks, "What were you doing in the shop?"

"Decided I ought to get that greenhouse built sooner rather than later; had to figure how many two-by-four's I would have to buy."

"Oh, that's great. I've been hoping we could have one by next spring."

"I am going to build it so it will be used year round. It will stay above freezing even in winter so we will be able to have fresh vegetables all year."

"Will it be heated?"

"Yes, by the sun."

"What about night time, won't it freeze? It is sometimes below zero, I don't understand," she says.

"It is fairly simple actually. The material covering the dome will let the light through, but is also acts as an insulation to hold heat. There will be a tank of water inside, it will be painted black. During the day the water will heat up and at night that heat will be released into the surrounding air. We won't be able to grow normal summer vegetables during winter, but spring and fall plants; root vegetables, and many of the leafy things like lettuce and cabbage."

"Wow, I always thought we'd have to heat a greenhouse to have things through the winter. This is exciting!"

It takes him a couple of days to cut all the 2x4's to length and the ends to the proper angles. There is a company that makes metal brackets to hold the ends together making the structure stronger; they can be nailed or screwed together, but sometimes a split in the wood near the end can leave a significant weak point. They are not very expensive so he ordered them and the plastic covering online. The cover is the same thing commercial greenhouses use; it has a better insulation quality than just clear plastic sheeting, and it is also UV resistant; it will last much longer in the intense sunlight of the plains. After the last board is cut, he arranges them in a neat stack in the shop and goes to the house.

"How is it going out there?" she asks.

"I just found the board I'd been looking for the past two days."

"The last one?"

"That's it. Sure takes time to get them right; each end is a compound cut so the miter saw has two different angles to cut on each end. I messed up a couple of times and had to scrap a couple, but all in all it went fairly well."

"How long will it take for you to put it all together? "Not sure, I'm sure there is a learning curve doing that just as there was in cutting the ends. I'll have to wait for those brackets to come in before I can start fastening them together, but I can get the site ready. Probably get that finished yet today."

"You taking a break now?"

"Thought I would. I'm going to get a glass and watch the news a bit, haven't really seen anything all day, you?"

"No, haven't been in one place long enough; I'll join you."

They both fill glasses with tea and settle into the black leather sofa and he turns on the TV. A commercial for an online dating service is on as the TV comes on.

"Maybe I should try that some time … ouch!" She jabs him in the ribs with an elbow. "You keep punching me like that and I might."

"Sure you will … you'd miss me; and you'd never find anyone as good as me … at least not who'd also put up with you," she grins.

"I'm sure that's true …"

The commercial is over and the news anchor begins the next segment. The report is on next year's presidential election and the run up to the primary season. They watch in silence for several minutes until the next commercial break.

"That's odd," she says, "I thought there would be some mention of the Middle East situation."

"Maybe there will be something after the commercial. I remember when I first was able to vote, there was never much mention of the presidential race until the conventions. Now the election begins almost as soon as the last one is over. Gets pretty old by the time it arrives."

"I sure get tired of it. I suppose in a way it is not all bad, at least there are no surprises by the time we have the actual election."

As the break ends the anchor is covering a story of a young mother who called 911 as two men tried to break into her home. She had a small child … and a shotgun. The men broke the door in, one had a knife and met a shotgun blast at close range …his partner fled the scene. He was caught a short time later, the one that was shot is pronounced dead at the scene.

"At least she was prepared; I can't imagine having that happen with your child right there. She must have been terrified."

He replies, "I'm sure she was.

They watch a while longer, but there is no mention of the Middle East situation.

"This is worse than hearing something awful is going on over there," she says.

“I agree. I can hardly believe they don’t have a bunch of pundits sitting around a table telling us every possible scenario.”

Chapter 35

ON THE OTHER SIDE of the world there is a discussion as to all possible scenarios, but it is by the leaders of the various countries involved. Directly, it is just Iran and Israel; indirectly, however, every Arab and Muslim country is and will be affected. American's have been short changed in their education. Most are unaware of the root of the word from which the former Persia gets the name Iran … Aryan. Originally a linguistic difference between Aryan and Semitic, we now recognize this has been taken to a different level since the Nazis and Hitler. Bottom line, it is like oil and water.

The whole nation of Israel has been on high alert since the attack. They do not wonder if there will be retaliation, just when and how much. Their nation is under constant threat by crude rockets fired at them daily even on a good day; this will be organized and relentless. They felt backed into a corner; the U.S. was not a dependable ally and if Iran obtained a nuclear weapon it was just a matter of time before a device was delivered killing millions; best to strike the first blow and then try to control the retaliation as much as possible.

What on the outside might appear to be a problem for Israel; the change of governments in Egypt, Tunisia and Lybia to more Islamic and extremist regimes, may turn to their favor. Little is known as to just who or what controls these new governments, the fact they are new and in disarray plays to Israel's advantage. They have no organized military machine, no hierarchy of military leadership, and their governments have no experience in anything other than overthrowing a government from within.

The president of Iran has had little sleep since the attack, primarily due to the rage that is seething within. He says to himself, "It is I who will bring forth the 12th Imam … it is I who will destroy the "Little Satan" dogs." How dare they take his precious plan and turn it upside down? The Supreme Leader has been patient, but he must be very careful. He will be the "fall guy" if things do not go well. He may give the orders and hold the power of life or death over the generals, but he can and will be replaced if he makes the Supreme Leader look bad or if Israel comes out on top. "Most of the world hates the Semitic dogs; there is no way they will win this conflict."

Sitting in a penthouse suite in an undisclosed location outside the US, Jorge Volar sits pensively as he looks out over the lights of the city below. Not one who answers questions from anyone, he left the country soon after receiving the phone call from Mike. He had been furious and was still quite angry, but he had learned years ago to not do things in haste when angry. "Always best to give things a little time and deal with them after careful consideration." He will take care of this fellow who has complicated things in time; first he has to do some damage control.

There are a number of companies that offer free conference calling and there is one he has used for years for various things, including the group for the project. When he sent the letters for the next meeting he gave them the info for a new conference line with a different company, just to add a little extra security. With the time for the call approaching, he turns on his pre-paid cell and goes out on the deck. It is a nice evening for this time of year and the coverage is better outside the oak log walls anyway.

He dials the number; it is a few minutes early so no one is on. He listens to the elevator music until there is a chime and, "Brenda" is heard on the line. "Evening, Bren … how are you tonight?"

"I'm great, how about you?"

"Doing well, thank you. When are you and John coming to see us?"

"You know, we were talking about that the other day. We want to take a road trip this coming summer, coming to see you and Janis is on the list."

"Awesome, looking forward to it!"

Suddenly everyone else is coming on at once. John, Keith, Knut, John, and Bernie all check in.

"Glad you all made it. Sorry for the cloak and dagger routine, but with all I've been through I'd rather be safe than sorry."

Bernie says, "I don't think any of us would blame you after all you've been through."

"That's right," says Keith. "Whatever it takes is fine with me."

There are multiple voices of agreement.

"Thanks everyone, let's get started. I'm afraid the reason for this call is a possible complication due to the attack in Iran."

Professor John asks, "Why would that affect us directly, or indirectly for that matter?"

"Well, I may be a little goosey or overly cautious, but I see a scenario of a "Perfect Storm" of sorts that could lead to some serious consequences in America."

His pilot buddy John says, "You have my attention now."

"First off, all of your efforts have been wildly successful; beyond my expectations for sure … you are all to be commended for your hard work and success. This leads to the first problem; with your success comes the chance the people behind the scenes will do something to try and stop the trend in some way. This could come in a push of violence or something to create a crisis."

"Why would someone do that," Brenda asks?

"Money and control … and ultimately, power. Remember, we will not understand these people because we do not think like they do.

"That's for sure," Bernie says.

"Now, throw in the situation in the Middle East and even in Europe, I'm afraid we are in for serious times."

"Wasn't the whole idea of our projects to prevent this from happening? Does this mean our efforts are a waste of time?"

"Oh, no … never. Your work will be vital to survival. The foundation you all have built will be the basis for everything. I just think we need to add another element to our plan. If things melt down in the Middle East and oil supplies are disrupted, we could see serious shortages and huge spikes in price. Europe is a mess, this could be the end of the Euro as a currency and several countries could fail."

"As you said, a Perfect Storm." This from Professor John.

"Unfortunately."

"So what can we do to stop this? Seems impossible!" says Keith.

"We can't stop it, no one can. If things happen separately, so each problem has some time to be dealt with, we might slide through without serious consequences; but then there's Murphy's Law. What we can do is help people prepare and survive. As I said, your projects have laid the groundwork; people are thinking about the future, helping others, getting back to our founding principles. We just need to add some things; bartering principles, growing food, hunting, investing in silver or gold and things along these lines. Most people in rural areas already live like this and these things come naturally, but city dwellers will need help."

There are a few moments of silence as this soaks in, and then Brenda speaks. "I can see this fitting nicely with the Mom Project. We're already teaching people to educate their children, get by on less, change priorities. I've been thinking about adding some recipes for homemade laundry soap and other ideas to save, so this would be easy to incorporate."

From Bernie, "I can see easy ways to incorporate gardening and other basic principles in our efforts.

The others voice similar sentiments and he says, "Excellent, I was sure you could see ways to make this work. We may be too late to fully prepare people, but it is never too late to do the right things. Most of us in this country have grown used to having enough money we take the easy and lazy route. I remember my dad talking about the Great Depression; he was raised on a dirt farm. The family was largely self-sufficient, they bartered and traded for things they did not have. They did not know the Depression existed, it was life as usual … it was the cities that suffered deeply … It will be similar this time, except many in rural areas have become lazy as well; and not so many live in the country as they did in the Thirties."

"I hope you are wrong about this," says Professor John, "but I'd say we have no choice but to take action and do what we can … it will not be a wasted effort regardless."

"Oh, I hope and pray I am wrong …nothing would make me feel better than to be wrong about this."

A few more brief comments as to how to move forward, but everyone is onboard with the ideas and agree it should be incorporated. They sign off and he walks from the deck back inside.

"How did the call go?" she asks.

"Very well … everyone agrees this is a good thing and is making plans to incorporate more survival ideas into their programs."

"Did you have any doubts they would accept it?"

"No, not one."

Chapter 36

THE NEXT SEVERAL WEEKS go by; he leaves for his trips and returns home, she does her 24-hour shift every third day. The greenhouse is completed, seeds planted for the garden in the spring. Amazingly, nothing has happened in the Middle East … this baffles him. There have been threats, saber rattling, and then nothing. Europe is experiencing some serious setbacks economically, Germany is holding things together … for now. In America the "Occupy Wall Street" protests have fallen to a few camps in major cities, including Washington D.C., but it is just a presence and few take notice. Likely the winter weather has kept the numbers low.

The timing was good for the projects to include more basic training. People seem to like having more control over their personal destiny and it has been liberating for many. The one thing people notice is the inflation. The government reports inflation is not a problem; it is at historic lows. The people are not so blind as to fall for this … they see their paychecks just do not make it as far as they did. Looking at how the reports are made; food and energy are viewed as "too volatile" and are not included. Whether they are trying to avoid a panic, or just lying, it is more evidence of a government that is not "Of the people, by the people and for the people."

The people should be educated and allowed, even taught to prepare. Keeping the people in the dark serves the politicians; the people will look to them for help. They are sheep headed to slaughter looking to the packing-plant processor to save them. "Come this way …"

Knut's project to oust sitting politicians and replace them with constitution-loving people with business experience is having a serious effect. While the presidential primary season is in full swing, the project is not involved at that level but at the U.S. Senate and Congress and the state and local level. Luckily there are those who are willing to set their lives aside for a time and answer the call; motivated only by a sense of national duty and pride. There are some districts where entrenched incumbents are safe, however even some of them have announced retirement; seems they do not relish taking a chance on being in the minority. And being in the minority is not all; it is being tied to all that has become so unpopular.

This of course leads some to try and conceal their true motives; wolves in sheep's clothing as it were. Luckily, with the internet it is easy to research a person's history and see just who or what they are. It is one thing to learn from your mistakes and change … it is quite another to try and hide your true colors. The latter is a trait held by far too many politicians.

He can almost sense a change in the country's mood. It is hard to put a finger on anything in particular; it is probably dozens of little things. Looking at the day to day news and events there are just hints; possibly because of the tendency to report largely negative things. However, there are occasional reports that make it very clear the various projects around the country are having an effect, plus the reports he receives from time to time. In some ways the best clues might be the unease he senses from the "other side." Occasionally, their verbal attacks go off the rails … a sure sign of desperation.

One such example he just heard on the news. A year ago a mentally disturbed young man went on a shooting spree in a southwest city, killing several and seriously injuring many, including a loved politician. At the time there were immediate accusations of it being a right-wing extremist tied to the Tea Party movement. Quickly, however, it was learned this nut had zero ties to any political groups, he was simply mentally ill. Of course, don't let a crisis go to waste. Cast blame, insert doubt in people's minds. Over time these claims died out due to lack of evidence, until today. Seems the chair of the Democratic Party has decided this is a wedge she can drive in; blaming the

Tea Party for a "change in tone," and making their opposition "the enemy." "These things lead people to take extreme measures and lead people to do violence such as happened when my friend and colleague was shot last year."

Saying such things is very volatile; bells cannot be "unrung." If someone in a community is accused of being a child molester … and then later it is discovered the accusations were false, the person was not even charged. There is a lingering doubt in many people's minds; some will whisper, wonder and in many people's minds even regard them to be guilty. The planted idea that the Tea Party members might foment or condone such actions is a hard obstacle to overcome. Such are the tactics of progressives.

Computers can be wonderful things. Tied to the Internet, research is no longer camped in a library and looking at encyclopedias and microfiche … and no longer takes days. They can also be a tremendous thief of time … if someone allows it. He is very aware of this and has a tendency to stay away from it maybe more than he should. Today he plans to do some research, just for his own education. It is unfortunate the media has agendas and reports in a way that skews the news. Going to original sources takes time, but is the only real way to learn the truth.

He sits at his desk in the small office and fires up the desktop. As it comes to life he takes a long drink of iced tea, and with a satisfied sound begins the keystrokes to start up the search engine. It does not take long to find that Mr. Volar has not disappeared from the scene, not that this was expected. Volar strikes him as one who does not get mad, but gets even. He knows his life will likely be at risk again one day, he just hopes to have the time to see America back on track. His one hope is that enough people know about him and there is evidence of Volar's involvement. Volar might be forced to just let it go and write this one off.

One report catches his eye right off the bat. The current administration has become nearly a dictatorship; using regulations to control business and activities. While stopping oil companies from offshore oil exploration and with the nation swimming in red ink, they have given Brazil several billion dollars to help their offshore exploration efforts … a key investor in the Brazilian company? Jorge Volar.

Another report is on the U.S. sending troops to the African country of Uganda. “Why are we doing this?” he thinks to himself. It seems there is a fledgling oil industry in the nation and we are sending troops to help protect the oil interests, to insure the free flow of oil to the world. The company that owns most of the exploration has an interesting investor … Mr. Volar.

An investigative reporter has made literally dozens of connections between government agencies, officials and non-profit organizations, and Volar. All this affecting energy prices and politics; Volar buys influence to get what he wants. The more he gets, the more he makes. The more he makes, the more influence he has … it never ends.

Capitalism and free markets are wonderful things and he believes deeply in them. People risk capital and life to not only to make money, but to make lives and country better. Are there some who take advantage of this and hurt people in the process? Of course, but is it a free market when some get special access, guaranteed advantages? Hardly, and Mr. Volar is apparently one of those … one who then uses some of the billions earned to “grease the skids” and make inroads to get more and more. He thinks to himself, “It is great to have this guy on your side as long as you get some of the gravy, but no one will control him and when someone’s usefulness is over, so is that relationship.” “This is why virtue is so vital to our nations’ survival, especially in government,” he thinks aloud.

He shifts his searches to another topic. National security is as much military as it is policy and how you are viewed by the rest of the world. He remembers a trip to Romania and learning much of the gypsy’s lives and customs. He was told, “If you have a ladder in your back yard, the gypsies will believe you have given him permission to take it unless you put a chain and lock on it. They would never cut a lock off, which would be stealing." Okay, we view that as crazy … but it is the rule they live by and if you are in that country and want to keep your ladder, live by the rule. This is what many do not understand about dealing with the world … not every country lives by the same rules … what makes sense to us seems nuts to others, and vice versa. What we do might make perfect sense and be a friendly gesture, but to another might be provocative or show weakness … you have to know the rules.

This is a case where our government is one of two things; stupid or devious. Our behavior with allies has put distance between countries historically close, and has caused countries that have and should fear us to become bold and do things previously thought impossible. Europe and Israel do not know what we might do; our messages and signals are confusing. North Korea, the Middle East and even Venezuela in our hemisphere treat us with disdain and contempt. He does not think we need to worry about what our enemies think of us as long as they are terrified of us and believe we are capable of anything. This is why President Reagan was so successful, most foreign leaders thought him a bit crazy and that he might do something just for amusement; they were not about to set him off to find out.

For some reason when there was an apparent revolution brewing in Iran, the administration stayed on the sideline, said nothing and let the government squash the peaceful movement with violence and death. Just as mystifying was their sudden interest and involvement in Egypt and Libya's overthrow of their government which was not peaceful, in fact we sent personnel and equipment. All this added to the uncertainty … not only by foreign leaders, but by U.S. citizens as well.

He understood the reason the U.S. went into Iraq and Afghanistan, but not why we are still there ten years later. Did we learn nothing from Viet Nam? The military's job is to kill people and break things; not spread democracy, not build schools, not protect women's rights. When we try to "make Americans" in other countries we are doomed to fail. We are not feared in the world, we are hated and not trusted. This is not how our founder's envisioned our place in the world.

Iran's president has not lost any of his rage, but he has controlled his temper and the way he has been viewed in the eyes of the Supreme Leader; and he is about to be rewarded for his control and patience. The meeting has gone well; reports of preparedness by the generals, plans for the attack, missiles, aircraft, warships, tanks and artillery, and soldiers. At the conclusion of the last briefing, the President looks at the Supreme Leader and is rewarded with a slight nod of approval. He can barely control his elation; at last he will be able to claim credit for ridding the world of the Little Satan and beginning of the next Caliphate. He will be revered in the annals of history for his accomplishments; the embarrassment at the hands of the Israeli dogs will turn into a glorious triumph.

The de facto leaders of Egypt and Libya along with Jordan, Lebanon and Syria are meeting. Syria has been at odds with Israel since the beginning of time and they are anxious to participate in any way possible. They have their eyes on some of the most fertile land in the region and the elimination of the Jewish State will cause no tears on their side of the border. Egypt had lived at peace with Israel since a treaty was signed in 1979; however that treaty was rejected by the new leadership after the revolution. They have no love of the Jews, but they have no money and no army. They can only give moral support. Libya is in a similar situation and can only offer some financial help now that they control the substantial oil resources in the country. Lebanon is heavily influenced by Hezbollah and is eager to join in the fight. Jordan is a very stable country and has lived under a treaty with Israel since 1994. While they see the formidable power of Iran and the potential for Israel's destruction, they are well aware of Israel's abilities militarily and are inclined to hold their cards close to the vest participating only peripherally.

Iran's president tempers his disappointment after receiving a call from Syria's president. He had hoped to have full cooperation from the countries surrounding Israel. Iraq is no help. While they dislike the Jews as well, the tensions of Iran's meddling in Iraq while the US was fully engaged there and before that, the Iraq/Iran war that raged for 10 years, participation is not going to happen and cooperation is going to be very limited; over flight authority and some overland transportation. It will have to do.

Israel has not let down her guard, not for a minute. And beyond just being prepared, they are keeping watch. For a small country, Israel has one of the largest intelligence organizations in the world … and also one of the most effective. In addition to information from satellite images, they have eyes and ears on the ground. The buildup of personnel and equipment does not escape notice.

Officials with the Pentagon, NSA (National Security Agency) and CIA are reviewing photos and intelligence data from the Middle East. They had been surprised something had not happened sooner, but now their expectations are being realized. Information is sketchy at best from Egypt and Libya, and as far as that is concerned, from Israel. Israel is wary of the administration and has no desire to share her plans until the last moment. The people in the room are well aware of this and are forced to just roll with things. They have no more idea than Israel what the U.S. might do, but then their job is to take intelligence data and deliver it with a recommendation; the final decision is not theirs. Israel has been in defensive positions ever since the initial attack, nothing has changed there. It was expected Iran would likely fire some missiles in retaliation, but nothing happened; nothing until now. The Iranians are amassing troops, equipment and supplies near their western border. Additionally the navy is moving assets in the direction of the Strait of Hormuz, the vital shipping corridor between the Persian Gulf and the Gulf of Oman; 35 percent of all seaborne oil shipped worldwide goes through this 34-mile wide strait. The senior representative from the Pentagon lifts the phone receiver from its cradle and pushes an auto-dial button.

"Yes?"

"We have a situation developing."

"I'll be right there."

In Europe, the situation is much different, but no less dangerous. For years the European countries had been the shinning success stories of Marxists and socialists; proof that centralized governments controlling every aspect of people's lives was the ideal way of life. Free healthcare, free higher education, pensions, housing assistance, guaranteed vacations and other job perks are all accepted as rights. The problem, as Margaret Thatcher once said, "The trouble with socialism is that eventually you run out of other people's money." They never would have lasted this long except for the U.S.; military spending by European nations is at a bare minimum as the U.S. foots the bill for worldwide security. The chickens have come home to roost, as the saying goes. All good things must come to an end. The debt has been piling up for years, and with the worldwide recession tax revenues have plummeted making a bad situation worse. No one wants to be the one to admit the emperor has no clothes. Greece is the worst and its credit rating was downgraded months ago, however overnight Spain, Portugal, Italy and France are downgraded as well. This sends shockwaves throughout the world; the U.S. and the IMF announce they will take measures to avoid a collapse of the Euro; but everyone is operating on borrowed money. It is a house of cards that is sure to collapse; it is just a matter of time.

Mr. Volar welcomes the news of Europe's plight. He has been involved in the collapse of several currencies over the years, actually playing a vital role in their demise. He sees all the signs and knows just how to position himself to profit and with billions on hand with which to speculate, an enormous windfall is essentially guaranteed. His wealth is not tied to any currency, it is tied to gold. He picks up the phone and places a few calls. Nothing wrong with making sure the failure of the Euro is assured, at least in his mind. He has done this before and knows just what to do.

Chapter 37

HE IS LISTENING TO the radio while working in his office and hears something that makes him stop and listen closely. One of the presidential candidates is at a local gathering prior to one of the early primaries. A man asks this potential president about his understanding of the constitution compared to one of his rivals.

In response to the question the candidate says, "The Constitution has to be read in the context of another founding document, and that's the Declaration of Independence. Our country never was a libertarian idea of radical individualism. We have certain values and principles that are embodied in our country. We have God-given rights.

The Constitution is not the 'why' of America; it's the 'how' of America. It's the operator's manual. It's the rules we have to play by to ensure something. And what do we ensure? God-given rights; and so to read the Constitution as the end-all be-all is, in a sense, what happened in France. You see, during the time of our revolution, we had a Declaration of Independence that said *We hold these truths to be self-evident, that all men are created equal, [that they are] endowed by their Creator with certain unalienable rights, that among these are life, liberty and the pursuit of happiness.*"

The candidate continues, "So we were founded as a country that had God-given rights that the government had to respect? And with those rights come responsibilities, right? God did not just give us rights. He gave us a moral code by which to exercise them."

"See, that's what my opponent sort of leaves out. He leaves out rights and responsibilities that we have from God that this Constitution is to protect. And my opponent says, *No, we just have rights, and then that's it.* No, we don't. America is a moral enterprise …"

"My understanding of our founding documents and the purpose of this country is different. I would argue that *his* understanding of the Constitution was similar to the French Revolution and the French understanding of the Constitution. The French had 21, I think, constitutions, but their constitutions were initially patterned after the American Constitution. It gave radical freedom, like ours does. But their founding document was not the Declaration of Independence. Their founding watchwords were the words, "liberty" and "fraternity." Fraternity, brotherhood, but no fatherhood; no God. It was a completely secular revolution; an anti-clerical revolution. And the root of it was whoever's in power rules."

"Wow," he says aloud. "I've never heard a politician have an understanding of the constitution like that." He is suddenly buoyed by the prospect someone like this has stepped forward to run for president. Politics in America have become a blood sport; good men seldom will attempt a run at the highest office in the land lest they be pilloried by the media and their opponents. Character is vital, and no one is perfect; but just as Jesus was falsely accused so are good people who dare upset the status quo. Charges of improper associations with women seem to be a popular way to take down a candidate, and this year is no exception. Charges are made, it becomes a "he said, she said" scenario … no proof is offered or needed … once the bell has been rung it is impossible to "unring" it. He hopes and prays this man will make it through the gauntlet of attacks; the country needs him.

After joining the assembled group and being briefed by the senior Pentagon official, the President's Chief of Staff asks, "What will be their first move, and when do you think it will happen?"

A general replies, “We are dealing with people who have a history of being unpredictable, and Iran’s president is very narcissistic and unstable. That being said, our best guess is the first move will be in the Strait of Hormuz in an attempt to shut down oil shipping.”

“Why would they do that? Israel will not be affected much by that.”

“It will have a dual purpose; we and our allies will have to respond to keep the flow of oil going, it will take resources … and it will help to shift attention away from the coming attack. Iran’s navy is not significant compared to what the rest of the world has, but with mines and using speed boats to harass it will be like bees swarming a bear … an irritation, but not a fatal blow.”

“What happens next?

“Most likely they will fire some missiles, their air force is not much of a threat, but they will attempt to soften the defenses before making a full ground assault.”

“What are the odds Iran will be successful?”

“Normally I’d say Israel would have little trouble defending itself, but this is not the same as in previous wars that lasted only days; things are different now. Israel historically has not had to deal with a country such as Iran. Egypt has never had the power of Iran, and Syria has a smaller military, but more militia type personnel as is Lebanon.”

“Who will help Iran?”

“Egypt and Libya are still in disarray from their revolutions and cannot participate in any meaningful way. Sources say Jordan is not too keen on becoming involved; they have a good relationship with Israel and do not want to jeopardize that, especially if Israel were to win. So, it appears Iran, Lebanon and Syria will coordinate. They have the equipment and manpower to overwhelm Israel …”

“But?”

“Well, Israel fights like no country you’ve ever seen; tactically they are far superior, but the sheer numbers might be too much to overcome, and that gives us cause for serious concern.”

“You think Israel might lose?”

"Sir, you don't understand. Israel will not lose, at least not militarily. They have nuclear weapons; before they are overrun, they will use them."

The Chief of Staff lets that sink in, "Dear Lord, what would happen then?"

"We are in uncharted waters here, but it will have worldwide ramifications."

Europe is dead, but does not yet realize it. He remembers over the years seeing examples of this in real life; the chicken with its head cut off running across the yard, a snake with its head missing yet striking at imagined threats, even businesses that had failed but refused to see the reality of the situation. Europe is probably a cross between the chicken and the business; running day by day as if everything is wonderful. Some of the people know, but under their system there is nothing the people can do.

He has a friend in France, Christine. She is originally from Germany, but lives and works in the southeastern part of the country. They are in contact from time to time and she is worried. She knows the government is lying about the debt and the dire situation; she knows it is bad, but just not how bad. She and her husband live as simply as they can, canning vegetables, making jams and jellies. They are not just frugal, they are preparing. They are too young to remember WWII, but their parents lived through it and made an impression on being ready for tough times.

Germany has by far the best economy in Europe, but it is not good enough to save all of Europe. The idea of the 17 countries leaving individual currencies and joining in the "Euro Zone" seemed a good idea at the time it was formed. He thought it an effort to compete with the US, but it was to compete on a global scale. They gained the strength of the unified group, but each gave up some of their sovereignty and their individual currencies; thus losing their identity…and the weak are dragging the strong down with them.

Greece and Portugal are already essentially bankrupt. The rest of Europe and the IMF have poured money into the hole with little hope of doing anything but delaying the inevitable, in a way as a severely injured patient receives units of blood yet nothing is done to repair the damage and stop the bleeding. Several of the countries have allowed mass immigration, mostly from Muslim countries, and allowed them to live as if in their home country, even under their home countries laws. With no assimilation into their new country, there is no allegiance felt or given. This will prove to be a serious mistake.

The European social experiment is a colossal failure, yet the efforts in America to move in that direction is unabated. The progressive idea of Utopia is a long held goal, an unattainable one. Most Christians realize there was once a Utopia; the Garden of Eden. No type of government is perfect, some are better than others … much better. Some view capitalists as evil and greedy, and some are. He agrees with many that a number of politicians are evil and greedy. The big difference being; a CEO might cheat you, be a poor employer or sell an inferior product … even pollute the air and water … a politician can pass laws which control your life, confiscate your money, infringe on your rights…he'd rather deal with the CEO.

Europe's cradle to grave entitlement system is making her demise like a slow motion train wreck. Germany has become weaker as she has tried in vain to stop or slow the process, and the countries that do fail weaken the group. Next will be Italy and Spain, then France and England. As the dominos fall with economies in shambles, citizens who have come to depend on the largess of the more prosperous will turn on their benefactors. Riots, death and destruction loom on the horizon. Two entities will be ready to pick the bones in the aftermath; Middle Eastern regimes with their Caliphate, and Jorge Volar.

Iran's president tries to look calm and cool as he prepares to launch the attack; inwardly he is doing back flips. This is the moment he has waited for, ever since … ever since he was part of the group who took the U.S. Embassy hostage during the Carter administration. He has the honor of launching the first missile, but dozens others are on their rails awaiting the impulse that will send them hurtling toward Israel.

The SCUD missile was made famous during Desert Storm, the first Iraq war with the US as Saddam Hussein Launched them toward Israel. They are little more than glorified "bottle rockets," the ones kids fire off on the Fourth of July. There is no guidance system, only a general aiming using basic elevation and windage. Once fired there is no way either guide it or destroy it should the missile go astray.

Iran's version is an improved version … the only improvement being increased range and a little larger warhead. Winds aloft can and do have a dramatic effect on accuracy … or lack thereof. Prevailing winds in this part of the world are west to east as it is in the United States. Timing is not good for this missile launch as the winds are stronger than normal at altitude, blowing from the southwest. They will significantly reduce the range and push the eventual landing northward. The missile commanders try to compensate, but it is only an educated guess.

"Sir, all missiles are ready, the range is clear. We are ready to fire on your command," this from the missile commander.

He has waited for this moment his entire life. He now has the chance to rid the world of the Israeli dogs and hasten the return of the 12th Imam, he closes his eyes and says a silent prayer and pushes the launch button. "Allahu Akbar! Complete the sequence please."

"Yes sir, thank you sir." The commander then begins the sequence of launching the remaining SCUD missiles. It will take a few hours as missiles are launched and the launcher is reloaded and the process begins again. The attack is underway.

In a bunker in Israel a young lady is intently watching live satellite feed when she sees the obvious bright flash of a missile launch inside western Iran. She keys her mic and announces, "Missile launch." After her initial report she again sees the flash, "Multiple missiles launched," she reports.

After so many years of attacks and wars fought, Israel is more prepared than any other nation in the world, both the military and the civilians. Within a few seconds of the initial missile launch, a signal is sent throughout the entire country.

Sirens blare, it is never a drill. Military personal move into action, civilians scurry to shelters.

In the Situation Room beneath the White House alarms are sounding. The U.S. has sophisticated imaging equipment that recognizes a missile launch and highlights the launch area.

"What do we have?" asks a senior Pentagon official.

"Multiple missiles fired from western Iran, appear to be heading for Israel."

"How much time before they hit Israel?"

"About fifteen minutes for the first one to hit."

"I'll tell the President, dear lord ... where will this lead?"

In the bunker containing the missile control and radar tracking equipment, the missile commander is nervously watching the missiles as they streak up to their apogee. Once their fuel is spent the SCUD is much like a rock falling to earth, only much more deadly. Their trajectory was not quite what he'd planned; they did not go as far down range as they needed and are a little to the north.

The President asks, "How much longer?"

"Just a few more minutes, sir."

"Are they on target?"

"Yes, sir," he lies. How can he explain this? If he admits they had had faulty winds aloft information it will be viewed as an attempt to cast blame elsewhere; best to lie, keep lying and hope for the best.

In the control bunker in Israel, human eyes are not the only thing tracking the inbound missiles. Made famous in the first Gulf War, the Patriot missile radar is also locked on. While the original Patriots were fairly successful, the latest generation is much more dependable and accurate. It becomes obvious to the trained eyes of the radar operators some of the missiles will not even reach Israel, but several will and although they will not threaten the larger more important cities such as Jerusalem and Tel Aviv, a missile hitting anywhere in Israel is not acceptable. Suddenly a Patriot battery swings into action, the intruder has come within range. Two missiles streak toward their target, in less than a minute they connect with the inbound SCUD and the 90 kg high-explosive warhead destroys it. While the SCUD's warhead has exploded and the trajectory is interrupted, hundreds of pounds of shrapnel from both missiles begin a freefall toward the earth.

Over the next several minutes this scenario is repeated a number of times and every missile that might have exploded inside Israel's borders is reduced to a lesser, but still deadly collection of recycle material crashing to the ground. Most of it lands harmlessly in the desert, however some remnants do cause a minimal amount of damage and injuries and a few deaths. Jordan is not so lucky.

The missiles which were not going to reach Israel were not engaged by the Patriot missiles and they cause significant damage as their warheads explode on impact. Luckily most of them land in the desert here as well; however two of them land on the outskirts of Amman. Impacting in primarily residential areas, the death and destruction is palpable. No warnings were sounded here and neither citizens nor emergency personal are prepared. The Prime Minister and King are notified. To say they are not happy with this is an understatement.

In Iran the missile commander is nonplussed. He was aware of the Israeli Patriots batteries and knew it was likely several of his SCUD's would be taken out, but he'd believed the number would overwhelm the defenses and at least some would make it to the target area. However, the winds deflected enough that the Israeli dogs took every one of his SCUD's out. Maybe this is his salvation …

The President is awaiting the commander's analysis of the attack. "Sir, it appears the enemy's missile defenses are better than we thought. I am saddened to report none of our missiles reached their target." He is sure the following scream is heard all the way in Tehran.

"Impossible! How can this be?" He is furious; no, furious is not strong enough for the emotion he is feeling now. He had hoped the initial attack would cause enough destruction and chaos the next phase would have a more significant impact. No use crying over this, he picks up the phone and calls his general who is leading the joint forces involved in the next phase. “You have a green light for all operations to begin immediately, Allahu Akbar!”

In the Situation Room of the White House various people are on phones, watching radar and satellite feeds. As the information comes in the senior Pentagon official gathers it and then summarizes to the others, including the Chief of Staff. “It appears the Patriot missile batteries did their job. No intact SCUD’s reached Israel and all the debris fell harmlessly in the desert.”

“Thank God for that,” says the Chief of Staff.

“Well, that is about the extent of the good news. It seems two SCUDS impacted in Jordan just outside Amman. Early reports are they hit residential areas and damage and casualties are high. The King of Jordan has already lodged complaints with the UN.”

“Anything else?”

“Yes, the Iranian Navy is moving assets in the direction of the Straits of Hormuz, ground equipment is moving west out of Iran and aircraft have been detected westbound, most likely to try and further soften Israeli defenses before the attack.”

The Chief of Staff lifts a phone, calls upstairs and gives a report. He listens, nods and says, “Yes Mr. President,” and hangs up. “NATO is going to handle the Straits, you are clear to coordinate a response to Iran and do whatever is necessary to keep the ship traffic flowing. We will watch closely as see how the rest materializes.”

“Yes sir, I’ll make the calls.” The Pentagon official lifts a phone and makes a call halfway around the world. He relays the orders; there are also encrypted digital copies of the orders sent as verification.

The carrier group had been on alert for possible action, so this did not hit them cold. They had been observing the Iranians for several days; from time to time the Iranians sent speed boats out to harass the navy ships … sort of like a gnat buzzing around a bear … an irritation, but not a threat. The commander calls his counterparts with the British and French to coordinate their actions.

In an apartment in New York City, "Yes sir, I understand; Aunt Martha will arrive on the twenty-eighth. We will have things ready for her, goodbye." As the Middle Eastern man clicks off the cell he looks at his partner across the room. "We have been activated; we are to carry out our mission on the twenty-eighth."

"Praise be to Allah!"

"Yes, Allahu Akbar!"

Similar calls are made and received all over the United States and Europe; this action is not tied to any of the ongoing world events. During the Cold War there were "sleeper agents" for both sides going to work every day and seemingly part of the locals. A phone call or a letter with a certain code was all that was needed to send the agent on his or her mission; possibly years or decades after being inserted.

These assets have a similar mission, but in today's world of immigrants it is much easier to accomplish. And they do not represent or answer to any government … but to an idea … a belief system.

"Anything on the news?" she asks.

"It just started; Iran has fired missiles at Israel," he replies with a grim look on his face.

She sits by him on the sofa and they watch for several minutes as reports come in and various pundits surmise what Iran's next move will be and how the Israeli's will respond.

"What do you think will happen next?" she asks.

"I'm guessing Iran will attack from the air and ground, likely will try something to stop or slow the flow of oil. Israel does not mess around. I saw some re-enactments of some of their wars. Tactically they are far superior to Iran; however Iran has a much larger army and likely help from some of the surrounding countries.

"It is not official, but it is generally accepted that Israel has nuclear weapons. It will be a last resort, but they will use them before they are defeated. If that happens, all bets are off.

There is no telling where the lines will be drawn, who will do what; this could be catastrophic."

"What will happen here, I mean in the U.S. in general … and here … where we live?" She is obviously quite upset and worried.

"I really don't know, babe. It could be as basic as higher gas and related prices …"

"Or this could be the beginning of the end, couldn't it?"

He takes a deep breath and responds, "Yes, it could be. Not the end of the world, but certainly the end of life as we know and enjoy it. There are so many variables, it will be impossible to know much before it happens."

"What will people do, I mean people in the cities who are not in a position to be self sufficient?"

"It won't be pretty."

Chapter 38

EFFORTS TO SAVE THE Greek economy with cash infusions and loan guarantees are about exhausted. The government is afraid of riots and for their personal safety if further cuts are made, so they refuse to make the necessary cuts to secure the aid. Without the aid, loans cannot be paid, without payment, default. The Europeans in general and the Germans in particular shake their heads and walk away. The Greek politicians don't understand whether they save the country or not, they will not survive the aftermath.

With the default, an emergency meeting is held in Brussels, and Greece is unceremoniously booted from the EU. With no outside support, a worthless currency, and all government employees suddenly unemployed, the country implodes. Museums are looted of priceless art and artifacts. People with any money and the ability, flee the country in the hours following the default. The country falls to anarchy almost overnight; riots, fires, theft from stores and people with assets. The death toll is in the thousands, and there is little press coverage, no one is safe.

In a coordinated act, dozens of fast boats leave the Iranian shore in the area of the Straits of Hormuz. On board are mines to be dumped in the Straits to stop all ship traffic. The NATO forces are not actually in the Straits and are not in a position to stop the sudden launch. In fact, they would not have tried to stop it because they did not know what was going on until it was too late.

In a relatively short time, hundreds of mines are laying in the Straits and the fast boats all return to their ports. The U.S. Navy Admiral in charge of the operation sends an alert to all ship traffic to stop, warning them of the danger. A North Korean tanker carrying a load of oil to the isolated Asian country ignores the warning believing it is some sort of trick. A mine explodes ripping a huge hole in the hull, spilling the cargo into the water and in time, sending the ship to the bottom. Not only are there mines in the water, but millions of gallons of oil in addition to the structure of the ship which is close enough to the surface in the shallow waters to be a danger to navigation.

With the tension and war in the Middle East, oil prices spike overnight. Already over $100 per barrel, every $1 increase in crude raises the price of gas 2.5 cents per gallon. Forecasters predict oil could reach $150 per barrel, and if the war persists $200 oil is not out of the question. This will cause the price of gas to increase $1.25 to $2.50 from an already high $3.50 per gallon. Five-dollar gas will seriously damage the U.S. economy … seven-dollar gas and diesel will send the economy into a tailspin.

As the senior officials in the Situation Room watch live satellite feed of the troops and equipment moving westward toward Israel, they receive word of the mining of the Straits. The Admiral mutters an expletive as he cradles the receiver. "The Iranians have mined the Straits, all ship traffic is stopped. A North Korean tanker ignored the warnings and hit a mine; it is sinking and losing its entire cargo in the water … about two-million barrels."

"How did this happen?" asks the Chief of Staff. "I thought we could control the area and over power the Iranians."

The Admiral explains how it happened.

"The President is not going to be happy about this."

"I'm not happy about this! But it is what it is; now we have to deal with it."

"How long before the shipping lanes are clear and traffic can resume?"

"Several days, likely a week."

"We don't have that long, it will have to be faster."

"You don't understand, we are limited to the equipment we have on hand. Once the mines are in the water and armed we have a much more difficult job on our hands. Certainly you don't want us to rush this and lose one of our ships?"

"I don't appreciate your tone, Admiral."

"I don't want to lose a ship or any men. We will do the best we can in the safest manner possible. We did not anticipate this sort of deployment by the Iranians. We will have air assets in place to prevent any such move in the future."

The Chief of Staff knows the Navy is doing the best it can, but he knows the President is going to rip them a new one and this call upstairs is not one he relishes; but he lifts the receiver and punches the red button.

Italy has been run for years by a wealthy playboy; acting as Prime Minister has been sort of a game to him. He and his parliament have been lying to the public for quite some time now. The debt is crushing them, he hoped a growing economy would pull them out of the mess, but the growth never came. Fear of embarrassment and failure made them continue to "whistle past the graveyard," but payments are due and there is no money. The banks are quiet about it for a period of time; however they are short and can wait no longer. Thinking the Prime Minister is holding out on them and doing some sort of shell game, they go public with their demand for payment; and the charade is over.

The EU is caught off guard and in an effort to save the rest of the group; Italy is cut off and left swinging in the wind like Greece. While chaos does not immediately take off as it did in Greece, panic does. Stores are emptied in hours and the stage is set for anarchy to rule this once noble state, the wait is not long.

The failure of Italy scares many other countries as well it should, but some make poor choices in the ensuing hours. Portugal has suffered much as Greece for the same reasons and has been teetering on the brink of collapse for months. Spain made a huge gamble several years back to "go green," sending the country in to tremendous debt as the government subsidized what it was sure would lift the country up as a shining example for the future of the world and energy production. Instead, over 20 percent unemployment crushed the country's ability to raise revenue and the new energy investments have been a colossal failure. Within hours of Italy's announcement of default, Spain and Portugal join in the demise.

As word of these new failures reach Mr. Volar's ears, a look of satisfaction crosses his mouth. He rarely smiles … well; sometimes one of his young female companions manages to elicit a slight smile from time to time.

As all this news hits the financial world, investors panic knowing how volatile things will be in the weeks and months ahead. Beginning in Asia, markets start to plummet. Some markets have automatic stops in place so that when a loss of a predetermined percentage occurs, all trading is stopped … others just about fall off the cliff. As markets open around the world, each one continues the precipitous drop, including the United States and other western-hemisphere markets. Trillions of dollars are lost by average investors; however, Mr. Volar is not the average investor. Shorting currencies and certain stocks while investing in others, his profits will be in the billions as others lose everything.

He has been on a trip and unaware of some of these latest developments around the world. Before catching his commuter flight home he calls her, "Hi babe! I'm on my way to catch the flight home, how's things going?"

"Pretty good, I'm having a good day at work. A few calls, but nothing terrible; how was your trip?"

"It was a long one, weather did not cooperate, had to hold waiting for our approach. I was afraid we'd be late enough I could not catch my flight home, but we made it. I'm just about to the gate; I'll call you on my way to the truck in a couple of hours."

"Great, talk to you then."

She is not aware of the situation either, most of her co-workers like to watch worthless TV; reality shows and such … they are woefully uninformed and in the dark regarding current events.

He checks in at the gate and gets his pass for the cockpit. It is just a few minutes before boarding so he takes a seat in the gate area, there is a TV tuned to a news channel. He watches for a moment and then thinks to himself, "Dear God, it's happening." He then says a silent prayer for the world, for his country … for his wife and family.

Israel has no intention of waiting for the Iranians and their allies to strike first; the best defense is a good offense. The military has been on alert ever since the initial air strike, so no large movements are required … everything and everyone is in place. The Prime Minister and Knesset have met and are in general agreement. There had been hardliners at one time who were dead set against anything provocative; however Iran's President and Supreme Leader made it clear in recent months that Israel's demise was not a matter of if … but when. Waiting was no longer an option. Washington had begged them to postpone the strike, to give diplomatic efforts more time. "Those fools would think differently if Mexico or Canada had threatened to wipe out the U.S., and then started a nuclear program to carry it out," was the consensus of the group. The Prime Minister calls his Defense Minister, "You are clear to begin operations as planned."

"Yes sir, Mr. Prime Minister. I'll report back soon," and he clicks off.

"God help us all," says the Prime Minister as he cradles his handset.

In the Straits, the mine sweeping process has begun. The U.S. commander of the NATO forces in the Gulf was pleasantly surprised to learn the British and French both had ships equipped for sweeping operations; he had thought the United States had the only one close at hand. Hopefully they will be able to clear the lanes in a few days. He is keeping an observation plane aloft watching for a repeat of Iran's mine launching operation as well as eyes on live satellite feeds. If they detect boats are being loaded with mines for a repeat performance he has clearance to strike them in port.

His commuter flight lands and as he heads for his truck, he calls her.

"Hi honey, you getting closer to home?"

"Yes, made it just fine and am on the way to the truck. Have you seen any news?"

"You know these guys, I never get to pick what I want and they all hate to watch the news. What's going on?"

"It's started, I think things are in motion that will bring about what we worried might happen. Iran has mined the Straits of Hormuz, so problems and tension there will cause oil prices to go through the roof, and their ground forces are moving towards Israel."

"Will that cause the U.S. to have such a big problem … other than a spike in fuel prices?"

"There's more; Greece defaulted a few days ago and that had been expected and likely factored in, but Italy, Portugal and Spain all defaulted today. Europe will be in chaos soon, certainly the affected countries, but the rest will surely follow in short order … they are simply too connected.

"I had no idea …"

"The markets are tanking all over the world and oil is climbing higher by the minute. The world economies are just tied too closely together, we rely on each other too much. As European economies fail, trade disappears. As trade disappears, everyone connected to that process will be devastated. Take away the entire economic stimulus, and add skyrocketing fuel prices …"

"I see, and inflation will climb overnight…and I bet there are banks in the U.S. who will be affected by the defaults …"

"Without a doubt ... and I'm sure there will be more bad news in the coming days. Israel will defend herself, who knows where that will lead."

"I wish I could be home with you tonight!"

"Me too. I'm about to the truck; I'll call you when I get home. I'm going to call the group on the way home and touch base with all of them."

"Okay, love you!"

"Love you too, bye."

He waits until he is out of town and the related traffic before starting his calls. He reaches everyone but his pilot buddy, but he knew John was on a trip and might not be where they could talk just now. He just wants to make sure they are all on top of things and realize what is ahead. He is not disappointed; they all are ahead of him as they've had the day to start preparations. These will not be easy times, but things will be better with some preparations than with none.

Chapter 39

ISRAEL'S PLAN IS BOLD and will have their air assets spread thin, but the element of surprise will be on their side. To most observers she is just sitting tight waiting to defend herself, armed to the teeth.

Knowing a mass launch of aircraft would certainly raise suspicion, fighters and fighter/bombers have been steadily taking off, some returning to land while others stay aloft over the Mediterranean. A number of aerial refueling tankers are prepared to have everyone fueled and on their way.

A code is received by all operations stations and aircraft putting the mission in motion. Some aircraft depart from ground bases while the rest are fueled in the air; armed with precision bombs they suddenly break for their targets.

Lebanon and Syria have been coordinating with Iran for their coming attack on Israel. As the columns of Iranian troops and equipment are closing on the Syrian border with Iraq, the commanders in Syria and Lebanon begin briefing their subordinates on the plans. Lebanon will push from the north as Syrian and Iranian forces push in from the east. They will cut south some into Jordan without permission, but what will they do? After Israel is destroyed and a smoking ruin, Iran has plans as well for these traitorous Arabs; there is no room in the Middle East for any country what will not cooperate.

They expect the Israelis to fiercely defend herself, but the sheer numbers should allow them to overrun the Zionists in a few days. Iran's air force will soon arrive in Syrian and

Lebanon airports for aerial support. They lack the aerial refueling capabilities, so runways are essential.

The Iranian operations commander receives an urgent message: "Multiple aircraft inbound from the west at high speed."

"What is this?" he asks himself. The Israeli airfields have been monitored for days and there have been no indications of anything unusual. Might the U.S. or NATO be helping Israel? Not likely, every indication is they are not happy with Israel's initial attack.

There is little the column can do other than "hunker down." They have no surface to air missiles other than some shoulder fired versions which are more suited to bringing down a helicopter than an advanced tactical fighter. Initially, precision bombs begin hitting the leading vehicles, destroying the road and plugging it with burning debris. After the ordinance has been dropped, guns are used to systematically strafe and wipe out nearly the entire line of equipment. The most devastating of these is the A-10 Warthog with its 30mm rotary cannon firing depleted uranium shells firing 3,900 rounds per minute. These projectiles go through tanks and armored personnel carriers and about anything else they hit. Heavily armed, they are not easily brought down by anything short of a missile. Within about 30 minutes the carnage is reminiscent of the "Highway of Death," the road from Kuwait to Bagdad during the first gulf war.

At the same time, attacks are happening on the front lines of Syria and Lebanon. These lines are more permanent and on home territory, while they are harder to penetrate and they do have some missile defenses, other than downing a few Israeli planes with missiles the results are similar. In recent history wars involving Israel have been measured in days. Even though this one had the potential to wipe Israel out, it will be measured in hours. However, neither Israel nor the world is out of danger.

In the Situation Room the occupants keep up with the Middle East via satellite feed and real time intelligence sources. As they observe the devastation visited on the enemies of Israel they know this is not the end of the matter.

The rage seething through the veins of Iran's president is at the boiling point; word of the attack and the destruction of his forces in such a sudden and complete fashion are unfathomable. The loss of such a large portion of the military machine is devastating and will take years to replace. His overall plan was to destroy the "Little Satan" first, then put things in motion to bring the 12th Imam forth. There will be no stopping his next move; he lifts the phone and calls his head of intelligence services giving him to green light to commence the planned operations there. He hangs up the phone and suddenly calm comes over him, the knowledge he is going to be exalted in the world to come for his part in bringing about the necessary world events. Of course, that is in his mind … what actually awaits him is far more sinister.

His first night at home alone is not a good one. The world events weigh heavy and his mind does not slow down, sleep comes in bits and pieces. He is up at first light, makes coffee and does the morning chores. She has some things she planned to do, but they can wait; she is anxious to see him and be home. It is a pleasant morning and he is drinking coffee on the deck when he hears the guineas herald the arrival of a vehicle. He steps to the edge of the deck where he can see the driveway. As she opens the door she sees him, flashes a smile and a wave. He walks inside as she enters the door into the kitchen.

"I'm so glad you are home early," he says as they embrace.

"Me too!" They stand there for a few moments holding each other before she continues, "What's the latest in the news?"

"At this point Israel has pretty much cleaned house. Before Iran could get into position they hit the Iranian forces in a column and at the same time hit an unsuspecting Syria and Lebanon. All three are pretty decimated with only minor damage to Israel, a few planes shot down."

"That's great news isn't it? I mean, if there is not a protracted war, isn't that a good thing?"

"Maybe, at least for now; NATO has cleared the Straits of Hormuz but shipping companies are not anxious to go through there. If they are caught and cannot get through the ships could be tied up for who knows how long."

"Or even blown up or hijacked."

"Exactly."

"Gas was up twenty-five cents overnight. A friend called me wondering why … she pays no attention to the news and did not have a clue as to any of this, and she did not understand why something over there affected us."

"I suppose that is why we are in the mess we are in, too many people are ignorant."

She pours a cup of coffee and they go out on the deck to relax and visit, and enjoy the view of the open country and fresh air.

In the Situation Room the Chief of Staff asks, "Any developments overnight?"

"The Iranians, Syrians and Lebanese are licking their wounds. We are not picking up any indication of a counter attack, but there is something else happening that is disturbing."

The Chief of Staff raises an eyebrow.

"There has been a dramatic increase in "chatter" picked up by all the intelligences services, just as before the 9/11 attacks and other events around the world. We believe something is in the works, but we have zero information as to what or where."

The Chief of Staff closes his eyes and rubs his forehead. "Why didn't I retire to spend more time with my family before all this happened?" he says to himself. "Nothing from anyone, nothing from Mossad?"

"We're not exactly on the best of terms with Mossad these days; they claim they know nothing and that is entirely possible." He thinks to himself, "And I don't blame them one bit for not trusting us … I wouldn't trust us either."

"Call me if there is any news, I'll be with the President."

"Yes sir."

Europe's slow motion train wreck is about to pick up speed. As banks close to avoid runs, businesses close with no operating capital, government entities lay off workers as they have no money to pay; people begin to take to the streets. At first it is fairly peaceful; loud, but without violence.

However this does not last long. Madrid, Barcelona, Valencia, Cartagena, Lisbon, Rome, Florence, Genoa and other cities are soon on fire ... literally. Islamists, as part of the overall Caliphate plan are ready to go into action. They take to the streets and stir up the masses. Communists who have been anxiously waiting for the chance to push things over the edge join in ... the enemy of my enemy is my friend. Police are outnumbered hundreds to one and concentrate on key facilities and buildings to protect. If things do not resolve quickly, martial law will be required and that will certainly add to the death toll.

Even though other countries in the EU are not directly affected, the loss of such important countries in the alliance puts a definite chink in the armor of the group. Once activists in other countries see what is happening, they quickly begin to gather groups to start protests and marches. Within a couple of days all the major cities in Europe are on the verge of meltdown. Hundreds of innocent people caught off guard are killed, hundreds of protesters die, and many simply caught up in their own actions ... friendly fire of sorts.

Governments enact Martial Law in most of Europe. The crackdown results in the death of thousands. Many of the rioters melt into the cities and begin a type of guerilla warfare with the military. Elderly citizens have flashbacks of the late 30s and 40s; life is once again a hard existence. Food is scarce, being in public is dangerous. Rural areas are largely unscathed, but the cities are deathtraps.

Washington is all abuzz with congressional hearings, private meetings with advisors, House and Senate leaders meeting with the White House. The stock market has lost half its value in recent days, oil price has nearly doubled as has gas at the pump. The nation senses a panic and is anxiously watching for its leaders to do just that ... lead. Unfortunately most in higher office have become accustomed to reacting rather than leading and they are woefully ill-equipped to respond in any meaningful way.

The Middle East is beginning to boil just beneath the surface. Sheiks and other ruling classes, kings ... all who really control the wealth of the oil fields ... see the writing on the wall. With billions secured in secret around the world, they casually make their way out of the countries to remote parts of the world; much of their wealth converted to gold and silver over the past year. While difficult to transport, it was never in the Middle East so rather than taking it with them they go to where it is stored. The regular people are poor peasants and are ill prepared to handle what is coming.

Chapter 40

IT HAS BEEN A nice day weather-wise and he's been out doing chores and tackling a few things that have been let go. She is working in her sewing room catching up on some craft projects for the grandchildren. She hears him come in and is ready for a break as well so she comes down stairs as he's pouring a glass of tea.

"Thought I'd join you," she says as he looks up at her.

"Perfect, ready for the company," he says and pours her a glass. "Have you had the news on?"

"No, watching one of my decorating shows … big surprise there I bet!"

He smiles, "Hardly." He picks up the remote and turns on the satellite receiver and the TV in the kitchen; and they both freeze.

A red banner on the screen is flashing "Breaking News" and the scene is one of chaos. Ambulances, police cars, official personnel in uniforms are running as well as citizens. There is fire and smoke in the background, a reporter's voice is speaking as the camera swings to show all the destruction.

"Information is sketchy at the moment," the reporter says. "But this appears to be the work of a suicide bomber. Witnesses say a man appearing to be Middle Eastern entered the mall, screamed Allu Akbar and blew himself up. We are getting reports this is not, I repeat, is not an isolated incident. We are receiving information there may have been dozens of such attacks across the nation in the past hour."

She looks at him with tears in her eyes, "They're doing it, aren't they? I mean, Iran is behind this isn't it?"

"That would be my guess. This is likely that nut job's way to usher the world into war to bring the 12th Imam."

They watch for a while longer and other locations are shown around the country. People are terrified, rightfully so, about what is going to happen next. He turns off the TV and they sit together and pray: for their family, for the nation, for the world.

In Washington, meetings are happening in every possible place: the White House, the Senate, the House, the Pentagon and every cabinet office. As the dust around the nation settles and details come in it becomes quite evident this is a very coordinated attack of unprecedented scale. As a safety measure the President orders all air and rail traffic halted. As no one knows just who or what is behind these attacks, all major cities cut off entry and exit of all traffic. It cuts fathers and mothers off from getting home to their children; tensions, anger and fear grow by the minute.

As the preliminary numbers come in, the scope of the attacks becomes more fully realized. Ten to twelve bombs have been set off in every major city around the country, only the lesser populated states with no major cities are unaffected. Over 40 cities have been hit … over 400 bombs have been set off in malls or sporting events. The death toll will exceed that of the 9/11 attacks. Suddenly the events in Israel and Iran seem very small and insignificant. The Situation Room has changed its focus and efforts to find who or what is behind this begins in earnest.

A message from the President is essential to try and allay fears. Speech writers are given what information is to be used and a speech is hastily written and put on the teleprompter.

"My fellow Americans, I come to you tonight with a heavy heart for all who are directly affected by today's cowardly attacks. It is too soon to know for sure just who is responsible for these murderous acts, but rest assured the full force and resources of the federal government will be brought forth to see justice is delivered to those who are responsible. I ask for calm and please do not jump to any conclusions as to who might be to blame. Randomly picking out individuals from any group of people and taking the law into your own hands will only complicate our job of finding the perpetrators. Keep your local radio and TV stations tuned in for updates and information. I personally will not rest until those responsible have been brought to justice. God bless each of you, and God bless the United States of America."

Since air travel has been halted much as it was in the days after 9/11, he will remain at home until further notice. It is just as well, his mind is so full of the various happenings he's not sure it would be safe to fly anyway. The TV has been on the 24-hour news channel since they first heard. Most of the coverage is of course regarding the events in the US, but reports from around the world are even more worrisome.

Martial Law is in effect in most European cities. Banks and most commerce is shut down ... some by failure, some have been destroyed and some closed by fear. People for the most part are trying to stay at home, but most Europeans are used to shopping daily and have little in the way of food stored in their homes. Bread and fresh fruits and vegetables are non-existent. As in most parts of the world, those in rural areas are not so seriously affected by these shortages. Power is another issue, shortages and rolling blackouts are commonplace. Delivery trucks carrying anything do not venture near the cities for fear they will be attacked. The military has set up places for people to come at certain times during the day to get MRE's (Meals Ready to Eat). There are not enough to go around, so even the law abiding citizens lose their temper and composure.

Thousands have died across Europe; some by violence and some have become victims of disease and lack of medical attention. Medicines requiring refrigeration go bad, or run out and people die; it is a terrible time to live in a large European city. The violence continues sporadically, sometimes fomented by Islamists and other times by the communists. The end result is a very difficult undertaking by police and military to find and arrest or kill the instigators. This is something that will go on for weeks or months.

The Middle East is in a different turmoil. As it is learned the power structure has abandoned the countries, all hell is breaking loose. Fundamentalist regimes are taking the place of monarchies and dictatorships. The new Caliphate is in full implementation in much of the area. Israel is still stable, but is an island in a sea of confusion. Jordan has clandestinely maintained a relationship with Israel, understanding the option of throwing in with a bunch of Mullah's or Ayatollah's operating under Sharia Law is not really an option at all. Israel knows they are truly in a life and death situation day by day; nuclear weapons are at the ready and will be used if necessary.

The United States is in quite a bit better shape in the near term. Over 6,000 people were killed in the initial attacks; people are in shock, are angry and pulling together as they did after 9/11. This is by far the worst single attack in the nation's history. This has been a terrible blow, but people are helping each other and trying to make life as normal as possible. With the disruption in travel, most businesses have resorted to phone calls, teleconferences, web meetings. Travel by car is greatly hampered by the high gas prices, over seven dollars a gallon. Most people are staying home, which is not good for the economy.

On a remote island Mr. Volar punches a number on a sat phone. On the other end, "Yes?"

"The time is right, activate the plan now."

"Yes sir, consider it done."

Volar sits back and a slight smile crosses his lips. A casual observer would be unsure if the phone call was pleasant, or the 28-year-old bombshell blonde beside him was the stimulus of the facial expression.

His eyes snap open, it is still dark but a slight glow is beginning to be evident on the eastern horizon. He listens, wondering if a noise woke him … but the quiet of the country is all he hears. He slips out of bed, slips on some shorts and takes the .357 from the bedside stand and a flashlight just to be on the safe side. He pads silently to the other end of the house watching and listening … there is nothing. He peers out a couple of windows, everything appears normal. He begins to relax, slips the revolver into his pocket and lays the flashlight on the kitchen counter. He starts running filtered water into the pitcher for coffee and measures the beans to grind. Once the coffee is brewing he turns on the TV.

There are riots in the streets; police in riot gear are losing the battle as they are so greatly outnumbered. It is then he realizes this is not a shot from a European city … it is New York! The reports say that at first light large groups gathered without warning and began looting stores, starting fires and generally destroying everything in their path. The police were caught off guard and are unable to contain the mass of rioters. Similar scenes are happening in Boston, Philadelphia, Washington and other cities up and down the east coast.

"What set this off?" he asks himself. Then it hits him. They are taking advantage of the situation after the bombings. They are going to overwhelm the system. He watches as he sips his coffee, the sun comes up and he steps out to the deck. The air is still cool this time of year, but it will warm up nicely. He hears the guineas starting to make noise wanting out of the coop, the ducks making their muted quacks. He walks over and opens the gate as the ducks and guineas flee to freedom for the day. The chickens stay in the coop until about noon so they lay their eggs in the nesting boxes and not scattered out around the farm. Ducks lay their eggs at night, so he gathers those and heads back to the house.

"Morning!"

"Good morning, you see the news?"

"Just been up a bit, commercial was on as I poured my coffee; what's up?"

"There are rioters hitting our major eastern cities, I'm afraid they are taking this time when we are already down from the bombings to try and overwhelm the system. This is going to be very bad."

A worried look takes control of her face as she watches the scenes on the TV. "What will happen next?" she asks.

"There are still many variables, but the odds are getting slimmer we will get out of this unscathed as a nation."

As the sun marches higher in the sky and comes up in the western states, the riots pop up with the sun in most of the major cities. The White House is in touch with all the governors as to what the federal government might or might not do. Posse Comitatus makes it illegal to use the Army or Air Force for law-enforcement purposes; however the states can use the National Guard. Some of the central and western states are not really involved in the riot situation as their population centers are not very large and with more traditional values, an insignificant number tried to create mischief and the local authorities easily handled these events.

With visions of the Kent State shootings in 1970, National Guardsman equipped with M-16's face off against the rioters. The idea of citizen facing citizen with military force is not why these young men and women joined the Guard. Smoke and tear gas are used, fire hoses and other non-lethal methods; it slows the rioters, but they are hurling bricks and debris at the police and Guard. These are mostly a distraction given the protective gear worn by the authorities, but Molotov cocktails are also thrown from the back of the group. These fiery bombs create serious problems; many receive serious burns after the flaming liquid hits clothes and skin.

The young guardsmen have been restrained and followed orders to use only non-lethal methods. However when one young man is consumed by fire, as he screams in agony, he also without thinking flips the safety off his weapon and fires a burst. His muzzle is pointing toward the ground, but bullets ricochet off the pavement and strike others nearby. Hearing the gunfire and seeing men falling, guardsmen start firing at the rioters. The rioters at first don't believe what is happening, but as several of them fall to the street reality sets in and they begin to retreat and take cover. The commander on scene is screaming to cease fire. In moments the entire future of the nation may have been changed by this event.

Word of the shootings spreads like wildfire, the fact it was initiated in a bizarre combination of events is of no importance to those who use it to their advantage … stirring up the rioters and adding to their ranks with the memory of the martyrs who have fallen. The fact the rioters were breaking the law and the soldier who was burned to death was the result of illegal violent activity is of no importance to those who have been convinced in their minds the nation has to be transformed. They view themselves as the early revolutionaries who fought against England. Minor technicality that one group fought to create the constitution, and the other is fighting to destroy it.

In storage facilities all over the country, gasoline has been stockpiled; in the past days volunteers have put the gas into bottles and jars with lids so all that needs to be done is to remove the lid and put a rag in the opening. Tens of thousands of these lethal bombs have been readied for this moment. The targets of the rage will be facilities and symbols of commerce and capitalism; banks, shipyards, power generating facilities, rail switching yards, airports and passenger rail stations. The idea is to shut down commerce long enough to have a serious effect on the nation's economy … overload the system in every way to bring it down.

As those in power in Washington work to try and figure out the best course of action to get the nation back on track following the bombings, they receive word of the shootings. This is a complication that is entirely unwelcome. There are immediate calls for calm from the White House and congressional leaders from both sides of the aisle. Of course those in the streets do not see or hear any of this, and those pushing them from behind the scenes are euphoric; the shooting places them in the best possible light. The guardsmen are the villains and the rioters are the victims. The pot is stirred even more while the rioters gain momentum. Police and the Guard pull back to more of a defensive position; from the lowest Buck Private to the highest commander, they are all afraid to act.

Europe is crashing, crashing hard. Banks close, businesses lose everything, and the EU is powerless. Some of the smaller countries are still functioning, but there is no one with which to trade. National currencies were abandoned for the Euro, and the Euro is now worthless. Individual countries would normally turn to the U.S .for some sort of aid or support, but she is struggling with her own problems … and after the Fed has monetized so much of the debt, the dollar is hanging by a thread in the best of times. Power companies are not able to maintain fuel to generate power; rolling blackouts are more and more commonplace.

Washington is busy calling CEO's, major banks and governors to reassure them, but Washington is hardly convinced herself and does nothing to allay fears. As word of defaults and problems in Europe continue to come in, America's banks are devastated by the losses. The failure of countries, companies and the loss of trade internationally has taken once powerful entities and rendered them insolvent. The Fed comes in with an infusion of dollars to prevent a complete collapse, it helps for the moment. The idea of mutually assured destruction in the financial realm was designed to protect each country from rogue actions by a single nation, but the idea of a national calamity taking all down was never deemed a realistic prospect.

China and Japan are scared to death. They remain mostly unscathed by the maladies directly, but the indirect effects are devastating them as well. The sudden virtual shutdown of trade will have a terrible effect on their economies. Both countries rely heavily on trade with Europe and the US; and both rely heavily on the U.S. dollar. While China has the reputation of holding most of the U.S. debt, Japan actually holds more. A default by the U.S. will sink both countries, but no one wants to think this is even possible. And in fact, it is not possible, technically speaking. The Fed will just create the money to pay, but this has been going on so long already the value of the dollar will eventually be the same as passing out blank pieces of paper.

There is a story from the effects of the staggering hyperinflation in the Weimar Republic. Menus did not have amounts on them as prices would climb just in the time you ordered to the time you paid. Two ladies were carrying a basket full of cash to buy some things at a local market. A fight broke out on the street and in the confusion they had to set the basket down. When they returned to pick it back up, the basket was gone, but the cash was still there … the basket was more valuable than the cash.

There is no warning again when the fast boats race towards the Straits from numerous ports. Radar and visual reports verify their departure, this time NATO is better prepared. Aircraft are in the air and race to the area to engage the fast boats. These smaller craft are designed to harass, carry mines, landing parties … they do not have any antiaircraft defenses, with exception of a couple of AK47's … which is about like firing on a charging lion with a BB gun.

Missiles will not work for targets such as these, so for the most part guns will be used. There are 16 fighters ready to engage, a formidable number, but there are over 50 boats. An AWACS aircraft is "running the show" so to speak, 16 fighters screaming in from all directions at over 500 miles per hour is a disaster in the making without coordination. The AWACS directs each aircraft in for an attack just as an air traffic controller would direct airliners in for landing at a major airport.

Initially it appears NATO has the upper hand, but it is harder than one might think and several boats get through and drop their mines. Each boat is taken out before it returns to port, but several mines are released into the vital Straits. The number only matters in relation to how long it takes to clear. One is enough to close shipping down again; the NATO commander makes the call. While he is alerting the ships in the area and the ports, an alarm goes off … there is an incoming threat. The Aegis destroyer in the fleet is the first line of defense for such threats. Armed with guns and missiles, the sophisticated radar will lock on to an inbound missile or aircraft and engage at a distance, leaving Gatling-type rotary guns as a backup.

Iran has been mass producing an anti ship cruise missile for a couple of years. It has a range of about 185 miles and travels MACH 3 … it is a formidable weapon. If fired at its max range it will only take about five minutes to reach target, these are a little over two minutes out at launch. Ten missiles have been launched which is well within the Aegis system to track and attack. Everything is automatic, when target acquisition is made, two missiles are launched. With a closure rate of 4,000 mph, it does not take long. In some cases the first missile scores, other times it is the second … unfortunately in two cases, both missiles miss. Guns automatically engage and take out one more; one strikes a nearby cruiser just above the waterline, the high explosive ripping a huge hole in the hull. Five sailors are killed instantly and another 10 are injured. The ship lists noticeably, but the crew is able to isolate the damaged area and prevent her from sinking.

The Aegis is not finished; she is also an offensive platform. The launch point has been pinpointed and cruise missiles are armed and ready. After verifying a green light to return fire, four missiles leave their rails and streak toward their targets. The Iranians do not have nearly the level of radar and defensive measures the NATO countries do and they can do little more than watch as each missile finds its mark. All four launch sites and a number of cruise missiles are destroyed. It has only been thirty minutes since the fast boats started this skirmish, and although not officially declared, the U.S. and Iran are at war.

In Washington, the President is wondering what he has done to deserve this. "Why did this have to happen on my watch?" A phone rings in the Situation Room every few minutes and everyone is jumpy about each call. It seems none of the calls are just information, each one carries bad news for the country and the administration. With so much happening in the Straits, shipping companies have decided to just avoid the area rather than take a chance of getting trapped in port, or worse. Oil prices are going up by the minute, the Fed has kept the door open on the banks, but businesses are scared to death. Fuel prices have thrown all pricing out the window, it is impossible to project and set prices when expenses are in such flux. People are staying at home, so restaurants and hotels take an immediate hit, much as they did after 9/11. If businesses are scared, the average citizen is terrified. Unsure of employment as businesses are reassessing their employee needs, unsure if they can afford groceries as inflation is in double digits, unsure if they can keep the utilities going.

The word that a U.S. ship has been hit by an Iranian missile and that the U.S. has returned fire is hardly welcome news. Now, even if NATO can keep the Straits cleared of mines, the proven ability and willingness of Iran to strike a ship with a missile will shut down the entire shipping industry in the area. A tanker with no defensive capabilities would not stand a chance.

Europe is fighting for her survival. Muslims who have gathered in huge areas to live essentially under their own laws are taking over large sections of cities all over Europe. The local authorities along with some military have their resources spread thin on two fronts, fighting communists on one hand and the extremist Muslims on the other. Initially the authorities are responding as more of a riot control, using non-lethal methods to try and stop or breakup the rioters; however it has become more and more obvious this is not rioting ... it is a definite attempt to overthrow the governments.

Up until now, it seemed important to keep the force limited so as not to stir up public opinion against the authorities...that is up until now. Public opinion will not matter if the governments are toppled, so police and military units move from defensive maneuvers to offensive ones. Casualties have been relatively light up to this point, but the change is dramatic. Armored vehicles, automatic weapons and rocket launchers are all employed. The rioters do have some weapons, but with European laws on guns only the Swiss have access to significant weaponry as private citizens. An occasional sniper picks off a few here and there, but the losses of the rioters are in the hundreds. Panic spreads like wildfire across Europe; military law is in full effect. As people are kept at home, the countries all grind to a halt; power generating plants shut down, no commerce moves, no fuel for vehicles, no food, and no medical supplies. The problems for Europe will only get worse in the days and weeks to come.

Israel is not yet out of the woods either. Since her military stopped the military attacks, smaller groups and terrorists turn their attentions on destroying the Jewish nation. It is much harder to stop smaller rockets that can be launched from just about anywhere, suicide bombers and kamikaze-style attacks. The sheer number of attacks is staggering and death on both sides is enormous. Normally public opinion around the world keeps Israel from responding too harshly, but the rest of the world is busy with its own problems and takes little notice of the level of power with which she responds. Previously it is the military that has suffered most losses on each side, but the terror attacks have taken a terrible toll on Israeli civilians; and the response has been devastating to civilians in the surrounding territories where the attacks have been launched. The Arab countries cry foul, but the cries fall on deaf ears.

Chapter 41

IRAN AND THE NATO fleet are in an all-out war. While Iran's air force has limited ability, it does tie up NATO forces and keeps them defending the fleet more than performing offensive strikes. While the ships are able to launch missile attacks well into the interior of Iran, they also are spending time defending themselves against a relentless onslaught of incoming ship killers. The sheer numbers and odds are overwhelming and it is impossible to stop every one. The fight has been going on for just a little more than 24 hours, and everyone is fatigued. All the naval assets were already in the area, so any relief is still days away.

Tehran is a mess as are most of the military installations around the country. Between cruise missiles and a few fighters which made the trip, enough infrastructure has been destroyed or rendered useless to seriously cripple the military and citizens as well. Still smarting from the beating by the Israelis, they have the ability to do little more than function day to day. A large number of their missiles have been either fired or destroyed on the ground; their ability to defend themselves or attack is pretty much over. Calls from the generals to the President are neither answered nor returned; his whereabouts unknown.

On the water, NATO has survived the battle for the most part. Several ships took hits from missiles and suffered significant damage taking them out of the fight directly, but thankfully none of them were sunk. A sort of unofficial ceasefire exists, on Iran's side as she regroups and determines what they have left while the NATO forces put planes on the ships to perform maintenance and give the crews a much needed rest. As the U.S. Admiral in charge of the NATO forces takes everything in and is formulating the next move, he receives a disturbing call. The events in Europe have nations like France and England in dire straits; they are bringing their ships home where they are needed to help prevent the overthrow of the governments. He does not know the extent of the damage inflicted on Iran and wonders if his reinforcements will arrive in time.

He has been on the phone with his friends in the groups. Everyone is as prepared as possible but when no one knows what to expect, it is a daunting job. People in the cities are feeling things already, food shortages and fear of people wandering about … who can you trust?

"You talk to everyone?" she asks.

"Yes, things are getting rough in the cities, and none of them live in the major metropolitan areas, more in the suburbs. I would think the cities themselves are like war zones."

"That would be horrible!"

"Yes, yes it would. I have a few chores to do; I'll be back in a little later and watch some news with a glass of tea.

"I'll make a fresh pitcher for you."

He flashes a smile, gives her a quick peck and goes out the door. Once outside he heads for the barn, but about half way there he stops and listens. He remembers after 9/11 when air traffic was suspended how strange it was to not see a jet contrail, or hear the engines in the distance of a jet or general aviation plane for days. He looks at the clear blue sky, knowing there will be no vapor trails. He wonders how long this might last. Will it be days, weeks, months … or even years?

He takes care of the chores and spends some time with the animals. It is always relaxing to spend time with them and in a way they seem to enjoy it just as much. The alpacas hum gently and nuzzle him for attention and are rewarded with strokes on their long necks and under their chin. He sits in the pen holding the goats and a pot belly pig they rescued. One of the young goats climbs in his lap for attention while Miss Piggy lies at his feet to have her belly rubbed. Last chore is to feed the fowl and put them in their coop. There is a cacophony of calls by ducks, chickens and guineas as he fills their water container and dumps feed in the feeders. A few of the chickens like special attention and he picks them up one at a time to stroke their necks and talk to them as they cluck softly in return. Chores finished, he walks to the house.

"I saw you coming and poured you a glass."

"Thanks!" He takes a long drink and makes a satisfied sound. "That hits the spot!" He sits in a chair at the breakfast table and turns the TV on to cable news.

When the picture comes on the camera is panning back and forth showing buildings ablaze. No fire-fighting personnel or equipment is in sight, only rioters pressing themselves against outnumbered police. They both sit in silence, mouths agape as the report shows scenes from several cities around the country. The rioters have started fires in large bank buildings, corporate headquarters, warehouses of large department stores; anything that represents business, commerce, or finance is a target.

"Why don't they stop them? How can they let this go on?" she asks.

"They'd probably have to shoot a number of them and I guess no one has the courage to make that call … yet."

A news alert flashes on the screen and the reporter says, "An official message has been released from the White House. The President will address the nation this evening at 7:00 Eastern. In the meantime he pleads for calm and civility from both sides asking all involved to return to their homes and wait for further announcements later today."

"Oh good, he's going to give a speech … that ought to fix things."

He does not respond to her snide remark right away. As she looks at the stern look on his face he speaks, "This will not be any ordinary speech; I believe he'll declare Martial Law. He delayed the announcement until this evening to give them more time to get ready."

"They can't do that can they? I mean, is that legal or constitutional?"

"Well, our last president signed a law that sort of weasels around it. Our military cannot take control, but this law allows the military to take control of National Guard units which are state units in a state of emergency; this overrides the Governor's authority."

"That's not right … I mean that's like passing a law that allows you to break another law!"

"Pretty much … of course, since when did Congress or the president seem to worry about laws and the constitution? They have become accustomed to passing what they want and wait and see if some court will overturn it."

Information is flowing in and out of the Situation Room much like bees to and from a hive. Coming in are reports from the Straits, Israel, Europe and around the country. As data and numbers are crunched, decisions are made and orders flow out. Everyone is stone faced and determined, no one is joking or standing around talking small talk as one might find in more normal situations … this is anything but normal; it is more as one might imagine if there had been a nuclear strike … and in some ways it is worse. In a war enemies are clearly defined. With all that is going on around the world and the country there are so many different players, the variables are many, possibilities nearly endless; and the unintended consequences of any decision could have disastrous consequences for entire nations … including the United States.

In another area of the White House the President's speech writers are working to get the words just right, lawyers are looking at every word to make sure the exact message is delivered in a way so as not to leave any room for doubt or confusion. This will be relatively short, but will be the most important speech of his life.

In the Straits, U.S. Naval ships are arriving as reinforcements to the battle weary contingent. There has been no significant action since the initial battle. Aircraft are in the air at all times as observers and defenders. Satellite images indicate many of Iran's missile launch sites are severely damaged and there is little indication of military activity. At this point their mission is to just maintain presence in the area and hold it; there is no ship traffic to protect.

In Iran, the Supreme Leader is meeting with the military leaders trying to get a handle on what went wrong and what might be done to salvage any modicum of respect in the region. The President seems to have vaporized. No one knows, or is saying, where he is ... but it is very unlikely anyone would dare to lie to the Leader. These will be very difficult times. It has not been very long since the government forcefully squelched a rebellion and blood was shed. The people might sense a weakness and take advantage to overthrow the government. Great care must be taken to shift from the offensive against Israel and protect their positions of power.

Europe is barely hanging on. Between the communists and the Islamists the police and military are struggling to stay on top. In a war, the military can come in with overwhelming force and destroy buildings and launch assaults at enemy forces. This is not only an urban setting, it is their cities and to destroy their own buildings will likely create more problems than it solves. So, they slog it out; often having trouble determining just who the enemy is within cities full of frightened citizens. In the rural sections of the various countries, the people are coping fairly well. Power is off in much of the countries, but they are more accustomed to austere living. However, any in need of medicine for their daily lives in much of Europe are beginning to suffer, and many will die in the coming days and weeks. Add to that the lack of sufficient food, water and sanitation; the death toll outside of the fighting will climb to the thousands quickly.

Israel is suffering terribly. The relentless attacks are taking a horrific toll on the citizens. Israel's military continues to exact a serious revenge on her neighbors as well. Normally they try to hit only the spots where rockets are launched, but helicopters and fighters are being less discriminate in their retaliation. Civilians on both sides of the borders are suffering loss of life and property. Serious consideration is given to using lower yield nuclear devices. There are two schools of thought; one, it might scare the Arabs enough they will back off … or it might inflame them to intensify their attacks. That debate will continue for the time being.

"The President's speech will be on in a few minutes. I normally don't really care to hear his speeches, but we'd better listen to this one."

"Me either," she replies. "But you're right. What he says tonight might have a direct impact on every person in the country."

"Do we have any ice cream? I'm in the mood for something fattening and sweet," he says with a grin.

"Yes, I know there is some vanilla and I think there is some chocolate almond as well."

"I'll take an extra-large bowl of ..."

"Chocolate almond … I'll have it in there in time for the speech. Go sit and relax for a minute and I'll be right there."

He gives her a big smile and thumbs up as she goes toward the freezer. He sits on the leather sofa in the living room and turns on the TV. Reporters and pundits are guessing what the President might say tonight. "Only reporters and pundits would try to guess what someone might say, only moments before it is said."

"What?" She is coming in with two bowls of ice cream. "Were you talking to me?"

"No, I was talking to the TV. I was remarking that who in their right mind would prognosticate about what the President will say only minutes before he speaks? You'll likely be proven wrong in just a few minutes!"

"That's because no one really listens to them or cares, here's yours," as she hands him a huge bowl of a rich chocolate ice cream filled with toasted almonds, plus some dark chocolate syrup drizzled over the top.

"Wow, death by chocolate! The world may be coming to an end, but we've got chocolate, so it's okay," he jokes.

The reporters quiet suddenly and a voice says, "Ladies and gentlemen, the President of the United States."

The President is sitting behind the Resolute Desk in the Oval Office. "My fellow Americans, our nation is in turmoil tonight as is much of the world. I'm sure you are all aware of the attacks and fighting in and around Israel. There has been terrible loss of life on both sides and people are hurting in every way. Tonight it is quiet, and I join the leaders from other nations around the world calling for calm and to engage in talks to settle things rather than fighting.

"All military action in the Straits of Hormuz has come to a close as well. We are attempting to work with the Iranian government to make sure no further action is taken is this area so that normal shipping operations will be able to resume as soon as possible.

"Our friends and allies in Europe are facing the gravest challenge since World War II. At least two separate groups are fighting in an effort to overthrow the individual governments and the citizens are caught in the middle. As nations fight for survival, the people are also fighting to survive without power, fuel and food. The situation there is dire and we all need to keep them in our hearts and minds.

"Our great nation is also at a crossroads. After suffering the bombing and suicide attacks, lawless groups have tried to take advantage of the situation and have launched their own deadly attacks. These cowardly groups, rather than engage in dialog and using the election process, have chosen to resort to violence and destruction of property. This clear violation of law and people's property rights is egregious and we will not allow this to continue.

"Under the powers granted this office by the Defense Authorization Act of 2008, I am declaring Martial Law throughout the entire country until further notice. All law enforcement will answer to military units I have pre- positioned strategically around the country. There will be a curfew for all civilians from dusk to dawn; anyone out during these hours will be considered to be part of the rioting groups and will be dealt with accordingly. Stay tuned to local TV and radio stations for updates.

"These will not be easy times, but with your help we will put these days behind us and put this great nation back on track to be the greatest nation in the world. God bless each of you, and God bless the United States of America."

He mutes the TV, "Well, what do you think?"

"Sounds scary and I don't trust Washington D.C. to run the law enforcement for the whole country."

"I don't either, luckily we are in a very rural area and we likely will not have any reason to ever have any contact with any of this. Hopefully this will all be put down in a couple of weeks and we can start healing the country."

"Quick, un-mute the TV!"

He hits the button on the remote, there is a news flash alert.

A reporter is speaking, "We just received confirmation that OPEC has announced they are concerned about the worlds' economy as are other nations including China, Japan and India. OPEC has taken the position they no longer have confidence in the U.S. dollar and with backing from these countries and the World Bank the decision has been made to no longer price oil in dollars. We have no further information at this time and no one seems to know what currency they will use or what this means to the dollar and the country … but it can't possibly be good."

"That has to be the understatement of the year," he says. "The good news just keeps coming … should we leave the TV on or …"

"Like turning it off will stop the news?"

"I'm about on overload now, not sure I can digest much more tonight. At least more news, I need to finish my ice cream before it melts."

They spend a quiet evening together, something that has become all too rare. The weather is pleasant and they sit on the deck talking some, watching the brilliance of the night sky, and listening to sounds of the night; the occasional coyote, frogs, crickets and a train on the distant tracks to the south. It is very late when they decide to turn in. There is nothing pressing on the schedule for tomorrow and the time together is more important than sleep tonight.

When his eyes open in the morning it is light, very light outside. He glances at the clock by the bed, nearly eight o'clock. Usually the only time he sleeps this late is after a long trip. He slides out of bed and quietly steps into the bathroom. He looks out the window, looks as if it will be another beautiful day. He slips on some shorts and moves quietly through the bedroom and to the kitchen, starting coffee before going outside to open the coop to let the fowl out to forage for the day.

Ducks lay their eggs at night and normally on the ground. After "releasing the hoard" as he calls it, the combination of sounds from ducks and guineas as they rush through the gate, he gathers a couple dozen duck eggs and returns to the kitchen. As he pours a cup of the steaming coffee he notices the red light for the burner is not on. He flips on another and it does not illuminate either, so he flips a wall switch and that light does not come on either. "Hmmm, power's off," he thinks to himself. Being in a very rural area this is not as common as it once was, but it does happen from time to time. If the weather is not bad; ice storm or possibly a windblown limb on a line, it could be as simple as a fire or an accident somewhere on the line.

Just in case, he picks up the wired handset for the land line to call it in so the Rural Electric Coop power company knows … the line is dead. This is strange. He takes his cell phone to try, and the phone cannot make the call due to "No Service" available. "Okay, this is now officially bizarre," he says aloud to himself. Whatever happened, it was while he was out tending to the fowl.

"What's wrong?" She is coming in from the bedroom rubbing the sleep from her eyes.

"Power's out … everything's out … electric, phone, cell …"

"That's strange."

"Very."

"We've got a couple of radios that run on batteries and that one with the dynamo you can wind up and use, I'll get one out."

"Thanks, I could go out to the truck and try there, but I'll sit here and have some of my coffee."

She returns with a radio and a package of batteries, sits at the table, installs the batteries and turns it on. "What station should I try?"

"1450 AM would be a good start."

"Nothing there."

"Hit scan, see if it will find something."

The numbers quickly change and suddenly lock on 580, a strong station about 200 miles northeast. The monotone voice speaking is obviously on a loop, as it finishes and starts over they hear, "This is a message of the Emergency Alert System. A state of national emergency has been declared by the President of the United States. It is requested that all citizens remain in their homes for their own safety. The entire nation is now under Martial Law until further notice with a curfew of 9 PM local time. Anyone violating this curfew is subject to immediate arrest. All electric, phone and other communication services have been shut down to prevent their use by enemies of the state. Tune in to this station for additional information and updates in the hours and days ahead. Thank you for your cooperation."

"Dear God, what does this mean?"

"It could be fairly straight forward, or it could be quite sinister … I sure don't trust the government from what they've shown me recently.

"What's going to happen to us … what about our children … our grandchildren?"

He stands and goes to her side, "It will be alright … everything will be alright," he says with more hope than surety. "Let's say a prayer." They hold hands and pray for the nation, the leaders, and the military that this might be a chance for a renewal, a return to virtue.

Chapter 42

NEWS IS SLOW TO come in the days and weeks that follow. They wonder how much is accurate, and how much is left out. They did not realize how much they depended on the Internet and satellite TV until it did not exist. Before the military was able to be in position, anarchists working with the various groups associated with OWS attacked power generating plants around the nation. Damage ranging from serious disruption to complete destruction of many conventional plants took place. Several nuclear plants suffered severe damage from near meltdown. A number of hydro plants were relatively unscathed; however their capacity to produce meaningful power around the nation was woefully inadequate.

Fuel is available for the military and emergency services only. Farmers have no fuel to plant or harvest, losses for them will be devastating … as well as the loss of food production will be for the population. Medical care and supplies including medication is scarce. The military has done the best it can, but the loss of life from this alone has been staggering. The military and National Guard units set up in communities the best they can to hand out MRE's, but people are hungry and there is not enough to go around. Violence raises its ugly head; more lives are lost; some in neighbor-to-neighbor fighting, some to the military having to take drastic action firing on its own citizens.

They can only imagine what life is like in the cities. They know the large cities are deathtraps, and even the smaller cities are struggling mightily. Rural families are not really used to living without the modern conveniences, but they are better equipped to do it. As a result of the project there are groups set up all over the country that are prepared to help the community. Often the help is physical aid and support with clothes, finding food the best they can, sharing whatever they can. There is a stark contrast between the rioters and looters; and neighbors helping neighbors, working together to make the best they can of a terrible situation.

On the farm things are going as well as one might expect, maybe better. He made one run to town to bring their oldest daughter and her children, along with their friend Dawn, back to the farm. Their oldest son and his family live nearby and have moved out as well. The old farm house had a wood cook stove which is moved closer to use for cooking meals. While the house has a gas stove, he prefers to not use it so as not to run the gas low … best to keep it and never need it, than to use it and wish you hadn't. They are lucky to have a wind mill on the property to pump water, but water does have to be hauled to the animals and the garden area.

With no refrigeration they are reduced to doing some things as were done in the past. His grandparents had what they called the "milk house." Water pumped by the wind mill goes into a tank within the building. The cool well water keeps things such as milk, eggs and cheese chilled, and then the overflow is piped to a cattle tank for their drinking water. In their situation, the location of the well does not work for the animal's water, so they direct the overflow into the pond.

The pond is stocked with fish, so this becomes a food source that is readily available … and the grandkids enjoy being a help for supper as well. The ducks and chickens do a fine job of supplying eggs, and the abundant wildlife supplies plenty of meat. Thankfully the garden had been planted and was nearly producing vegetables when things fell apart. There is plenty of help, and with the greenhouse there should be a reasonable amount of fresh food well into the winter should that be necessary. It is not perfect, but they are living quite well compared to most of the country … or the world for that matter.

Unknown to most of the world because of the turmoil and the shutdown of normal services and communications, a constitutional crisis has arisen. The President decided to take the crisis as an opportunity to make some bold moves, one of which is to cancel the fall national election. Military leaders had become increasingly uneasy with some of the orders, and when this occurs, they have had enough. After conferring with the Speaker of the House and members of the Supreme Court, a decision is made. The President and Vice President are both "on the same page" so to speak, so removal of the President would not solve the problem. The Speaker agrees that while this action is unprecedented in our nation's history, so is the effort by the President to essentially take over the country by force.

In a coordinated move with the military and Secret Service, an elite Special Forces unit arrives at the White House and the Naval Observatory taking the President and Vice President into custody. The Chief Justice of the Supreme Court is brought in and in front of numerous witnesses, the Speaker of the House is sworn in as President of the United States. He never aspired to reach this position, and he is unsure he is up to the task under the circumstances. He calls an immediate joint session of Congress.

Speaking to the assembled group, he tells the stunned audience about the events leading up to this moment. He pledges to make sure elections do in fact take place and that he will not run. He also pledges to make every effort to return the nation to some sense of normalcy as soon as possible. Some of the senators and congressmen are outraged at this takeover, but most even from the President's party are relieved this has happened and are anxious for a move back to a constitutional republic.

In the weeks and months following the change in Washington, America is slowly putting herself back together. The military had already contained the groups fomenting the violence; once the change in power took place it became evident to the anarchists, rioters and those pushing the buttons they were not going to be able to push the country over the edge. They pull back and melt into the communities. They will have to be dealt with in the future, but for now rebuilding the nation is more important.

Military personnel working with contractors begin rebuilding power plants and infrastructure destroyed by the violence. It is a daunting proposition, but necessity being the mother of invention … and the fact that essentially all federal regulations that typically slow progress of projects like this are waived in the interest of getting the country back on track. Slowly but surely, power is brought back to cities and communities, and finally rural areas. Initially there is not enough to go around for all to have power 24 hours a day, so there are rolling blackouts as the power is shifted to different areas … but some power is better than none.

The mood of the country has changed as well. There are still those who have a vision of a socialist utopia, but a large number of people have had their eyes opened to the perils of such entitlements. Luckily, one of the projects was to find and promote people willing to run for office. As the elections near there are a number of solid citizens who have stepped up to the plate to help on the local, state and federal level. The candidates who had been running for president against the incumbent had been set for some time. While none of them are the Washington or Lincoln the country really needs at this time, it is hoped the combination of new blood in Congress and the recovery of the nation after the collapse will help them rise to the occasion. The former president's party is still reeling from his removal from office. Legal action is attempted, but no court wants to become involved. They hurriedly find a candidate willing to run, knowing it will be a futile effort.

By Election Day things are still a long way from normal. Power is still sporadic as rolling blackouts give everyone a little power every day. The airlines are running very limited schedules, people are slowly getting back to work, but unemployment is still nearly at 40 percent and gas prices are still at historic highs; demand is down, but so is the supply. Businesses have limited supplies and replenishments will be very slow. Manufacturing, transportation, banking, and exploration of resources, will take from months to years to recover ... tourism likely longer. While these are staggering realities to face, there *is* a recovery taking place. Some nations are not so lucky.

The politics of the world are changed for generations to come. Israel survives, for now. Isolated even more, an island in a sea of Muslim anarchy. Most Muslim nations are now under Caliphate domination which will plunge these countries into deep isolation, leading to the death of thousands who have fought for freedom in these nations. Much of the world's oil comes from this region as well, and time will tell how the balance will play out; the world's need for oil versus the region's need for income, yet the deep seated hatred of the non-Muslim world remains very complicated.

While China and India along with many other countries in Scandinavia and Africa remained relatively unscathed by the revolutionary violence, the world-wide deep depression crashed their respective economies ... the result of mutually assured economic disaster. Russia had terrible losses as a result of Islamic uprisings in the south; and she had become enough a player in international trade she suffered as well from economic collapse. Most of South America suffers as well.

Europe has not been so lucky. She started with the economic collapses and then suffered the violence. Each country was able to fight off the attack to overthrow the governments, but the loss of life and facilities are staggering. Much will take years to rebuild as it did in the wake of WWII. While the European's determination is strong, they are left with a realization the path chosen previously was perilous at best. The entitlement society, the European Socialist lifestyle, while appealing, could not be sustained.

The United States in recovery is becoming a much different nation. It will be neither easy nor without protest, but enough people woke up to the disastrous path the nation was on to help put her back on the path the founders devised … the Constitution. The newly elected president, congressmen and senators first order of business is to attempt to undo much of the recent years march toward a centralized government. It cannot be accomplished overnight, but the march can be halted and a reverse course plotted. There is much healing needed, and much loss from which to recover. The destruction of property while widespread and totaling in the billions of dollars, the loss of millions of lives was far greater; deaths from violence, starvation, and medical needs unmet … it is a period in America's history that will never be forgotten … unless the progressives once again succeed in rewriting history.

Epilogue

One year later …

He is sitting on the deck with a wide-mouth Mason jar full of ice tea. He listens to the muted sounds of the ducks as they feed on the pond. The late day sun is shining brightly, the sky a deep blue marred only by two jet contrails high above. He can see the planes in the sun well enough, even at this distance, to recognize the company colors. One is his company, and the other jet is from John's. As he watches them move across the sky toward the sun he thinks to himself, *How fitting*.

"What are you looking at?" she asks as she comes from the house.

"Just a couple of westbound jets."

"You never miss a plane that flies by here, not surprised. Guess what I just heard on the news?"

"Ah, I give up."

"Volar was found dead by his aide this morning. Looks like a stroke or heart attack."

"That's terrible news … really?"

"Really … maybe all that is actually behind us now."

"We can hope. I actually feel that after he lost about everything last year we were not terribly high on his list anymore."

"Maybe so. You have everything ready for your trip tomorrow?"

"Yes, I wanted to have it all out of the way so we could just relax tonight. You ready for your shift?"

"Pretty much, just a few things left, my uniform's in the dryer."

"I thought you got used to the power being off all the time and would just use the clothes line I put up," he says with a grin.

"I did what I had to then, but that was then … this is now."

"I was just kidding you know."

"I know, but that was a rough time for all of us. I really don't like to even think about it."

"But we did it, we survived … we did more than just survive. We grew, we learned, we taught our grandkids … I hope none of us, I mean the nation, forgets the lessons — not only the lessons of survival, but the lessons of departing from the Constitution."

"Me too."

"The projects are ongoing; everyone agrees the principles of the various projects to be vital to not only the recovery, but staying on course. Besides, they all love what they are doing … they may not have saved the country, but they made it better."

She sits beside him and holds his hand. They look at each other and smile; she then rests her head on his shoulder. They quietly watch the ducks on the pond, occasionally putting their heads underwater with tails pointing skyward, bobbing like corks on a fishing line as they feed on algae and underwater plants.

"You know," she says, "I'd still like you to get that big wardrobe cabinet of your dad's moved to our bedroom."

It is a huge piece that will require three people to move, she has wanted it for quite some time and has been very patient with him. He sighs, "I'm sorry, I guess I sort of conveniently forgot about it. I promise, I'll get it moved … in my spare time."

She pokes him in the ribs and they share a smile.

He says, "I think I'll take a shower."

"I need one too, maybe I'll join you."

"You in a hurry?"

"No, you?"

"No."

They stand and hold hands as they walk inside and turn toward the back of the house and their room.

CPSIA information can be obtained at www.ICGtesting.com
Printed in the USA
LVOW101519011212
309601LV00005B/9/P